Tara Pamm ... wasn't lost in a book ... much more excitin ... later, Tara's wild i... word revealed what she really wanted to do. Now she pairs Alpha males who think they know everything with strong women who knock that theory and them off their feet!

Leah Ashton has been a lifelong reader of romance. Writing came a little bit later – although in hindsight she's been dreaming up stories for as long as she can remember. Now she lives in Perth, Western Australia, with her own real-life hero, two gorgeous dogs and the world's smartest cat. By day she works in IT-land; by night she considers herself incredibly lucky to be writing the type of books she loves to read and to have the opportunity to share her own characters' happily-ever-afters with readers. You can visit Leah at www.leah-ashton.com.

Fiona McArthur is an Australian midwife who lives in the country and loves to dream. Writing Medical Romance gives Fiona the scope to write about all the wonderful aspects of romance, adventure, medicine and the midwifery she feels so passionate about. When she's not catching babies, Fiona and her husband Ian are off to meet new people, see new places and have wonderful adventures. Drop in and say hi at Fiona's website: www.Fionamcarthurauthor.com.

Dreaming of…
COLLECTION

April 2018

May 2018

June 2018

July 2018

August 2018

September 2018

Dreaming of...
Bali

TARA PAMMI

LEAH ASHTON

FIONA MCARTHUR

MILLS & BOON

Published in Great Britain 2018
by Mills & Boon, an imprint of HarperCollins*Publishers*
1 London Bridge Street, London, SE1 9GF

Dreaming of... Bali © 2018 Harlequin Books S.A.

The Man to Be Reckoned With © 2015 Tara Pammi
Nine Month Countdown © 2014 Leah Ashton
Harry St Clair: Rogue or Doctor? © 2011 Fiona McArthur

ISBN: 978-0-263-26664-1

09-0618

MIX
Paper from
responsible sources
FSC® C007454

FSC
www.fsc.org

This book is produced from independently certified FSC™ paper to ensure responsible forest management.

For more information visit: www.harpercollins.co.uk/green

Printed and bound in Spain
by CPI, Barcelona

A MAN TO BE RECKONED WITH

TARA PAMMI

From mathematics class to masters degrees, through crushes on boys to crushing debts, through fights with our moms to marriages and babies- you've always been constant and unflinching in your support and love. This one's for you, Sushma.

PROLOGUE

"He might die any minute of any day or he might live to be a hundred. There's nothing to be done for it."

Nathaniel Ramirez looked up at the snowy, whitecapped mountain peak and gulped in a big breath. The words he had overheard the cardiologist say to his mother all those years ago reverberated inside his skull. The cold air blasted through his throat, his lungs expanding greedily.

Would this be the day?

He raised his face to the sky as his vision cleared and his heart resumed its normal beat.

At some point during the trek, he had realized he couldn't finish the climb today.

He didn't know whether it was because, after almost twelve years of courting death, he was finally bored of playing hide-and-seek with it, or because he was just plain tired today.

For a decade, he had been on a constant go across the world, without planting roots anywhere, without returning home, making real estate deals in corners of the world, making millions.

An image of the roses in the garden his mother had loved, back in California, their color vividly red, the petals so soft that she had banned him from touching them, flashed across his mind's eye.

A stab of homesickness pierced him as he followed the icy path down. Sweat drenched him as he reached the wooden cabin he had been living in since he closed the Demakis deal in Greece six months ago. Restlessness slithered under his skin.

And he knew what it meant. It meant he was thrashing against the cage he had made for himself; it meant he was getting lonely; thousands of years of human nature were urging him toward making a home, to seek companionship.

He needed to chase a new challenge, whether clinching a real estate deal or conquering a new corner of the world he hadn't stamped with his name yet. Fortunately for him, the world was vast and the challenges it presented numerous.

Because staying still in one place was the one thing that made him weak, that made him long for more than he could have.

He'd just stepped out of a hot shower when his satellite phone beeped. Only a handful of people could reach him via this number. He pushed a hand through his overlong hair and checked the caller ID.

The name flashing on the screen brought an instant smile to his face.

He connected the call, and the sound of their old housekeeper Maria's voice coming down the line filled him with a warmth he had missed for too long. Maria had been his rock after his mom passed.

Suddenly he realized he missed a lot of things from home. He clamped down on the useless yearning before it morphed into the one thing he despised.

Fear.

"Nathan?"

"Maria, how are you?"

He smiled as Maria called him a few names in Spanish and then asked after him as if he were still a little boy.

"You need to come home, Nathan. Your father... It's been too long since you've seen each other."

The last time Nate saw him, his father had been the epitome of a selfish bastard instead of a grieving husband or a comforting father. And despite the decade and the thousands of miles that Nathan had put between them, the bitterness, the anger he felt for him was just as fresh as ever.

Maybe there was no running away from a few things in life.

"Is he ill again, Maria?"

"No. He recovered from the pneumonia. They, at least that woman's daughter, she took good care of him."

Praise from Maria, especially for *that woman's daughter*, as she put it, meant Jackie's daughter had slaved to take care of his dad.

Nathan frowned, the memory of the one time he had seen his father's mistress's daughter leaving a sour taste in his mouth. She had been kind even then.

That day in the garage, with the August sun shining gloriously outside with blatant disregard to the fact that Nathan's entire world had crumbled around him. There had been blooms everywhere, the gardeners keeping it up for his mother even though she had stopped venturing into the garden for months.

The grief that his mother was gone, the chilling fear, the cold fist in his chest that he could drop dead any minute like her, and the little girl who had stood nervously by the garage door, a silent witness to the choking sobs that had racked him.

He hated everything about that day.

"I'm so sorry that your mother died. I can share my mother with you if you want," she had said in a small voice.

And in return, he had ripped through her.

"He's getting married, Nathan." Maria's anxiety cut through his thoughts. "That woman," she said again, refusing to even speak Jacqueline Spear's name, the loathing in her voice crystal clear even through the phone line, "she'll finally have what she wanted, after all these years. Eleven years of living shamelessly with him under his roof..."

Nathan grimaced as Maria spouted a few choice words for Jacqueline Spear. Bitterness filled his veins at the thought of his father's mistress, the woman he had taken up with even before Nathan's mother had passed.

"It's his damn life, Maria. He has every right to spend it as he pleases."

"He does, Nathan. But your mama's house, Nathan... she's preparing to sell it. Just two days ago, she asked me to clean out your mother's room, told me to take anything I wanted. Your mama's belongings, Nathan—all her jewelry's in there. She's putting the entire estate on sale—the grounds, the furniture, the mansion, everything."

Every piece that had been painstakingly put together by his mother with love. And now in the hands of a woman who had been everything his mother hadn't been.

"If you don't come back, it will forever be gone."

Nathan scrunched his eyes closed, and the image of a brick mansion rose in front of him. A strange anger gripped him. He didn't want that house to go to someone else, he realized.

He had lived the life of a loner for a decade, and the image of the house he had run away from hit him hard in his gut. "She doesn't have the right to sell it."

The silence on Maria's end stretched his nerves taut. "He gave it to her, Nathan. As a gift."

Nausea rolled around in his mouth. His father had killed his mother, as clearly as if he had choked the life out of her, with his disgusting affair, and after he'd lived in her house with his mistress and now... His knuckles turned white around the phone.

This he wouldn't, couldn't, tolerate.

No matter that he didn't want to live in the house any more than he wanted to put roots down and settle anywhere in the world.

"He's giving away my mom's house as a wedding gift?"

"Not to Jackie, Nathan. To her daughter, from her first marriage. I don't know if you ever saw her. Your father deeded the house to her a few months ago. After he was dreadfully ill that first time."

Nathan frowned. So Jackie's daughter was selling his mother's house. Getting rid of it for the monetary value it would yield, he supposed.

The restlessness that had simmered inside him a few hours ago dissipated, washed away by furious determination.

It was time to go home. He didn't know how long he would stay or if he could bear to even stay there at all after so many years.

Neither could he let the house, his mother's house, fall into some stranger's grubby hands. He just couldn't.

He bid goodbye to Maria and switched on his laptop.

In a few minutes, he was chatting with his virtual manager, Jacob. He gave orders for a local manager to look after his cabin, for his airline tickets to be booked to San Francisco and last but not the least, for any information the man could dig up on his father's mistress's daughter.

CHAPTER ONE

"I HEARD THE investors sold the company to some reclusive billionaire."

"Someone in HR said he's only bought it for the patented software. That he intends to fire the whole lot of us."

"I didn't realize we had value to attract someone of that ilk."

What ilk? What billionaire?

Riya Mathur rubbed her temples with her fingers, slapping her palms over her ears in a gesture that in no way could silence the useless speculation around her.

What had changed in the week she had been gone for the first time in two years since Drew and she had started the company? What wasn't he telling her?

Her chat window from their internal IM program pinged, and Riya looked down at her screen.

A message from Drew: Come to my cabin, Riya.

Riya felt a knot in her stomach.

Things had steadily been going from bad to worse between her and Drew for six months now. Since New Year's Eve to be exact. And she hadn't known how to make it better except to put her head down and do her job.

Stepping out of the small cubicle she occupied, only separated from the open cabins in the huge hall by one movable shelf, she marched past an anxious, almost hyper group of staff amassed in the break room toward the CEO's cabin. She had spent the better part of the morning waiting on tenterhooks, walking around the different teams and trying to persuade them to get back to work while Drew's door remained resolutely closed.

But his continuing silence, even after an email from her, peppered with little tidbits of gossip, was making her head spin. Running her damp palms over her baggy trousers, she came to a halt at the closed door.

She tapped a couple of times cursorily, and every whisper gathered momentum in pitch and volume. Without waiting for an answer, she turned the handle and the pandemonium behind her descended into a deathly silence.

Stepping inside, she closed the door.

Drew's lean frame was molded by the sunlight streaming through the windows, the San Francisco skyline behind him.

He opened his mouth to speak but stopped abruptly. Her heart in her throat, Riya took a step in his direction. He stiffened a little more and tilted his head.

That same awkwardness that had permeated their every conversation filled the air thickly now.

But this was work. Their company truly had been a product of them both. "The whole office is buzzing with rumors…" She came to a stop a couple of steps from him. "Whatever our personal differences, this is our company, Drew. We're in it together—"

"It was your company until you took the first seed capital from an investor," a new voice, every syllable punctured with a sardonic amusement, said behind her.

Riya turned around so fast she didn't see him for a few seconds. Blinking, she brought her focus back to the huge table and the man sitting at the head of it. The chair faced away from the window. With his long legs sprawled in front of him, only his profile was visible to Riya.

The entire room was bathed in midmorning sunlight and yet the man sat in the one area of the room that the light didn't touch. Ungluing her feet from the spot next to Drew, Riya walked across the room so that she could see better.

She felt the newcomer's gaze on her, studying everything about her. Her usually articulate mind slowed down to a sluggish pace. The feeling that he had been waiting to see *her* tugged at her, a strange little premonition dancing in her gut.

"I've been dying to meet you, Ms. Mathur," he said, turning the vague feeling into solid dread. "The smart mind that built the software engine that drives the company," he added silkily. He had left something else unsaid. She knew it, just as surely as she could feel her heart skidding in her chest.

He had even pronounced her last name perfectly, elongating the *a* after the *M* just right. After knowing her since her freshman year at college, Drew still didn't say it right. It was a small thing, and yet she felt as though this stranger knew her entire history.

Taking the last step past the overfilled bookshelf, Riya came to a halt. Her stomach did a funny dive, her sharp exhale amplified to her own ears.

Her first thought was that he belonged in a motorcycle club and not in a boardroom.

Electric eyes, a brilliant shade of ice blue, set deep in a starkly angled face, collided with hers. That gaze was familiar and strange, amused and serious. A spark of recognition lit up inside her, yet Riya had no idea where she had seen him.

Dark blond hair, so unruly and long that her fingers itched to smooth it back, fell onto his forehead. Copper

highlights shimmered in his hair. The sunlight streaming
in played hide-and-seek with the hollows of his cheekbones,
the planes darker than the hollows. Which meant he spent
a lot of time outdoors.

His skin, what she could see of it, was sunburned and
looked rough. An untrimmed beard covered his jaw and
chin, copper glinting in it too.

That beard, those haphazard clothes, his overall appearance—they should have diluted the intensity of his presence in the small room. It should have made him look less
authoritative. Except those eyes negated everything.

They had a bright, alert look to them, a sardonic humor
lurking beneath the sharp stare he directed at her.

He wore a dark leather jacket that had obviously seen
better days, under which the collar of a faded shirt peeked
through.

A cough from behind her brought her up short and Riya
felt her cheeks heat up.

Amusement deepened in those eyes.

"Who are you?" The awkwardly phrased question
zoomed out of her mouth before she realized. Suddenly it
was tantamount that she remember him.

Because she did, Riya realized with a certainty.

He leaned back into his chair, not in the least affected
by her tone. There was a sense of contained movement
about him even though he remained seated. As though he
was forcing his body to do it, as though staying still was
an unnatural state for him.

"Nathaniel Ramirez."

Riya's mouth fell open as an article she had read just a
few months ago in a travel magazine flashed through her
mind's eye.

*Luxury Travel Mogul. Virtual Entrepreneur. Billion-
aire Loner.*

Nathaniel Ramirez had been called a visionary in developing hotels that were an extension of the environment, a man who had made millions with zero investment. The string of temporary hotels, which he'd envisioned and built with various landowners in different parts of the world, were all the rage for celebrities who wanted a private vacation, away from prying eyes.

He had tapped into a market that not only had met an existing demand but had opened a whole new industry to the local men in so many remote corners of the world.

And more than any of that, he was an enigma who'd traveled the world over since he was seventeen, didn't stay in one place past a few months, didn't own a home anywhere in the world and worst of all, had no family ties or relationships.

Even the magazine hadn't been able to get a picture of him. It had been a virtual interview.

The quintessential loner, the magazine had called him, the perfect personality for a man who traveled the world over and over. The fact that he made money doing it was just a perk, someone had heard him remark.

He'd only said his name, and nothing more about what he was doing here, in San Francisco, in Travelogue, in their start-up company's headquarters.

Why? Why would he give his name instead of stating why he was here?

She threw a quick look behind her and noticed Drew still stood unmoving at the bay windows, his mouth tight, his gaze swinging between her and Mr. Ramirez.

"You make a living out of traveling the world. What can a small online travel sales company do for you?" She shot Drew a look of pure desperation. "And why are you sitting in Drew's chair?"

The intensity of his gaze, while nothing new to Riya,

still had a disconcerting element to it. Men stared at her. All the time.

She had never learned how to handle the attention or divert it, much less enjoy it, as Jackie did. Only painstakingly cultivated an indifference to those heated, lingering looks. But something about him made it harder.

Finally he uncoiled from his lounging position. And a strange little wave of apprehension skittered through her.

"I bought controlling interest in Travelogue last night, Ms. Mathur."

She blinked, his soft declaration ringing in her ears. "I bought a gallon of milk and bread last night."

The sarcastic words fell easily from her mouth while inside, she struggled not to give in to the fear gripping her.

"It wasn't that simple," Nathan said, getting up from the uncomfortable chair. The whole cabin was both inconvenient and way too small for him. Every way he turned, there was a desk or chair or a pile of books ready to bang into him. He felt boxed in.

Walking around the table, he stopped at arm's length from her, the fear hidden under her sarcastic barb obvious. Gratification filled him even as he gave the rampant curiosity inside him free rein.

Like mother, like daughter.

He pushed the insidiously nasty thought away. True, Riya Mathur was the most beautiful woman he had ever seen, and as a man who had traveled to all the corners of the world, he'd seen more than his share.

She was also, apparently, extremely smart and as possessed of the talent for messing with men's minds as her mother, if everything he had heard and Drew Anderson's blatantly obvious craze for her was anything to go by.

But where Jacqueline met the world with a devil-may-care attitude, flaunting her beauty with an irreverent smile, her daughter's beauty was diluted with intelligence and a carefully constructed air of indifference.

Which, he realized with a self-deprecating smile, made every male of the species assume himself equal to the task of unraveling all that beauty and fire.

Exquisite almond-shaped, golden brown eyes, defiant, scared and hidden behind spectacles, a high forehead, a straight, distinctive nose that hinted at stubbornness and a bow-shaped mouth. All this on the backdrop of a golden caramel-colored silky smooth complexion, as though Jackie's alabaster and her Indian father's brown had been mixed in perfect proportions.

She had dressed to underplay everything about herself, and this only spurred him on to observe more. It was like a cloud hovering over a mountaintop, trying to hide the magnificence of the peak beneath it.

A wary and puzzled look lingered in her eyes since she had stepped inside. Which meant it was only a matter of time before she remembered him.

Because he had changed his last name, and he looked eons different from the sobbing seventeen-year-old she had seen eleven years ago.

He should just tell her and get it over with, he knew. And yet he kept quiet, his curiosity about her drumming out every other instinct.

"I had to call in a lot of favors to find your investors. Once they were informed of my intent, they were more than happy to accommodate me. Apparently they're not happy with the ways things are being run."

"You mean disappointed about the bucket loads of money they want us to make?" A flash of regret crossed her face as soon as she said it.

She was nervous, which was what he'd intended.

"And that's wrong how, Ms. Mathur? Why do you think investors fund start-ups? Out of the goodness of their hearts?"

"I don't think so. But there's growth *and* there's risk." She took a deep breath as though striving to get herself under control. "And if it's profits that you're after, then why buy us at all?"

"Let's just say it caught my fancy."

Frustration radiated out of her. "Our livelihood, everything we've worked toward the past four years is hanging in the balance. And all you're talking about is late night shopping, things catching your fancy. Maybe living your life on the periphery of civilization all these years, cut off from your fellow man, traipsing through the world with no ties—"

"Riya, no...." She heard Drew's soft warning behind her. But she was far too scared to pay heed.

"—has made you see only profit margins, but for us, the human element is just as important as the bottom line."

"You make me sound like a lone wolf, Ms. Mathur."

"Well, you are one, aren't you?" She closed her eyes and fought for control. "Look, all I care about is what you intend to do with the company. With us."

Something inched into his features, hardening the look in his eyes. "Leave us alone, Mr. Anderson."

"No," Riya said aloud as Mr. Ramirez walked around the table and toward her. Panic made her words rushed. "There's nothing you have to say to me that Drew can't hear."

Stopping next to her, Drew met her gaze finally. The resignation in his eyes knocked the breath out of her as nothing else could. "Drew, whatever you're thinking, we can fight this. We own the patent to the software engine—"

"Does nothing else matter to you except the blasted company? Statues possess more feelings than you do."

Bitterness spewed from every word, and the hurt festering beneath them lanced through her. She paled under his attack, struggled to put into words why.

"I'm done, Riya," Drew said, with a hint of regret.

"But, Drew, I…"

His hands on her shoulders, Drew bent and kissed her cheek, all the while the deep-set ice-blue gaze of the arrogant man who was kicking Drew out stayed on her without blinking.

Something flitted in that gaze. An insinuation? A challenge? There one minute, chased away by a cool mockery the next.

But Riya didn't look away. Locking her hands by her side, she stood frozen to the spot.

Stepping back from her, Drew turned. "I'll set up something with your assistant, Nathan."

Without breaking her gaze, the hateful man nodded.

"Goodbye, Riya."

The words felt so final that Riya shivered.

Leaving her flailing in the middle of the room, Drew closed the door behind him. It felt as if she were locked in a cage with a wild animal even as her mind was sifting and delving deeper.

Nathan…Nathan…Nathaniel Ramirez. Owns a group of travel and vacation companies called RunAway International, has traveled the world since he was seventeen…

A strange shiver began at the base of her spine, inched everywhere. She pushed her fingers through her hair, a nervous gesture she had never gotten over. "What did Drew mean?"

"Mr. Anderson decided he wanted to move on. From…"

His gaze swept over her, a puzzle in it. "...*Travelogue*," he finished, leaving something unsaid.

Riya felt as if he had slapped her. He had said so much without saying anything, and she couldn't even defend herself against what she didn't understand. She had never felt more out of her depth. "Who the hell do you think you are? And you can't just kick him out. Drew and I own—"

"He sold his share of the stock. To me. I now own seventy-five percent of your company. I'm your new *partner*, Riya. Or boss, or really...there are so many things we could call each other."

CHAPTER TWO

AND JUST LIKE that, her name on his lips, spoken like a soft invocation, unlocked the memory her mind had been trying to grasp from the moment she looked into that ice-blue gaze.

"She's dead. And she died knowing that your trashy mother is just waiting at the gates, ready to come in and take her place. I hope you both rot in hell."

The memory of that long-ago day flashed through her so vividly that Riya had to grab the chair to steady her shaking legs.

Robert's wife had been Anna. Anna Ramirez.

Little shivers spewed all over and she hugged herself. She had brought this on herself. "You're Nathan Keys. You're Robert's son. I read about you and I never realized..."

He nodded and Riya felt her breath leave her in a big rush.

Her little lie had worked and here he was, with the largest of her company's stock, her livelihood in his hand.

Robert's son, the boy who had run away from home after his mother's death, the son of the married man with whom her mother had taken up, the son of the man who had been more a father to her than her own had ever been.

The son she had been trying to bring back to Robert.

She had lied to Maria about selling the estate, hoping it would lure him back home. Thought she would give Nathan a chance she had never had with her own father.

A hysterical laugh rose through her.

Leaning against the far wall, his legs crossed together in casual elegance, he smiled, his tanned skin glinting in contrast against the white of his teeth. "What? No 'welcome home' greeting for your almost stepbrother, Riya?"

There were so many things wrong about his fake greeting, the worst of which was how aware she was of him in the small room. Mortification drenching her inside, Riya glared at him. "You're kidding me, right?"

"My acceptance of your offer for familial solidarity is almost a decade late, but—"

Her chest fell and rose as she fought for a breath. "You... you *waltz* in here, get rid of my business partner, wave the biggest chunk of my company in my face—" she pushed her shaking fingers through her hair "—and you want welcome?"

He stayed silent and her stride ate up the distance between them. Fear was a stringent pulse in her head. "If this is revenge for my mother's affair with your father, let me tell you—"

"I don't give a damn about your mother *or* my father."

The very lack of emotion in his words stilled Riya's thoughts. He was going to be livid when he learned what she had intended. "Then what is this?"

"You refused every offer I had my lawyers put forward for the sale of the estate."

Her gut twisting with fear, Riya flopped into a chair. Hiding her face in her hands, she fought through it. He had moved to acquire her company because she refused his escalating offers for the sale of the estate.

What would he do when he learned she had never intended to sell it in the first place? What had she brought on herself?

Nathan stared at the lustrous swath of dark brown hair that fell like a curtain over Riya. Even as impatience pulled at him, he stood transfixed, stunned anew by the sharpness of his reaction to her.

Every minute they spent in this confining room, his awareness of her grew like an avalanche that couldn't be stopped.

How she wore no makeup and yet the very lack of it only heightened her beautiful skin and sharp features.

How everything about her beauty was underplayed like her professional but bland brown dress shirt and trousers.

And how utterly she failed at masking that beauty.

How exquisitely expressive her wide, almond-shaped eyes were and how she fluttered those long lashes down when she wanted to hide her expression.

Her slender shoulders trembled and he felt a pang of regret. "All I want is the estate. However high I went, you kept refusing my offers. Refused to even give a reason."

She looked up, the flash of fear in her eyes still just as obvious. But now there was a resolve too. "So you made a play for my company?"

"Yes. It's called leverage. Believe me, as innovative as your software engine is, your little company is not Run-Away International material. Sign on the dotted line today and you'll leave here a rich woman. I'll even leave you to run your boring company. Of course, you'll run it into the ground in two years the way you're going, but being the uncaring bastard that I am, I'll let you ruin your and your staff's future."

"What about all the money you spent on acquiring it?"

"A drop in the ocean. I'm sure the stock will be worthless in a couple of years anyway."

Riya chafed at his grating confidence that she would only ruin the company. But she couldn't focus on that now, and there was no good way to put it.

"I didn't accept those offers because I never intended to sell the estate *to anyone*. I still don't."

"Then why did Maria assume that…"

Every inch of his face tightened as if it had been poured over by concrete and had permanently set with the fury in those chilling eyes. He was still leaning against the table, and yet he looked as if the seams of his control would burst any second.

But he didn't move, didn't lose control even by the flicker of a muscle. Only the sheer frost in his gaze was testament to the fury in his eyes. Finally he blinked and Riya felt the tightness in her chest relent infinitesimally.

The most unholy glint appeared in his eye, sending a ripple of apprehension through her.

"You manipulated Maria and me." His words rang with awe and derision, his gaze studying her, as if he was reevaluating and coming to an unsavory conclusion. He moved toward her slowly. "You laid bread crumbs very cleverly to make sure I trailed after you."

"Yes."

The single word sounded like a boom in the wake of his silent chill.

"You took advantage of my attachment to that estate. You knew I would go as high as you wanted."

Forcing a laugh, which sounded as artificial as it felt, she took a step back, her nerves stretching tighter and tighter.

"Actually I took advantage of your hatred for me and Jackie." And because his silence confirmed it, she continued, battling the ugly truth. "I wasn't even sure it would work. Maria just barely tolerates me. How would I know she would come tattling to you?"

Shaking his head, he covered another step. Though it was cowardly, Riya couldn't stop herself from stepping back again. "Don't minimize your accomplishment now. You knew exactly what you were doing."

Heat flamed her cheeks. "Fine. Something she had said a few months ago stuck with me. About how you might have considered coming back long ago if only Jackie and I were gone. About how much you loved the estate, even the staff, and how dare Robert give it to me? About how I was stealing even this from you."

"So you decided luring me here would make you the maximum amount of money on the estate."

"That's not true. I felt guilty. I never asked Robert for the estate. I know it's not—"

"And your guilt, your insecurities give you the right to play games with me?"

The depth of his perception awed Riya. Despite constantly reminding herself that she had been too young to change anything, she had remembered his grief-stricken words again and again, felt guilt carve a permanent place inside her gut.

His gaze met hers, an icy resolve in it, and Riya forgot what she had been about to say. There was not an inch of that grief-stricken boy in him. Only a cold fire, an absolute detachment.

He reached her, and her heart slammed against her rib cage. She couldn't blink, couldn't look away from that piercing blue. And a slow tremor took root in her muscles. Like the time when she'd had the flu. Only in a less hurting and more disconcerting way. As if every fiber of her were a stringent pulse vibrating in tune to his every move.

His lean body neatly caging her against the alcove, his gaze was a fiery frost. "Why are you doing this?"

"You were gone for eleven years. Eleven years during which time I helped Robert with the administration of the estate, with the staff, with everything. You were off doing who knows what and I slogged over every account, every expense and income number, in the face of a staff that hated the very sight of me. I did everything I could to keep that place going." She had tried to be a model daughter to Robert and Jackie, had taken care of him when he fell sick.

Nothing she had done had removed the shadows of guilt and ache in Robert's eyes.

"That's what this is all about? What I offered wasn't enough?" Nathan said, coming closer. Satisfaction practically coated every word. "Name your price."

"I don't want money. I was trying to explain how much that estate means to me…I was—"

"Then what the hell do you want? How dare you manipulate me after your mother turned my mother's last few days into the worst of her life?"

It took every ounce of her will to stand still, bearing the judgment in that gaze. The pain in his words cut through her. "I want you to see Robert."

The silence that dawned was so tense that Riya felt the tension wind around them like a tangible rope. The knot in his brow cleared; the icy blue of his eyes widened. It was the last thing he had expected to hear. That she had surprised him left her only shaking in her leather pumps.

"No."

Fisting her hands behind her, Riya pushed the words that refused to come under his scornful gaze. "Then I won't sign it over. Ever."

She could practically hear him size her up, reassess his assumptions about her in the way disbelief and then pity filled his gaze. He looked at her as though he was seeing her anew.

"Don't lose what you've built trying to alleviate some weird guilt. Don't push me into doing something I don't want to. That estate, it's the one thing in the entire world that means something to me."

His words were laden with emotion and so much more. And she understood that attachment, because she loved the estate too. But she couldn't weaken now, now that he was here in San Francisco, so close to Robert.

"I've already made my decision."

He ran his fingers through his overlong hair, his gaze a winter frost. There was a tremble in the taut line of his shoulders, a hoarse thread in his tone when he spoke. "I'll drag you through the courts. Your company, I'm going to tear it to pieces. Is it still worth it?"

Riya swayed, the impact of what he was saying sweeping through her with the force of a gale. To see her company pulled apart and sold for pieces… Every inch of her revolted at the mere thought. Desperation filled her words.

"I deceived you. My staff has nothing to do with this. Can you be so heartless to take away their jobs?"

Their gazes locked and held. And every second felt like an eternity to her.

Finally he spoke, his mouth a tight line. "Yes."

The fight deflated out of Riya and she held herself together by sheer will. Her company was everything to her. But if Robert hadn't been there for her when she needed an adult with a kind word, Riya couldn't bear to imagine what her life would have been today.

"Fine. The estate, it's rightfully yours, I believe that. And eventually it will be. But a legal battle will take years.

Robert said he made sure the deed was ironclad, exactly to avoid this kind of battle if he died suddenly."

"Because he's determined to rob even this from me?"

"No. You're misunderstanding him. He thought he was going to die. He... A long, drawn-out court battle is what you want for your mother's house? For Maria and the staff who have looked after the house all these years, for your mother's memory?"

His jaw flexed tight, the vein in his temple flickering threateningly. "You have no right to speak of her."

The utter loathing in his words slashed through her. Because he was right. His fury was justified.

She had no right to even speak of his mother, no right to her estate. To this day, she was equal parts amazed and perplexed that Robert had even deeded it to her.

For the first time in her life, she truly wished she was more like her mother—carefree, blissfully ignorant of everything around her but her own happiness. Wished she could turn her back on this man who threatened everything she had built, wished she could turn her back on the shadows that haunted Robert's eyes.

"I've no right to speak of her, true, but I'm sure she would never have wanted you to hate him all your life. Everyone's always talking about what a generous and kind lady she was and—"

He flinched as though she had laid a hand on him. "You have no idea what she'd have wanted." He stood at the window, just as Drew had done, his wide frame blocking the sunlight from coming in. Contrary to the cold, heartless man she had called him, he looked like a volcano of simmering emotions.

"Get out. I have nothing more to say to you."

Riya closed the door behind her, her legs shaking. Panic pounded through her.

Would he break Travelogue into pieces? How could she fight to keep what was hers? How was she to convince him that it was only Robert's haunting pain that had driven her to this?

Her head reeling, she stepped into the huge, open area laid out with open cabins.

The staff had already figured out that Drew was gone. The faint scraping and shuffling of chairs, the concerned glances in her direction—they were looking to her to provide some direction.

But Riya had no way to save the day, no answer to give to those hopeful looks. She grabbed her handbag and left, unable to think of anything else but temporary escape.

Nathan stared at the closed door, still trying to control his raging emotions. One flimsy, fragile woman had so nearly eroded his self-control.

It had taken him a few years to get over the grief of his mother's death, to accept the fatality of his own condition. He'd been so scared, alone and he'd lashed out at the world.

But in the end, he had not only accepted it but also tailored his life to live it without being haunted by the fear of dying every minute. Had made sure he'd not formed an attachment to anyone, made sure that no relationship could leave him weak. Like the way it had left his mother in the end.

Had gloried in each day he had, lived it to the fullest.

Today, he hadn't been able to help himself from taunting the manipulative minx, from pushing her. But for all the steely will with which she had manipulated him, there was a naiveté to her that cooled his interest. In a million years, he wouldn't have expected his father to command such loyalty in anyone. So much that she was risking everything she owned.

But nothing he did or could do would shake that resolve. Despite the very clever way she had manipulated Maria and taken advantage of his attachment to the estate, he had to admire that resolve. And she was right about one more thing.

Engaging his father in a legal battle would gain him nothing but a deadlock for years to come. He would win in the end, but when, he didn't know.

Time was the one thing that Nate didn't have the luxury or certainty of.

He wanted that estate, and convincing Riya to sell it back to him as soon as possible would be the biggest win of his life. He couldn't dismantle her company for no good reason, couldn't just play with the livelihood of so many people.

But he had learned enough about the smart, steel-willed beauty. Just the thought of those beautiful eyes widening with awareness and shock, the way she held herself rigid when he had neared her, brought a smile to his face.

He was going to enjoy convincing her to sell the estate to him.

CHAPTER THREE

BY THE TIME Riya drove past the electronically manned gates and along the gravel driveway lined with the tall century-old oaks, she was still wondering what she would say to Jackie or how she would bring up the subject of Nathan. Jackie had the most singular way of looking at the world and the people in it. Only interested in how they affected her own life and happiness.

Riya pulled the window down and took a deep breath. The smell of pine needles and the fragrance of the roses greeted her.

The sight of the mansion emerging just as the driveway straightened always revived her, filled her with an indescribable joy. For her, the brick mansion meant home.

Driving around the courtyard, she pulled into the garage, parked and leaned her forehead on the steering wheel. Disappointment and a perverse anger filled her. Nathan didn't love the estate as she did, had been gone for a decade without a thought for it.

Would probably kick them all out, *her especially*, without a second thought. And to leave this place, to say goodbye finally? The very thought made her chest hurt.

Grabbing her laptop bag and her handbag, she stepped out of her car. All she wanted was to have a bath and sink into her bed and deal with everything tomorrow. She entered the vast, homely kitchen through the back door intending to go up quietly when Jackie called her.

Dressed in a cream silk pantsuit, she looked perfectly put together, as always. Except for the frown marring her brow.

"Riya! I've been calling you for hours and you didn't answer a single time." Her painted mouth trembled. "He's here, just…appeared out of thin air, after all these years."

Riya froze, her gaze flying around the house, her heart ratcheting in her chest. Fighting the rising panic, because of course it had always fallen to her to be the calm one, she straightened her spine. "Mom," she said loudly. "Calm down."

She called her that so infrequently now that Jackie looked at her with alarm.

"Now tell me clearly what happened."

"Nathaniel is here," her mother said, awe coating her words. "Apparently he's some big-shot billionaire who can ruin us with one word or—"

"He said that to you?"

"Of course not. He won't even meet my eyes. It's as if I'm not there, standing right in front of him. That witch Maria said it. He looks so different too, all lean and so coldly distant and arrogant."

Riya nodded, surprised that Jackie had noticed it too. There was something she couldn't pinpoint about Nathan either. A sort of cool detachment, a layer of frost as if nothing or no one could touch him. And yet he had been so angry when she refused to sign over the estate.

"Even Maria took a few seconds to recognize him. He just stood there looking as if he owned the place, when he didn't even ask after Robert all these years." Riya bit the inside of her cheek to keep from correcting her mother that the estate *was* his. "He arrived a couple of hours ago. Showed up at the front door and sent the staff into a frenzy.

They were all crying and laughing, and Robert's not even in town. He won't say why he's here."

How? She hadn't even seen his car in the garage. "Where is he? Did he say what he wants?"

"He's been wandering around the estate, drops in every half hour or so. Maria said he wants to see you."

Riya's heart sank to her feet.

A calculating look emerged in her mother's eyes, her panic forgotten. "Why *is* he looking for you? I'm still shaking from the shock of seeing him, and all this time, if you'd known that he was—"

"Hello, Riya."

Every time he said her name, it was like flipping a switch on inside her. A caress. An invitation. For what, she didn't even want to speculate. Her skin tingling, Riya turned.

He stood at the huge arched entrance into the kitchen.

Once again, Riya felt the impact of his presence like a magnet pulled toward a slab of iron.

The beard was still unshaved, but he had changed. Now his clothes reflected the casual power he exuded so easily. The rumpled shirt had been exchanged for a white dress shirt and a formal jacket this time. The snowy-white collar a contrast against his sunburned skin. His hair gleamed with wetness, looked more black than brown.

He looked knee-meltingly gorgeous. Case in point, her knees practically buckled beneath her.

"You didn't come back to the office, haven't been answering my calls," he said, waving his cell phone.

"I didn't realize I was supposed to be at your beck and call," she retorted, not trusting the invasive intimacy of his smile. In fact, she had liked him better when he was angry and threatening. "Not everything I do is about you."

That small smile turned into a grin, and his teeth gleamed against his tanned skin. It lit up his whole face,

softening the harsh angles of his features. And the mouth…
she had been right. It was made for smiling and something
else that she didn't want to think about.

"From now on, it's going to be all about me," he said,
stretching his arms by his sides. The casual gesture drew
her gaze to the breadth of his shoulders. That jacket was
cut perfectly, following the wide swath of his shoulders and
the narrowing of his waist.

Alarm spiked through her. "No."

"I have a proposition for you." Something glimmered
in his gaze. "You're not chickening out already, are you?"

Jackie gasped, and Riya wondered if her mother could
explode from the tension radiating from her. She infused
steel into her voice. "We don't have a deal."

"We do now. You've…*persuaded* me to take a chance
on you, Riya."

There was no way to arrest the heat blooming up her
face. He was doing it on purpose. Saying her name like that,
insinuating with that smile that there was more between
them than his hatred and her risky gamble. She wanted to
run away and hide in her bedroom, hope it was all a bad
dream.

Next to her, Jackie began again. "Riya, how dare you
not tell me—"

Nathan shot Jackie a look. Pure arctic frost, it was the
only way Riya could describe it. Granted, he probably was
the one man who could shut Jackie up without meaning to,
but Riya had a feeling he would have the same effect on all
of them, even if he had just been Nathaniel Ramirez. And
not the adored heir of the estate.

He had that kind of a presence. Contained and controlled with a violent energy brimming underneath the
calm facade.

How was it possible that she could notice so much, understand so much about him just in a few hours?

"Come," he said in a cajoling tone as if she were a recalcitrant child. When she still didn't move, he caught her wrist and tugged.

Her bare skin tingling at the contact of his rough fingers, Riya followed, past the nonplussed staff, who had gathered in the huge dining hall, and her pale mother, through the door and out into the lush acreage behind the house.

A cold breeze blew her hair in her face, and with a soft huff, Riya pulled it all to the side. The night was inky black, only the moon and carefully placed lights on the ground illuminating the path for them.

But instead of dulling his presence, the dark intensified her awareness of him. The graceful line of his shoulders, the taper of his lean chest to his waist and the corded energy of his thighs when she stumbled and he steadied her.

Her own senses revolted against her mind, determined to observe and absorb every little thing about him. They'd reached the well-lit-up gazebo in the south corner of the estate when Riya realized his long fingers were still wrapped around her wrist.

Dragging her feet on the grass, she tugged her hand away.

The splish-splash of water from another fountain, the relentless whisper of the cicadas, a hundred different fragrances carried around by the breeze greeted her. The very place she had always found blissfully peaceful was now ruined by the man playing a cat-and-mouse game with her livelihood. And something much worse.

Grasping the fear that was the only way to puncture her awareness of him, she lashed out. "You couldn't have given me an evening to brace myself? Let me figure out how and what I'm going to tell my mother, to figure out my future?"

"You left without a word to anyone. Is this how you run the company?"

"The very company that you threatened to tear into pieces?" she threw at him. "You asked me to get out. Very clearly."

"You were blackmailing me."

She bristled at the outrage in his voice. "I was doing no such thing." And because she couldn't bear to simply stop thinking of it as her company, she continued. "Even if your plan is to dismantle the company and sell it for bits, you'll need a skeleton staff to see through the memberships for the rest of the year. I recommend you keep Sam Hawkins on. He's been there from the beginning and Martha Gomez too. She needs this job and she'll be invaluable to—"

All of her panic ground to a halt as his long-limbed stride ate the distance between them.

"I don't remember firing you. Are you resigning, then?"

Riya reached behind her and grasped the wooden column. But there was nowhere to go and he was standing too close.

The lights from around the gazebo cast him in shadows. Close enough to realize how many different shades of blue his eyes could turn depending on the light. Close enough for her to see the shape of his mouth, which had a hint of gaiety to it. Close enough for her to breathe and learn the scent of him and realize why he affected her so much.

She had never before experienced the weird pull in her stomach, the feverish tremble that gripped her, the constant fascination with every aspect of him.

Fisting her hands by her sides, she clamped down the shaky realization.

His gaze rested on her mouth for a nanosecond. Only an infinitesimal fragment of time, but her lips tingled. "I didn't quit. But have you left me a choice?"

As if the tension became too much even for him, he moved to her side and leaned against the structure. "The staff's murderous glares after you left would have turned me into dust if I hadn't told them you were just having a tantrum."

Her breath left her in a huge whoosh, the sound amplified in the silence. "Building up their hopes that everything's okay is just cruel. Does nothing get to you?"

"No."

His response wasn't threatening or emotional. Scarily, it was honest.

His watch glinted in the light as he folded his hands. "I'll give you and your staff one chance. Prove that Travelogue and you are worth taking on as part of RunAway International."

Catching the immediate thanks that rose to her lips, she turned toward him. Her heart thumped hard in her chest. Whether it was because of how close he was standing or because he was giving her a chance, she had no idea.

Ruthlessly killing her own hopes, she shook her head. "I don't want to work for you."

"Why not?"

"What do you mean *why not*?" She moved away, exasperated by him and her reaction to him. "Because you and I have a history, that's why. And not a good one. Whatever you think of me, I lied because..."

He gave her such an arch look that she backpedaled quickly. "Fine. I manipulated Maria and you with good intentions. Whereas you...you are doing this out of some twisted need for *revenge*. That's it. You want to torture me, guilt me and then—"

He grinned, and his blue eyes glittered. Her knees wobbled. "Have you always been this prone to drama or is it me that brings it out in you?"

How she wanted to say he affected her in no way, but they would both know she was lying. Better instead to focus on fighting it. "Why the sudden change of heart, then?"

"A strong sense of familial duty? A core made of kindness?"

Rolling her eyes, she swatted him. Deftly, he caught her hand in his.

Her breath stuck in her throat. Her fingers moved over his in the dark, registering the different texture of his palm—rough and abrasive, devoid of any softness, so different from her own.

It was his absolute stillness next to her, just as powerful as that latent energy, that made her realize what she was doing.

She jerked her hand away, the air she had been holding rushing out of her.

What the hell was she doing, *pawing* him like that? He was her employer, her enemy…

No man had been so dangerous to her internal balance as him. No man had ever spun her senses so easily.

Rubbing shaking fingers over her face, she struggled to think back to their conversation. "You're agreeing to see Robert, then?"

"If you give me a date now as to when you will sign the deed over to me."

"Stay here in San Francisco until their wedding. See Robert, let him speak to you. And I'll sign over the estate the day after the wedding. Also, none of my staff will be made redundant. When this is all over, I want you to go away and leave Travelogue alone. Forever."

"That depends on if Travelogue stays intact that long."

"If you give us a fair chance, I have no doubt it will."

His eyes gleamed ferociously. "You've got a lot of nerve, setting conditions to sell my mother's house back to me."

"You're a billionaire, you're your own boss and as far as I understand, you have no one in your life that you're answerable to. What's two months in the big picture of your life, Nathan?"

"Everything, Riya." There was no humor in his smile now, only a dark warning. "This is your last chance to let it go."

She didn't take even a beat to think it over. "No. Robert... he...I'll do anything for him."

His curious silence swathed her and Riya felt like the rabbit in the story her father had told her when she was little. The rabbit had gone into the lion's den, determined to change his mind about eating one animal every day.

At that point, she had stuck her fingers in her ears and begged him not to continue. A few days after that, she and Jackie had left. Her father had never seen her again, never called her, never sent a birthday card.

For years, she had wondered if he thought of her, hoped he would write to her, call Jackie to ask about her.

Only utter and absolute silence had greeted her hopes.

Now...now she didn't even remember his face clearly. On the road with Jackie, hearing her crying at night, not knowing where they would go next—it had been the most uncertain time of her life. Until Jackie had met Robert and he had taken them to his estate, Riya had thought she would never know a stable home again.

And to see Robert ache to see Nathan, to speak a few words to him, she couldn't back down now. Not when Nathan was finally here.

"Fine. Come to work Monday morning."

She saw the shadow of something in his eyes—a promise, a challenge.

"I'll stay two months. I'll even dance with you at the wedding."

"I don't want to dance with—"

"You started this, Riya. I'm going to finish it."

She breathed in cold gulps of air, only then seeing the faint shape of a chopper. "Stop saying my name like that," she said, not sure when the words had exactly left her lips.

Frowning, he stepped closer. "Am I saying it wrong?"

There was that strange little tension again. Winding around them, tugging at them.

"No. I just...we're..."

The helicopter blades began whirring, and he bent toward her to make himself heard. A firestorm danced through Riya as his breath played on her nape.

It was a heated brand, a molten caress. The simple touch of his fingers on her waist as she swayed seared through the cotton of her shirt.

"Mr. Ramirez and Ms. Mathur are too formal when we're going to work in close quarters for a couple of months. And calling each other brother and sister, especially when we..." Her heart drummed in her ears, a flash of heat bursting all over her as he paused dramatically. "...*obviously don't like each other* will just earn us a place on a daytime soap opera, don't you think?

"Nathan and Riya, it has to be."

She felt his smile instead of saw it, the faint graze of his beard against her jaw making her hyperaware of him. He lifted his head and Riya stared mutely at the striking beauty of the planes of his face.

All wicked, from the twinkle in his eyes to the dimples in his cheeks. And sexy all the way.

"See you Monday morning." He stepped back, sending

her heart pitter-pattering all over her chest. "And FYI, I'm what they call an exacting boss."

By the time Riya walked the long way around the acreage back to the house, she was hungry and tired and her head hurt.

Turning the gleaming antique handle on the side door into the kitchen, she stepped in. Even though her stomach rumbled, all she wanted was to get into bed and forget that this day had happened.

She couldn't believe that Drew had sold her out so easily, couldn't believe what she had set in motion. And of all things, she couldn't believe the sharp and stringent quality of her awareness of Nathan, of his every word and gesture, of the flash of the same awareness in his. But she had no doubt, where she was floundering and flailing in the wake of it, it was nothing but a game to him.

The overhead ceiling lights came on, bathing her in a blaze of light.

Jackie stood near the curving staircase, her eyes glittering with fear and fury. "If you knew he was coming, why didn't you stop him?"

Guilt settling heavily on her shoulders, Riya sighed. If only life were as simple as her mom thought it was. "It's his estate we're living in. One of these days, he was bound to return."

"Just when Robert has finally agreed to the wedding and—"

Unable to hear another word of her mom's self-absorption, she cut across her. "Robert will be happy to see him. I can't just send him away, even if I wanted to."

Her elegant hands wringing in front of her, Jackie walked around the huge dining table. "What does he want with you?"

"He wants the estate back."

"No," Jackie said, her tone rising, her gaze stricken. "He'll probably just kick us out if you do that. You can't—"

Even as she wished her mother would think of Riya's feelings for once, she softened her tone. Whatever her weaknesses, Jackie had found stability and peace here with Robert and the estate. "I can't stop him from taking what is rightfully his, Jackie."

Jackie's gaze zoomed somewhere far away, and Riya locked out the urge to shake her mom. That look meant nothing she said was going to get through to her now. "I don't care what you have to do. Just make sure he doesn't have the house back. Do something, anything to send him back, Riya."

"I can't take him on," Riya said, looking away. If Jackie found out he was here because of what Riya had done... "If I fight him on this, he threatened to drag us through the courts. I don't have a choice."

"Of course you can. You have Robert on your side. He'll never agree to Nathan taking the estate from you. If there's a long court battle, then so be it. You can't lose the house, Riya. I can't take this uncertainty, this kind of stress at this stage of my life."

And there was the heart of the matter. Bitterness pooled in her throat, but Riya shook it away. As she always did. "Robert will look after you, Jackie. Nothing will happen to you."

"Does it occur to you that maybe it's you I could be worried about?"

"There's no precedent for me to think that, is there?"

Jackie paled.

Now Riya felt like the green scum that lived under a rock.

Jackie sighed. "You slogged over the estate for years.

Where was Nathan when he was needed? Do whatever you have to do, but make sure you hold on to this house.

"You have just as much right to this as he. Or even more."

Nathan's dark smile as he'd stood close to her sent a shiver over her skin. His offer for Travelogue was more than she'd hoped for, but she didn't like the look in his eyes.

It wasn't just that ever-present energy between them. It was more. As if he could see through her, into the heart of her. As if he could see her fears and insecurities and found them laughable. As if he knew how to use them to trip her up.

She just had to remember that whatever he threw at her, she could cope with it. The only danger was if he had true interest in her. He didn't. Nathan was a man who traveled the world over.

Like everyone else in her life, she would matter very little to him once he realized she wouldn't budge from her goal. And then he would leave her alone.

For years, she had lived with the knowledge that her father hadn't cared about her. For Jackie, she was nothing but a crutch of safety, the one who would never leave her. For Robert, she had been the means to assuage his guilt about Nathan and his mom. Not that she didn't appreciate his kindness.

But the truth was no one had ever really cared about her, about her fears, her happiness. And Nathan would be no different.

CHAPTER FOUR

WHEN RIYA ARRIVED at work Monday morning, it was to find Nathan leaning against the redbrick building, head bent down to his tablet.

Pulling in a breath, she forced her nerves to calm down. She had agreed to this, actually forced him into this. Now she had to see this through for Robert and for her own company.

The shabby street instantly looked different, felt different. And more than one woman sent him lingering looks as they walked past. But he was unaware of the attention he was drawing.

Today, he was dressed in a V-necked gray T-shirt coupled with blue jeans that hugged his lean hips and thighs in a very nerve-racking way. His hair gleamed with wetness, his beard still hiding his mouth. The veins bulging in his forearms, the stretch of the cotton across his chest. Every time she set eyes on him, something pinged inside her.

So early in the morning, with no caffeine in her system, he was just too much testosterone to stomach.

"You're wasting my pilot's time." His gaze didn't waver from his tablet.

"Pilot? What are you talking about?" Feeling heat in her cheeks, she dug through her bag for her phone.

For the first time in two years since she and Drew had

started Travelogue, she had resolutely refused to check her work email. Now she just felt stupid because she had obviously missed some important communication.

"Not completely together still? Had to abandon the mother ship early today?"

"I need coffee before I can deal with you," she muttered. "I turned off my email client all weekend."

She had hardly finished speaking when his chauffeur appeared by her side with a coffee cup. Nathan's gaze lingered on her as she took a few much-needed sips.

His perception surprised her, but she wasn't going to confide about Jackie to him. Or anything for that matter. For all his generous offer, she didn't trust his intentions.

"I thought you slaved night and day, weekends and whatnot to build Travelogue. Didn't have a life outside of the company and the estate. Apparently you're a paragon of hard work and dedication and every other virtue. Except for the 'small incident' with Mr. Anderson."

Feeling like a lamb being led to slaughter under his watchful, almost indulgent gaze, she gulped too much on her next sip and squealed. He was instantly at her side, concern softening his mouth.

She jerked away as his palm landed on her back, scalded by his touch more than the coffee. Feeling like an irresponsible idiot, she cleared her throat. "Just...tell me what's on the agenda today."

Wicked lights glinted in his gaze. "British Virgin Islands."

Her leg dangled midway over the footpath as if she were a puppet being pulled by strings. "Like going there? Us?"

"Yes."

Alarm bells clanged in her head. "Why?"

He moved closer. She caught the instant need to step back. "A project of mine has come to the execution stages.

It'll suit very well to see what your precious team and you are made of. Sort of a test before I flush you guys."

"A trip to Virgin Islands just to test us seems like the kind of extravagance that adds a lot of overhead to small, itty-bitty companies. I would rather—"

"Didn't I tell you? Your finances, your projects—everything's on probation." Arrogance dripped from his every word, every gesture. "A skeleton crew will keep the website and sales going."

She swallowed the protest that rose to her lips. She'd have to just show him what she and her team were made of. Navigating to the calendar on her phone, she synced it and opened his shared calendar. Tilting her head up, she leveled a direct look at him. "Robert is back tonight. Should I go ahead and block your time, then?"

A mocking smile lingered on his lips as he studied her. Her breath felt tight in her chest as she willed herself to stay still under the devouring gaze. "We won't return for a few days."

"I don't see the need for—"

"I'm beginning to see why your investors were so eager to jump ship. You don't want to make money, and you don't listen to advice or input of any kind. It's almost as though you live and work in isolation."

"That's not true. I…"

Folding his hands, he raised an eyebrow.

Something about the look in his face grated on her. But she didn't want to give him a single reason to back out of their deal. "Fine. I'm ready to go."

Faced with her increasingly unignorable reaction to him, she found it tempting to just accept defeat, sign away the dratted estate and walk away. Except she had heard the stunned silence when Jackie told Robert that Nathan was here. She had heard his hopes, his pain in the one request he had made of her.

"Whatever he wants, please say yes, Riya. I want to see my son."

It was the first time Robert had ever asked anything of her.

Guiding her along with him, Nathan crossed the small, dingy street that housed their office to the opposite side. Every inch of her tautened as the muscled length of his thigh grazed hers.

"Which island are we visiting?" she said pushing her misgivings down. Robert and her company, she must keep her reasons at the center of her mind.

"Mine."

She slid into the limo and crossed her legs as he occupied the opposite seat. "You own one of the Virgin Islands?"

"Yes."

"But you don't even own a home."

Amusement deepened his gaze. "Been reading up on me?"

She shrugged, as if she hadn't devoured the internet looking for every scrap of information on him over the weekend. "There wasn't really much."

"What were you hoping to find?"

"Not the list of your assets," she said, remembering the article he had been featured in in *Forbes* about the youngest billionaires under thirty. It galled her to admit it, but the man *was* a genius investor and apparently also one of the leading philanthropists of their generation.

He donated millions to charity and causes the world over, but there hadn't been a byte about his personal life. What was she to make of him?

"I was looking for something of a personal nature."

He leveled a shocked look at her. "Why?"

"Jackie told Robert you were back and he asked me a thousand questions about you. I had nothing to tell him apart from the fact that you're a gazillionaire and an arrogant, heartless SO..."

He narrowed his eyes and Riya sighed. Antagonizing him was going to get her precisely nowhere.

"So, all this interest in my personal life is only for your precious Robert, right?"

She would jump from the thirteenth story before she admitted to him how scarily right he was. Ignoring the charged air of the luxurious interior, she went through her email. "This whole trip is just an excuse for you to—"

"Excuse for what?" he interrupted, a thread of anger in his voice. He leaned forward, his muscled forearms resting on his thighs. Gaze zeroed in on her with the focus of a laser beam. Lingered over every inch of her face until it was a caress. The decadent sides of the vehicle seemed to move inward until it was as if they were locked in a bubble.

"You're welcome at any time to sign the papers and walk away. And I'll do the same."

Shaking her head, Riya looked away, trying to break the spell he cast around them. She was nowhere near equipped to take him on. On any level.

Soon they arrived at a private airfield. A sleek Learjet with RunAway International's logo, a tangled-up R&A, was waiting. They boarded the aircraft and it was easy to keep her mouth shut, greeted by the sheer affluence and breadth of Nathaniel Ramirez's standing in the world.

The interior of the plane was all cream leather and sleek panels. Her brown trousers and ironed beige dress shirt had never looked quite so shabby as they did against the quiet elegance of her surroundings. While Nathan spoke to the pilot, she took a quick tour and came away with her head spinning.

The master suite in the back was more opulent than her bedroom at the estate.

Still reeling from the sheer breadth of Nathan's wealth, she made a quick call to Jackie and Robert, informing them of her sudden trip.

It took her a few minutes to settle down, to regain her balance that he tipped so easily. Soon they were leveling off at thousands of feet, with nothing but silence stretching in the main cabin.

"Robert asked me to tell you that he can't wait to see you," she said.

His mouth narrowed into an uncompromising line, his whole posture going from relaxed to tense in a matter of seconds. "Tell me what happened between you and Mr. Anderson."

"That's none of your..." Sighing, she tried to collect herself.

The last thing she wanted was to talk about herself and with him of all people. But if he couldn't even tolerate Robert's name, what was he going to say when he saw him? What was the point of all this if he just sat there and glared at Robert with that frosty gaze?

How hardhearted did he have to be not to wonder about Robert all these years?

If the price was that she answer questions about herself, then she would.

"There's nothing much. Drew and I shared a professional relationship. For the most part." Time for attack again. "Where did you go when you left all those years ago?"

Challenge simmered between them. If she went down this road, he was going to make her pay.

"New York City first and then I backpacked through Europe." Promptly came the next shot. "So Mr. Anderson was just a hopeful candidate you were trying on?"

"For the last time, I was not trying him on. I never even went on a date with him."

"That's not the story I've been hearing."

"I have no intention of humiliating myself or Drew just so that you can sit there and play us off against each other."

He leaned back into his seat as they leveled off, and the gray fabric stretched over his chest. "You managed it quite well all by yourself. I reviewed all of last quarter's reports, and he did nothing but run the company into the ground. With his head buried in love clouds and you averse to any risk, Travelogue would have died within a year."

Drew and she had known each other for a while, their relationship always in a strange intersection between friends and colleagues. But things had slowly spiraled to worse in the last few months. "I never expected him to sell me out to you."

"Selling out to me was the wisest thing he did. There hasn't been a lot of financial growth in the last quarter. And anyone who had good ideas, Drew fired them. Like the marketing strategist."

The sparkling water she had ordered came and she took a fortifying sip. "All the marketing strategy suggested was that we increase the cost of membership for customers who have *been* with us since the beginning, and take a bigger cut of the profits from the flash sales for vacations packages.

"These are middle-class families who come to us because we provide the best value for their buck, not international jet-setters who don't have to think twice about buying and sinking companies like a little boy buys and breaks his toys."

Nathan countered without blinking at her juvenile attack. "That marketing strategy is spot-on. Different tiers of membership is the way to go. An executive membership that charges more and provides a different kind of experience. There's a whole set of clientele that Travelogue's missing out on. If you don't grow, if you don't expand your horizons, you'll be pushed out of the market."

"That's a huge risk that might alienate us to our current clientele."

"It is. And it's one I'm willing to take."

Neatly put in place, Riya bristled. It was all her hard work and his risk. And the consequences would be hers to bear. "Does it ever get old?"

"What?"

"That high you're getting from the casual display of your power and your arrogance?"

He laughed, and the deep sound went straight to her heart, as if it were a specially designed missile targeted for her. It seemed every little gesture of his went straight to her heart or some other part of her.

Parts she shouldn't even be thinking about.

How did he get past all of her defenses so easily? Why did he affect her so much?

She had no answers, only increasing alarm that she would never figure out how to resist whatever it was that he did so easily.

"What will you do once I sign over the estate to you? Kick Robert and Jackie out?"

"Maybe. Or maybe we can all live under one roof like a happy family. Would that pacify your guilt?"

The idea of it was so absurd that Riya stared at him, taken aback.

"Horrifying prospect, isn't it? Me and you, me and your mother, me and Robert—it's a disaster every which way."

"This is all so funny and trivial to you…you don't care…" She had to pause to breathe. "You have all these resources, you own a damn plane and yet you couldn't have visited Robert once in all these years?

The cabin resounded with her outburst.

"It's not a one-for-one anymore, Riya."

He slid some papers toward her, and the words *Disciplinary Action* printed neatly on top stole the remaining breaths from Riya's lungs.

She fingered the papers, her heart sinking. "What is this?"

"His mismanagement of the company in the last few months meant Drew was the dispensable one between the two of you, for now. But it doesn't mean you're without culpability. I need to know the source of the problem between you two."

"Ammunition to make me dispensable too?"

"I'm making sure it's documented properly. It's a standard HR policy in my group of companies."

Nathan leaned back into his seat, wondering at the puzzle that Riya Mathur was. The software engine she had built, he'd been told by one of his own architects, was extraordinarily complex. And yet she blanched at using it to its full potential by expanding the client base, at spreading her wings in any way.

"This is your one chance to clear it all up," he said, softening his voice. He wasn't bending the rules, but he was also very curious about what happened between her and her colleague.

"Last year, on New Year's Eve, a week after we had signed up the half millionth member, we had a party. Drew was drunk. I…I had a glass of white wine. We…ended up next to each other when it struck twelve. He…kissed me. In front of the whole company." She looked away. But the small tremble that went through her couldn't be hidden. "I kissed him back…I think. Before I remembered to put a stop to it."

"You think? It's not rocket science."

She glared at him and pushed her hair back. "I don't know what happened or how I let it happen. Just that it was the stupidest thing I've ever done. In my defense, I had got the news that day that Robert was out of danger and with Travelogue making such a big milestone…" She ran shaking fingers over her face. "I've been kicking myself for losing control like that. I never meant to…"

"Enjoy a kiss?"

"Yes. For one thing, it was unprofessional. For another, it was reckless on so many levels. A relationship with any man is not in my plan right now. Career is my focus."

Nathan frowned, seeing embarrassment and something else. He admired her drive to succeed in her career, understood that it might leave very little time for a personal life. If not for the thread of wistfulness in her face.

Every time he had a conversation with her, he was struck sharp by how innocent she was. Yet from everything Maria had told him with grudging respect, Riya had always worked hard, pretty much taken care of herself even when she was a child. Had helped his father every way she could.

The parameters of her life—Travelogue and its current client base, the estate, his father and her mother—they were all so rigidly defined. To step out of any of them, he realized, sent her into a tailspin.

And the one kiss reflected her age, she was calling it a momentary lapse in judgment.

"You have a plan for your life?" he asked, disbelief slowly cycling into something far more insidious.

She fidgeted in her seat. "A road map, yes… Drew is too volatile, unreliable. When I'm ready to settle down in a decade or so, I want a stable man who'll stand by me for the rest of my life, who'll be a good husband and father. Right now I can't allow myself to be sidetracked by—"

Slow anger simmered to life inside him. "It seems your plan allows for everything except living."

Her gaze flew to him.

Nathan uncurled his fist, willing the unbidden anger to leave him. She was of no consequence to him. None.

What did it matter to him if the naive fool spent the rest of her life slaving over the estate and company, wasting her life instead of living it?

"Do you have a list of qualities and a timeline for when you'll meet and mate with this ideal specimen of manhood too?"

Her gaze flashed with warning. "My personal life has no bearing on you. I'm only telling you this because you're questioning my professional behavior."

"Yet you dare ask me questions about my visits, about where I've been all these years."

"That's because I've seen the pain you've caused Robert for so long. Much as I try, I can't help wondering what kind of man stays away from everything he knows for a decade, without once looking back. You didn't even stay for your mother's funeral. You didn't care about what happened to your father for a decade. You didn't come when Maria... If I hadn't realized that she knew where you were—"

"Enough."

He leveled a hard look at her and Riya knew she had crossed a line.

"I want a new software model created within three weeks for an executive membership and a package from your team on the front end. You'll see the launch event."

Her mouth fell open, her stomach dropping into a vacuum. "It can't be ready in three weeks. I'll need to redesign the whole software engine, and we don't have any of the product development team to put the package together. I have only worked behind the scenes till now."

"Then step into the front. Work smarter and learn to delegate. Use your staff as more than your cheerleader. And the next time a colleague professes undying love to you on office premises and continues to harass you, you'll immediately file a report with HR."

She slapped her palms against the table between them, something snapping in her. "How long will you hate me for what my mother did?"

"Don't overestimate your place in my life, Riya." Each word dripped with cutting incisiveness. "Although thanks to your manipulation, I'm veering toward moderate annoyance."

"Then how long will you punish me for lying?"

"Punish you?"

"Yes. Lording it over me, dragging me across the world, setting goals that ensure my failure, enforcing this…this…"

He stood up from his seat and she craned her neck.

"You've got quite the imagination for someone who's determined to live her life by a plan. We made a deal, one that you started. You're bending all out of shape now because I'm holding you to your end of it?"

His voice was soft, all the more efficient for it. The angrier she got, the calmer he grew. And perversely she wanted to ruffle that frosty, still exterior, wanted to make him angry, hurt, feel something.

That scared her more than anything.

"Or is it me personally that you can't deal with?"

She stood up, meaning to get away. "I don't know what you're talking about."

He grasped her arm, the lean breadth of his body too close. "If we're going for all-out honesty, one of us has to state it for what it is."

Panic unfurled in sharp bursts in her belly.

As long as it was unsaid, as long as it was just in her

head, and in their glances and in his knowing, arrogant smile, she could still ignore it, she could still believe it to be just a by-product of how much power he held in her life right now.

"There's nothing to state." She tugged at his fingers but his grip was relentless. Bending down, he neatly trapped her against her seat. His gaze moved over her as if it could touch her. Lingered over her eyes, her nose, her mouth. The sound of their breaths, labored and fast, surrounded her in the silence. She didn't understand where this energy was coming from or why it was so strong.

When she kissed Drew, it had been pleasant, nice. Like a breezy day on the coast, like sitting in front of a warm fire in cold winter.

When Nathan touched her, it felt as if she would come apart from the inside if he continued. Left her feeling shaken when he stopped. Probably how someone would feel when jumping off a cliff. How someone felt when playing with fire.

"Please, Nate, let me go."

A smile wreathed his mouth. It was full of satisfaction, of understanding, even a little glimmer of resignation. The pads of his fingers pressed into her skin. His breath caressed the tip of her nose, his gaze dipping to her mouth. "You didn't wonder what would happen if I came back and turned your life upside down. You didn't expect this current that comes to life when we look at each other. Do you have a plan for what to do in this twisted situation we're in?"

Emotion, that emotion she wanted to see in him, it coated every word. This unbidden fire between them, for all his forcing the matter, he didn't like or want it any more than she did.

"Do you think your life is still completely in your control?" he asked.

"It would be if you weren't so determined to play games with me."

"I haven't done one thing today that I wouldn't have even if you weren't the most beautiful, most infuriating, the strangest creature I've ever met."

A soft gasp left her mouth at the vehemence in his words. The small sound reverberated in the quiet cabin.

Releasing her, he stepped back, his gaze a wintry frost again. Glanced at her with unease. As if he didn't know what had happened.

"You are the problem, Riya. Not me. It rattles you when I come near you, when I lay a finger on you. You fight it by attributing motives to me. Tell me you'll sell the estate, and I'll have the pilot turn the plane around. Tell me you've had enough."

"Why are you fighting me so much on this?" she said, desperation spewing from her. "What do you lose by talking to Robert a few times? What do you have in there, a big hard rock for a heart?"

Her attack took him by surprise. A scornful twist to his mouth, he stared at her. And Riya could literally see the minute he decided she wasn't worth it. Whatever it was.

Perverse disappointment flooded her and she stood immobile in its wake.

"I have no heart. At least not a working one." His mouth barely moved, his jaw clenched tight. "I'll never forgive him for what he did to my mother. He let her down when she needed him. Flaunted his affair with Jackie in her face. Just the mere thought of him fills me with anger, reminds me of my own weakness."

CHAPTER FIVE

RIYA STRAIGHTENED IN her leather seat as they touched down on the runway. She had spent the entire flight alternately staring at the screen and catching sneaky glances of Nathan. He, however, seemed to have very effectively removed her from his mind.

The new software model that he had demanded loomed high at the back of her mind, but she was way too restless to focus.

As much as it galled her, the infuriating man was right.

All these years, she had drowned herself in work, focused on the estate and Robert and Jackie. Had spent it all denying herself a normal life.

What was the point in inviting anyone into her life when all she faced in the end was pain and disappointment? When, inevitably, she would be deserted? A small mistake, and look how easily Drew had walked away from her. Wasn't it better than the hurt that followed if she allowed herself to form any kind of attachment, to constantly look inside and wonder what she was lacking?

For years, she had wondered why her father had given up on her so easily, why she wasn't enough for Jackie as she struggled herself...

Safer to focus on work, to develop her career. At least, the results were dependable. But it also meant she was woefully unequipped to deal with her attraction to Nathan. And all the ensuing little things she was sharply becoming aware of.

Simple things like how different the texture and feel of his hand was against hers. How the scent of him invaded her senses when he stood so close. How there was a constant battle within her between reveling in what he evoked and fear that she was losing control.

How slowly but surely his words were beginning to affect her...

As she followed him down the plane's stairs, she stilled on the second step, taking in the vast expanse of land, a beautiful landscape of beaches and water. Her mouth slack, she blinked at the sheer magnificence of it.

The island was a paradise and apparently Nathan's next billion-dollar venture.

A team of engineers and architects greeted him, all dressed in casual shorts and T-shirts. "Is Sonia still working?" he asked, and was told yes.

Her curiosity about the island and the project he had mentioned trumping everything else, Riya stayed behind him. His attention to detail, his incisive questions...it was like watching a super computer at work.

The island, she learned, was to be rented out as a private retreat to celebrities who wanted a slice of heaven to get away to, at a staggering half a million dollars per day. The tour they had been given, driving around in buggies, had permanently stuck her jaw to her chest.

There were a hundred acres of heaven, with six Balinese-style abodes, a submarine that could be chartered to see the untouched coral reef, a Jacuzzi that could apparently house two dozen people at once and an unnamed attraction that everyone mentioned with sheer excitement. Also included on the island were private beaches, infinity pools that led into the ocean, tennis courts, a wide array of water sports and every single abode came with a personal chef, a masseuse and a housekeeping staff of ten.

No small detail was beneath Nathan's attention. He had even asked after the scientific team dedicated to studying an almost extinct gecko that was native to the island.

The more Riya saw, the more guilt and awe gripped her insides.

He owned all this and he still wanted that small estate. He had chosen to accept her little deal when he could have done anything with her company, with her and not looked back. That didn't speak of a heartless, uncaring man, and Riya struggled to accept what it did mean.

Just the mere thought of him fills me with anger, reminds me of my own weakness.

His words pinged incessantly in her head all afternoon. Beneath the cold fury, there had been so much pain, an ache that she understood. All she knew was that his mother, Anna, had died of a heart condition. But why say Robert reminded him of his own weakness?

Seeing his dynamic interactions with his team, however, his face wreathed into laughter at something, she found it hard to see any weakness in him. He was gorgeous, wealthy and possessed of an incisive mind that had made him a billionaire.

Sometime since they had arrived, he had changed into khaki shorts and a cotton T-shirt. The relentless sun caressed his face, glinted in his beard, reflecting myriad shades of blue in his eyes. The watch on his wrist glinted expensively as he signaled to someone, and his hands and arms caught her attention.

His gaze found her right then, as though he was aware of her fascination, and she dragged her own back to the delicious food that they had been served. They were lunching on the covered terrace of one of the villas.

Fresh water cascaded into a whirlpool on the terrace below and poured into the enormous swimming pool, its water as clear as crystal. The living area was cavernous with tropical sunlight streaming in from every direction.

Using local stone and Brazilian hardwood floors, the villa was an architectural beauty that boasted ten bedrooms. Decorated with priceless antiques, Indian rugs, art pieces and bamboo furniture from Bali, the villa was situated above a hill providing a spectacular view of the beach.

The chocolate soufflé had barely melted in her mouth when Nathan sat down in the chair next to her.

"What do you think?" he asked, and his entire team had come to a grinding halt as though his very question to her demanded utter silence.

Riya had met his captivating gaze, warning herself not to read so much into a simple question. "Everything is brilliant, gorgeous," she replied, feeling his scrutiny like a warm caress. "But you don't need Travelogue to find high-end customers for this place."

She had known he had dragged her along only to make her uncomfortable. Still, disappointment slashed through her. For a few hours, she had forgotten their little deal, had felt like a part of his dynamic team, had realized how much she had been missing living in her own world.

"I have something else in mind for Travelogue. The island is the place we're testing it out. Also, every year, there will be three months when we'll offer up the six villas independently for a deal. A special sale for our low-end customers, a chance for an average man to experience a little slice of heaven."

"And the income from those three months? It goes to a charity, doesn't it?"

The Anna Ramirez Foundation, she remembered, her heart feeling too big for her chest.

"Yes."

"I don't know what to say. Nathan, I—"

"You get to do the work." He cut her off on purpose. "I want you to build a new server plus a front-end package from your team that will tie this to the software model you will be designing. And we'll need—"

"Different tiers for pricing, and packages and even log-in portals for different members," she replied, a keen sense of excitement vibrating through her.

She had a feeling she had scratched not even the surface of the man he was. And yet she had judged him for not seeing Robert all these years. It scared her and excited her, like nothing else, what else she might learn about him in the coming weeks. And there was no way to turn back from this, no way to curb the curiosity that swept through her.

"Maybe you'll last long enough with me, then," he said, standing up.

Riya looked up, hanging between the urge to apologize, why she had no idea, and to leave the status quo. There was something about the tone of his voice that said he had neatly pushed her into the employee box. That he regretted the tiny little fracture in his control earlier.

The easy humor, the carefully constructed indifference, they were all a foil for something beneath, something deeper. Riya wanted to run away and delve deeper at the same time.

"Take a couple of hours off. The island heat can be too strong for newcomers."

She nodded, feeling a strange sense of disappointment as he walked away.

Nathan was e-signing a bunch of documents for his virtual manager when he heard more than one long sigh from his engineering team and a subdued curse fall from the local construction crew they had hired.

Baffled by the sudden change in the tenor, he looked up from his tablet.

His own breath fisted in his chest. Languid energy uncoiled in his belly.

Clad in a white stretchy top that hugged the globes of her lush breasts, and denim shorts that showcased the lean muscles in her long legs, Riya was coming down the steep path. Her hair was tied into a high ponytail and swung left and right with her long stride. She wore flats, the strings of which tied around her ankles in the most sensual way.

He couldn't fault his team for losing their focus, nor fault her for her simple attire. The weather was a combination of damp and stifling heat.

Every inch of him thrummed with tension and anticipation. Locking his jaw, Nathan turned away. Fought the insidious thought supplied by his mind that he could have her if he wanted.

Her skin glistened golden in the sun. And it felt like raw silk, he knew now. And her brown eyes took on the darkest shade when he touched her. The faintest whiff of roses clung to her skin. Two tiny things about her that he would never be able to erase.

Even as he warned himself, his gaze traveled over the modest neckline of the sleeveless T-shirt that draped over her lush breasts and dipped to her waist.

She stopped and looked around her with a smile that only added to her appeal.

The need to run his fingers over that graceful line of her neck, to sink his hands into her hair, to shake loose the safe, sterile world she had built for herself, to be the one to wake her up to her own potential in every way was almost overwhelming.

She was like a beautiful butterfly that refused to leave the cocoon, and he wanted to be the one to lure her out.

With a curse that punctured the stunned silence around him, he shot up from his seat. Turned away from the temptation she presented. Reminded himself that he had conquered obstacles and fears that were far more dangerous.

Things were already too twisted between them. And from her episode with Drew, he knew she could never handle him.

Nathan needed the rule-following, road-map-for-my-life female in his life the way he needed a heart attack.

What he should do was to put her on a flight home immediately and forget her or her little deal.

And yet with the excitement thrumming through her as she reached them, her wide eyes taking in the equipment around, he couldn't find it in him to break his word.

Three more months of this torture, and he was already chafing against his own rules.

Pushing her shades on to keep the orange glare away, Riya looked around herself. All the guesses she had made were off by a mile. It was not a casino, or a resort or a theater or an architectural marvel of any kind.

A huge crane stood behind the working team. An enclosure that was as tall as her surrounded the crane.

Her heart beating with a thunderous roar, she stepped inside and stilled.

A raised platform with an exquisitely designed, waisthigh iron railing that went all around sat center stage in the enclosure. The most luxurious little sofa with legroom in the front sat against the back wall, and Riya noted that it was riveted to the wooden floor of the platform. As she watched with spiraling curiosity, tiny little lights, strategically placed around the perimeter of the floor turned on, casting brilliant light around.

Two small tables sat on either side of the sofa. Exotic orchids in vases along with an assortment of other things like expensive chocolate and even a bucket of champagne in ice sat on the tables.

And the final thing she noticed was safety tethers on each side of the sofa.

Her breath hitched in her throat as she realized what the elaborate setup meant.

She turned around, determined to find out if the fantastic idea was really true, when Nathan and a tall brunette stepped inside the enclosure.

Meeting her gaze, Nathan tilted his head toward the newcomer. "This is Sonia Lopez. She's the project manager."

A kind of suspended silence hung in the air where the woman obviously waited for him to say more and then gave up.

"Riya Mathur. She's the software architect on a company I acquired recently."

Relief sweeping through her, Riya shook the woman's hand.

Sonia cast another quick look toward Nathan before stepping out of the enclosure.

Leaving her alone with Nathan.

She jerked as he clasped her wrist and tugged her toward the raised platform. "Let's go."

Her eyes wide, fear beating a tattoo in her head, she shook her head. "No. I would very much like to be a spectator, thank you."

The most unholy delight dawned in his eyes, a wicked fire that turned them into a fiery blue. His mouth curved into a smile; it was the most gorgeous he had ever seemed to her. There was no facade, no frost. Only pure, undisguised laughter at her cowardice. "Not a choice. If you want—"

Surprising him, she took a few steps forward and cast a quick glance at the setup. "It's not fair, Nathan. My going on this has nothing to do with my company's abilities."

"Life's not fair, Riya. But you have to grab your thrills where you can."

With that, he pulled her and they stepped through the railing.

"You sound like a little boy going on an adult ride for the first time."

He clasped her hand and pulled her down to the sofa. Her knees quaking, she managed to stay still as he clipped the safety belt around them. And now, instead of an intangible one, there was a rope binding them together.

Breathe, Riya.

Within minutes, a faint whirring began and the crane unfolded, lifting them up into the sky.

Riya gasped and clasped his hand tighter, at the sheer magnificence of the feeling. Her mouth dry, she laughed giddily as they went higher and higher.

The whole island was laid out beneath them like a glittering jewel. The villas, the infinity pool, the beautiful grounds, she had never seen a more breathtaking sight. Her heart raced at a thunderous speed, a strange pull in her stomach.

When it felt as if she could extend her hand and touch the clouds, they came to a standstill. She found her gaze drawn to Nathan's profile.

His nostrils flaring, he looked around them, his eyes glittering with thrill and energy.

It was the most exhilarating thing she had ever been part of, the most beautiful sight she had ever seen. And the effect of it still paled against the sheer masculinity of the man holding her hand.

Panic surged within her and Riya breathed in greedy gulps. He tightened his clasp on her fingers. "You okay, Riya?"

She nodded and met his gaze. "This is your true thrill, isn't it?"

The safety belts forced them much too close for her comfort. When he turned, his thigh pressed against hers and Riya sucked in a sharp breath through a dry throat. "Yes."

Laughing, because it was just impossible not to when you were hundreds of feet in the sky, Riya nodded. "It's spectacular."

"I think so."

"I hope it's not going to be limited to this island," she said, thinking of how many people, average people like her, would miss it if it were. "Something like this, everyone should have access to it."

He turned to look at her, a warmth in his eyes. "We're aiming for Las Vegas, Paris, Bali, São Paulo, Mumbai, London in the first round. As soon as the approvals are in, we'll launch the new level of membership and also offer an exclusive offer to our low tier members at a discounted price."

Riya glanced around once again, her heart swelling in her chest. "It's going to be magnificent. What's it going to be called?"

He shrugged and smiled. And Riya felt a different kind of pull on her senses. "Haven't decided yet," he said.

Before she could blink, the safety tether loosened. Imagining them plummeting to death, Riya gasped and held on tighter.

Only to realize that Nathan had undone the belt.

"No…no…no…Nate…Please *Noooooo*," she screamed as he tugged her up until they were standing. He dragged her forward to the railing, and the whole setup swung in the air. Her stomach lurched, and Riya plastered herself to him from the side, breathing hard.

He stiffened for an infinitesimal moment even as the ridges and planes of his lean body pressed against her.

Adrenaline pumped through her, her muscles trembling with a thousand little tremors. She was shamelessly plastered against his back, but for the life of her, she couldn't seem to peel herself away from him.

His fingers tugged at her arms around him. His smile dug grooves in his cheeks. His hair was wind-ruffled; his eyes were glowing. "Don't worry, Riya," he whispered, tucking her tight against his side. "I won't let you fall."

Sandwiched snugly against his side, Riya looked around at the magnificent sight.

Her heart boomeranged against her rib cage; her senses spun. It was a moment of utter perfection, of glorious beauty.

When he pulled her back down, she went reluctantly, suddenly loath for it to be over.

Letting her breath out slowly, she settled into the moment, grateful to him for allowing her to be a part of it. They sat like that for a while. Everything about the evening cloaked them in intimacy.

Gratitude that he had given her a chance, that he'd let her be a part of this, and some unknown sensation she couldn't stem welled up inside her. And beneath it, Riya felt a sliver of fear that she was crossing into unknown territory. "Nathan, I'm very sorry for everything that...for all the hurt we caused you. I can't imagine what you must have felt learning about Jackie and me so soon after she died. I'm so—"

His arm around behind her, he turned, and his finger landed on her mouth. "I don't require an apology from you."

Raising her gaze to his, Riya forced herself to focus on

his words rather than the sensation of how her own mouth felt. "Is Maria right? All these years, would you have come back if Jackie and I had been gone?"

"No, I wouldn't have. Leave the past where it is, Riya. Come out of your cocoon, and live your life, butterfly."

The warmth in his endearment caused minute little flutters all over her.

"Just because I don't stand hundreds of feet in the sky and touch the clouds on a regular basis doesn't mean I'm not living," she countered.

His long fingers landed on her jaw, the abraded tips pressing into her skin. Their legs tangled in front of them. He shifted sideways until he was all she saw. Found herself staring into languid pools of molten hunger.

Desire punched through her, every inch of her thrumming with alarm and anticipation.

They were hanging in the sky with a slice of paradise laid out beneath them for as far as she could see. And the man in front of her, the most gorgeous, the most complex man she had ever met. In that moment, something she had held tight inside her, something she hadn't even realized existed, slowly unraveled.

Just a little movement of his head and suddenly his breath feathered over her nose.

Her fingers landed on his chest, to push him back. But the thudding roar of his heart beneath muted any rational thought. A slow fire swirled low in her belly, spreading to every inch of her.

One long finger traced her jawline in reverence, the tips of the others grazing her neck. "I think it's the most terrible thing in the world that you don't know whether you enjoyed a kiss or not, butterfly. The most horrible thing that no man has shown you, without doubt."

Liquid desire darkened the ice blue into the shade of a cloudy sky.

Every other thought faded from her mind except this man, every other sound faded except the loud peal of her own pulse. Every other sensation fled except for the insistent and answering thrum of her skin at the hunger in his eyes.

The brush of his lips against hers was at once cool and hot, testing and assured, bold and yet inviting. His beard rasped against her tender skin, wreaking havoc on her. The contrast of his soft lips and the roughness of his beard... her entire world came crashing around her.

It was her own response to the press of his soft mouth that blew her apart, the strength of the deep longing that jolted to life inside her. Her fingers crinkled against his shirt as he increased the pressure and the back of her head hit the leather.

Heat, unlike any she had ever known, slithered and pooled in every molten muscle as he licked her lower lip. His body teased against her own, a soft invitation to press herself against the hardness.

She purred, like a stroked cat, and gasped at the curl of pleasure and instantly, he pushed on. Only when it vibrated through her did she realize that it was a groan that fell from her mouth. Pleading for more, demanding more.

And it wasn't just their mouths that were touching anymore. His fingers inched into her hair and held her slanted for him; his lean body enveloped her; he was everywhere.

He felt alien, yet familiar. Her thighs trembled, locked against the tensile strength of his; her belly dipped and she groaned.

The tenor of the kiss went from slow, soft appraisal, a testing of fit and sensation to pure, exploding, ravenous heat.

He bit and stroked, nibbled and licked. He kissed her as if they would both drown if he stopped, and that's how it felt. So she let him. Stayed passive and panting under his caresses, let him steal her breath and infuse her with his own.

A freeing desperation joined the molten warmth inside her.

When he stopped, when he sucked in a shuddering breath, everything inside Riya protested that he did. She flushed as he pulled back and locked eyes with her. His gaze was the darkest she had seen yet, his breath coming in and out a little out of sync. The pad of his thumb moved over her lower lip, and she shivered again.

"Did you enjoy that kiss, butterfly?"

Riya fell back against the couch, her fingers on her still-trembling mouth.

That kiss had been beyond perfect. But the mockery in his eyes grated; the laid-back arrogance in it stung. It was nothing but a challenge to him. Whereas the entire foundation of her life had shaken.

"I would have been surprised if I hadn't," she said, dredging up the cool tone from somewhere. Her fingers still on his chest, she glared at him. Her heart still hadn't resumed its normal pace. "Very altruistic of you," she said, a little hollow in her chest, waiting for him to deny.

He grinned instead. "I haven't been called one of this generation's greatest philanthropists for no reason."

"Forgive me if being your charity case doesn't fill me with excitement."

Turning away from him, Riya sought silence. Fortunately for her, she felt them coming down again. They had just stepped out of the enclosure when they saw Sonia waiting there, her gaze stricken, her features pinched with pain.

Mortification came hard at Riya. Had the entire crew

seen them kissing? If Nathan hadn't been satisfied with proving his point and stopped, how far would she have let him go?

Next to her, Nathan turned into a block of ice, and Riya fled fast, wondering what she had stepped into. Reaching the villa, she couldn't help casting a quick look at Nathan and Sonia.

The way they stood close but not touching, the tension that emanated from them, their body language so familiar with each other—it was clear they were or had been lovers. And the pain in Sonia's eyes had been real enough.

Here was one clue to his past, an answer to the unrelenting curiosity that had been eating through her. A streak of jealousy and self-doubt held her still.

Shaking, Riya wiped her mouth with the back of her hand. If only his taste would come off so easily. But her mind rallied quickly enough.

He had stopped so easily when he was done. She was nothing but a naive, curious entertainment to a man who built castles in the sky, to the man who made billions by selling an experience.

Riya avoided Nathan over the next few days. With enough workload to challenge her and the very real threat of losing Travelogue, it was easy. Not that she had been able to get that toe-curling kiss or Sonia and her stricken expression out of her mind.

Determined to assure Sonia, and herself, that there was nothing between her and Nathan, she had gone looking for her the next evening. Only to find that Sonia had left the island that morning.

The fact that Nathan had so neatly, and quietly, dispatched her infuriated Riya. How dare he comment on her conduct when he possessed no better standards? Was this the true Nathan, flitting from woman to woman and walking away when he was done? Why did she even care?

But she kept her thoughts to herself, the very absence of his easy humor over the next few days enough of a deterrent.

He was her employer, and Robert's son.

She spent the rest of her days between work, fixing any defects for Travelogue's software, and her nights, soaking up the sultry beauty of the island. One afternoon the day before they were set to leave, she was working in one of the bedrooms in the villa she was sharing with four other female members of the crew.

The bedroom had open walls, with three-hundred-and-sixty-degree views of the island, bringing cool breezes in. Riya smiled, having finally hit on a solution to a design problem she had been trying to solve for two days.

She stood up and took a long sip of her fruity drink with a straw umbrella when Nathan appeared at the entrance. The cold drink did nothing to fan the flames that the sight of him dressed in a white cotton T-shirt that showcased his lean chest and hard midriff and tight blue jeans ignited.

Wraparound shades hid his expression, but Riya couldn't care. Her gaze glued itself to his freshly shaved angular jaw, traveled over his chin. The beard was gone, although there was already stubble again.

And the mouth it revealed sparked an instant hunger in her.

Men didn't have, *shouldn't* have mouths like his. Lush and sensual with the upper lip shaped like a perfect bow. A cushion of softness that contrasted against the roughness and hardness of the rest of him.

She had the most insane, overwhelming urge to walk up to him and press her lips to his again, to see how it would feel without the beard. She pointed her finger at him and heard the words fall from her mouth. "You shaved it."

Instant heat flared in his gaze, and Riya gasped, only then realizing she had said it out loud.

"What did you say?" he said, coming farther into the room, and she wished she could disappear.

"Nothing," she managed, lifting her gaze to his. "Were we supposed to meet?"

He looked behind her and saw the papers she had been scribbling on and her laptop. "Riya, why didn't you go with the rest of them for the submarine tour? The marine life you get to see here is unparalleled. With your record, it'll be another decade before you leave California again."

His remark grated even as she was aware that it was true. "I was stuck on a tricky design problem and I wanted to resolve it. And I did. I have an initial model ready."

The surprise flashing through his gaze went eons toward restoring her balance. "Already?" he said.

"You did put my life's work under scrutiny and up for assessment," she said sweetly, handing him her laptop.

More than once, her work had come to her rescue. From a young age, she had been comfortable around numbers and equations and then code. Because you could be sure y would come out when you put in x.

Not like people and emotions. Not like the crushing pain of abandonment and the cavern of self-doubt and longing it pushed you into. Nothing like this incessant confusion and analysis their kiss had plunged her into.

He made no reply to her comment. Took the laptop from her and sat down at the foot of the bed. After a full ten minutes, he closed her laptop and met her gaze. Shot her a couple of incisive questions. Finally he nodded. "It's better than I expected." A deafening sound whooshed in Riya's ears.

"Upload the docs into the company's cloud. I'll have my

head of IT take a look too. Travelogue can have this project based on how the rest of your team brings it together for beta testing. But, irrespective of your team, you're Run-Away material."

The whooshing turned into a roar. Exhilaration coursed through her and she damped it down. Too many questions lingered in her, and Riya couldn't untangle professional from personal ones. Only that he would always do this to her...make her wonder about things she shouldn't want. "I don't want another job. I want my company back."

He stood up and faced her, close enough to see the small nick on the underside of his jaw. The scent of his aftershave made her mouth dry. "You're halfway there, then."

"Until you remember why I'm not signing over the estate?"

"Excuse me?"

"I would like to know what you have in store for me, how far you're willing to go for..." When he waited with a grating patience, she said through gritted teeth, "You kissed me."

Nathan frowned, fighting the impulse to kiss that wide mouth again. It was bad enough that damn kiss was all he could think about. Even the incident it had instigated with Sonia hadn't been enough to temper the fire it had started in him. "And you kissed me back. I don't see your point exactly."

Something combative entered her eyes. "What happened to Sonia?"

The question instantly put him on guard. The hurt expression in Sonia's eyes had been haunting him the past few days. And the fact that he had caused her pain, even after he'd been careful not to, scoured through him.

"None of your business," he said, turning away from Riya.

Her hand on his arm stalled him. "Just answer the question, Nathan."

"You think one kiss gives you the right to take me to task?"

"No. I'm trying to understand you."

"Why?"

"You hold the fate of my company in your hand. You hold my fate in your hand. I don't think it's worth killing myself if you're unscrupulous. If you make a habit of taking your employees as lovers and then firing them when things turn sour, I'd rather cut my losses now."

"That's quite a picture you paint of me," he said, laughing at the nefarious motives Riya attributed to his actions.

Even preferred it to the truth. Because the reality of losing a friend who had known him for over a decade was all too painful, the hollow in his gut all too real. The number of people who were constants in his life over the past decade were two—Sonia and his manager, Jacob.

The realization that he was condemning his very soul to loneliness still shook him.

But then Sonia had left him with no choice, giving him an ultimatum between her love and her friendship. One time of seeking comfort with her, of breaking his rule, and she had forgotten he didn't do relationships, forgotten that he lived his life alone by choice, that he'd turned his heart into a stone painstakingly over the years.

That he couldn't let himself become weak by giving in to emotions.

He'd immediately told Sonia that it had been a mistake, that it changed nothing. That they could never repeat it.

It was his fault that he hadn't held her at arm's length like with everyone from the beginning, that she was hurt. His fault that he'd given in to temptation with the woman in front of him, even more ill-suited to handle him than Sonia.

Her fingers bunched in his shirt, Riya's brown eyes blazed with anger and confusion. "How can you be so... so careless about someone's pain? So casual about the havoc you're wreaking?"

"On her?" He gripped her hands with his, feeling a powerlessness course through him. He had punished himself by sending Sonia away, and that Riya judged him for that only fanned his fury. "Or on you and your plan? It was a damn good kiss, Riya, but don't let it distract you from your plan."

She let go of him as if he had struck her. "I know I'm nothing more than an entertaining challenge to you. And that kiss...it's nothing but you proving to me that I'm out of my element with you. But she and you have known each other for a decade, and now no one knows where she is."

He turned toward the stunning vista, his knuckles showing white against the brown of the wood paneling. "No injustice has been done to her. Sonia is a twenty percent shareholder in RunAway. She'll be all right." It was the only thing that gave him solace.

"Then why did she leave?"

"Because I told her in no uncertain terms that she has no place in my life anymore. Pity, because she was my only friend," he said in a low voice.

Riya reeled at how easily the words fell from Nathan's mouth. But the affected disinterest didn't extend to the pain in his eyes. Whatever he had done with Sonia, it hadn't left him untouched. "Why?"

"She messed up at the one thing I asked her not to do."

"What could she have done that you removed her from your life like you would delete a file?"

He smiled at her consternation, but there was no warmth in that smile. There was no mockery, there was no humor in his gaze. Only the shadow of pain, only unflinching honesty. "She fell in love with me. Despite knowing I'm allergic to the whole concept."

The impact of his words came at Riya like a bucket of ice-cold water.

"She knew I didn't want her love. She knew nothing was ever going to come out of it. But she didn't listen. Now she's cost us both a friendship that should have lasted a lifetime."

It didn't matter that it hurt him to lose that. He had still cut Sonia out of his life. He had never turned around for Robert. He was exactly the kind of man who walked away without looking back. The why of it didn't matter in front of his actions.

It was all the proof Riya needed to realize that of all the men on the planet she could have been attracted to, Nathan was the most dangerous of all.

CHAPTER SIX

FOR THREE WEEKS after they returned to San Francisco, Riya slept in one of the extra rooms that had been booked at a downtown hotel in addition to the conference room for the Travelogue team.

Nathan had given her team three weeks to put together a package for the launch event, and for her, to build the software model that would support that package. Even though he could still dismantle them if they didn't come up to scratch, he was definitely giving them a chance first.

It didn't help knowing that his own team from another company was also putting something together at the same time. He expected her company to fail and she was determined to prove him wrong.

Three weeks in which Riya had backed off from pestering him about their deal, in which she had slept only minimum hours to develop the final model for software, in which he had set a relentless pace, driving every member of Travelogue and his own team crazy. Three weeks in which Jackie had figured out somehow that Nathan was back because of Riya, that she had willingly offered to sign away the estate.

Nothing Riya said helped, not that she had a lot of time.

Nathan worked just as hard as they did, putting in long hours, giving much-needed direction and expertise. If they encountered a problem, there was nowhere to go until a solution was found.

As manic as he had been in his energy, he also had tremendous motivating capabilities. With the entire team working together in a conference hall, exchanging ideas and finding instant solutions for challenges they encountered, it had been the best workweek of her life.

There was something to his energy, to his credo of doing everything right then, of implementing an idea as best and as soon as possible.

Now the beta testing they had done of the model had been a spectacular success, and they had entered the next iteration. It was three weeks since Nate and she had struck that deal, and he had yet to see Robert.

She'd been trying to get a word with him for two days and failed. The man was a machine, traveling, working, managing teams all over the world... Knowing that tonight he was just a few floors above her, in the penthouse suite, she had to take this chance.

Squaring her shoulders, Riya took the elevator. The doors swished open and she entered the vast black-and-white-tiled foyer.

For a few seconds, she was lost in the brilliant San Francisco skyline visible through the French doors. Subdued ceiling lights cast a hushed glow over the steel and chrome interior.

She spotted Nathan in the open lounge, clad in gray sweatpants that hung precariously low on his hips, doing push-ups.

The line of his back, defined and pulling tight over stretched muscles, was the most beautiful thing she had ever seen. The copper highlights in his hair glinted and winked in the low lights.

Sweat shone over the smooth, tanned skin of his back,

his breathing punctured by his soft grunts. Warmth uncurled in Riya's belly, her own breathing becoming choppy
and disjointed.

In a lithe movement that would have made a wild animal proud, he shot to his feet and grabbed a bottle of water.

Her mouth dry, Riya watched as his Adam's apple
bobbed. A drop of sweat poured down his neck and chest,
which was lean with sharply bladed muscles. A sprinkle
of copper-colored hair covered his pectorals and formed
a line down his hard stomach. His shoulder bones jutted
out, his throat working convulsively as he swallowed. He
wasn't pumped up with bulging muscles, but what was
there of him had such sculpted definition that her fingers
itched to trace it.

She had the most overwhelming urge to cross the hall
and to press her hands against that warm skin, breathe in
the scent of him.

Shivering from a heat that speared across her skin like
a fire, she was about to clear her throat when she saw him
sway. He was so tall and lean that it was like seeing an immovable thing buck against a faint breeze. Her heart lurched
into her throat as his knees buckled under him.

Riya didn't know she could move so fast. Working on
auto, she grabbed his shoulders just as he sank onto his
haunches, his head bent. She tapped his cheek, fear twisting in her gut. "Nathan…Nathan…"

She ran her hands all over him, his shoulders, his neck,
her throat aching. "Nate, honey? Please look at me…"

His fingers closed on her upper arm, almost bruising in
their grip, and he slowly raised his head. His gaze remained
unfocused for a second longer, before it rested on her face.
He blinked then. "Did I scare you, butterfly?"

Fear still clawed at her, but she fought it. This was

ridiculous. He was right in front of her, solid and arrogant, as always.

"Riya?"

"Yes?"

His fingers moved from her arm to her wrist, firing neurons left and right. "Don't leave just yet, okay?"

She nodded, the stubble on his jaw scratching against her palm. He didn't look dizzy or disoriented.

Slowly he peeled her fingers from his jaw but didn't let go. "Are you all right?"

Breathing hard, Riya pulled her hand, but his grip was firm. "Me?" She licked her lips and his gaze moved to her mouth. "I'm fine. I thought you...Nathan? You almost fainted."

Something flickered in the depths of his eyes. For a second, Riya could swear it was fear. But it was replaced by warmth.

He flashed a grin that stole her breath. He dragged her hand to his chest.

Skin like rough velvet, hot as if there were a furnace under it, stretched taut over his chest. His nipple poked the base of her palm. His hand covered hers as his heart raced beneath it. "See? In perfect working condition," he murmured, but Riya had no idea what he meant.

And his gaze locked with hers again.

It lingered there with such focus that she wouldn't have known her name then. All she wanted was to sink into his touch, to make sure he was all there. He was always so incredibly focused, so unbearably driven that the seconds-long spell fractured something inside her. Something knotty and hard sat uncomfortably in her throat, and giving in, Riya threw her arms around him. Buried her face in the crook of his neck and closed her eyes. "You scared the hell out of me, Nathan."

He was like a hard, hot statue for a second, and then his hands moved over her back slowly. For a second, his arms were like vines around her, holding her so tight and hard that her lungs struggled to work, and Riya felt her armor shatter.

"Shh. I'm okay," he finally said, releasing her. Pulling her hands forward, he clasped her face with his hands, a burning resolve in his eyes. "I do, however, need a little fortification, butterfly." His breath came in little pants as he made a lithe movement and tugged at her lower lip with his teeth.

A peal of shuddering pleasure rang through Riya and she shivered all over. Gasping at the sharp nip, she braced herself against him. Had every intention of pushing him back. But the moment her palms landed on his shoulders, she was a goner.

With a ragged groan, he covered her mouth again.

He was hot, sweaty, hard, trembling and he was everything she wanted right then. His fingers crept into her hair, held her hard as he stroked her mouth, changed angles and kissed her again.

As if he couldn't stop, as if he couldn't breathe if he did, as if his entire universe was reduced to her.

At least that was how it felt to her.

He pushed her to the floor, and her limbs folded easily.

"Nathan," she whispered as he covered her body with his and claimed her mouth again. He didn't just kiss; he devoured her, ensnared her senses. He made her feel giddily excited and incredibly safe at the same time.

"Please, Riya." His tongue traced the seam of her lower lip; his fingers tightened in her hair. "Open up for me."

The guttural request sent Riya over the edge.

He teased her tongue, nibbled her mouth, bit her lower

lip and when she gasped into his mouth, he stroked it with his tongue. She couldn't breathe with the pleasure as he sucked at her tongue.

This kiss was so different from the first one. It wasn't about give or take. It was about claiming, possessing, about wringing an earthy response that she couldn't deny. It was all about what their bodies did together, how perfectly soft she was against his hardness, how a simple touch and gasp could send them both shuddering.

Her breasts became heavier; her nipples ached. Her spine arched as he locked her hard against him, every inch of him pushing and pressing against her trembling body.

Because lying underneath his shuddering body, lying underneath all the rippling muscle and heated hardness, she felt he was her universe. She opened her legs to cradle him and he moaned against her neck, ground himself into her pulsing heat with a hard grunt.

To feel the hard length of him throb against her aching core, to hear the violent curse that fell from his lips as she moved her pelvis against that unrelenting hardness…it was bliss. It was heaven. And it was nowhere near enough.

"Oh, please, Nate…" Her whisper was raw, close to begging.

She wanted to peel her clothes off, wanted to feel the rasp of his rough skin against her softness, wanted to touch the rigid shaft that was pressing against her sex.

He traced a heated path to her neck and Riya gasped, finding purchase in his shoulders. When he sucked at the crook of her neck while his hand closed over her breast, she bucked off the floor.

And hit the tiled floor with a thud. The impact vibrated through her and she gasped again, her head reeling with pain.

With a curse, Nathan pulled them both up to their knees, his fingers sinking into her hair. Her chest rising and falling, Riya stared at him, shock holding her still under his concern. She felt winded and yet every inch of her also tingled, throbbed. Deprived.

What had she done? What was happening to her? Another few minutes and she would have let him make love to her right there, on the floor. *Begged* him to finish what he had started. A shudder racked through her.

His touch gentle, Nathan clasped her jaw. "Riya, look at me."

Jerking away from his grasp, Riya rose to her feet and straightened her clothes and her hair.

He approached her and she scuttled away again toward the door.

"Stop, Riya." His brow tied into a fierce scowl. "I just want to make sure you're okay."

She shook her head, incredibly frustrated and scared and wound up. "I needed that thud," she said jerkily. "Because it's obvious I've lost all sense. You took my company, you want to take the one place that's ever been home to me, you keep kissing me and I don't stop you and now you've made me bang my head on that hard tile and it hurts like the mother of all…"

Her voice rose on the last few words until she was shouting at him.

"It does seem like you only bring pain to me, so I should be afraid. At least hate you, but why the hell do I not feel either?"

"Don't know." He sounded inordinately pleased with her unwise declaration.

She risked a look at him, saw his mobile mouth twitching and burst into laughter herself. "It's not funny," she yelled at him, even as more laughter was on the way.

She was doubling over then, both laughing and something else, everything piling up on her.

Before she could breathe again, she was in his arms again with his arms locked tight around her, him whispering, "Shh...Riya... You're in shock..."

Male heat, hard muscle, smooth skin...irresistible Nathan. But beneath all that, it felt incredibly good to be just held, to laugh with him, to be in this place that was both strangely intimate and thrilling. A thrill she had had too much of for one evening.

Extracting herself from the cocoon of his arms, she wiped her mouth on her sleeve. "Will you please cover yourself?"

Throwing a strange look at her, he pulled on a sweatshirt and she hurried toward the door.

He appeared between her and the door, his gaze concerned. "You hit your head pretty hard. Check and see if there's a bump."

"I'm fine," she said.

This was not okay; this was not good. Only three weeks in his company and she was ready to throw away all the lessons she had learned, ready to forget all the pain relationships caused, the clawing self-doubt they left.

This heat between them, it was nothing but a challenge for him. He could kiss her and shake it off after a few minutes while the very fabric of her life shook. He would tangle with her and walk away unscathed, while she would wonder and spiral into self-pity and anger. Would forever wonder why it was so easy to walk away from her.

"You're not stepping out until I'm sure you're okay. If you don't check properly, I'll have to do it. And it won't stop there if I lay a hand on you again."

When he stepped toward her, she held him off. Fighting the furious heat climbing up her neck and chest, she poked her fingers under her hair. "There's some swelling."

His pithy curse echoed around them. Riya suddenly remembered.

He had almost fainted, she was sure now. "I thought you were going to collapse. Yet you weren't even surprised. What does it mean? Are you okay? Shouldn't you be the one that should see the doctor?"

Shadows fell over his eyes instantly and Riya knew with a certainty he wasn't going to tell her the truth. Was he unwell? "I think I just overdid it with the exercise." He exhaled in a big rush, ran a hand over his jaw. "I'll be fine. Why did you come here?"

Since they had returned, they danced around each other, avoided even talking to each other without anyone around. And today was a testament to what they had both known.

Apparently even his cold treatment of Sonia wasn't enough to make her see sense.

"I heard that you were leaving for Abu Dhabi. I won't let you leave without seeing Robert."

His hands landed on his lean hips, the bones jutting out at the band of his sweatpants. The hollow planes of his muscles there were the most erotic sight she had ever seen.

"Excuse me?" he said with such exaggerated arrogance that she lifted her gaze to his.

"Yes. To remind you that it's been almost three weeks and you haven't seen Robert yet. You said—"

"Heaven help a man who tangles with you." He shook his head, resignation filling his eyes. "I'll see him tomorrow, fine? Now shut up and sit down."

Switching his cell phone, he rattled off orders for a physician and his chauffeur.

"I don't need to—"

"Doctor or me, Riya?" he challenged.

"Doctor," she said, sinking into the couch.

Even without looking at him, she was aware of his movements at the periphery of her vision. Heard the Velcro rip of his watch. What had happened to his Rolex? Frowning, she turned and saw him look at the display and note down something in a small notepad.

He wiped his face with a towel and Riya pulled her gaze away.

Not that she had missed the rippling muscles or the small birthmark he had on the inside of his biceps. Or that instead of turning her off, even being sweaty, he muddled her senses and filled her with an unbearable longing. Or that he kissed as if he could never stop. Or that he liked having utter control even as he shredded hers.

Or that she had liked it—the way he couldn't stop, the way he took control, the way he just made it hard for her to think, the way he knew exactly what would drive her wild with longing. That she had liked how good it felt to give herself over to him, body and mind, that she trusted him as she had never trusted anyone.

All of them were things she shouldn't know about him. A bunch of things she didn't want to know about herself.

She felt raw, exposed. All she wanted was to run. Far from him, far from herself.

Handing her a chilled bottle of water, he dropped to the couch, and Riya shot up from the couch. He tugged her down. Riya slinked to the edge, her breath coming in choppy bursts. Panic weaved through her.

"You and me, this can't happen, Nathan."

"You can't control everything in life, Riya. I don't want this to happen either, but I've learned the hard way that you can't have everything the way you want it."

She turned to him, desperation raising her tone. "Don't say that, don't just...accept this."

His mouth took on a rueful twist. "What do you want me to do? Wave a wand that'll make it go away? The only solution I can think of is dragging you inside and giving us both what we so desperately want. Maybe we should get it out of the way, and things will be much clearer then."

"This is probably your MO. Seduce a woman, say good-bye and walk away. And cut her out if she doesn't accept your decision. Like you did with Sonia. But I won't fall for you. You have no heart. You're the last kind of man that I should kiss, or want, or…"

Fury dawned in his eyes, turning them into blue fire. "Is it helping, then? If my being here is turning you inside out, how about you give me the blasted estate? I'll leave tonight."

"No. I can't."

"Damn it, Riya. You're not responsible for Jackie or Robert or anyone else. You were what? Twelve? Thirteen, when my mother died?"

"Robert regrets his mistakes. I know he does. He gave Jackie and me a home when we'd have been on the streets. He always had a kind word for me. He gave me shelter, security, food. He treated me like a daughter when my own father didn't bother to even ask after me in a decade."

"Where is your father?"

"How the hell should I know? He never asked about me, never checked how Jackie has been all these years. And this is after he divorced her because she was emotionally volatile. And he let her take me. He let his volatile wife have charge of his eight-year-old daughter.

"For all her weak nature, Jackie at least looked after me in her own way. That's more than I can say for—"

"She didn't do you a favor by doing that, Riya. It was her minimum responsibility. And she failed you in that. She exposed you to her fears, to the staff's hatred at the estate. Don't you see the effects of that in yourself?"

"My life is perfectly fine, thank you. And my professional one even better, thanks to you. The last few days, working with you, have been amazing. I love your energy, I love the way you do things, Nathan. And if Travelogue can—"

"As of this morning, Travelogue has an investment of ten million dollars from RunAway International. I have ordered my lawyers to put the papers together."

RunAway International Group. The brilliant boutique of his companies offering flights, vacations, adventure trips through faraway lands... And now Travelogue was a part of that prestigious group.

Her small company...it was at once the most exciting and breathtaking prospect. She had no words left.

"I'll double the figure you make now and you'll have stock options in RunAway too. I've started the headhunt for a new CEO, and we'll find one by the time I leave."

He was going to leave. That was what she had wanted; that was what she needed. That was their deal.

Then why did the prospect sit like a boulder on her chest? What had changed in a mere three weeks?

Concealing her confusion, Riya forced a smile and thanked him just as the physician knocked on the door.

All the way through him checking on her and the limo ride back to the estate, she couldn't figure out why reaching the goal she had set for herself, why impressing someone of Nathan's vision, why achieving the financial freedom she had always craved was suddenly not enough.

Whatever his behavior toward Robert, Nathan was unlike any other man she had ever met. All her rules, all her fears and insecurities, nothing stayed up when she was around him. He made her want to know him on a visceral level, made her want to abandon her own rules, made her yearn for a connection that she had denied herself for so long.

Nothing mattered with him. Not the pain of the past, not the fear for her future, only the present. And she couldn't let this continue. Already she was in too deep, lost at the thought of him leaving.

Nathan had no idea how long he stood staring at the closed door after Riya left, the silence of his suite pinging on his nerves. Everywhere he looked, he saw her now.

Laughing, smiling, arguing, kissing, moaning, gasping, glaring...even as she denied her nature, there was such an innocence and intensity to the emotions that played on her face.

He wanted her with a sharp, out-of-control need that crossed all lines. Now that he knew how she felt underneath him...

Everything inside him wanted to make her his. Ached to own her, possess her, show her how wild and good it could be between them, longed to make her admit that she felt something for him.

Why not? a voice inside taunted him.

They were both free agents. They were both adults. And she wanted him. There was no doubt about that.

No.

How could he tangle with her knowing what she wanted in life? Even if she was determined to hide from it. How could he touch her knowing that when it was time to leave, she wouldn't be able to handle it?

She hadn't recovered even now from her father's abandonment, from her mother's negligence. Even his father's acceptance and caring of her hadn't been enough to erase that ache from her eyes.

It was in the way she was hiding from life, had slaved herself over her company and the estate, the way she took responsibility for the adults who should have looked after her.

In the way she had risked his wrath and her ruin just to make Robert smile. In the way all the light had gone out of her eyes when she mentioned her father.

And yet she was loyal, she was caring and she was strong. Exactly the kind of woman who could plunge him into his darkest fear if he let her. But by the same token, how was he supposed to walk away without stealing a part of her for himself?

CHAPTER SEVEN

NATHAN PACED THE study in the home he had avoided thinking of for so many years, fighting the surge of memories that attacked him. The study had been one of his favorite rooms with huge floor-to-ceiling shelves covering two walls completely and French doors on the opposite side that opened onto the veranda.

Thick Persian rugs that had been his mother's pride covered the floor. He remembered playing with his toys on those rugs sitting at her feet.

The smell of old books and ancient leather stole through him swiftly, shaking loose things he had forgotten beneath layers of hurt and fear.

Emotions he didn't want to feel surged inside.

They had laughed here, the three of them. Spent numerous evenings in front of the fire—his father reading to him while his mother had sat in the cozy recliner with her knitting. There had been good years, he suddenly realized, years of laughter and joyful Christmases before ruined football games and hospital visits had become the norm. Before fear had become the norm, before fear had infiltrated every corner and nook.

Had it begun with his fainting and near dying at the football game? Had it begun when his mother had been gradually getting worse and worse? Or had it begun when his father had started his affair with Jackie?

Did it matter anymore?

"Hello, Nate," his father said softly, and closed the door behind him.

Even having learned all the details of his father's illness from Maria, Nathan still wasn't prepared for the shock his father's appearance dealt him. As much as he wanted to not give a damn, he found he couldn't not care, couldn't not be affected by how frail he looked.

His blue gaze seemed dulled, haunted by dark circles underneath. His frame, always lean and spare, now looked downright skinny.

Alarm reverberated through Nate.

He didn't want to feel anything for his father. Damn Riya for forcing him to this. The blasted woman was making it hard on herself and him.

"It's so good to see you, Nate. Riya's been telling me all about your ventures and how powerful and successful you are. I'm very proud of you."

Nathan could only nod. He couldn't speak. Was he as big a sap as Riya? Because one kind word from his father and he couldn't even breathe properly.

Fury, betrayal and so much more rose inside him. And that kind of emotional upheaval scared him more than the little fracture in his breathing the other night.

If he let one emotion in, they would all follow. Until all he felt would be fear.

There were too many things out of his control already. And to be in control, he had to remember things he'd rather forget, remember things that had driven him from his home, things that had driven him to live his life alone. "Let's not pretend that this is anything but the fear and regret a man faces once he sees death coming for him, Dad."

His father flinched, and this time, nothing pierced Nathan. Not even satisfaction that he had landed a shot. Tears flooded those blue eyes that were so like his own. "I'm so sorry, Nathan, that you felt you couldn't stay here after she was gone."

He couldn't bear this, this avalanche of fear and love, of need and despair that it always brought. "It was so hard to lose her like that, so hard to see my own fate reflected in her death. But to learn that you were with that woman. Can you imagine what that must have done to her?"

"I made a mistake, Nate, a ghastly one. I couldn't bear to see her wilt away. I let that fear drive me to Jackie. I was so ashamed of myself. And your mother…I instantly told her. And she forgave me, Nate."

Shock waves pounded through Nate. "I don't believe you."

He collapsed onto the settee and buried his head in his hands. There was an ache in his throat and he tried to breathe past it, but his dad's words already stole through him.

Because Jacqueline Spear was the one thing his mother hadn't been in that last year—vivacious, brimming with life, an anchor for a drowning man. He had assumed that his dad had done that to his mom. But what if it was the reverse?

What if seeing his mom lose all her will for life had driven his father to Jackie? It was still the worst kind of betrayal, but didn't Nathan know firsthand what fear could do? How it could turn someone inside out?

His dad reached him. "I don't blame you for not believing me. All these years, I have regretted so many things and the worst of it was that my cowardice drove you away. How many times I wished I had been stronger for you."

"If you were sorry, then why did you bring them here? Jackie and Riya? What was that if not an insult to Mom's memory?"

Wiping his face with a shaking hand, his father met his gaze. "What I did was abhorrent. So much that I couldn't bear to look at Jackie for years after that, much less marry her. She was my biggest mistake given form. But I couldn't do anything to hurt Riya.

"I couldn't turn away from the child who needed a proper parent, and Jackie...she was still reeling from her separation from her husband. It was fear that drove us toward each other, that made us understand each other.

"Riya made me think of what I should have been to you, gave me a chance to rectify the mistake I made."

Nathan nodded, his throat raw and aching, a ray of pure joy relieving the burden in his chest. Something good had come out of all the lies and betrayal.

Because this man who looked at him now, this man who had cared for someone else's daughter, he knew. This was the man he remembered as his father before everything had been ruined. "Is that why you gave her the estate?"

"I had no idea what had become of you. I had no way of reaching you. And when I thought I would die...I thought it a good thing that she have it.

"Riya loves this house, this estate, just like Anna did. Everything she touches blossoms. Jackie and Riya gave me a reason to live for, after I lost everything. I thought it fitting that it went to her."

Nathan shook his head, the most perverse emotion taking hold of him. He should be a bigger man, he knew that. His mother had been generous and kind. She wouldn't have minded the estate going to Riya, going to someone who loved it just as much as she had. But he couldn't just walk away, couldn't sever the last thing that had some emotional meaning to him.

Couldn't let himself become a complete island severed from anything meaningful in the world. "She can have as much money as she wants instead. The estate is mine. If she'll listen to you, ask her to stop playing games with me and sign it over."

His father frowned. "What are you talking about?"

"I asked her to sell it to me, and the condition she put in front of me was that I see you. That I remain here for two months."

"Oh." His father sank to the couch, and Nate reached him instantly.

"What is it? Are you unwell again?"

"No. I…" His father sighed, regret in his eyes. "I ended up being another person who leaned on her too much. When she told me you were back, I told her to do whatever she could to keep you here. After all this, tell me you'll stay for the wedding, Nate."

Nathan didn't want to hear the hope in his father's eyes, fought the sense of duty that he had ruthlessly pushed away all these years. His father had needed him just as much as Nathan had needed him.

But he hadn't been alone. Gratitude welled up inside Nathan for everything Riya had done for his dad.

The more he tried to do the right thing and stay away from temptation, the more entrenched she was becoming in his life.

Lifting his head, he met his dad's gaze. "I had already decided to stay for the wedding."

A smile broke out on his father's face, transforming it. Clasping Nate's hand, he pumped it with joy. "I'm so glad. Will you live in the house again? Anna would have—"

Nathan shook his head.

He wished he could say yes, wished he could let his father back into his life, wished the loneliness that ate at him abated.

The bitterness inside him had shifted today. And the estate was the one place that meant something to him. It was also the one that would forever remind him that his time was always on a countdown, remind him of how his beautiful mother had turned into a shadow because of her fear.

Because Nathan remembered that fear, remembered what his father had left unsaid, realized that he thought he could protect Nathan from the bitter memory. But beneath his anger for his father, his fury toward what Jackie represented, Nate remembered his darkest fear now.

For the last year, his mother had become but a shadow of herself. It was what had driven his father, as deplorable as his action had been. It was what had filled Nathan with increasing fear for his own life. She had willed her heart condition to leach her life away, had only dwelled on being gone, on being parted from Nathan and his dad.

And in the end, she had become a self-fulfilling prophecy. Her fear had leached any happiness, every joy from her life until death was all that had remained.

His father squeezed his shoulder, his voice a whisper. "You've achieved so much, Nate. You won't become like—"

And Nathan swallowed at the grief that rose through him. How perfectly his dad understood him without words.

Turning around, Nathan smiled at his father. "No, I won't. And that's why I can't stay."

"I'm strong enough to face anything, Nate. I would never—"

Clasping his dad's hands, Nate smiled without humor. It was Riya's face that rose in front of his eyes. "I don't know that I am."

Just as he had accepted his own limitations, Nathan

accepted this too. Riya was dangerous to him like no other woman had ever been. Already he had broken so many of his own rules; already he was much too invested in her well-being, in her life.

He couldn't risk more.

He could never care for anyone so much that the fear of being parted would pervade every waking moment. Couldn't let any woman reduce him to that.

Over the next week, Nate arrived at the estate every evening to see his father. As if determined to create new memories for Nathan, his father insisted that he was too weak to leave the estate. And Nathan found a simple joy in indulging him.

The evenings would have been perfect, the most peaceful moments he had known in a while if not for Riya.

Every evening, he found the anticipation of seeing her build inside him. Only to learn that she was out on another errand, one of hundreds apparently and gone all evening. And the couple of times every day that he dropped into the offices of Travelogue, she was nowhere to be seen either.

One evening, he had even walked through the entire grounds and the house itself wondering if she was having his dad and the servants lie to him.

How could she be always out when he was visiting?

It had taken him a week to recognize the pattern.

The woman was avoiding him, going out of her way to make sure they didn't even lay eyes on each other. He remembered the fear that had leaped into her eyes when he suggested he give them both what they wanted.

There were three weeks until the wedding, and Nathan realized, with simmering fury, that she intended to avoid him until that day.

He should have been happy with that knowledge. Riya was not equipped in any way to take him on.

But as another day fell to dusk, he found himself thinking of her more and more. He was working long hours, negotiating a deal with an Arab prince about building a travel resort in his country, and yet every once in a while, he would look up from his laptop in his penthouse and imagine her on the floor, writhing beneath him, her curves rubbing against him, her gorgeous eyes darkened with arousal, her legs clamped around his waist.

His name falling from her lips like a languid caress.

Running a hand through his hair, he slammed his laptop with a force that rattled the glass table.

Pushing away a hundred other warnings his mind yelled at him, Nathan looked at his watch. It was a quarter past noon on Saturday, one where he should be on his private jet in less than half an hour, flying to Abu Dhabi for the weekend.

A fact that Riya was aware of. Switching his cell phone on, Nate called his virtual manager and ordered him to cancel all his plans for the day.

He found her in the grounds behind the house, knee deep in mud, pruning the rosebushes in the paths leading up to the gazebo.

The white sleeveless T-shirt she wore was plastered to her body, her skin tanned and glistened. Her long hair was gathered in a high ponytail while tendrils of it stuck to her forehead.

She looked as though she belonged there.

Nathan swallowed at the sensual picture she presented. Her skin was slick with sweat, and the cotton of her shirt displayed the globes of her breasts to utter perfection.

His reaction was feral, instantaneous, all-consuming.

His mouth dried, all the blood rushing south. Never had deprivation of oxygen to his lungs felt so good. Never had the dizziness he felt just looking at her been so pleasurable before.

He cleared his throat and she looked up. A bead of sweat dripped down the long line of her throat and disappeared into her cleavage.

Nathan fisted his hands and shoved them in his pockets. He wanted to touch her, he wanted to push her down right there on the dirt, spread her out for him and cover her body with his own. He wanted to feel his heart labor to keep up as he plunged himself inside her and pushed them both over the edge.

"You've been avoiding me."

"I've been busy with the wedding preparations. Jackie's been waiting for so long for it and she's so excited that she's practically useless and of course, Robert is ecstatic that you're here. There's a lot to do."

"Then why didn't you ask for my help?"

Her movements stilled. He realized with a pang that she hadn't even considered it.

He got onto his haunches, and her gaze flew to him. "You really think hiding is the solution? Will you hide at the wedding too? Will you hide from everything that threatens to shred your damn rules? One day, you'll be a hundred years old, Riya, and you'll be alone and you'll realize you didn't live a moment of your life."

Her mouth fell open on a gasp, and the shears clattered to the ground. She looked as though he had struck at the heart of her deepest fear. Feral satisfaction filled him.

"Get out, Nathan. This estate is not yours yet. I could dangle it over your head just as you dangled the company over mine."

He laughed and inched closer, the challenge in her gaze playing with his self-control. "You're becoming reckless, butterfly."

"Maybe. Maybe I'm tired of being dictated to by you. I danced to your tunes for my company, for Robert. Now I have a new condition. Stay away from me. Or else—"

"Or else what?" he said, a fierce energy bursting into life in his veins. A hot rush of lust swamped him. "You'll be all alone at the wedding too."

"No, I won't. My plan needed modification, true. And you just happened to be the one that made me realize that. I already found someone I like very much, someone I've known a long time. I even have a date with him tonight."

He tugged her toward him until their noses were almost touching. Until the scent of her, dirt and sweat and something floral, infused his very bloodstream. "With whom?"

"Do you remember Maria's son, Jose? He's stable and nice and dependable."

Clenching his teeth, Nathan released her, awash in burning jealousy. Because that was what it was.

The very fact that the knowledge was sweeping through him with such impact should have warned him. But he didn't heed. He couldn't even see past the red haze covering his vision.

That Jose would kiss that luscious mouth, that Jose would make love to her, that Jose would have her loyalty forever because she would give it all.

"No, you went for him because you think he'll never leave you. Jose might as well be the oak tree in the estate. You're using him. But he'll realize one day that he's nothing but a security blanket for you, that the reason you actually chose him is that you think he'll never leave you. And he'll resent you for it, even hate you for it."

She fell against the dirt, a stark fear in her eyes. "I don't need advice from a man who could cut his best friend out of his life. Now, if you'll excuse me, I have a date to get ready for."

Nathan watched her walk away, his blood boiling in his veins.

He told himself that he had no interest in her. He just couldn't stand by and watch her make a colossal mistake, waste her life like this anymore. If it was up to her, she would never leave this estate, never leave her mother and Robert, never experience anything.

Everything in him wanted to fight the chain of responsibility he felt for her, shackling him.

He made a quick call to his PA and then went back toward the house, intent on finding the woman who was going to marry his father.

He'd first hated her for a decade and then avoided her for the past few weeks. But it was time to talk to Jackie, high time for someone to think of Riya.

CHAPTER EIGHT

TWO DAYS LATER, Riya was rooting through her closet searching for a beige, ankle-length dress she'd once bought in a small designer boutique in downtown San Francisco. It would do very well for the Travelogue Expansion Launch event.

She'd asked Jose if he would come with her after the longest evening of her life. It wasn't Jose's fault that she kept imagining Nathan all evening or that Nathan pervaded her every thought.

In the end, Jose had kindly and laughingly kissed her cheek. With a twinkle in his eyes, he'd told her that, as flattered as he was that she wanted something between them, there was nothing.

She heard a knock at the door and turned around.

Jackie stood at the door. Terrified was not an exaggeration to describe her expression.

Unease clamping her spine, Riya walked around the empty cardboard boxes she had brought for packing. "Jackie, what is it? Is it Robert?"

"No. Robert's fine." She straightened a couple of books on the chest of drawers, her hands shaking.

Her unease deepened. "Jackie?"

"I've been lying to you," she said in a rush, as though the

words wanted to fall away from her mouth. Her arms were locked tight against her slender frame, her words trembling.

Riya clutched the wooden footboard, anxiety filling her up. "About what?"

"About your father."

Her entire world tilting in front of her, Riya swayed. She felt as if she were falling through a bottomless abyss and would never stop. "What do you mean?"

"He didn't abandon you, Riya. Things had begun to go downhill for a couple of years already. But he and I…we tried to work it out for you. Nothing helped. We were just too different. One night, he said he was considering returning to India. I didn't know how serious he was. But I panicked. If he took you, I would lose you forever. So when he went on one of his weeklong conferences, I grabbed you and I ran.

"I'm so sorry, Riya. I never intended it to be permanent. I kept telling myself I would get in touch with him. But then I realized what I had done and I was so scared he would never let you see me again…"

Tears running over her cheeks, Jackie sank to her knees.

Riya heard the hysterical laugh that fell from her mouth like an independent entity. Hurt splintered through her, as if there were a thousand shards of glass poking her insides.

Her father hadn't given up on her. He'd never abandoned her. The biggest truth she had based her life on was a lie.

"You ruined my life, Mom. All these years, you let me think he didn't care about me."

"I'm sorry, Riya. I couldn't bear to part with you then. And every time I thought of telling you, I was so afraid you'd hate me."

Her head hurt so much, and Riya wanted to scream. "You, you, you… It's always about you. My whole life has been about you. You were afraid to be alone, so you ran.

You were afraid I would hate you, so you hid the truth from me all these years."

Jackie clutched her hands and Riya recoiled from her, everything inside her bursting at the seams.

"That's not true. I...I know you must hate me. But I did it only because I was so scared. I...please, Riya, you have to believe me."

"Get out," Riya said, her words barely a whisper. "I don't want to look at you. I don't want to hear a word you have to say."

Casting one last look at her, Jackie closed the door behind her.

Riya sank into a heap on the floor and wrapped her arms around her, every inch of her trembling. Her heart felt as if it were encased in ice. Why else couldn't she shed even a tear?

Everything she had believed about herself had been a lie. She had let the one fact that her father had given up on her permeate every aspect of her life. Had built a wall around herself so that she was never hurt like that again.

"You're a coward, Riya."

Nathan had been right. She had done nothing but hide from life all these years. He'd even been right about her desperate date with Jose. Something even Jose had realized.

Fury and shame pummeled through Riya. And she latched on to the wave of it.

She was done hiding from life.

The launch event for the expansion of Travelogue was being held in the ultra glamorous banquet hall of the luxury hotel where Nathan was staying in the penthouse suite.

He tucked his hands into his pockets and looked out over the crowd. A smile broke out on his face as the Travelogue crew stared around the luxurious hall.

The crystal chandeliers, the uniformed waiters pass-

ing out champagne, the vaulted dance floor to the right…
he had wanted everything to be on par with RunAway International.

The Travelogue crew had slogged to create the new
package and had surprised him and his own team with
their dedication and creativity.

He shook his head as a uniformed waiter offered him
champagne. Anticipation had never been his thing, but
searching for Riya, he felt as if he were looking up at the
snowcapped peak of a mountain.

He had set something in motion. Something that couldn't
be taken back and he felt the truth of it settle like a heavy
anchor in his gut.

The fact that Jackie had told Riya nothing but lies had
only urged him on. She had helped Nathan see the truth,
hadn't she? He didn't think he could ever forgive his father,
but he, at least, understood. Now he was returning the favor.

More than once, he wondered if he was doing it for all
the wrong reasons, wondered if he was being incredibly
selfish again. Had even considered picking up the phone
to stop what he had set in motion. But in the end, he had
persisted.

No one had ever looked out for Riya. Her whole life was
built on the foundation of a lie.

Running a hand through his hair, he looked at the dance
floor. And felt the shock of his life jolt through him in
waves.

She was moving to the music, her gaze unfocused. And
she didn't look like the Riya he had come to know in the
past few weeks.

He heard the soft whispers from the women around,
the shocked gasps of the men, and yet he couldn't shift his
gaze away from her.

The red dress, the hair, the spiky gold heels that laced around her toned calves…she screamed only one word.

Sex.

The dress was strapless. It cupped and thrust up her breasts to attention, lush and rounded. Her skin glinted under the bright lights, casting shadows of her long eyelashes on her cheekbones.

It cinched at her waist, contrasting the dip of her stomach against the curves of her breasts and hips. Ended several inches above her knees, displaying a scandalous amount of toned thigh.

The dress so scandalously short that he wondered…

And as though as a direct answer to his licentious question, she turned around and Nathan swallowed.

Too much of her back was bare, with only a strip of fabric covering her behind.

And as he watched, she laughed, threw her hands behind her and did a little thing with her shoulders.

His mouth dried up, lust slamming into him from every direction.

Her hair, all that glorious, lustrous hair was combed into a braid that rested on one breast, calling attention to the shadowed crook where her neck met her shoulder.

She wore no jewelry. Her face, usually free of makeup, was made up, and yet not in a garish way. The bloodred lipstick matched her dress perfectly, making her mouth look even more luscious.

Suddenly Nathan was incredibly hot under the collar. His erection turned stone hard as she looked around herself aimlessly, her tongue swiping over her lower lip. It seemed the butterfly had finally come out of the cocoon, and God help the male population.

She moved again, in tune to the soft music, and this

time it was a subtle move of her hips. Threw her head back and laughed.

Her hands above her, she moved in beat to the tune. Rubbed the tip of her nose against her bare arm in a sensual move that knocked the breath out of him.

Where had this woman come from? Where had she been hiding all that sensuality?

Just then, she turned her head and caught his gaze.

Across the little distance that separated them, something zinged between them. Like a juggernaut, he weaved through the crowd toward her.

Their gazes didn't break from each other. And for the first time since she'd stormed into the office that morning a few weeks ago, Nathan saw a challenge, a daring in her gaze.

He moved fast and caught her as she turned in tune to the languid jazzy beat again.

Her breasts pressed against him and he hissed out a sharp breath. Aware that she was beginning to attract unwise attention from colleagues she would have to work with for years to come, Nathan tapped her cheek and tilted it up. "Riya? Riya, look at me."

Her gaze found him instantly and he breathed out in relief. She was only mildly buzzed. He felt her mouth open in a smile against his arm.

Sinking his fingers into her hair, he tugged until her gaze settled on him. Shock, shame and finally recklessness settled into her beautiful brown eyes. Recklessness that had his blood pounding in his veins. "Hi, hotness."

Nate didn't know whether to laugh or throw her over his shoulder and carry her out. Probably both.

She was all toned muscle and soft curves to his touch. His imagination running wild, Nathan swallowed. "This public display is not you, Riya."

"Even I don't know what I'm supposed to be." She sounded sad, wistful. "Anyway, don't be a party pooper, Nathan. I want to do one thing I've never done before the buzz in my head evaporates."

His fingers around her arms, he tugged her toward him.

"Let me go. I'm having fun. For once in my life, I'm behaving the way I should."

"And what is that exactly?"

"To live for the night. And you...you're getting in the way of my fun."

This was going all wrong. It wasn't what he had intended.

Isn't it? a voice mocked him. *Isn't this what you wanted all along?*

For her to throw off the shackles she'd bound herself with? For her to be reckless and wild? For her to realize what it was to truly live? For her to embrace life and make it impossible for him to walk away without giving them both what they wanted without guilt?

Gritting his teeth, he clamped down the questions. It was too late now. For regrets or guilt.

His arm around her waist, he tugged her off the dance floor. "This isn't what you want, Riya."

Her fingers clutched the lapels of his coat. Stretching on her toes, she tilted forward until she could whisper in his ear. Her warm breath feathered over his jaw, making every muscle clench. His entire frame shook with hunger, with lust so hard that he swayed on his feet.

"Do you know what you want, Mr. Ramirez?"

She must have licked her lower lip. But the stroke of her tongue against the rim of his ear burned through him. Turned every drop of blood in him to molten desire.

Keeping his arm around her, he pushed at her chin, until she was facing him again. "I do, Riya, with a blinding clarity. And I know why it would be wrong to take what I want too."

Large, almond-shaped eyes widened. The edge in his voice hadn't gone unnoticed. She would back down now. She would retreat under that hard shell. She always did.

She didn't and Nathan felt something in him unravel.

Long, pink-tipped fingers fanned over his jaw, and their restless wandering drove Nathan crazy. With the tip of her forefinger, she traced his lower lip, sending a shiver down his spine. "You know, you have the sexiest lower lip I've ever seen on a man. The upper one is the mean one, the one that declares to the world that you're heartless. But the lower one betrays you, Nate."

Her gaze caressed him. And Nate struggled to control his own desire under it. "It shows that you're kind underneath, that you have a softer side. Why are you so bent on keeping everyone at a distance?"

Nathan felt like the lowest scum of the world. The trust in her eyes, he didn't deserve it. He didn't even deserve to stand next to her here. "Tell me what happened."

"Why am I finally living my life like a twenty-three-year-old should? Why am I having fun?"

He steered her around. "I'll take you back to the estate."

"No." She shuddered, her balance still precarious. "I don't want to see Jackie. I can't bear to be even near her," she said with such bitterness that it stopped Nathan in his tracks. "I hate her. I didn't know it was possible to hate anyone so much."

He ran his fingers over his eyes, wondering what he had started. To see her turn from a sweet, caring person to this? It was like watching a train wreck happen knowing you had instigated it.

He sighed, fought against the panic rising through him.

Panic because he could see clearly where it was headed and still it seemed he couldn't stop it.

"Riya, you're not yourself. Let me take you back to the estate."

She tugged away from him and stepped back, her mouth pouting. "Leave me here if that suits you. But I won't go back there." She reached out for the pillar and moved toward it. "I've always taken care of myself, did you know? I'm sure I can handle tonight. What's the worst that could happen? I'll fall and land on my rear. The best? I'll go home with some stranger like every other partying twenty-three-year-old over there."

And those words...they sank into Nathan like sharp claws.

The picture they painted, her bare limbs tangled up with some faceless stranger, was enough to root him to the spot.

Nathan clasped her wrist and dragged her behind him. The swish of the elevator doors, the soft ping as it began to ascend. Everything felt magnified. As if every breath was rushing up to the moment where he would have her in his suite, dressed like this, and he and his control and his good intentions in tatters.

He still made one last attempt at keeping his sanity, at doing the right thing. "As soon as I pour some coffee down your throat, I'm taking you home."

She laughed then, her hands tucked tight around her, her entire body trembling. "Home? I have no home, Nathan. That estate belongs to you. I have no one and nothing."

"Riya, it doesn't have to be this way. I understand that you're angry. I understand how it feels when someone who should take care of you betrays you...when someone you—"

"Do you? She lied to me. About my father. She practically stole me from him."

If she had cried, Nathan wouldn't have been so scared for her. But she didn't. It was as though her shock was much too deep for mere tears. "Everything I have believed about myself, everything is a lie. I thought he abandoned me. I thought he didn't love me. I will never forgive her for this. She stole my childhood and she made me into this frozen coward who hid from everything in life. No one has ever cared about my happiness.

"Not her and definitely not my dad. If he had, knowing how emotionally weak she is, would he have threatened her that he would take me from her?"

What the hell had he started?

He had never meant to hurt her. He had never meant to make her feel alone, had never meant to unravel her like this. He understood the weight of it, he knew better than anyone how painful, how awful it felt.

"Shh, Riya. Enough," he said in a stern voice. "Look at me, butterfly."

When she raised her gaze to him, the depth of feeling that filled him scared the life out of him. Her mouth trembled and he jerked his hand back, the urge to touch that soft cushion overwhelming him. "This will pass, Riya. Believe me, let me drive you back to the estate and—"

"Please don't send me away, Nathan. Tomorrow, I'll be back to myself again. Tomorrow, I'll be strong again. Tomorrow, I might even forgive her. Tonight, I want to be selfish. Tonight, I want it to be just about me."

What could he say to that?

His chest was tight with guilt. All she had tried was to make his father smile. And he…he had unleashed nothing but hurt on her.

Because he had coveted something he could never have.

CHAPTER NINE

TIGHTENING HER ARMS around his neck, Riya nudged closer to Nathan, the warmth of his body a cocoon she didn't want to leave. As though sensing her reluctance, he didn't put her down. Not when he lingered outside the sitting area, not when he walked through it into the bedroom.

Finally he sank down in the armchair and settled her in his lap.

How had she never learned how good it felt to be held like this, to be cherished as if she was precious? How many more things had she missed tucked away in her own world?

She had erected a fence around her heart, around herself, and she had missed out on so many things. While other girls had been going on first dates and experiencing first kisses, she had been studying for a place at the university, giving Robert a hand when she could, managing her mother's moods.

She had bound herself so tight that a little truth from the past had splintered through her. Nothing had really changed. And yet everything had.

It felt as if someone had stuck a pin in her side to jolt her awake from a slumbering state. She sucked in a breath and opened her eyes. His gaze clashed with hers, his long fingers splayed out over her bare arm.

An infinitesimal tension spun into life around them.

His other hand tipped her chin up. "Why this dress? Why drinking? Why this route to show your anger, your hurt?"

And just like that, he shot straight to the heart of the matter. "I don't remember when I had decided that no man would ever hurt me like my father's abandonment did, when I decided I would live my life in this frozen state. I wanted to prove to myself that she didn't ruin me forever with her lies."

"And?"

She tucked her head into his shoulder and sighed. "It's not that simple, is it? A lifetime of sticking to the safe side, suppressing any small urge that could be deemed unsafe, that could risk pain, it's a hard habit to shake." She gave a laugh, tinged with sadness. "I was dancing and I had a little to drink, but I realized it wasn't that simple to change myself inside. Like flipping on a switch. I can't suddenly do something I've trained myself not to do."

"No, it's not simple." There was a roughness to his voice, an edge, a desperate sense of being tightly leashed. As if he was forcing himself to laugh instead of…something else.

Her hand clasped in his. Long fingers with blunt nails and hers, slender and pink tipped, coiled around his.

"It takes years to defeat that kind of conditioning, years to conquer that fear. Doesn't take much to trigger it back either." He sounded strained, almost resigned. He squeezed her arm and Riya caught the sigh that rose to her lips.

How did he understand her so well?

"How about you start with small steps, butterfly?"

She smiled and nodded, the scent of his cologne drifting over her. And the huge chasm that she couldn't cross toward living her life suddenly didn't feel so daunting.

In the shifting confusion of her own emotions and thoughts, he was constant, her awareness of him sharp and unwavering.

Nathan, who had brought so much upheaval into her life, felt like an anchor. All he lived for was the thrill, the fun, the moment. Who better to show her what she'd been missing? Who better to show her what it meant to be daring, to be wild, to grab life by the horns and shake it? Who better to start on her path to living than a man who would never affect her in any other way?

With Nathan, there would be no expectations, no disappointments. When it was time to leave, he would, and this fact had nothing to do with her. Therein lay her safety net.

A sharp hunger bursting inside her, Riya slid her fingers toward the nape of his neck. Pressed her mouth to the pulse flickering on his throat. "Is a kiss a small enough step, Nate?"

Instantly he stiffened beneath her. His fingers landed on her jaw, pushed her face away from his neck in a gentle but firm grip. Desire was a relentless peal in her, as if her pulse had moved just from some points to all over her body.

Fear and safety were taboo. Daring and living were her words of the moment.

She clasped his wrist with her hand and laid kisses against the inside of it. His palm was rough and warm, and as she pressed her lips again to the center of it, she felt the rightness of it.

"Tonight's going to be your lucky night," she said, her throat working to get the words out. She had to brazen it out, didn't want him to know how huge this was for her.

A sharp grip at the nape of her neck caused her to look at him. "My lucky night?" he said.

He looked as if his face were carved from pure stone, his blue eyes molten with desire. There was no frost, no ice tonight.

Nathan was all fire and passion, and she wanted that fire;

she wanted to lose herself in him. "Don't make promises you might not be able to keep, butterfly."

Straightening in his lap, she pushed into his touch, determined to have this. "It's okay if you're not up to it, Nate. No one wants to be a pity f—"

His fingers tightened their grip in her hair. His breath landed on her mouth, until there was nothing to do but breathe the same air as him. "You're doing this for the wrong reasons, Riya."

Feeling gloriously alive, she bent and kissed a spot just beside his mouth. The bristle on his jaw rubbed against her mouth. Heat spread everywhere, incinerating a need she had never known. So she did it again. And again. Like a cat rubbing herself against her favorite surface. Until her lips, her cheeks, her chin stung in the most delicious way, scraping against the roughness of his jaw. Until he made a feral sound that in turn scraped against her very senses.

And her desire went from a risk, a dare, to need for him. Only for Nathan.

Finally her mouth landed at the corner of his luscious mouth. And she spoke the words against his lips, felt a shudder vibrate in his lean frame. Reveled that she could do this to him.

He was like a fortress of leashed desire around her.

"I'm doing this for the only reason that it should be done for."

"And that is?" he whispered back against her mouth, and Riya ached. Ached to feel that mouth everywhere, ached to lose herself.

"That it feels so good, Nate." She moved, to get closer to him, and felt the hard evidence of his arousal against her thigh. "From the minute you stepped into my life, this... it's like a fever." She pulled his hand and pressed it to her chest. "And in all the lies and confusion, this is the one thing that's unwavering. Make love to me, Nate. I want to do all the things that I told myself I didn't feel."

She didn't wait for him to deny her. She just jumped off the ledge, hoping he would catch her. Kissed him with everything she had in her.

When her lush mouth touched his, it was all Nathan could do to pull in a breath. There was no hesitation, no doubt in the way she pressed little kisses over the edge of his lips, over his chin, over his lips, her breath coming in little pants all around him, her scent filling his nose, her fingers scraping against his scalp, holding him in place for her pleasure.

No one had ever quite so thoroughly seduced him. No one had even come close.

She was an explosion. She was a revelation. And under her honest, raw hunger he came undone. No amount of honor could compete with the liquid longing coursing through him, could puncture the desire to return her kiss, to give her what she wanted. And to allow himself what he had been craving.

When she stroked his lower lip with her tongue, tentative but still powerfully maddening, he was done being a passive participant.

Clasping her jaw, he sucked her lower lip with his teeth and she shuddered. Gasped into his mouth.

And they were sucking, nipping, their teeth scraping, their tongues licking with a searing hunger that brought the world down to only them. Pasts and futures were forgotten, only the present mattered.

Panting, he moved away from the temptation of her mouth. Sank his hands into her hair and tugged at the lustrous locks until she was looking at him.

Golden skin flushed, pink mouth swollen, beautiful brown eyes dazed with desire and daring, she looked at him without blinking, without hiding. Pushed into his touch. She was inexperienced; her kisses told him as much. But the sensuality of the woman, the way she responded, so hot and fiery. This was a battle he'd already lost.

But this was a defeat he welcomed.

When she thought of him, he wanted her to do so with a smile and a sigh of pleasure.

He leaned forward and dug his teeth into her lower lip. A gasp fell from her mouth and he blew softly over the trembling lip. "This means nothing to me except that I want you with a madness that knows no reason." He could leave no doubt in her mind. And if she wanted to stop, he was going to head straight for a cold shower. But he couldn't take a chance on risking her emotions. "I'll leave when it's time, *butterfly*. And if you want to stop this, do it now. We'll forget about it. You can take the bed and I'll take the couch."

Her gaze flickered to him, a shadow in it. And then she smiled. Her gorgeous, perfect, dazzling smile. "Falling in love, risking my emotions, it's never going to be easy for me. And with you…I could never fall for you. We're really the worst kind of person for each other, aren't we? But that's what makes this easy, that makes one night with you everything I want it to be."

Her honesty stung him, but he slashed the feeling away.

One night to satisfy this craving, desperate need for each other. That was all they could afford of each other.

Pulling her arm to his mouth, he kissed her wrist, licked the vein flickering there. Kissed a path upward, all the glorious skin warm to his touch.

Her soft tremble, her gasp as he reached the crook of her neck swept him away hard. "Shall I shock you and tell you all the different ways I've imagined having you?"

He licked the pulse there, sucked on her skin. She shivered, sank her hands into his hair. Shuddered, writhed, but he didn't let go. He continued until she was panting, moving restlessly in his arms, rubbing her breasts against his chest. He was rock hard, her volatile response tightening his own need, fraying his control.

He fisted his hands, fighting the urge to push her dress up, to drag her on top of him and thrust up into her wet heat.

Sweat beaded on his brow. And that couldn't be borne. He would enjoy this; he would drown himself in the scent of her, but his control couldn't falter.

It was all about release, all about his body. As long as he kept it to that, as long as he didn't think about what this might have meant to her, to him in a different world, beyond tonight, it was good.

Laughing, she tugged her hair away from her shoulder and looked down at herself. A blush spread upward from her neck as she ran a pink-tipped finger over the blemish. A soft pant fell from her mouth, and it was the most erotic sound he'd ever heard.

There was innocence in it and there was a raw hunger in it. For more. He had been right. She had repressed so many things, and that flicker of undisguised hunger now, of playful curiosity, turned him inside out.

Her gaze moved to his mouth and stayed there. "It stings."

Picking her up, he mumbled his apology into her mouth.

She kissed him with a searing hunger that rocked through him. Scraped her teeth against his mouth. Stroked it with her tongue when he groaned.

"Only in the best way," she whispered when he let her breathe. "I want more."

Laying her down on the huge bed, Nathan shucked his jacket and loosened his tie.

Raising an eyebrow, he let his gaze travel all over her. "Unzip, Riya."

Coming to a kneeling position, she reached for the zipper on her dress. Her fingers trembled around it. But she slowly tugged it down.

His mouth dried as the dress came loose around her chest. He was dying to see those lush breasts, those long legs, every inch of her. Just as the fabric flapped down, she held it to herself, her cheeks flushing. "Can we turn off the light, Nathan?"

"Nope," he said so loudly that she smiled. "Those prim dress shirts and trousers have been driving me mad." When she still hesitated, he stilled his hand on his shirt. "You can't see me either, then."

Something flickered in her gaze. Lifting her chin, she straightened to her knees and pulled her dress down. Over her chest, over her midriff. Leaned back onto her elbows and kicked it from around her feet.

Nathan felt his heart pump harder and harder, and for once, something else took precedence over the malfunctioning organ. His breath balled in his throat.

Her slender shoulders bare, her lush, rounded breasts thrust upward, the shadow of her brown nipples visible through her strapless bra, the concave dip and rise of her stomach, the flare of her hips, the V between her thighs hinting at dark curls...

If his heart stopped right then, Nathan would have had no fear, no regrets.

And the lack of fear, the lack of any other emotion except his feral hunger to possess the woman in front of him, was a sensation he reveled in.

Because it made him feel alive as nothing else could.

Riya had never understood what the fuss was about sex, how it drove people to the most unwise decisions.

Until now.

She'd never understood how completely it unraveled you, this desire, how completely it exposed every part of a person, how it connected one so deeply with another.

They hadn't even undressed completely, but the look in Nathan's eyes—so demanding and all-consuming, the possessive challenge that lingered there—would have sent her running to the hills.

He would demand complete surrender, of her body, her mind, even her very soul. And beneath the flicker of fear, there was also a freedom in giving herself over.

The soft fabric of her bra chafed against her nipples and her thong, which had been a necessary evil for this dress, suddenly felt intrusive, making her sharply aware of the ache between her legs, the incessant peal of need there every time his gaze traveled over her.

She was wet there and she was hot all over, and together, the sensation continued to build.

His gaze never leaving her, Nathan unbuttoned his white dress shirt, pushed it off.

All that bronzed, glinting skin, the whorls of copper chest hair, the black string hanging with a pendant over his pectoral muscles, the jut of his shoulders, the flat male nipples so unlike her own, the washboard plane of his stomach, the line of hair that went down below his navel. He was so utterly male.

And all of it was hers tonight to do with as she wished.

With sure movements, he unzipped his trousers and kicked them away. Then his boxers.

Riya licked her lips at the sight of him completely naked. Her heart thudded incessantly, her sex pulsing.

His guttural groan surrounded them, and she raised her gaze to him.

He moved closer, in touching distance. Riya raised her

hand, eager to touch that hardness, eager to learn every-thing about him. "You won't touch me, is that clear?"

Frowning, she tilted her head up. "Why not?"

He didn't answer.

Pushing her back against the bed, he climbed into the bed and on top of her in such a predatory, masculine way that all of her possessive claims, all of her risky resolve fled.

Leaving nothing but gloriously alive sensations toppling against her, drowning her, demanding her utter enslave-ment.

He was heavy over her, he was hard against her, he was hot all over and he didn't let her move. His arms cradled her upper body, raising her to him, locking her so tight against him. She was aching to touch him, dying to feel his muscles harden under her fingers…

But he locked her, leaving her no escape but to feel every assault of his fingers, his mouth, his tongue, his breath.

He kissed her until there was no breath left in her. He played with her hair…

Her toes curled into the sheets as he dragged his open mouth down her neck and to the valley between her breasts.

Need knotted at her nipples as he cupped her breasts reverently, kneaded them, lifted them to his mouth. She bit her lip, scrunched the silky sheets with her fingers, bucked against his grip. "Nate, please let me touch you, let me move or—"

"No."

"What do you mean no?" she cried.

He rose above her like a dark god, intent on pulling her under, every inch of his face carved from stone. His icy blue eyes wide, he was panting too. And Riya realized what tremendous control he was exercising, how tightly reined in his desire was. How, even being in the moment, he wasn't truly with her.

But before the thought could take root, he licked her nipple and she lost all coherence again.

"Do you want me to stop, butterfly?" he whispered hotly against her breast, his tongue laving the skin around her eager nipple.

"No," she said so loudly that the word reverberated in the silence.

His fingers tweaked her other breast, pulled at her nipple, while his mouth closed over the first one. Riya kicked her legs against the bed, and still he didn't let her move.

She gasped under the attack, she sobbed, she twisted and turned as he suckled, laved with his tongue. And a frantic pulsing began at her sex.

"I wondered," he whispered against the valley between her breasts, taking a shuddering, reverent breath.

All she could manage between catching her breaths was to say "What?"

"Your nipples," he said, rolling off her and lying on his side. His muscular leg covered her legs, his arm holding her tight against him. He dipped his mouth and suckled the swollen tip again and she arched her spine as sensations rippled and splintered through her.

The heat built intolerably between her legs and she rubbed her thighs restlessly.

His large hands stole between them, denying the friction she needed, and Riya was ready to beg. "I wondered what color they would be." This against the underside of her breasts.

"I guessed it right." This against the planes of her stomach. "Like chocolate."

He looked up then, and Riya looked down, her skin slick with sweat. She saw his gaze move over her face, her mouth and her breasts again, and felt a shyness come over her.

This was so intimate, intrusively so.

This moment when something else arced beneath the simmering chemistry between them was everything she had avoided her entire life. Here, lying naked below him, all of her exposed to his eyes, was the biggest risk she had ever taken.

For a startling second, she wondered what she had started. Wondered how she would face him tomorrow, how she would…

Moving up, he devoured her mouth in a kiss that left no breath in her. Pressed another one at her temple. "You okay, butterfly?"

Riya nodded, not at all surprised at how easily he read her. She had never met anyone who had understood her so well. Grabbing his forearm, she pressed a kiss to his biceps, flicked her tongue over the birthmark that had fascinated her so.

"You're still thinking. And I won't tolerate that, Riya," he said, traveling down her body again, trailing wet heat over her skin. His mouth hovered over the waistband of her thong, his teeth dragging against her skin. His breath sounded harsh. "You're driving me insane and I very much want to do the same to you," he said, sounding almost angry.

She could do nothing but sink her fingers into his hair.

Moan loudly as he tugged the string of her thong tight against her clitoris. And pulled it, up and down.

She bucked off the bed as his fingers explored.

Jerked as he learned her with clever, lingering strokes.

Dug her nails into his shoulders as he tweaked the spot aching for his touch. Dragged her nails over his back as he eased a finger and then two into her wet heat.

The softness of her sex felt amplified around the intrusive weight of his fingers. Every inch of her contracted and pulsed at that spot, and Riya sobbed.

"Nathan!" she said, the invasion of his fingers, the relentless rub of the pad of his thumb, the building pressure,
driving her out of her own skin.

She laughed or cried, she didn't know which, her body,
her heart careening out of control.

"Look at you!" His hot mouth pressed against her midriff, and her muscles clenched. "You're the wildest thing
I've ever seen."

He moved his head between her thighs. The stroke of his
tongue against the tight bud was like touching a spark to
a building storm. "Let go, butterfly," he said, and without
warning, sucked at the slick bundle of nerves.

Screaming and thrashing, Riya shattered around his fingers in a dizzying whirl of such exquisite sensations that
she thought she would fall apart. Sobbing, she tried to bring
her knees together, but with his fingers still inside her, he
clasped her against him. Continued the relentless pressure
of his fingers so that the small tremors continued until she
was nothing but a mass of sensation and pleasure.

As the tremors slowed down, she opened her eyes, saw
the stark need, the possessive pride written in his face.
He'd watched her explode and liked it. Took her mouth in
a possessive kiss that knocked the remaining breath out of
her lungs. "You're a screamer, Riya..."

Fighting the shyness that he had witnessed it with such
blatant thoroughness, Riya pressed her mouth to his chest.
If she stopped to think, she would stop altogether.

And she didn't want to stop. She wanted all of him.

She moved her fingers down his hard stomach and down
farther. Clasped the hard length of him. Flicked the soft
head with her thumb, heard the guttural groan that fell
from his mouth. His chest was hollow with his breath held.

The most powerful feeling exploded inside Riya. He was

so hard in her palm, and he was big. She felt the sharp need begin in her all over again as she stroked him.

He moaned so loud that she did it harder.

He jerked his hips into her hands, and whispered the filthiest words she had ever heard. Gasping at the renewed urgency in her own body, she moved her fist up and down.

He dug his teeth into her shoulder and she gripped him harder, going hot all over. Sweat beaded his skin, every muscle so tight that she wondered if he would break into a thousand shards.

Moving down, she kissed her way down his body, licking, tasting, reveling in the shudders that racked through him. When she reached his shaft, his fingers tightened in her hair, staying her. Looking up, she jerked her head. "Let go, Nathan."

His eyes were the darkest she had seen yet, his nostrils flaring, his control nearly shredded. "Tonight's about you, Riya."

"No, tonight's about what I want to do," she said boldly. Leaving him no choice, she licked down the long, hard length of him. He cursed.

She closed her mouth over him and sucked experimentally, a wet heat gathering at her own sex. She felt no shame, no shyness, only the gloriously alive feeling coursed through her. Licking the tip, she looked up at him.

And before she could blink, she was on her back and he was lodged between her thighs. "Enough," he said with such vehemence that Riya stared at him.

She watched increasingly boldly as he sheathed himself. She hadn't even given thought to protection. Coloring, she pushed up and kissed the hollow beneath his pectoral, tasted the salt of his skin, breathed in his musky scent.

The head of his shaft rubbed against her entrance. Feeling restless again, Riya met his gaze and held it, wanting all of him in that moment.

He pushed slowly at first, letting her accommodate to his length. Long fingers left deep grooves on her hips, holding her still, the way he wanted her. Kissing her mouth again, he dragged her closer, tilted her hips so she was right for him. And then swept in with one hard thrust.

Her head thrown back, Riya gasped at the sharp sting and the heavy intrusion, every inch of her stiffening. Her hands clasped his shoulders, the bones protruding out of them pressing against her palms.

His head went back in a recoil, the corded length of his neck stiff. Thick veins pulsed in his neck, his face clenched tight in satisfaction. His gaze was unfocused; then he blinked, as though fighting for control. In that moment, he looked savage, like a roaring volcano of emotions and needs, the hard shell he encased himself in falling away by the heat between them.

"Riya, you'll be the death of me," he said in such a grave tone that her focus shifted from the already receding pain.

But instead of being scared, Riya felt like a victor. Because this Nathan who wore his needs and passions in his eyes was the true Nathan.

Hiding his face in her neck, Nathan breathed hard. "You're a virgin." Of course she was. *Damn, damn, damn.*

He heard the accusatory, sinking tone of his words, but for the life of him, couldn't do anything about it.

Couldn't think about anything except the need surging through him, demanding release. She was like a fist around him, smooth and tight, and he was going to burst at the seams if he didn't move. For a man who abhorred having sex merely for the release it provided, this need to plunge into her until she was all he felt…he was drowning in it.

What had he done?

He was truly gone if it had taken him until now for that little fact to filter though.

Somehow he found an ounce of his shredded self-control, and raised his head.

Her pinched look slowly fading, Riya looked up at him. Beads of sweat glistened over her upper lip, and he fisted his hands to stop touching her.

"Do you want me to stop? You should have warned me, slowed me—"

"Would you have done it differently if I had?" the minx demanded. She sounded husky, a ragged edge to her words that seared him. "Would it have stung less? Was there a pain-free way of deflowering that you would have employed?"

Damn it, he had no wish to hurt her. In any way. "No."

This was getting too complicated. He was breaking each and every one of his rules with her. "But I would have resisted you better." *Lies, all lies.*

He saw the hurt in her eyes before she hid it away. "Then I'm glad I didn't."

"Damn it, Riya, this is not what—"

"It's just my hymen, Nate, not my heart. Except it played the gatekeeper to my heart until now."

"If you waited this long, it means you wanted it to be special."

"I waited this long because I was like Sleeping Beauty, except I wasn't sleeping but just functioning. Isn't it better I'm doing it with someone I know than a stranger? With someone I trust?

"You're my best bet, Nate. And I took it. Now it's up to you to make sure I made a good one."

She wiggled her hips experimentally, and Nathan felt

the walls of her tight sex grip him harder, the slow rub of friction driving him out of his own skin.

"Please, Nate. I swear, I won't fall in love with you. Do something. I want—"

He licked her already swollen lower lip, the pleading tone of her words sending him over the edge.

She ran her palms over his thighs and sighed. His thighs turned into hard stones. Wiggled again.

"Stop doing that."

This time, she rotated her hips, and his hips responded of their own accord. He pulled out and thrust into her. Pleasure spiraled up and down his spine. He cursed again. "How do you know how to do that?"

She smiled and winked at him, arched her spine, thrusting those beautiful breasts up, and Nathan felt himself move another inch.

Nothing was in his control anymore, not the situation, not his body and not his heart.

Her fingers moved to his hips, and she scooted closer and sighed. The rasp of it grated against his skin. The blunt tips of her nails dug into his buttocks as though she couldn't wait to be as close as possible. "I think I'm going to be a natural at this. How stupid that I waited this long… ah…"

And that broke the last thread of his control. Grabbing the rounded cheeks of her rump, he tilted her hips up, pulled all the way out and thrust back in. Slow, but letting her feel him every inch. And again. And again.

Until he thought he would die from the pleasure building in his veins, until she was sobbing his name again. But she didn't look away, didn't let him look away, and Nate wondered who was in charge, who was in control, even though he was the one who set the rhythm.

His heart pounded, raced as sensation built and clawed up his spine.

And he wanted her with him. He wanted her as unraveled as she was making him. On the last thrust in, he bent and dragged his teeth on her nipple and she exploded.

As she climaxed around him, Nathan pumped into her heat. And the tremors in her sex pushed him over. His own climax thundered toward him, splintering him into a million shards of pleasure and sensation. And nothing else.

He felt as though he was done for. His heart rushed in his ears, and he smiled, in defiance.

Take that, you useless organ, he challenged it. *Stop this moment and it would all still be worth it.*

Riya was still trembling beneath him, he realized, and he was crushing her with his weight. He meant to move off her, but her fingers clenched around his biceps, holding him still.

"I'm too heavy for you. Let me go."

She hid her face in his chest, and his muscles clenched under her tender kiss. "I can breathe. Just a minute… Please, Nate."

For a few minutes, which actually felt like an eternity, Nate cradled her face in his hands. Rubbed his lips against hers, heard the thundering roar of her heart and her breaths trying to keep up with his.

Lingered in the moment until his heart swelled in his chest.

And slowly, as the haze of the pleasure faded, as his breathing resumed normality, regret and remorse rushed in.

He felt her kiss his forehead, wrap her arms around his shoulders.

Found his own arms moving to wrap around her, to hold

her close, to tell her how explosive it had been. To tell her that sex had never been this personal for him.

"Nate?"

The whisper of his name at his ears was an intimacy that had him hardening inside her again. "Hmm?"

"Is it always like that?"

No, it wasn't always like that. In fact, it had never been like that for him.

Looking into her eyes, he said in a matter-of-fact tone, "With the right partner, it could be."

Her palms traced the ridges of his back. "Oh."

He pushed a lock of hair that fell forward. "And you were right. You're quite the natural at it. You're explosively responsive and any man would..."

The very idea of Riya with another man made him sick to his stomach.

Sudden panic surging up within him, he jerked away from her. Rose from the bed and walked into the bathroom without looking back. Turned the shower on and stood under it.

He never indulged in the intimacy of holding his lover or sleeping with one in his bed. He had never wanted to, if he were honest. In that first year after he left home, all he had done was take, as if the whole world were for his own personal enjoyment, everything in it his prize.

And waking up tangled with a woman whose name he didn't know and would never know, in an unending cycle of seeking comfort and escape from his fate and fears, bitterness had risen in his mouth one day.

Until he'd realized that at the end of all of it, the truth had never changed.

It hadn't made him stronger or smarter or healthier. It had only made him disgusted with himself. And he had realized that even this total loss of control, this gorging on things, was also driven by fear. So instead he'd put rules in place for himself.

Never get involved. Ever. Sex, even as he hated the casual, transient nature of it, had to remain impersonal.

Traveling as he did, working as he did, he'd found it easier to keep to his tenet. He had never had a girlfriend; he had never had a first date or a second date. He'd never taken a woman to dinner, never gotten to know one.

He had never even hugged one or comforted one as he had done tonight. Never let a few minutes of his life be about anyone but himself. Never let anyone get under his skin.

And now everything inside him roared with a savage intensity, raged against an unknown fate. He pummeled his hands against the tiles, bent his head in defeat as the water pounded over him.

A longing like he'd never known burst free inside, spreading through him like an unstoppable virus, and he shivered under the hot spray.

Because he wanted to go back into that bedroom.

He wanted to hold her, kiss her, he wanted to tell her that what they had shared was special. Even his untried heart knew that. He wanted to tell her that he was glad that she'd trusted him for her first time, that for all the hurt she had lived through, there was an intrinsic purity and courage to her emotions.

He wanted to tell her that the thought of her sharing her body with anyone else lanced him like a hot poker, that the thought of her sharing her emotions, her fears and her joys with someone else filled him with a hot fury.

But if he did, he would only make it harder on both of them. Make it awkward for the rest of his stay. Would push her into making more out of it.

He'd never let anyone close in his entire life. And he didn't intend to start now.

Even if she was the most extraordinary woman he had ever met.

He was gone.

Riya opened her eyes and felt the silence around her, touched the empty silk sheets and closed her eyes again. Locked away the sting of his withdrawal. Pulled the sheets up to her neck and scrunched tight into herself.

She ran the tip of her finger against her lips and found them swollen. Her arms trembled, her thighs felt as if she had run a marathon. Her body throbbed and ached after his deep thrusts. Even her scalp tingled, an aftereffect of how tightly Nathan had held her when he climaxed. Her hips bore the evidence of his loss of control, of his passion— pink grooves where his fingers had dug into her.

He had lost control in the end. He'd come as undone as she had. And Riya hugged the fact to herself.

She had known, after all these years of denying herself the simplest touch, it would be strange, weird. But she felt as if she had died and come out alive again.

She gazed at the corridor through which he had walked, his lean frame radiating with tension.

She had broken a rule she hadn't known. That much was clear.

Had it been the kiss? Had it been the way she clung to him? Or had it been her question about it always being that good? Emotions, he didn't do them. She knew that.

But whatever it had been, it was done. In a way, she was glad she had angered him. That left her alone to face what she had done, gave her a reprieve from what she felt around him.

Because nothing, she realized, could take away from the

moment, from the beauty and wonder of what she had experienced. She wasn't going to regret it; she wasn't going to ruin it.

It had been the best few hours of her life, the most alive she had felt. The most fearless she had been. Free to look and touch and taste without wondering about the consequences.

And now it was over.

For a few more seconds, she let herself linger in the moment. Buried her face in the pillow. Breathed in his scent again. Remembered the heady pleasure of being locked under him, her every breath, every moment, every inch of pleasure she felt, all his to give.

Her emotions and herself, under his total control and how good it had felt.

Imagined that he was still there, pulling her into that lean body of his, wrapping those corded arms around her and holding her safe.

This was not a rejection. And even if it was, she couldn't care.

It took only a few moments under the hot spray of the shower for Nathan to realize how heartless he had been. He didn't have to break his self-imposed rules, but he could have at least said a kind word to her. Could have made sure she was okay.

For goodness' sake, it had been her first time.

When had he turned into such a thorough bastard? He felt a distinct unease in his gut. Walking away shouldn't have become this easy. All she'd asked was a simple question.

How could he forget that Riya was new to this, and not just physical intimacy? The hardened cynic that he was, even he'd been moved by the intensity of it.

Wrapping the towel around his hips, he trailed water all over the marble floor as he walked back to the bedroom.

The empty bed felt like a punch to his stomach. He looked around the bedroom and the sitting room and returned to the bedroom again. Her dress was gone. Her sandals were gone. Her clutch was gone.

She was gone.

His phone pinged and he picked it up with a vicious curse. He switched it on, suddenly unsure of where all the anger was coming from. He hated to be so emotional, so unbalanced, and she had done it to him.

"I never asked you to leave," he said.

A short silence reigned before he heard her clear her throat. "I know. I thought it was best. I called to say I found your chauffeur and he's driving me back."

Another silence while Nathan fumed at himself. There was no accusation in her tone. And yet it grated at him.

"Nathan?"

He had taken her virginity and he had forced her into fleeing his bed after the night she had had.

"Nate? Please say something."

Now she sounded wary, tired. And he remembered the emotionally draining day she had had, all thanks to him. "Riya, I'm sorry, I should have—"

"Thank you, Nate," she said, cutting him off. There was no sarcasm or mockery in her tone. Only genuine gratitude.

His throat closed off.

"For...for everything tonight."

"Hell, Riya. You don't have to thank me for sex. I'm not a..."

What? What was he not? And what was he? What was he doing with her?

She laughed, and the ease of the sound only darkened his mood. Had it really been that simple for her? Just been about one night? Had he ruined all her innocence, changed her forever?

"Thank you for being there for me tonight, for your kindness. No one's ever done that for me. No one's ever let it be about me. That's what I meant earlier. I…I will always cherish tonight. And the…sex…"

He had a feeling she was forcing herself to sound breezy.

"…it was more than I would ever have known if left to my own devices. Would never have known how beautiful it could be." Another laugh, self-deprecating this time. "So yeah, thanks for that too, I guess."

He couldn't say a word, couldn't get his vocal cords to work, couldn't manage anything but a stilted silence. He didn't deserve a word she said; he didn't deserve her.

"Good night, Nathan."

She didn't wait for him to speak before she hung up, probably realizing he wasn't going to say anything.

Her face disappeared from his screen, and he clenched his teeth, a soft fury vibrating through him.

He threw his phone across the room, his chest incredibly tight. He sank to the bed and instantly the smell of her, the scent of sex, hit him hard, and he buried his face in his hands. Gulped in a greedy breath.

There was an ache in this throat, something he hadn't felt since his mother told him about his condition.

It was self-pity, it was fear, it was how he felt when his emotions were out of control.

With a curse, he swallowed it back.

No.

She wasn't allowed to do this to him.

No woman was allowed to send him back to being that boy. No woman was allowed to pry this much emotion from him.

With a ruthlessness he had learned to survive without

fear, with the resolve that had turned him from a runaway to a millionaire, he put her out of his mind. Dressed himself and ordered some coffee. Called housekeeping to change the sheets.

He didn't want any reminder of her, of what they had done together, of how he had felt with her beneath him, of how incredibly good the intimacy with her had been. Neither could he focus on how much he wanted to repeat the night, of how he wanted to find her at the estate and sink into her bed, of how much he wanted to hold her slender body in his arms and drift into sleep...

She made him think of Nate Keys, the boy who had been desperately afraid for himself, who wanted to love and live, who wanted to be invincible. But he couldn't be.

He turned on his laptop and went back to being the man he had trained himself to be.

Nathaniel Ramirez—billionaire, survivor and loner.

CHAPTER TEN

OVER THE NEXT couple of weeks, Riya threw herself into the wedding preparations with a rigor that left her with zero headspace. Between her increased responsibilities at Travelogue and the wedding preparations, not to mention the toll it was taking on her to avoid her own mother while living in the same house, it was a miracle she was managing as well as she was.

But she liked it like that. Her days were busy to the point of crammed and when she fell into her bed at night, she was so exhausted that she went right to sleep.

It was only when she was doing some mundane organizational task for the wedding that she found herself thinking of Nathan. She had tried to keep her thoughts free of him. But seeing him every day wasn't conducive to purging him from her mind. After a while, she had just given up.

"Are you well?" he had asked her the following Monday at work, his gaze intent.

She hadn't been able to stem the heat spreading up her neck. "I'm fine," she had said, pleased that she had sounded so steady.

He had tucked her hair behind her ear, clasped her cheek for a moment.

Her heart had thundered in her chest, everything in her yearning to keep his hand there. Because that gesture hadn't been about heat or attraction. It had been about affection, about comfort.

Before she had done anything, however, he had jerked back. He had nodded, looked at her some more and that had been that. And taking his cue, she had thrown herself into work.

Training her mind was still one thing. And absolutely another was her body.

Every time she saw him—either at work or the house, because of course, to her growing annoyance, Nathan apparently couldn't stay away from the house and Robert, she remembered the night they had shared.

Their one night of pleasure. Her one night of freedom from herself. And it was in the most embarrassing and humiliating ways too.

Humiliating because he didn't seem to be facing any such problem. He was back to being the intensely driven slave driver and perfectionist Nathaniel Ramirez. The man really had to have a rock for a heart.

Embarrassing because the memories of that night crept upon her all of a sudden.

The taste of his sweat and skin when she had licked his wrist intruded on her when he extended some papers to her in a meeting full of people. She had stared at his wrist for a full thirty seconds before she grabbed the papers from him.

The velvet hardness of him moving inside her, the stroke of his fingers at her core, the way his spine had arced and the way he had shuddered when he climaxed…she couldn't look at him and not think of what she had let him do to her.

With her late entry into the realm of physical pleasures, she understood her fascination with him. Like how he caught his lower lip with his teeth when he was thinking hard. The way he sometimes placed his palm on his chest and rubbed when he frowned.

But what she missed the most was the man she had come to know. His irrepressible energy around her, his constant teasing of her…now one of them, or both, had erected a wall of politeness. They worked together perfectly, but now they were strangers.

Having finalized the menu once again on the caterer's online website, Riya shut her computer down.

"Riya, I want to speak to you," her mother's voice came from behind her.

Shaking her head, Riya shot out of her chair and grabbed her laptop. "I have nothing to say to you."

"Then why on earth are you doing so much for the wedding?"

"For Robert. I'll do anything for him." Which was why she hadn't packed her stuff and left the estate as her initial impulse had been to do.

Jackie flinched and Riya felt a stab of regret and shock. The fact that anything she said or did could even affect her mom, except in the most superficial way, was a shock in itself. But however hard she tried, she couldn't find it in her to forgive or even forget for a little while.

Her jaw clenching and unclenching, Jackie stopped in front of her, blocking her exit. "I knew it. I knew it from the moment he stepped on the estate that he was going to ruin it all."

Despite every intention not to fall into the guilt trap her mom was so adept at laying, Riya still found herself getting sucked in. "What are you talking about?"

"Nathan. He's doing all this. Robert can't stop talking about him. He wants us to leave the estate without complaint, says we can't have the wedding here anymore because Nathan doesn't want it. And when I argued, he raised his voice to me. Nathan's all he can think about—"

"Robert thought he would never see Nathan again. Can't you be happy for him? For them?"

Because Riya was incredibly happy. For both of them. A little part of her was even envious. Of course, Robert had cared about her. And she was so thankful to him for everything. But the light that came into his eyes when he spoke of Nathan made her a little sad too.

"You're so strong, Riya. Not everyone is so…self-sufficient. I made a bad decision. It doesn't mean I don't love you. You can't give up the estate just because—"

"Are you kidding me, really?"

"I'm telling you the truth. That's what you want these days, right? I love Robert. And yes, I begin to panic when he gets mad at me. Just as I panicked when I thought your father would take you away from me."

Her insecurity was at the root of everything Jackie did. For the first time, instead of helplessness and then anger in the face of it, Riya felt pity for her mother.

"Just because Nathan's back doesn't mean Robert doesn't love you anymore. I don't think it works like that."

"No? Look how he's turned you against me. For years, we've been each other's support, all we've had, Riya. And now, just weeks after he's back, you won't even look at me. All these years of—"

"You were never my support. I was yours. You leaned on me when you shouldn't have. If I've had even a little bit of a carefree childhood, it's because of Robert. And if I've known, even for only a few hours, what it means to live, it's only because of Nathan. So excuse me if I don't—"

"Few hours? What're you talking about?"

At Riya's silence, she became even tenser. "It's none of your business."

Her gaze filled with shock, Jackie shook her. "You slept with him, didn't you? Riya. How stupid are you?"

As dramatic and distasteful as she was making it out to be, Riya refused to let Jackie ruin the most perfect time of her life. "That's grand coming from the woman who fell in love with a married man," she shouted, hating Jackie for reducing her to this.

"At least Robert still stuck with me all these years. Nathan will leave and never look back. He's the wrong man for you."

The fact that Nathan was going to leave was something Riya absolutely refused to think about. But she was aware of it, at the back of her mind, gaining momentum, beginning to rush at her from all sides.

"This has nothing to do with the estate or you, or Robert. It concerns only Nathan and me. No one else. As hard as it is for you to accept it, I have a life. Am going to have a life that's beyond you. I'm leaving after the wedding," she said.

She had been thinking about it, but there was no doubt in her mind now.

She had made to move away when Jackie gave a laugh, and the genuine pity in it rooted Riya to the spot. "Now I see why he insisted. He's planned it all along. And you went straight to his arms."

"What on earth are you talking about?"

"Nathan. He was the one who insisted I tell you about your father. He manipulated you into his bed, Riya. He doesn't care about you."

The urge to slap her hands over her ears was so strong that she dug her nails into her palms. "No," Riya denied, something inside her shaking at the revelation. She closed her eyes and his face, kind and resigned, flashed in front of her. "He didn't manipulate me. He never could." She kept whispering the word, too many things shifting and twisting in front of her.

"He didn't plan anything. He wanted nothing but for me

to know that I was throwing my life away. He's the first person in my life who thought about me, who cared enough to do something about it."

Her mom would never understand. And she needed to be okay with it. It wasn't that she hated Jackie now. Only that she realized that she had a life beyond Jackie, beyond her father, beyond Robert and beyond the estate.

On some level, she knew she should be angry with Nathan. He had been high-handed; he had brought her nothing but hurt. He had set it up without breathing a word to her.

But she couldn't be.

Wasn't it the truth that hurt her? Jackie who had hurt her? Even her father, to some extent, by threatening Jackie to take her away?

Nathan had only liberated her from under the burden of the truth. And then he'd been there to catch her when she was falling. It felt precious, momentous, this molten feeling inside her, this expanding warmth in her chest that he had cared.

She went looking for him later that afternoon when she heard Maria mention that he was visiting. Found him sitting at the gazebo.

He sat with his denim-clad legs stretched in front of him, with his head resting behind him, his face turned up. Sunlight hit his face in rectangular stripes. Kissed the shadows under his eyes. Caressed the planes and hollows of his cheekbones. The breeze ruffled his hair, the copper in it glinting in the sunlight.

His tan was fading a bit and his mouth, not smiling, not teasing, was a tight bow, his lower lip jutting out.

He looked strained, she thought with a pang. He was always such a dynamic, go-go-go, bursting-with-unending-energy kind of man that she didn't like seeing this stillness in him. There was a melancholic quality to that stillness, a dark shadow to the quiet enveloping him.

A sharp need gripped her. Not to feel his touch, although that was there too. But this was a clamoring to reach him, wrap her arms around him, hold him close. For herself, yes, but for him too.

In that moment, there was a loneliness around him. The same one inside her that she had covered up as the need for security.

The realization brought her up short. And she shook her head. It was ridiculous. Just because she felt alone in the world didn't mean Nathan was. It was his choice in life. It had been her choice too, but she hadn't even been aware of it.

As though he could hear her thoughts piling on top of each other, he looked up. His eyes were a different blue in the sunlight, but even the sharp gaze couldn't hide the strain around them.

There was that instant heat between them. He leaned forward onto his knees and frowned. "Is something wrong?"

She shook her head.

For a full minute, she stood there, holding his gaze, not knowing if she wanted to step forward or turn back.

He sighed, a harsh expulsion of breath and anger, she thought. "Come here," he said.

And she went, silencing the clamor inside her. Settled down next to him and stretched out her own legs.

It was a beautiful day with a soft breeze that carried all kinds of fragrances with it. The silence between them, even though a little tense, slowly drifted into a comfortable groove. And she didn't fight it, didn't seek to cover it up or change it.

Was this where they were going to settle? In this place between simmering heat and a strange intimacy?

Slowly she covered the gap between them. Scooted closer until her thigh grazed the hard length of his. Leaned back and sideways until she hit the wall of his chest. Wound her arm around his lean waist. Held herself tight and still, bracing for his rejection.

Seconds piled on top of each other, her breath balled in her throat. He didn't push her away. Her heart thundering just as fast as when she had stripped in front of him, she wrapped her arm around his torso and leaned her head on his chest.

She almost flinched when his right arm came around her shoulders and pulled her closer. Her breath left her in a shuddering whoosh and she settled into his embrace. He smelled familiar, and comforting. He felt like home. And this time, she knew it wasn't the estate. It was the man.

She didn't know how long they sat like that.

"You don't want the wedding to be here?" she finally asked, loath to ruin the peace but needing to. Because if she didn't, she had a feeling she would never let go.

And that was definitely reason to panic.

He tensed, but when he spoke, there was no anger in him. "No."

Feeling his gaze on her, Riya looked up. He ran his thumb over her temple. Pressed a kiss to her forehead. And yet there was no shock in either of them that he'd done it.

Because how could anything that felt so right be wrong?

"I have no anger for her, your mother," he said, and her chest expanded at the kindness in his words, at the rough edge of emotion coating it. "I just want this place to remain my mother's."

Riya nodded, her throat clogging. "Do you miss her very much?"

His mother...she was asking about his mother. The woman who had died with fear in her eyes. She couldn't have jolted him out of the moment better than if she had electrocuted him, reminded him of everything wrong that he was doing. Sitting here, sharing this moment with her, comforting her, finding something in her arms, this was wrong.

All of it, every precious second, every incredible touch.

Nathan jerked away from her and shot up from the bench, fear filling his veins. Every inch of him vibrated with a feral need to ask her to come with him, to show her the world, to have her in his bed for as long as they wanted each other.

And he couldn't let her have this much power over him, couldn't yearn for things he could never have. He steeled himself against her beauty, her heart, and willed himself to become cold, uncaring.

It was the only way to save her from a bigger hurt.

"My manager's taking care of all the arrangements to have the wedding somewhere else. You don't have to redo them. And Robert too. There will be a nurse who will check on him once every day. He and your mother, I'll take care of them, Riya. You've carried their burden long enough."

He had thought of everything. He was making arrangements. Before he… And suddenly she couldn't lock away the questions. "Thanks. So you'll be at the wedding?"

He laughed, and now there was no more easy humor in the sound. The moment was fractured. And she didn't know why. He tucked his fingers into the pockets of his jeans. Looked anywhere but at her. And Riya tried not to show her utter dismay.

It was obvious withdrawal, painful retreat.

"I would like nothing but to leave this very instant and not look back. I've stayed too long already and I'm getting restless. But I did give you my word."

He was not joking and the utter lack of any emotion in

his words shocked her. She had barely made friends, or any other relationship for that matter. And he...he was one relationship she didn't want to lose. "Are we friends, Nathan?"

His jaw tight, he stared at her for several seconds, anger dawning in his gaze. "We are nothing, Riya."

She flinched at the cutting derision in his words. The entire tenor of the conversation had changed. "Why are you acting like this? What did I do wrong?"

"You were fun that night." Her palm itched to knock the derisive curve of his mouth. "Today, you're falling into a pattern that I'm allergic to."

"Because I want us to be friends? I know that it was you that forced Jackie to tell me truth." When he opened his mouth, she put her hand over it to hush him. And felt the contact jolt through her. "I know you did it because you cared. I don't want explanations. I just...I think I would like us to be friends, Nate. I..." She stopped, arrested by the look in his eyes.

"I did what I did because I felt sorry for you, for what your mother and this estate—for what they all did to you."

"Sorry for me?"

"Yes. You manipulated the truth to bring me here, risked everything to patch things up between Dad and me. It has brought me a peace unlike anything. I thought I would pay you back the favor, lift the veil from your eyes, so to speak.

"We're not anything, Riya. We can't even be called a one-night stand. Because you weren't even there for the whole night, right? And we're definitely not friends."

And now she was angry, very angry. And stunned, because there was nothing but finality in his tone. "Why not? Why are you being such a jerk?"

"Because there could be no friendship between us, Riya. Not after that night. When I leave here, you won't see me again, hear from me again. *Ever.*"

Her breath knocked around in her lungs. It didn't feel as though he was stating a fact. It felt as though he was making her a promise. A painful one.

"You never plan to visit the estate that you went to all this trouble for? You'll kick us all out and just let the house be?"

"Yes." The word kicked her in the gut. "I could say otherwise now to make you happy, but it would be a lie. And I can't bear lies."

Something glimmered in his eyes, but Riya had no idea what. He was hurting her with his words. He was aware of it and he was still doing it. Very efficiently even.

Suddenly the cold stranger from the first day was back. Nathaniel Ramirez was back. And the man who had learned more about her in a few weeks than anyone else in her entire life, he was gone.

"Don't do this, Riya. Don't fixate on me because I'm the first man you slept with. Or because I'm the first man who showed a little bit of concern." He clasped her cheek, devouring her as if he were starving, as if he was memorizing every feature, every angle of it. "What you feel for me is only attraction. Only your body asking for—"

"A repeat performance? You think I'm naive enough to sugarcoat my words when all I want is one of those fantastic orgasms you deal out? And for the record, if that's what I wanted, I'm sure you would oblige me, wouldn't you?"

Now there was anger in his eyes. And Riya was glad. She wanted him to be angry, she wanted him to be hurt.

"I think you don't know the difference between a good friend, a great lover and a man who deserves your love. I'm only good for one of those roles. I think you haven't seen enough of the world to know yourself."

"Right. Because Nathaniel Ramirez knows what's best for everyone." She pushed his hand away, hating herself for wanting to revel in his touch. "Will you do me two favors while you're still here, then? Or have I run out of luck with you?"

He looked pale, drawn out. As if there was nothing more left in him. And she was the one who was hurt. "Yes."

"Can you find out where my father is? Put all your power and wealth to use?"

"Yes, I'll put someone on it. What's the second one?"

"There's a week to the wedding. It would make me really happy if you didn't come here. Robert can come see you at the hotel."

"Why?"

Stepping back, she ran her fingers over the wood grain, her throat clogging. "This has been my home for more than a decade. You have the rest of your life here. I only have one week. I want to enjoy it. And if you're around, it'll ruin it for me."

He nodded and then walked away. Riya sank to the bench, her limbs sagging.

For some reason, the tears came then.

They hadn't come so many times when she wished for them, when she needed an outlet for the ache in her heart. They hadn't come when she thought her father had let her go. They hadn't come when she learned that Jackie had lied. But they came now.

Sitting in the gazebo, in the place that had been home to her, Riya cried.

She didn't know why, and she didn't try to understand. Only tucked her arms around her knees and let the tears draw wet paths over her cheeks. She cried for the little girl she had been, for the lost and guarded teenager she had been, for the frozen woman she had become.

She didn't think about Nathan. He had no place in this. This was for her. Only her.

And when the tears dried up and her head hurt, she wiped her cheeks, took a shuddering breath and stood up. Looked around at the lush greenery.

What she had been doing was not enough anymore. That night with Nathan had only been the beginning. Something had to change in her life. She needed to live more. Not that she had any idea how to do that. But she had to start somewhere. After the wedding, she would leave.

She would have to quit her job. She would have to plan her finances, apply for part-time remote-access jobs. To give up all the stability she knew, to leave a job that paid well, the city she had grown up in, to leave Robert and Jackie…the excitement of it all, the fear of it, rocked through her.

There was a whole world out there. And staying still wasn't an option anymore.

Standing at the entrance to the kitchen, Nathan felt every muscle in him clench with a feral ache. Every soft cry that fell from Riya's mouth, every hard breath, landed on him like a claw, raking through him.

But he couldn't go to her. He couldn't hold her as he wanted to, he couldn't promise her that life would get better. That it would hurt less and less. That pain was just as much a part of life as joy.

He didn't make the mistake of thinking she was crying over him. He knew she was saying goodbye. Still, he wished he could be her support even as it was he who was forcing her to leave.

Ask her to come with you, Nate, a voice piped up, catching him unaware.

If he gave in to the longing inside him, if he asked her to come with him temporarily, just until this fire in him was at least blunted… Whether she realized it now or not, when this wave of risk-taking became too much, her natural world would reassert itself. There would be nothing for him except her rejection.

And that rejection would kill him as nothing else had done. To see that fear in her eyes would surely finish him off. And he couldn't blame Riya for being who she was, for the way she had survived.

He would never be the right man for her. And if he wanted to nip this…this yearning, this longing she made him feel, he would have to leave soon. Not risk seeing her again.

Before he forgot, before he started hoping for things that would never be, could never be his. And the distance between hope and fear was not that big.

And so he left, without looking back. As he'd always done.

CHAPTER ELEVEN

THANKS TO THE superefficient event management company Nathan had hired, the wedding preparations went without a hitch. All Riya had to do, even if reluctantly, was to keep her mother calm and turn up to the wedding. More than once, she had indulged in the idea of leaving even before the wedding. But doing that would have hurt Robert and, of course, her mother.

And she wasn't ruthless enough yet just to cut them out of her life.

But the week leading up to it, surprisingly, had been a pleasant one. Grudgingly she accepted that this fact was due to Nathan. She was aware he threw around his wealth as he pleased, but that he had actually cared enough to have the event organized for Robert, that she couldn't overlook.

Since he had kept his word and she had mostly worked from home, she hadn't seen him for the whole week. Having always been the one to take care of the logistics and details of their everyday life, she felt that having it all taken out of her hands had been the best. All she had needed to do was to pick a dress. And even that hadn't been left to her.

She had been presented with three gorgeous ones that a team from a world-famous fashion house, from whose designs she had never been able to afford even a pitiful scarf, had been waiting with for her one afternoon. A stylist and designer along with the dresses.

She had balked at the idea of wearing anything Nathan paid for. Had absolutely refused to even look at the selection picked out for her.

Until he had texted her: Am paying for the wedding. To show my father that I don't resent it.

Can buy my own dress, she had texted back. My boss is a heartless pig, but he pays well.

Thundering silence until…

It's a welcome-to-the-family gift. Accept it or I'll call you sis J

She had laughed, imagined the crinkles he got at the corners of his eyes when he did.

Gross and perverted, that's what you are.

Her heart had run a marathon as she waited. And slammed against her rib cage when her phone pinged again.

Please, Riya.

Her fingers had lingered over her phone's screen. Why? she wanted to ask him. He had rejected her friendship, so why did it matter whether she accepted this from him? Why was he playing games with her? Caring and affectionate one second and a ruthless stranger the next?

In the end, under his relentless will, she had given in. Let them fit her. Fallen in love with the frothy beige silk creation that somehow was almost the same color as her skin and yet stood out against it as if it were made for her.

Whispered sinuously when she moved, outlined her curves without being tacky.

Understated and yet elegant, it had shocked her at how much it suited her, her personality. Not the boring, dowdy clothes she had worn before and not the garish red of her wild night.

But somewhere in between, just perfect for her.

Her hair had been twisted into a sophisticated knot on the top of her head, with soft tendrils caressing her neck and jawline. She had refused the makeup artist's help, however.

The limo that had brought them to the hotel from the estate, the quiet but affluent luxury of the hall they were having the reception in, the delicious buffet—despite all the things clamoring for her awe and attention, despite her heart fisting in her chest with the thought that she was going to leave everything that was familiar to her very soon, Riya couldn't silence her need to see Nathan.

But when she entered the hall, shook hands with friends, he was nowhere to be seen.

And so she waited. Through Robert and Jackie exchanging vows, through their friends toasting them.

She stumbled through her own speech, her eyes still locked on the entrance.

And she waited.

She kissed Jackie's cheek, danced with Robert and only then it dawned on her that her waiting was useless.

Nathan had never planned on attending the wedding.

Riya was fuming when Jackie found her in the quiet corridor that seemed to absorb her anger and the sounds she made.

"Riya." Wary hesitation danced in Jackie's eyes. "I'm so sorry, but this is for the best. Let him go, Riya. It's got nothing to do with you."

Shocked at how perceptive Jackie was being, Riya stared at her. "Please, Jackie. Not today. Just enjoy your day."

"I'm learning, Riya. I've never provided you with security, but I do think of you, worry about you. After all this, you deserve happiness, you deserve someone who'll love you and take care of you for a long time. And Nathan is the last man on earth for you."

Riya didn't like the look in Jackie's eyes. And yet, for the first time in her life, she had a feeling that her mother was speaking the absolute truth. "What do you mean?"

"He doesn't deserve you. Isn't that enough?"

"Just please tell me what you mean."

"He has the same heart condition that Anna had."

Gasping, Riya grabbed the wall behind her. A violent shiver took hold of her, and her teeth chattered in her mouth.

She felt as if someone had pushed her off a cliff and the earth was rising to meet her without a warning, without a safety net.

Anna had been barely into her forties when she died. *No. No. No.* It couldn't be true. It couldn't be borne. Nathan was a force of life.

"I don't have a heart. At least, not a working one."

All the signs had been there right in front of her. That night in his suite, he had almost fainted. Did it happen often? That strap he had worn on his wrist sometimes instead of his watch, it had to be a heart rate monitor.

So many times she had called him heartless, had thrown his mother's name in his face, wondered at how easily he cut everyone out of his life... She shot to her feet and swayed, still feeling dizzy. "I need to see him."

"Riya? What's wrong? You look unwell."

She lifted her gaze to Robert's and swallowed. Tried to rally up her good humor, her strength. Because she had always been strong, hadn't she? They all left, they all deceived her; what else did she have but her strength?

But Nathan hadn't deceived her, hadn't lied to her. In fact, had told her that he would always leave.

"Nathan. Do you know where he is?"

"He went back to the estate. He's leaving in a few hours."

Shock traversed through her, a sudden cold in her chest. "He was here. Today? When? Why didn't he—"

"Yes. But he left just as you and Jackie arrived. Said he couldn't stay any longer. He's leaving tonight."

Let him go, Riya, the part of her that she had painfully trained into place screeched at her. *Let him walk out of your life. End it all before you sink.*

"Oh." It was a miracle Riya managed that, because inside it felt as if someone had pulled the ground from under her. "He didn't even say goodbye, Robert. I… He promised me he would be here tonight." She tried to breathe past the fear and spiraling hurt. "I don't understand any of this. How could I not realize? How could he not tell me? I…"

Wrapping his arms tightly around her, Robert hugged her. And enveloped in the love she had always craved, the lack of which had made her erect a shell around herself, Riya found herself unraveling. One question kept relentlessly pounding against her head.

Why did she care so much?

He had made it clear that they didn't mean anything to each other. Not even friends. Having faced abandonment and rejection all her life, she'd always worn retreat as her armor. She wanted to do that tonight too. But he had left her nowhere to hide.

"I'm sorry it came to this, Riya. But you have to know it has nothing to do with you."

Riya laughed because that was what everyone kept saying. "No?" she said, her voice echoing in the quiet of the carpeted foyer. She was so tired of fighting this, of telling herself that she was strong. "It seems everyone finds it so easy to walk away from me, so easy not to feel even affection for me. So easy to reject me. I hate him for doing this, hate myself for feeling like this. I have to be the stupidest woman in the world—"

Shaking his head, his heart in his eyes, Robert sighed. "It's the way he survives, Riya. He would despise himself if he became like Anna."

"*I don't care* what his reason is. I deserved at least goodbye."

"No, Riya. Wait."

Uncaring of the anxiety in his face, Riya tugged at her arm. Every inch of her was shaking with urgency, the rest of her body scrambling to catch up with her heart. "Let me go, Robert. If he leaves before I can get there, I'll never see him again."

Her throat closed up at the very prospect. "Never again." He'd pretty much promised her that. He'd cut Sonia out like that. And to never see him. "I have to talk to him—"

"Don't make this harder on him."

"What about how I feel?" She screamed the words, wondering how to stem the hurt. She'd been prepared to say goodbye tonight, but knowing what she did now… "I never saw my father again. If Nathan leaves before I see him, if something happens to him, I couldn't bear it, Robert."

It hurt as if someone were ripping out her heart from her chest. Had she and the time they had spent together meant nothing? Hadn't she mattered even a little to him? Shards of hurt and pain splintered through her.

Trembling, she patted her palms down her midriff in a rhythm.

"I'm so sorry, Riya. He had no right to do this to you. I'm sorry I didn't protect you—"

The sob that she had battling rose through Riya and she threw herself into her mom's arms. "He doesn't care, Jackie. He was perfectly willing to walk away…without a word. I wish it didn't hurt so much." She clenched her eyes closed. She couldn't give in to tears now. "This goodbye is just for me. Just for me."

Standing in that softly lit corridor, looking at Robert, who had the exact same eyes as his son, Riya calmed herself down. Her world was changing, slipping from her hands, forever shifting. But even for the fear rattling through her, she couldn't stop.

Only one more night, she reassured herself. Just one more night and she would never think about him again.

"You promised me a dance."

Hearing the soft whisper of her voice, Nathan turned around from the balcony. He hadn't been sure if she would seek him out. With a steely focus, he'd not speculated on whether he wanted her to find him.

Leaning against the wall, he let his gaze rove over her. She looked ethereal tonight, like some beautiful, other-worldly creature come to earth with the express purpose of tormenting him. The beige silk dipped and flared around her lithe body, her hair falling like a silk curtain on one shoulder.

Like a shadow, he had watched her step out of the limo. Hadn't been able to help himself from greedily drinking in her beauty. Had exercised every ounce of will when he saw her gaze wander through the hall, looking for him.

It had taken everything he had in him not to drag her away from the appreciative male gazes and there had been too many of those for his liking. But she wasn't his to protect or even to look at. After so rudely rejecting her small advance for a friendship, after witnessing the hurt flash in those beautiful eyes, he'd known he'd better keep his distance from her.

Not hurting Riya had somehow become the most important thing to him.

"If I remember right, you said you didn't want to dance with me," he said, willing himself to smile. His fingers gripped the railing so tight that the pattern would imprint on his palm. *"Leave Travelogue and go away, forever.* Those were your words."

Something shimmered in her gaze, but for the life of him, he couldn't tell what.

Stepping inside, she closed the door behind her. "I changed my mind. I've decided a lot of things have to change in my life."

"Like what?"

With a shrug, she looked away from him and he saw her chest rise and fall, her spine straighten as though she was bracing herself. For what?

He needed to get her out of here. Before he lost the tenuous thread of his control. Before he forgot how it had felt to have her look at him as if he was her hero, as if there was nothing he couldn't conquer. As if he would always be there for her.

She smiled then. There was fear in that smile, a bravery in it. There was something in her eyes that pulled at him, pierced through him. As if she was fighting to stand, as if she was fighting to keep herself together. And, as it had been from the beginning with her, every atavistic, male instinct in him rose to the fore.

Was she afraid? Of what?

He reached her, lifted her chin, looked into her eyes. "Riya, what is it?"

She shook her head, clasped his wrist, brought his hand closer so that his palm was wrapped around her cheek.

Pressed her mouth to the center of his palm. "I'm quitting Travelogue."

"What?"

"I found a remote-access job. It's a software architect position for a charity based in Bali. A six-month contract."

He frowned, worry for her trumping every other emotion in him. "Bali? Do you even know anyone there? Let me talk to some people I know and get the area checked—"

She shook her head. "No. I'm sure I'll be okay. I've taken care of myself so far, haven't I?"

"Why Bali? Why quit Travelogue?"

"Nothing here…nothing feels enough anymore. This life I've been leading, I want more. I want more excitement, more everything."

"Riya, I don't think you should just up and leave."

"Nathan?"

"Hmm?" He made a sound in his throat, incapable of anything else with her hands moving up his body. Sexual tension and anticipation arced and swelled between them, binding them together.

"A part of me wants to throw caution to the wind and live recklessly. A part of me will always hold me back. You are in between, Nate. Between risk and safety." Her hands clasped his cheek, and she tilted his chin up to meet her eyes. Lust and fire danced in them.

He frowned as her palm pressed against his chest, as if it wanted to confirm the thunderous roar of his heart. The intimacy of the gesture swelled inside him. "What do you want, butterfly?"

"That whole night that you promised me." Stepping back from him, she tugged the zipper of her dress down. With an elegant sensuality that sent lust rollicking through him, she pulled the fabric down, revealing the plump globes of her breasts, pushed it past her hips.

The dress pooled at her feet and she slowly kicked it away. Leaving her voluptuous body in a strapless bra and a thong.

He stepped back from her, only by the skin of his teeth. He couldn't be near her and not take what he wanted. He was painfully aroused, every nerve in him strung to breaking point. It didn't help that he'd had two drinks when he never drank, and now he had a simmering buzz in his head. "No."

She reached him before he could draw another breath. "Yes." She had somehow unbuttoned his shirt and now her palm rested against his hot skin, every line and ridge of it leaving an imprint on him. "You don't have to worry, Nate, I know precisely what I want and what I'll be getting. And come tomorrow morning, I'll bid you goodbye with a smile." Bending, she pressed an openmouthed kiss to his chest, flicked his nipple with her tongue.

Lust slammed at him from every direction.

With a punishing breath, he realized he couldn't send her away. She had come back here, hadn't she? She wanted him, and she owned her desire in a way that reduced him to nothing but heat and hunger.

Maybe with her he would always be weak. With the one woman who needed him to be honorable, strong, maybe he would always be this man who needed more than life had given him, who would always be reduced to the lowest denominator there was of him. Who wanted a few more stolen moments, a few more kisses…

It was exactly as he had feared.

Wasn't that why she was so dangerous to him?

All his armor, all his rules flew out the window when it came to her. She had brought forgiveness into his life. For a few weeks, she had banished the loneliness that was a part of his very bones now. She had brought him peace.

And tonight, it wanted pleasure, hers and his, and it wanted all of her, all night.

So he kissed her. Swallowed her soft gasp. Tasted her with hungry strokes of his tongue, learned her all over again. Drank from her until he was heady with lack of air. He was greedy, he was hot and he didn't grant them both even a breath.

His throat ached; his chest hurt at the sweet taste of her. Her touch, as her fingers wound around his nape, branded him. Her body coiled around his, stamped him forever, owned it, even if she didn't know it. Her breasts grazed him, the taut nipples rasping against his chest like tight buds driving him out of his skin.

And in that minute, he knew he would never again know the touch of another woman, the taste of another woman, the embrace of another woman. His breath harsh, he pressed his forehead against hers, the words rising through him like a tornado that couldn't be contained.

Because, as he had realized all those years ago, it wasn't the fact that his heart didn't work that was the problem. It was that it wanted more than it could ever handle in a lifetime. And all the needs and wants he had suppressed to live his life came rising to the fore when it came to Riya.

Everything he had done, everything he had achieved, felt so small compared to this moment when he couldn't say the words he most wanted to say. They burned on his tongue, fighting to be freed, weighed down on his chest, choking him.

He longed to tell her how much he loved her, how she had forever marked his heart, how she had brought forgiveness to his life, how she had, even if it was only these few minutes that he allowed himself, made him feel.

How alive he felt when he was near her, how much he

wanted to grow old with her, how much he wanted to be the one who would protect her, cherish her, love her.

Their teeth scraped, their tongues tangled. Their breaths mixed and became one. They became one.

The bed groaned as they fell onto it, devouring each other. He pushed his fingers up her thighs until he found her core. Only made sure that she was ready for him. Rubbed the swollen bud there. Let her soft moans surround him.

And she matched him in his hunger, giving as good as she got, digging her teeth into his chest, and there was nothing left in Nate but the desperate need to possess her.

He pushed her legs apart roughly in a frenzy of need. Undid his trousers. Tugged her thong out of the way. Holding her gaze, he entered her in a deep thrust that spoke of his desperate hunger rather than finesse.

Her wet heat clamped him tight, and Nate clenched his jaw to keep the words from spilling out.

Her legs wrapped around his hips; her spine bucked off the bed. She groaned and scratched his biceps with her nails as he pounded into her, only the haze of his approaching climax driving him. He touched the swollen bud at her core, glistening with moisture, calling for his touch.

She exploded around him and he thrust harder, faster, riding the wave of her release, forever changed by her.

His chest still expanding and contracting, he gathered her in his arms and rolled, until she was on top of him. But this time, she shied her gaze away from him and he wondered if she was bracing for his caustic words again. Cursed himself for changing her.

Running his fingers through her silky hair, he pressed a kiss to her temple. Tasted the sweat and scent of her skin. She was all around him, and it was the one place Nate never wanted to leave.

It was a place of belonging, it was home, it was what he

had always wanted in the corners of the heart that he had ruthlessly locked away.

Now, when his heart had found the woman it couldn't have but wanted with so much longing, he knew he would never again look at another woman as a man did.

Because he, Nathaniel Ramirez, apparently was a one-woman man. And he resigned himself to it.

If he couldn't have her, he didn't want anyone. With the realization came desperate need. Tugging her toward him, he pushed her onto her stomach. Breathlessly waited to see if she would protest. Turning her face toward the side, the minx smiled at him. "I'm yours tonight, Nate. To do with as you please."

With a hand under her body, he tugged her up until she was on her hands and knees. Splaying his palm on her lower back, he kissed along the line of her spine. Found the bundle of nerves that was already wet and slick for him.

He plunged his fingers into her and stroked the swollen tissue, a guttural sound escaping him. Felt the shudder that racked her. Bending down, he licked the rim of her ear. "Do you want me to stop, Riya?"

"No, please, Nate. Don't."

And that was all he needed. Holding her hips, he thrust into her. Felt stars explode behind his eyes, felt his body buckle at the waves of sensation.

There was no gentleness left in him. No honor, no control. Only excruciating love for the woman beneath him. It took him every ounce of will he possessed to wait for her before he let his climax take over his body.

Pulling out of her, he turned her face to find her mouth.

The spasms of her climax still rocking through her, Riya shivered, a cold dread pooling in her chest. With his explo-

sive lovemaking, Nathan imprinted himself onto every inch
of her, and she felt as if she were drowning in the wake of it.

"Did I hurt you, Riya?" Dragging her close until her
skin was slick against his, he pressed his mouth over her
temple in a reverent touch. Laced his fingers with hers so
tight that a stinging heat rose behind her eyes.

Flushing, Riya shook her head.

"Please, Riya, look at me."

"I'm fine. I just…I think I should go now."

With panting breaths, Riya willed the panic and pain
rising through her to abate.

She had meant to say goodbye, thought doing so would
give her closure. How could she have left without his touch,
his kiss, without feeling his tightly leashed control fray
around her one more time? Without feeling the closeness
she felt when he made love to her, without feeling the raw
edge of his emotion seek her, need her? It was the one time
she felt cherished, loved, the one time she felt as though
she mattered.

And now she had only dug herself deeper.

She couldn't break down now. If she did she would only
end up begging him for another second, another minute,
another hour. Of him holding her, kissing her, losing himself in her, of wondering if just another night would make
him want her, of eviscerating hope that he would ask her
to come with him.

Because another night or a hundred of them wouldn't
change him, wouldn't make him care for her. Just as she
had a sinking feeling only a lifetime with Nathan would
be enough for her. And she couldn't let him see how much
he had hurt her. She couldn't bear it if he told her in ruthless words that she was naive and a fool and that he had
warned her.

Pushing away from him, she wrapped the sheet around

her nakedness. Picked up the dress she'd discarded in such passion. Padded to the bathroom and splashed water over her face. Swallowed the sharp knot in her throat and sucked in a deep breath.

Even the silky glide of the dress over her skin felt like too much sensation to her hyped-up senses.

Keeping her spine straight, she walked back into the bedroom. Instantly her gaze sought and found him, standing at the French doors, looking up at the sky. It was the darkest of the night, just before dawn. He turned just as she found her clutch.

"Riya, before you go, I know someone in Bali who can—"

"No. I don't want your help. I'd like to get going now," she said, and walked toward the door.

He didn't move or speak. Only stared at her, with that utter stillness of his. His gaze devoured her, a maelstrom of emotions in it.

"Goodbye," she whispered, and turned the knob.

But something in her wouldn't calm down. Adrenaline spiking through her, she felt as if she were standing on a cliff.

"Are you ever coming back, Nathan?" When his mouth tightened, she hurried. "Not for me, don't worry. I know that in the scheme of things I matter very little to you. But for Robert, are you ever going to come back?"

She wished he would lie, wished she could believe him if he did.

"No."

Her stomach lurched, like the time it had on that fantastic ride with him. Only this time, he wasn't going to hold her through it. He was going to let her fall and shatter.

"Dad knows that I won't return." He closed the distance between them, something shimmering in his gaze. "Riya, my leaving has nothing to do with you. Don't make this harder than it has to be."

His words were a soft whisper, but the blaze of emotion in his eyes was unmistakable. And the evidence of his emotion birthed her anger, and it flew through her, an anchor in the drowning storm of hurt and fear.

"Has it become that easy for you, Nathan? Have you become that much of a bastard? Or are you just blind to what you have become?"

His chin reared back as though she had pummeled him with her fists. "I've always warned you that—"

"I know that you have Long QT syndrome like your mom. I know that you fainted and almost died when you were thirteen. I know that that night in the lounge, you almost fainted again. I know that you've cut out every ounce of emotion to survive, that you don't want to go..." Her voice broke. "...go like your mother did. But do you believe you're truly living your life, Nathan?"

"Get out, Riya."

Riya smiled through the tears blurring her vision. They had come full circle. "No, I won't. You pushed the truth on me when I wanted nothing to do with it. You made me hurt, made me feel so much for the first time."

"I already know my truth, butterfly. I've lived with it for more than a decade."

"You think you've conquered your weakness, but you're hiding behind it. You think love makes you weak. You think it'll rid you of your control, leave you at its mercy. You think it will leave you with nothing but fear for yourself and for the ones you love... But you're not your mother, Nathan.

"When I think of what you've achieved, the depth of your generosity...you've allowed yourself everything but happiness. How is it courage if you let it dictate how you live your life? How is it life if it has to be without love?

"You pushed me out of my comfort zone. You made me realize what a sterile life I'd built for myself. When my mother told me about you, I was devastated. I was so scared, Nate. In that moment, if I could erase ever knowing you, I probably would have."

He moved then. Grabbed her arms and hauled her to him. It was like being pulled into a whirlpool of roiling emotions. Like being sucked into the heart of a tornado. "If it scared you so much, then why did you come?"

"I came to say goodbye," Riya said, losing the fight. "I fought the fear that was roiling through me and came to see you. I came despite it, Nathan." She pressed a kiss to his jaw and released the words that she was courageous enough to speak. She knew now he would always plan to leave. But it didn't have to be today. "Tell me not to leave. Ask me to come with you."

Tugging her hands away, he let her go and stepped back. And Riya knew he was putting her out of his mind. "One day, you'll thank me for not taking you up on your offer, butterfly. One day when you find the man who'll love you forever, you'll be glad I left."

CHAPTER TWELVE

Three months later

RUNNING A HAND through his overgrown hair, Nathan waited as the cardiologist checked his heartbeat. It was always hard for him to sit still and even harder when it was this routine checkup.

His chopper was waiting on the roof of the hospital in a remote area of the island of Java. He had stopped seeing world-renowned specialists a long time ago. From day one, he had accepted that there was nothing to be done.

The doctor, who was seeing him for the first time, examined Nathan with warm brown eyes. "You're in remarkably good shape for a man with your condition, Mr. Ramirez," he said in perfect but accented English. "But I guess you know that. Just keep doing what you're doing."

Nathan nodded and thanked him.

"Your next checkup is in—"

"A month," Nathan finished for him.

Thanking the doctor, he was buttoning up his shirt when his cell phone rang. Seeing the face of his virtual manager, he switched it on. "Yes?"

Jacob sounded wary. "Those papers have come back unsigned again."

Nathan caught the fury that rose through him. It wasn't

Jacob's fault. It was that manipulative minx's. What the hell kind of game was she playing? Why was she bent on tormenting him? "From where?"

"From Bali again." So she still hadn't returned. "And there was no reply to our lawyer's question about what she wants."

It had been the same for the last three months. He would send the papers to her and she would send them back, unsigned. Without a reply.

Nathan clenched his teeth, the emptiness he had been fighting for months sucking him in. "Find her number for me."

A few minutes later, Nathan punched in her number and waited. His heart leaped into his throat, his pulse ringing very much like the peal of the phone on the other line.

"Hello?" her voice came across the line, and his stomach lurched. Just hearing her voice was enough to drive him into that crazed, out-of-control need to see her, to touch her, to hold her close, to wake up to her face.

"Hello?"

Stepping back from the sunshine, Nate leaned against the brick wall. Took a deep breath. "Why the hell aren't you signing the papers, Riya? What do you want now?"

The line was silent for a few seconds. And her face popped up in his mind's eye, her expression stricken as she had left him that night.

"I... Nate, how are you?"

"I'm alive, Riya." He heard her gasp and ignored it. At least now there was no need to pretend. "And if I weren't, you would be the first one to—"

"Bastard."

This time, he laughed, chose again to ignore the cutting pain packed into the single word. "Cut the theatrics and tell me why you're refusing to sign away the estate."

"I decided that it should be mine. That I don't want to part with it, after all."

Disbelief roared in his ears. And he let a curse fly. "Have you finally decided to listen to your mother, then?"

"I figured it was mine every which way it counted," she continued smoothly, as though he hadn't just insulted her and *this thing between them*, as though she wasn't tying him up in knots.

"And how did you come to that impossible conclusion?"

"Robert, who's my father as far as I'm concerned, deeded it to me with love. I'm strong enough to accept my right over it now. Of course, that's thanks to you. And more than that, I figured it was mine because it belonged to the man I love with all my heart."

He felt as if a fist had jammed up into his chest. He couldn't breathe as her words sank in. There was no hesitation in her voice. "You've lost your mind," he said, pushing the words out through a raw throat. "Gone over the edge."

"Actually it's the opposite. I've realized that my happiness is in my hands. Not Jackie's or Robert's or even yours. That I have to believe that I deserve love. That I have to risk pain to fight for it." Now she didn't sound that put together. "Admit it, Nate. If I asked you for it right now, you wouldn't fight me. You wouldn't deny me."

His butterfly was getting reckless, coming into her own. Despite the ache in his heart, he smiled. "Why would I do that?"

"Because you love me." She waited, as though she wanted him to feel the full impact of her outrageous announcement. "You can put thousands of miles between us, you can cut all connections from me, you might never even see me again. But you think about me all the time. That estate, that massive fortune of yours, that faulty but generous heart of yours…they are all mine."

"You sound very sure, Riya."

The sound of her laugh pierced through him. "I think I know you as well as I know myself now. I realized that I won't ever have to work a day in my life again and still live like a princess. Because one of the richest and the most wonderful man in the world…I belong to him now. How's that for security, huh?"

She sounded confident, even brazen, but he could imagine the tears in her eyes, her hands fisting at her sides as she forced the words past that beautiful mouth. "But the thing is, I would rather risk my heart for another moment with him than have all the security in the world." He heard her suck in a breath. "That estate is the best waiting place for me when I come back."

With every word she said, she was twisting his insides, unraveling him. And beneath his rules, his honor, his revulsion for fear, Nate saw something else. As if he had been sitting in the dark all this time, mistaking his cowardice for his guts.

He asked the question he knew he shouldn't. "Waiting for what?"

"For you to come home." The ache in her voice was as clear as the ache in his own heart. "For you to come back to me." And she was crying and unraveling, right along with him, even though there were thousands of miles between them.

He rubbed his eyes with his fingers, a stinging heat prickling behind them. Her words gouged a hole through the emptiness he felt. "That's never going to happen, butterfly. You're wasting your precious life. You want a stable life with a steadfast man who'll be with you for the rest of your life, remember? Me? I could be gone any time." His own cheeks were wet now and Nathan didn't feel ashamed or afraid, only ache.

"Yeah, well, you ruined all my plans for my life, Nate. Now I want something else."

"Yeah? What?"

"A decade, a year, a day, or even another moment with the man I adore. With the man who showed me how to live, and love. With the man I'll love for the rest of my life."

He heard her grasping breath, the catch in her voice. Heard her tear-soaked voice as if she were looking at him with those beautiful brown eyes.

"I love you, Nate, with every breath in me. I have been a coward all my life. I was a coward even that night. I let you walk away. But not anymore. I deserve happiness and so do you. My life is empty without you, Nate."

How he wanted to believe her; how he wished he had the courage to be the man she deserved. Because that was what he was lacking. Not the robust heart, not a body that would live for a century. But the courage to grab the love she offered, to trust her love and his, to risk his heart.

Whatever it was that was holding him back now, protecting his heart, this was fear.

He was in that moment he had dreaded his whole life. Fear and pain. And yet it was of not seeing Riya ever again, of not waking up to her, of not seeing her wide mouth split into a smile at the sight of him, of not holding her tight until they couldn't breathe.

"I'm waiting for you, Nate." She was crying now, in soft sobs and broken words. And the pain that caused him was more than any he had ever felt, hurt deeper than any other fear that he didn't want to feel.

"I think I'll always wait for you."

And then she hung up.

Riya sank to her bed in her hotel room, her breaths coming jerkily. Grabbing the edge of the T-shirt she had taken from Nate that night, she buried her face in it. Every inch of her was still vibrating at hearing his voice. Her fingers hurt with how tightly she had fisted them, how she wanted to touch him, feel his arms around her.

Had he known that she was falling apart? How much it had cost her to say what was truly in her heart, even knowing that it might never change his mind? How big a risk she had taken by binding herself to him, by giving him her heart?

But to this new Riya whom he had brought to life, nothing less than what she wanted, what she deserved was acceptable.

Without him, nothing in the world meant anything to her.

CHAPTER THIRTEEN

NATHAN FOUND HER a month later on a beach in Ubud, Bali, in one of the villas RunAway owned, sitting on the deck that offered spectacular views of rolling hills and valleys. The villa was the utmost in privacy and comfort. It perched atop a valley overlooking a lush river gorge.

It had been his very own slice of paradise. When Jacob told him that a request had come in from his property manager that a woman named Riya *Ramirez*, who'd claimed to be his close friend, had wanted to use it, he had laughed for a full minute. The woman was relentless, stubborn, manipulative, and he loved her for all of it.

And yet, with the setting sun casting golden shadows on her striking face, it was loneliness that enveloped her now. And it clawed at his heart.

It had taken him three weeks to consolidate his worldwide holdings, to find and hire efficient managers where he needed, to fight the voice that whispered *no* every second of the day.

But there had also been one that kept counting the time down, telling him that he had wasted enough as it was. And he realized, if he had lived without fear, he had also lived without joy for too long.

Once he had decided, it had taken him a week to find her, and every minute of waiting to hear more had been excruciating. Until the stubborn woman herself had sent him a clue.

Did she love him that much? Would she have stopped at nothing until she got through to him? Could he always prove himself worthy of it?

Feeling a knot of anxiety, he clenched and unclenched his fingers.

She was dressed in a sleeveless, floral dress that rippled around her knees with the breeze.

"Riya?" he said, unable to say anything else past the emotion clogging his throat.

She was off the lounging chair and deck before he could blink. Standing before him with her hair flying in her face before he could draw another breath. Her chest falling and rising, her mouth pinched.

And the love in her eyes undid Nathan as nothing had ever done. "I love you, butterfly," he said, and she swayed, a gasp falling from her lips. Threw herself into his arms like a gale of wind. Knocked the breath out of him, knocked him off his feet.

He buried his mouth in her neck, filling himself with the scent of her.

Her arms wound around him so tight that he laughed. Pulling her head back, she glared at him. "I'm never letting you go, ever. You even talk about leaving me again and I'll chain you to myself." A shudder swept through her in direct contrast to the bravado in her words.

"I love you so much, Nate. I've missed you so much. Every day, every night, wherever I want, I thought about you. It hurt so much that I wanted it to stop for a while. It felt like—"

"Like you were missing an essential part of yourself?" he said, and she nodded.

He tasted her in a rough kiss, needing the fortification,

needing tangible proof of her taste. She clung to him with just as much desperation.

"Do you know what you're signing up for, butterfly?" he said, when his desperation had blunted, when his heart beat normally again. When the shadow of a lifelong fear clasped him tight. "It would kill me much sooner to see—"

Her palm closed over his mouth and she shook her head. "I do feel fear, and sometimes I can't breathe thinking of this world without you. But I'd rather fight that fear every day than live another moment without you. I'll do it, Nate. I'll only ever try to be your strength. And all I ask is that you give me the chance. To love you, to be loved by you, for as long as possible, that's all I want."

Clasping her hand in his, he dragged her to the edge of the deck and looked out into the valley and beyond. Turned her toward him and dropped onto his knees.

"I love you, Riya, with every breath in my body, with every beat of my faulty heart. I was so lonely before I met you. I thought I was protecting you by walking away. When you called me, when you so bravely put into words what you felt for me…to hear you say what I felt for you, to hear you tell me you chose to love me even as you were afraid, it made me realize I wasn't living, merely existing. You've taught me what it is to be brave, butterfly."

Riya kissed him, tears stinging her cheeks. Running her hands over him greedily, she clung to him, fear and joy all bubbling inside her. Her biggest risk had paid off and her heart stuttered in her chest. "All I want is to be by your side for the rest of our lives."

His eyes shining with unshed tears, he kissed her temple. "Will you be my wife, butterfly? Will you tie yourself to me, then?"

Riya nodded, the small doubt in his tone doing nothing to abate the intensity of her own love. He had come for her;

he had shown her his heart. It didn't mean years of protecting himself from fear and hurt would be gone this very second. But she was strong enough for both of them. "Yes."

He dragged her into the cradle of his arms, his lean frame shuddering. "That's the sweetest word I've ever heard, Riya."

For the first time in his life, Nathan felt joy, and he felt complete. With the woman he loved with him, there was no place for fear.

Only love and utter happiness for the rest of his days.

EPILOGUE

One year later

HIS BREATH HITCHING in his throat, every inch of him thrumming with anticipation, Nathan turned around and froze.

With the blue sea and white sand as her background, Riya stilled beneath the arch that was decorated with sheer white lilies and cream-colored silk.

Her gaze met his, her mouth wreathed in a shy smile; she was waiting to see his reaction, he realized.

The red sheer silk sari she wore wound around her striking figure, baring her midriff, inviting his touch. When he had looked at the huge yard of the material and frowned a week ago, she had patiently and laughingly explained to him how it worked, and how much fun she was having with her aunt teaching her how to wear it.

And that she was learning it for him, she had said with a wink.

He was glad she did.

The silk draped over her left shoulder and hung behind her, hiding and showcasing her beautiful body. Her long hair flew in the breeze, but it was the glittering expression in her eyes that arrested him.

He couldn't breathe when he remembered her tears when they'd learned that her father had passed away a few years before they'd tracked him down. He had held her all night, her pain as much as his. And the smile in her eyes, when he'd told her about the aunt his PI had located... the only blood relative of her father still alive.

All his wealth and power, he had truly appreciated it that day. For it had brought such happiness to the woman he loved.

He mouthed, *I love you* and tears shimmered in her gaze as she walked toward him.

Her heart racing as if toward some invisible goal, Riya rubbed her fingers over her face. She blew out a breath, a shadow of fear marring her perfect day.

Beneath the cliff on top of which the villa sat, the sea was dark blue, the horizon where the sky met the sea not visible. It was the most beautiful place she had ever seen.

The wedding on the beach had been her dream come true. Robert, Jackie and her aunt, and the staff from the estate, Riya had never felt more loved or cherished.

And in between all of it was the man she loved.

It had taken all these months for Nathan to believe that she truly wanted this—that she wouldn't change her mind, that she would never stop loving him, that she would never let herself be driven by fear.

And now the truth she had realized just this morning.

Wrapping her arms around herself, she battled both excitement and fear.

She turned when the door of the main bedroom in the villa closed with a soft thud.

Nathan stood leaning against the door, and the raw heat in his eyes instantly sent an answering tremble through her. She wondered if she was betraying herself, if the small thing she had learned this morning was written on her face.

"I don't want you to wear a sari again."

"What?" She ran her hands over the silky folds, distracted by his expression. "You don't like it?"

"As your husband, I command you not to wear it in public," he added with a possessive glint in his eye, and she laughed.

"I've been waiting to say that since I saw you walking down toward me."

He caught the edge that trailed over her shoulder with one hand and tugged hard. And the silky soft material came undone around her and ripped at her waist.

He tugged until Riya was caught in his arms.

"You look utterly gorgeous and scandalously sexy in it. And I don't want any other man but me to see that."

He buried his mouth in the curve of her neck, his hands settling around her bare midriff. "Nate, wait, I want to—"

"It's all I've been wanting to do since I saw you, Riya. Please don't deny me."

Forgetting her own words, she pushed into him and sank her fingers in his hair.

As he whispered words that made her core pulse with spiraling need, his long fingers climbing up her midriff toward her breasts encased snugly in the blouse.

He groaned and pulled the hooks that held it together with a strong tug and Riya gasped as she heard the blouse rip at the hooks. With impatient fingers, he pushed the cups of her bra down.

She shuddered as his abrasive palms covered her breasts, the aching, tight nipples rasping against the roughness. Rubbing her buttocks against his hard body, Riya loosened the petticoat and let it pool at her feet.

His palms moved over her waist and then her thighs. When he picked her up and placed her on an exquisitely crafted sofa table, she laughed and gave herself over to the dark passion lighting up his eyes.

Their lovemaking was swift, desperate, coated with the awareness that they were now joined in the holiest of bonds, exalted by the promises they had made to each other. Sweat cooling on her forehead, she leaned her head against his chest, the superfast rhythm of his heart comforting under her palms.

She kissed the taut skin of his pectorals, breathing in the musky scent of him.

"You always do that," he said, his words a gravelly rasp against her senses.

Looking up, she smiled, her arms still around him. "What do you mean?"

He pushed sweaty tendrils of hair that stuck to her forehead. "Check my heart. Every time after we make love, you put your face to my chest as though you want to—"

Shaking her head, she put her fingers over his mouth. "I'm sorry, I didn't even realize that I did that. I didn't mean to make you feel—"

He laughed and swallowed the rest of her words in a sizzling kiss. "These last few months have been the happiest of my life. Every day, I can't imagine this is my life. I can't believe that I walked away from this. If you hadn't fought for me, for our love…" He sighed against her mouth, a shudder racking through him. "I love you, Riya. I love that you'll forever be mine and I yours."

An ache rose in Riya's throat at his words. Her gorgeous, powerful man never let a day pass without telling her how much he loved her, without showing her how precious she was to him. But they were both still so new to this. He was only now getting used to having her around after living alone for so long.

Underneath that easy humor, there was still a self-sufficiency that wouldn't leave so easily. But he made an effort for her and Riya was so glad for it.

Hiding her face in his chest, Riya gathered the courage to say the words. "Nathan, I have to tell you something."

"What is it, butterfly?"

"I realized yesterday that...I...we've been traveling so much and I lost track of..."

He lifted her chin, his gaze curious. "What's bothering you?"

"I took a pregnancy test this morning, and it's... I'm pregnant, Nate."

Shock flitted in his eyes, cycled to concern. "I don't know what to say."

Riya felt the happiness of her day pop.

"Riya, I know this isn't what we had planned. I mean, we didn't really even plan anything, did we? But, my little butterfly, that's how you came into my life, didn't you?" He tugged her toward him and hugged her so tight that Riya thought she would break under the avalanche of his love. Yet when he spoke, there was a restraint in his voice. "I know it's scary when we're so new to each other. I know that having a child is a huge thing, but, Riya—"

Riya pushed at his shoulders and studied his gaze. He was holding back his reaction for her. She pulled his hands to her stomach and spoke past the raw ache in her throat.

"Please, Nate. Will you be honest with me about this?"

He nodded and clasped her cheek. "It's the perfect gift you could have given me today. You'll have me every step of the way. You—"

And that was when Riya understood. And she laughed and hugged him tight, kissed his face. Looked into his beautiful blue gaze.

"Nathan, you and I made this. We created this with our love. Can you imagine anything more beautiful or wonderful in this world? It's true I'm afraid, I'm nowhere near ready or equipped to be a mom, but if you're with me, I can do anything. Tell me you want this just as much as I do. Tell me you want this baby."

Tears pooled in his beautiful blue gaze and he kissed her again. Now it was he who trembled and Riya hugged him hard to herself. "I do want this, Riya. I'll always want anything you bring into my life, butterfly."

* * * * *

NINE MONTH COUNTDOWN

LEAH ASHTON

For Regan – who thinks all my heroes are based on him, but they're not.

You're *my* hero though, baby. I'm having so much fun sharing my happy ever after with you.

CHAPTER ONE

IT HAD STARTED exactly eleven steps down the aisle.

Ivy knew this, because she'd been counting.

Step, together *one*. Step, together *two*.

Generally the counting happened when she could feel the famous Molyneux temper bubbling away inside her. Or on the rare occasions she was nervous—although she couldn't remember the last time that had been. But today, it was neither of those things. The bride—her sister April—was the one who should be feeling anxious. Marriage wasn't something Ivy could see herself doing any time soon. She dated, occasionally, but never anything serious. Right now, her focus was on her work, and the family business, and everything else took a back seat. Because in Ivy's experience relationships had an irritating habit of leaching into everything. And when it came to her career, well—anything that could damage *that* was just not acceptable.

But anyway... She'd been walking down the aisle, happily aware that the crowd seated in rows of white wooden chairs were peering around her for a glimpse of the bride, when she'd *felt* it. At exactly step eleven.

Someone wasn't looking around her. Not at all. Someone was looking right at her, in a way that Ivy wouldn't have thought possible. In a way that had *weight*.

And it was so strange, and so unexpected, that Ivy even stopped counting.

But she didn't stop walking, and she didn't shift her gaze from exactly where she was heading: the celebrant, a pretty wooden trellis temporarily constructed on the exclusive Nusa Dua beach, and the cerulean blue of the Indian Ocean beyond. Because today she was April's chief bridesmaid, and she took any job that she was given seriously. Bridesmaid or Board Executive—it didn't matter. Work was work, and Ivy *always* lived by the idea that you should never do *anything* if you weren't going to do it right.

So she started counting afresh, and then made sure she completed her bridesmaid duties to the best of her ability.

But that weight didn't lift until well after April had kissed her new husband. In fact, it wasn't until April and Evan stood together to accept the hugs and well wishes of their guests that Ivy could *finally* openly search the crowd without fear of raising the ire of the videographer.

But by then it was too late. That heavy, heavy gaze was gone.

Much later—what seemed like *hours* of smiling for the photographer later—Ivy stood with her two sisters and the rest of the bridal party at the back of the enormous marquee that would host the wedding reception.

The luxury hotel their mother had booked for the occasion loomed four storeys high on three sides, hugging the marquee as it stared out to the ocean. A welcome whisper of a breeze skimmed Ivy's bare shoulders and pushed the silk of her full-length dress against her legs. It was still warm, but Bali's famous humidity appeared to have let up just a little. Regardless, a blonde make-up artist hovered amongst them, busily 'fixing' Ivy and her sisters before their big entrance. *Can't have your faces melting!*

Ivy shifted her weight rather than rolling her eyes—which reminded her once again that crazily expensive, handmade, bespoke heels did not guarantee comfort. Not even close.

The Balinese wedding planner was barking out instructions in a failed attempt at a stage whisper, but having reviewed the day's minute schedule—and provided a few useful suggestions—Ivy knew exactly where she should be. She strode over to Sean, Evan's best mate—and best man—and hooked her arm through his.

'Are we going in?' he asked. Beer in hand, he clearly wasn't taking his best-man duties as seriously as Ivy would've liked.

In fact, the music April had chosen for their entrance had started, so Ivy used her free hand to pluck the beer from Sean, and to hand it to the wedding planner.

'And we just follow them?' Sean asked as he watched Mila and Ed disappear into the marquee.

'You *were* at the rehearsal, right?' Ivy said, but she was smiling as she tugged Sean behind her.

Inside, the marquee opened up—it was only the rear wall that had, well, *a wall*. Otherwise it was edged with white fabric gathered curtain-like against each support. April's two-hundred-odd guests sat at white-draped tables topped with ivory flower arrangements amongst dozens of sparkling chandeliers—and beyond them, framed by the marquee like a postcard, was the ocean. Of course, a Molyneux wedding would never be anything less than spectacular—but even Ivy was impressed. And timing their entrance *just* as the sun began to sink beneath the darkening blue of the ocean? Perfect.

Ivy was about halfway to the bridal table when she realised she was counting her steps again.

Thirty-two. Thirty-three. Thirty-four...

But this time it annoyed her. Maybe it was the distraction of...of whatever it was she thought she'd felt during the ceremony—or maybe it was just that it kind of made sense that she'd be a bit tense while walking down the aisle, given her feelings about love and relationships. So counting her steps then had been okay.

But now? No, it wasn't acceptable. Because now she recognised why she was doing it.

She *was* nervous. The way her stomach was flip-flopping all over the place made that crystal-clear.

Why?

She was used to having so many eyes on her. How many times had she been the spokesperson for Molyneux Mining? She had years of media training behind her. She'd been interviewed on live television, and she'd been splashed all over the newspapers—accurately and otherwise—her entire life.

So, yes, nineteen-year-old Ivy counted her steps *all* the time. Twenty-seven-year-old Ivy a hell of a lot less. Now, *thirty-one*-year-old Chief Operating Officer of Molyneux Mining Ivy shouldn't need to do it at all.

Thirty-one-year-old Ivy was an accomplished, confident—*powerful*, some might say—*grown-up*. Counting steps was just…juvenile.

Fifty-seven. Fifty-eight. Fifty—

'What did I do?' Sean asked as he pulled out her spindly chair at the long bridal table.

Ivy blinked. 'Pardon?'

'You just told me to "Stop it".' He looked at her curiously. 'With some force.'

'I didn't,' she said, very quickly. Then sat down and fussed needlessly with her silverware as Sean took his own seat.

Ignoring Sean's gaze, Ivy looked up to watch April glide across the marquee, arm in arm with her new husband—and both with stars in their eyes.

Her little sister had never looked more beautiful: like a princess with her blonde hair piled up high, and the oversized skirt of her dress floating about her like a cloud.

Ivy couldn't help but smile, the ridiculous mystery of the

step counting put aside for the moment. She was so happy for April. Today was her dream come true.

Slowly she relaxed into her chair, allowing that inexplicable tension to ease from her body.

And it was right about then—right about when she decided that *yes*, it was totally fine to slide her heels off beneath the privacy of the long table cloth—that she felt it again.

That look. *That* heavy concentration of attention that made the back of her neck prickle, but other parts of her... tingle. And Ivy was not one for superfluous *tingling*.

But this time there was nothing stopping her from looking up—from searching the crowd for this person, for this... Man.

There he was, on the opposite side of the parquet dance floor. With his close-cropped hair, and the broadest of broad shoulders, Ivy would've guessed he was in the military, even if she hadn't already known he was.

Angus. His name was Angus...Something. She remembered his name had stood out amongst April's seating plan and guest list—a name she didn't recognise, and who April also didn't know. An old school friend of Evan's: *All I know is that he's a soldier,* April had whispered with some awe, *one of those special ones. SAS.*

Amongst a million other wedding-planning things to do—and a million more work-related concerns—she hadn't given the mysterious Angus Somebody another thought.

But right now, the man had somehow taken up *all* her thoughts. And when their gazes finally connected—when she could truly *see* all that remarkable intensity—it was almost as if he'd taken over her body, too. Her skin was hot. Her mouth was dry.

And from this distance, she couldn't even see the colour of his eyes.

Oh, God. What would happen if he was close enough for her to see if they were blue, or green, or grey?

Based on her current reaction, she'd most likely burst into flames.

No.

Now she was being silly. He was just a man, just a guest at the wedding.

Just a distraction she didn't need.

She was April's chief bridesmaid. And she was Chief Operating Officer of Molyneux Mining. Neither of those things were conducive to gazing like a lust-crazed idiot across the dance floor at her sister's wedding.

Yet she was still doing exactly that.

And just as she was sternly telling herself that it really wasn't that hard to look elsewhere…*anywhere*…but at *him*…

Something happened.

He winked.

Angus Barlow always knew what he was doing. He was measured, methodical, structured. Calm. Not easily distracted, or swayed by others.

So he'd known what he'd been doing when his gaze had first collided with Ivy as she'd walked down that aisle. He'd been having a damn good look at a beautiful woman.

Her long black hair was looped and twisted up to leave her neck exposed above her bare shoulders. Her skin had glowed in the sunlight, and was still managing to do so now, even in the candlelit marquee without the help of the rapidly setting sun.

She had a great profile. A long, thin nose and a strong chin.

The sea breeze had done fabulous things to the pale purple dress she wore, plastering it hard against her curves as she'd walked. And if he'd continued to watch her rear

view, rather than turning to observe the bride's arrival—
well, Angus didn't really think anyone could blame him.

And now, hours later, he'd found himself again com-
pelled to look at Ivy.

Angus supposed it could be argued that Ivy wasn't the
most beautiful woman at the wedding. In fact, Angus had
heard that many considered her unlucky she didn't inherit
more of her father's movie-star looks, the way her two
younger sisters had. Although Angus couldn't agree. It
was true she did take more after her unusual mother—in
both looks and personality, given the way she was following exactly in her mother's business footsteps. But he liked
the angles to Ivy's face: the sharpness of her cheekbones,
the slant to her brows.

Plus he'd *really* liked the contrasting plump of her lips.
He'd never noticed before tonight, never really even looked
at the many photos of her that could be found in the paper,
or the footage of her on TV. But right now it seemed impossible he hadn't.

So yes, he did know what he was doing.

Right on cue, he felt a twinge in his bandaged right wrist,
as if to remind him at least partly *why* he was doing this.

Not why he was looking at Ivy Molyneux. But why he
was here, at this wedding, at all.

He wasn't supposed to be here, of course. He'd declined
the original invitation, only to break his wrist during a
training exercise in Darwin a month or so later.

So rather than where he *should* be, deployed with his
squadron in Afghanistan, he was at Evan's wedding. Surrounded by people who were part of a world he'd exited
so abruptly more than fifteen years earlier, and that he'd
truly not missed at all.

This was not his thing: an opulent, diamond-drenched
evening jammed full of the superficial and the vacuous.

He was on a singles table of sorts. His fellow guests

were a mixture of the different flavours of wealth he remembered from high school: old money, new money, and used-to-have money. Then there were the people aware of their luck and good fortune—and then those that were painfully, frustratingly oblivious. In his experience, most of the wealthy fell into the second category. But even then, they generally weren't bad people. Just not his type of people.

Ivy Molyneux was certainly not his type of people either. A billionaire heiress born into obscene wealth, how could she be anything but extraordinarily ignorant of what it was like to actually exist in the real world?

And yet that was the thing. Amongst the hundreds of faces here at this wedding, amongst all this glitz and glitter, when she'd met his gaze it had felt...

Real.

That he certainly hadn't expected.

That was why he hadn't looked away, and why his interest in her had become *much* more than a simple visual appreciation of a beautiful woman.

That was why he'd winked.

And Ivy's jaw had dropped open, then almost immediately snapped shut.

Then her eyes had narrowed, just before a near imperceptible shake of her head—and she'd turned her attention to the groomsman beside her, as if Angus no longer existed.

But somehow he knew, knew deep within his bones, that this wasn't even close to over.

It had taken considerable effort, but Ivy managed to avoid looking at Angus throughout her entire maid of honour speech. Thanks to years of practising public speaking, Ivy knew how to ensure the entire crowd felt she was talking directly to them. Unfortunately tonight the block of about five tables immediately surrounding Angus's might have felt rather ignored.

But, it couldn't be helped.

Not that the not looking helped a lot. Because he'd definitely just kept on looking at her.

She knew it, because her whole body felt his concentrated attention. It had only been sheer will that had prevented the stupid racing of her heart or the odd, inexplicable nerves that churned through her belly from impacting her voice. Honestly, she felt as though, if she let herself, she'd come over all soft and breathy and...*pathetic*.

But of course she hadn't, and April had given her the tightest of hugs after her speech, so that was a relief. That was all that mattered tonight, that April was happy.

Even her mother—on the parents' table in prime position near the cake—had lifted her chin in the subtlest of actions. Ivy had learnt long ago that that was about as effusive as Irene Molyneux ever got, so she'd take it.

With her formal duties out of the way, Ivy should now be able to relax for the remainder of the speeches. But of course she couldn't.

By the time dessert was served, and Evan had delivered his—hilarious by the reaction of the guests, even if Ivy registered barely a word—speech, Ivy was about to crawl out of her skin in frustration.

Finally the dancing began—and Ivy made her escape.

With the straps of her heels tangled in her fingers, the lawn outside the marquee was cool beneath her bare feet. She had to walk some distance before she could hear the ocean above the exuberant cacophony of music and voices of the reception.

The hotel gardens stretched along the beach from either side of the main hotel building. Lights dotted pathways that led to bungalows and villas, but they were all empty, with every guest at the hotel also a guest at the wedding.

And it felt empty, which Ivy appreciated. She'd flown in from London only...yesterday? No, the day before.

Ivy smiled—it was recently enough, anyway, that jet lag still had her confusing her days.

But after a series of intense business meetings, a thirty-six-hour journey from London after delays in Dubai, the madness that was the last-minute planning for the wedding, and then that disconcerting attention from Angus Whoever—Ivy was seriously happy to finally be *alone*.

She took a long, measured breath and waited for her muscles to relax as she exhaled.

But they didn't.

'Ivy.'

She spun around to confront the reason for the tension throughout her body. Angus wore a cream linen shirt, untucked, and dark knee-length tailored shorts—a variation of what the majority of male guests were wearing. Unlike the majority of male guests, he still managed what should be impossible—to look as if he was attending a wedding, rather than a barbeque. Maybe it was his posture? The extreme straightness of how he stood, combined with the way his clothing hung so perfectly from his muscular frame? Whatever it was, Ivy suspected he looked equally gorgeous taking out his garbage.

'You followed me,' she said.

He shrugged. 'You knew I would.'

Ivy's mouth dropped open. 'Don't be absurd.'

While his shirt was clearly visible in the limited light, the rest of him blurred into the darkness behind him, his face all angles and shadows. Even so, Ivy knew, *knew*, he was looking at her in disbelief.

'Look,' she said, in her no-nonsense work voice, 'I really don't have time for this.'

'This being?'

He really did have a fantastic voice. Deep and authoritative.

Not that it made any difference.

'*This,*' she said, waving her hands to encompass them both.

'I'm still confused,' he said. 'Can you elaborate?'

Ivy gave a little huff of frustration. 'I don't have time for whatever two random strangers might do when they meet at a wedding.'

And she didn't. It had been hours since she'd checked her email.

A laugh. 'C'mon, Ivy. I'm sure you can think up a far more interesting descriptor than *whatever*.'

'I could,' she said. 'But that would take more of my precious time. So—'

She was half a step towards the path when Angus's hand wrapped around her lower arm. He wore a light bandage that encircled his palm and extended halfway to his elbow, the fabric just the tiniest bit rough against her skin.

'Honey, *everyone* has time for...' his grip loosened and his fingers briefly traced a path across her wrist '...talking.'

Ignoring her body's traitorous shivery reaction to his touch, Ivy went on the defensive. 'This isn't just talking.'

But, of course, that was a mistake.

She sensed, rather than saw, his smile.

'No,' he said. 'That's the point, isn't it?'

Ivy shook her head, as if that would somehow help her brain reorganise itself. She was just...off. Unbalanced. If she was to walk away from him now, she'd be counting her steps, definitely.

'No,' she said. 'The point is there *is* no point. That's the point.' Seriously? Could she be any more ridiculous?

She tried again. 'You're not my type, Angus.'

The shadow of his smile told her immediately that she'd made a mistake. Now he knew she knew his name.

But standing so close to him, Ivy supposed she should be relieved she could speak at all. What did this man do to her?

'I don't believe you,' he said. As if that was that.

And then he surprised her by casually sitting on the sand. He leant right back on his elbows, his legs crossed at the ankles. 'Sit.'

Logic would've had her back at the marquee by now, so it came as no surprise that she found herself seated beside him. She sat more stiffly though, her hands rested on the silk skirt that covered her knees, her gaze firmly on the black of the ocean.

A big part of her knew she really needed to get back to the marquee. What if April needed her? Plus it really had been hours since she'd checked her email—maybe she could pop by her suite on the way back?

She'd levered herself onto her knees to stand when she felt Angus's hand on her arm. Electricity shot across her skin and she found herself completely still.

'Hey,' he said. 'We're supposed to be having a conversation, remember?'

'But, my emails—'

The man's laughter was loud, and strong and totally unexpected in the darkness.

'Emails? You're on a deserted tropical beach with a guy who is seriously attracted to you—and you're thinking about email? That cuts deep.'

Ivy smiled despite herself, and rearranged her legs so she was sitting again, his hand—unfortunately—falling away.

'You're seriously attracted to me?' she said.

'I'll take smug if it means no more talk of work.'

Ivy smiled again. 'Deal,' she said. For a long minute, she studied the ocean again. Her eyes had adjusted now, and she could just make out the occasional edge of foam along the crest of a wave.

Something had changed, Ivy realised. The stiffness in her shoulders had loosened. A tightness in her jaw was gone.

She couldn't say she was relaxed, not sitting beside this

man. But the tension she felt had shifted—maybe it was that her everyday tensions had lifted? Only to be replaced by another flavour of tension, but Ivy had to admit the tension that radiated between her and Angus was vastly, vastly preferable—no matter how uncomfortable it felt.

Uncomfortable, because she didn't know what to do with it. But also…different. Unfamiliar. Exciting.

She twisted to face him.

'Hi, I'm Ivy Molyneux,' she said.

'Angus Barlow.'

And she smiled. It had been an intense few days, so frantic that she'd barely acknowledged her beautiful surroundings.

For the first time, she really felt the beach sand beneath her toes. Felt the kiss of the ocean breeze.

She deserved a break, even if she didn't have time for a holiday.

And really, what was the harm of letting her guard down with a gorgeous, charming stranger, just for a few minutes?

Then she'd go check her email, and then back to the wedding.

Simple.

CHAPTER TWO

VERY CALMLY, IVY snapped the clear lid over the end of the test, and took a long, deep soothing breath.

She was sitting on the closed lid of a toilet. A very nice toilet in a very expensive Perth skyscraper, but a toilet, none the less. A public toilet.

This had been a very stupid idea.

Buying the test itself had seemed the rational thing to do this morning. Her driver, Simon, hadn't suspected a thing when she'd asked him to stop at a pharmacy on the way to her ten a.m. meeting. And even if he had wondered why Ivy Molyneux was bothering to run into a pharmacy for whatever lady thing he thought she needed—rather than asking one of her assistants—it wasn't as if he'd ask her.

Yet she'd still fidgeted in the back seat of the car as they'd driven away, as if Simon had X-ray vision and could see through the layers of her handbag and pharmacy paper bag should he glance in his rear-view mirror.

The plan had been to wait until she was home this evening. Safely alone in the privacy of her home in Peppermint Grove, where she could pee on a stick and irrationally stress and worry *alone* for the two minutes she was supposed to wait because—come on, it was *totally normal* to be two days late, even if that had never, ever, ever happened before...

Of *course* someone else had just walked into the bathroom, and now she had to wait in this excruciating state as she listened to the other woman pee—because it now seemed beyond her to look down, to look down at the test that by now would display the result.

The reality.

All she had to do was look down and this would all be over.

This *thing*, this *day*, this *moment* that she had not expected at all. *That* night seemed a lifetime ago. April was already back from her honeymoon. Ivy's work days had been as endless as ever and her weekends had been so blurred into her weeks that she'd barely noticed them. Life had gone on. She'd gone on, just as normal. That night— that *totally out of character* night—was long behind her. She hadn't given it, or Angus, another thought.

Well, barely. Maybe, just maybe, when she'd been in that space between wake and sleep when her brain finally emptied of all things Molyneux Mining, *maybe* she'd let herself remember. Remember the way her skin had shivered when Angus had looked at her. The way her heart had zipped to a million beats a minute when he'd finally touched her. How she'd felt in his arms. How *he'd* felt beneath her fingertips.

How it had *all* felt. To do that. To do something so crazy, so uninhibited, so...

Reckless.

The toilet flushed beside her, then footsteps, and then the cubicle door closed. The basin had some silly sensor arrangement to turn on, and Ivy had to wait as the other woman tried to work it out, and then listen to her jump and giggle when the water finally gushed out.

Just go. Just go, just go, just go.

But also just stay. Stay, stay, stay for ever, so she never had to look down, never had to know.

But then she wasn't into delaying things, was she? That was why she was here, in this public toilet, holding the test.

Because she couldn't wait. Couldn't even wait until her

ten a.m. meeting was over. She'd excused herself mid meeting, and now she'd taken way, way too long.

The bathroom door clicked shut, and Ivy was finally alone amongst all this marble and the softest of background music.

And now she had to look down.

And now she couldn't lie to herself that she was just being silly, and that there was *nothing* to worry about, and that she was on the pill and even if she couldn't be sure she hadn't forgotten a pill amongst all the time zones and delays on the way to April's wedding that surely the odds were *still* in her favour. Because people tried to do this for *years* and it didn't work. People who were trying, people who wanted this, people...

Two pink lines.

She'd looked down only to confirm what she already knew. What she'd known deep down for the past two-hundred-odd minutes since the absence of her period had suddenly dawned on her.

She was pregnant.

She was pregnant.

Ivy took a deep, audible breath, and willed the tears in her eyes to go still. Then she stuffed the test back into its box, back into its pharmacy paper bag and back into her handbag.

Then she went back to the meeting with her business face on and no one—she hoped liked hell—was the wiser.

No, only one person knew that Ivy Molyneux's life had just completely fallen apart.

And unfortunately, that number would soon have to increase to two.

Angus's feet pounded on the heavy rubber of the treadmill, his breaths coming slow and regular.

Sweat had long ago soaked his grey T-shirt black, and

the muscles of his calves and thighs had given up protesting and now simply burned.

This was the bit he loved. This time after he'd conquered the arguments from both his brain and body and simply *kept on going.*

He'd been like this since his late teens, since the sudden death of his father. He'd gone for his first run immediately after his mum had told him the terrible news—an impossibly long run fuelled by intense, raging grief. And that run had triggered a near addiction that had him craving the adrenalin rush of exercise, craving the burn, and craving the pain.

He had no issue admitting that one of the reasons he'd joined the army was so he could be paid to reach this high. On some days he couldn't believe his luck that he earned his living effectively living out many a childhood fantasy—the helicopters, the firearms, the boats, the tactical training...

Angus shook his head as he ran, shifting his focus back to his body.

Running on a treadmill was not his preference. Here in the gym at the barracks, he'd much rather be lifting weights, or, even better, completing a punishing PT session with the rest of his squadron.

But when it came down to it, the method was irrelevant. Winning the battle over his body was what mattered. Especially now, especially while injured.

Technically he was on medical leave, but clearly losing physical condition wasn't an option in his job. He'd been down at the barracks daily, excluding that weekend in Bali. Even there he'd made locating the hotel gym a priority.

Except the morning after the wedding. That morning he'd slept in.

Despite the sweat and the screaming of his muscles, Angus grinned.

Ivy must have worn him out.

He reached out to slow the speed on the treadmill, reducing his pace from near sprint down to a brisk walk as he cooled down.

It wasn't the first time the beautiful billionaire had popped into his head. It surprised him. There had been no question as to what that night had been. Neither he nor Ivy wanted anything beyond those few…admittedly incredible…hours on that beach.

Angus smiled again as he remembered the way Ivy had taken charge as they'd walked back to the hotel.

If anyone asks—I was in my suite, working.

He'd grinned then, too. *And how would I know that?*

She'd just glared at him, and protested silently when he insisted on walking her to her room. He had, of course, checked that no one would see them.

He wasn't a total jerk, after all.

Although kissing her on her doorstep had not been gentlemanly—or planned.

He'd seen it in her eyes—and felt it in her body—that she'd been about to invite him in. But she hadn't.

And he would've declined, anyway. He was sure.

It was for the best.

In his experience, keeping things simple was always for the best.

Later, after his shower and as he walked across the car park, he felt his phone vibrating in the backpack slung over his shoulder. Automatically he fished it out, then, on seeing it was an unknown number, considered for a moment whether he should bother answering.

Work-related numbers weren't stored on his phone, of course—but then, no one was going to be calling him while he was on leave.

But could it be to do with his mum?

So he answered it, if a bit gruffly, and was certainly not

expecting the contradictory soft but firm—and *familiar*—female voice he heard.

'Is that Angus Barlow?'

'Ivy Molyneux,' he replied, and then smiled when she gave a little sound of surprise.

'Uh—yes,' she said. A pause. 'I asked Evan for your number.'

She was nervous, her words brisker than normal.

'That wasn't very discreet,' he said.

Hell, it didn't bother him. Ivy could've announced the fact they'd had sex on the beach to the whole wedding reception and he wouldn't have cared.

But he knew she did.

Unease prickled at the back of his neck.

'No, it wasn't discreet at all,' Ivy said, her words pancake flat.

Then there was a long, long pause.

'Why did you call me, Ivy?' He *was* gruff now.

She cleared her throat. 'Are you free tonight?' she asked, much more softly.

Relief washed over him. He'd continued walking as they'd been talking, and now he propped a shoulder against the side of his black SUV.

He smiled. He remembered that tone from that night. That soft, intimate—almost *shy*—voice. So different from the brash confidence of Ivy Molyneux, mining executive.

He was jumping at shadows. Ivy Molyneux was a woman who went after what she wanted. This phone call was nothing more. Unexpected, but also—not unwelcome.

'I'm free,' he said. 'How about we meet at Ms Black at eight?'

A wine bar in Subiaco he'd visited with the rest of his squadron after they'd returned from their latest assignment—before they'd quickly relocated to the pub next door. It was sophisticated, intimate, stunning. Very Ivy.

'Fine,' she said. 'I—uh—guess I'll see you there.'

'Ivy—' he said, before she had the chance to hang up. 'I'm still not after anything serious.'

He felt it was important he was honest.

But judging by her almost shriek of laughter before she ended the call, he had nothing to worry about on that front, regardless.

How had she let this happen?

For what felt like the hundredth time, Ivy had to stop herself fidgeting. So far she'd swivelled her bar stool, kicked her heels against the foot rest and attempted to tear a coaster into a million pieces.

She'd counted every step she'd made tonight. From her house to her car, and then from where her driver dropped her right outside this incredibly trendy bar to this seat. It was *ridiculous.*

In front of her sat an untouched glass of champagne.

She didn't even know why she'd ordered it. Out of habit? Or denial?

Ha!

As if it weren't the only thought reverberating about her head.

I'm pregnant. I'm pregnant. I'm pregnant.

How had she let this happen?

This being pregnant. *This* being dressed in a cute cocktail dress on a Thursday night to tell a man *she didn't even know* something that would change his life for ever.

The dress was new. She'd dragged one of her assistants out shopping. Ivy had made sure she'd smiled a lot and dropped hints about her 'date' tonight while still being deliberately coy.

That was all that had kept her going as the seconds and minutes had crawled along—focusing on her...*plan.*

In all honesty, it was far from her best plan. In fact, it was most likely her worst.

But she needed a plan right now. She needed a way forward, a way to fix this.

Because Ivy Molyneux didn't make mistakes.

'Ivy.'

At the sound of Angus's already familiar deep voice, Ivy channelled Julia Roberts in *Pretty Woman* as she slowly pivoted her chair to face him. What she really wanted to do was disappear between the floorboards. So, so badly.

But then she saw him.

In Bali, in his casual wedding attire, he'd been undeniably handsome. Heck, he'd be undeniably handsome *anywhere*.

But in the intimate lighting of the bar, in dark jeans, boots and a slim fitting black shirt he was…just plain gorgeous. His clothes weren't particularly formal, but he somehow managed to still look effortlessly dressed to impress. He looked darker, taller, *broader* than she remembered.

Especially now that he was standing so close to her. Close enough to touch.

And then he did touch her. Casually leaning forward to brush a kiss against her cheek and to bring his lips to her ear.

'You are stunning,' he said. His breath momentarily tickled her neck.

Ivy shivered.

He stepped back, his appreciative gaze sweeping over her.

She loved the dress she'd bought today. Teal silk with a feminine wrap bodice and a fitted skirt that hit mid-thigh, it flattered her curves and on any other day would've made her feel on top of the world.

That it didn't helped bring her back to reality.

This wasn't a date.

This *so* wasn't a date.

Ivy slid off her chair, waving away the arm he offered her. Without a word she headed to the back of the bar. It was busy, with all but the three tables along the far wall occupied.

Each was marked with a small reserved sign, and it was towards the middle table that Ivy gestured.

'I booked a table,' she said.

She'd booked three, actually, and paid for a night's worth of meals on all. It was still hardly private, but it would have to do.

'Dinner?' Angus asked.

Despite everything, Ivy managed a smile. Clearly dinner and conversation were not what Angus had planned for the night.

He was close beside her, and she could practically feel his growing tension.

Well, that situation wasn't about to improve for him.

She took her seat, and Angus took his. He must have plucked her champagne from the bar, as he placed it before her, his wrist still bandaged as it had been in Bali.

That was nice of him.

Would he be a good dad?

She gave a little shake of her head. No. This wasn't fair, that she knew and he didn't. That he thought he was here for meaningless flirtation followed by meaningless sex, when he so, so wasn't.

'Ivy, what's going on?'

She'd been staring, unseeing, down at her fingers, which she'd been wrapping and unwrapping around the stem of her champagne glass.

She took a breath. The deepest breath she could remember taking.

Then she lifted her gaze, and met his.

Even in the moody bar lighting, she now finally had enough light to see the colour of his eyes. Hazel.

They were lovely eyes, sexy eyes, but right now they were hard and unyielding.

Yes, he'd worked out that this night wasn't going to pan out the way he'd planned.

'Angus—I'm pregnant.'

CHAPTER THREE

PREGNANT?

All the stupid, obvious questions were on the tip of his tongue.

Are you sure?

How…?

Is it mine?

But he knew all the answers:

Of course she was. That she wanted to be anywhere but here was clear in everything about her. She was one hundred per cent sure or she wouldn't be putting either of them through this.

The how hardly needed explaining. He'd been there, too.

And was it his?

Well, that was only a faint hope that this was all a terrible mistake, rather than a genuine question.

And he was grateful that a small smidgen of his brain told him to swallow the words before they leapt from his mouth.

Because of course it was his. He had known what he'd been doing in Bali—known he'd pushed her out of her comfort zone, known he'd pursued the electric attraction between them to what he'd felt was the only logical conclusion…

But that she didn't normally have random sex with a practical stranger on a beach had been abundantly clear.

So yes, it was his.

With the basics covered, he dropped his head, gripping his skull with his hands.

He swore harshly.

That was about the sum of it.

'Angus?'

He kept his head down, but he nodded.

'I know this is a shock. I know this is the wrong place to tell you. When I called I hadn't planned this...but...'

It didn't matter. Who cared where she told him?

His thoughts leapt all over the place, as if his brain was incapable of being still, or of grasping onto anything at all.

He'd never felt like this.

He'd been in combat many more times than once.

He'd been in the most stressful situations that most people could imagine. Real stress. Real life-and-death stress, not running-late-for-work stress.

And yet *this* had thrown him. This had sent his ability to think, and apparently to talk, skittering off the rails.

'Um, the thing is, Angus, I have a plan.'

His gaze shot up, linking with hers in almost desperation. 'A plan?'

Ivy nodded slowly. And then she seemed to realise what he was thinking.

She looked down, studying her untouched champagne glass again.

'No,' she said, so softly he had to lean closer. 'Not that.' Her gaze darted back to his, and she looked at him steadfastly now. With that directness, that *realness* he'd liked so much in Bali. 'I'm thirty-one, and I have money and every resource I could wish for at my disposal. In every possible way this is the *last* thing I want. But a termination isn't an option for me.'

She barely blinked as she studied him. Long, long moments passed.

Angus cleared his throat. 'I'm thirty-four with a career I love that takes me away from home for months at a time and could one day kill me. I don't want this. I don't want children.' Ivy's gaze wobbled a little now as Angus swallowed. 'But for no reason I can fathom, I'm glad you've made that decision.'

Now he glanced away. He didn't know why he'd said that, or why he felt that way. The logical part of him—which was basically *all* of him—didn't understand it.

It made no sense. But it was the truth. His truth.

When he looked back at Ivy she was again studying her champagne glass.

'Well, it's good we're on the same page, then,' she said, her tone now brisk and verging on businesslike. 'So, here's my *actual* plan.' By the time she met his gaze again, she was all business. Ivy Molyneux of Molyneux Mining—not Ivy the girl from the beach. 'I'll get straight to the crux of it: I'd like us to get married.'

Straight after the pregnancy news, Angus would've thought it would take a hell of a lot to shock him.

That did it.

'What?'

She held up a hand. 'Just hear me out,' she said. 'What I'm proposing is a business arrangement.' A pause, and then a half-smile. 'And, yes, marriage.'

Ivy might find this funny, but Angus sure as hell didn't.

He remained stonily silent.

'The term of the agreement would be twelve months from today,' Ivy continued, clearly warming to her topic. 'As soon as possible we would reveal our—until now—several months' long secret relationship to family and friends, and, shortly after, our engagement. Then, of course, our—' now she stumbled a little '—our, um, *situation* would mean that we'd bring our wedding forward. I thought that we could make that work in our favour. A Christmas Eve wedding would be perfect, I felt.'

A Christmas Eve wedding would be perfect?

Angus's brain was still requiring most of its synapses

to deal with his impending parenthood. But what little remained was functioning well enough to realise that this was *completely and utterly nuts.*

'Is this a pregnancy hormone thing?' he asked, quite seriously. 'Can they send you loopy?'

Ivy's gaze hardened. 'I can assure you I am *not* crazy.'

More than anything, Angus wished he'd had time to order a drink. For want of another option, he gestured at Ivy's champagne. It wasn't as if she could have it, after all.

She nodded impatiently, and then carried on with her outrageous proposal as he downed half the drink in one gulp.

'After the wedding we'd need to continue the illusion that we're a couple, but given the nature of your work that shouldn't be too hard. My house is huge, so we could live quite separate lives when you are home. Not being seen in public together will help, anyway, for when we separate a few months after the baby is born.'

She blinked when she said *baby*, as if she couldn't quite believe it was true.

'After the separation you're free to do whatever you like, and then, as soon as legally allowable, we'll divorce, and carry on with our lives.'

'Except for the fact that we're parents of a child we had together.'

A reluctant nod. 'Well, yes.'

Angus took a second long swig to finish the champagne he'd barely tasted. He plonked the glass down with little care, and then leant forward, watching Ivy's eyes widen.

'Why?' he asked.

Ivy actually shrugged. 'Does it matter? I can assure you that the remuneration you'll receive for this will be a life-changing amount. Millions of dollars.'

Pocket change to her.

'And a house, too, if you like,' she added, as if an afterthought.

'Before tonight, Ivy, I never wanted children, and I never wanted to get married,' he said. 'Now I'm having a child, but, I can assure you, absolutely nothing has changed on the marriage front. I wouldn't have picked you to be the old-fashioned sort, Ivy, but I'm not. Even with a diamond-encrusted solid-gold carrot.'

Ivy shook her head, as if she couldn't comprehend his rapid refusal. 'I promise you that this will cause you minimal impact, I—'

'It's *marriage*, Ivy. Nothing minimal impact about that.'

She gave a little huff of frustration. 'Don't think of it like that. Think of it as signing a contract, nothing more.'

'Signing a contract of *marriage*, Ivy. And you still haven't told me why.'

Now that he had her glass, Ivy had transferred her fidgeting to her fingers—tangling and twining them together.

Had she really thought he'd agree, just like that? An offer of a crazy amount of money and all sorted? Even if her proposal made no sense on any level?

He studied her. Was she was so detached and separate from reality in her billionaire's turret that she truly believed that money *could* buy her anything? It was his immediate and rather angry conclusion.

He could feel every sinew in his body tense in frustration at the thought of the level of entitlement, of arrogance that would lead to such an assumption...

But now as he looked at Ivy, it didn't fit. He hadn't seen it in her in Bali, and he still didn't recognise it now.

Sure, she was still some distance from *normal*, but he knew it wasn't entitlement, or arrogance, that had triggered her plan.

It was something he could understand. That he could recognise.

It was desperation.

Ivy didn't know what to do now.

Maybe he was right. Maybe pregnancy hormones *had* sent her loopy, because, honestly—had she really thought he'd just agree?

In her experience some people could be bought for the right price. Actually, make that many, many people. But nothing about Angus had indicated to her that he was one of those people. In fact, if she'd spent even a minute properly considering her plan, she would've seen this fatal flaw.

Which of course was the problem. She hadn't spent any time thinking about it, at least not thinking about such pesky details like: *what if he doesn't agree?* Because she'd been clinging to this plan as if it were a rope suspended over the abyss that was her pregnancy, and she just couldn't, could *not*, let it go.

But, the thing was, if this plan had something to do with mineral exploration or extraction, she certainly wouldn't give up this early in the fight.

And that meant that she'd have to—at least partly—answer his question.

'When I turn thirty-two,' she said, looking him in the eye just as she always did during business negotiations, 'my mother will relinquish her position as Chief Executive Officer of Molyneux Mining to me. It's the same age she was when my grandfather died and left her the company, and this has been planned literally from when I was born.' She paused. 'I turn thirty-two in July next year. Based on some useful internet calculators—pending me seeing a doctor—our baby will arrive approximately one week before that date.'

Our baby. A slip of the tongue, but Angus displayed no reaction.

'Although the succession plan was determined before *my* birth, I can assure you that I want this too. I'm very different from my mother in many ways.' A huge understatement. 'But in this way, we are in sync. We both live for Molyneux Mining. This is incredibly important to me.'

It is everything to me, she almost added. But somehow she didn't think that would help.

It was near impossible to read Angus's expression, but he nodded. 'I get that you love your job. I get that you don't want to give that up. What has this got to do with marrying me?'

'About ten years ago just under half of Molyneux Mining was listed on the Australian Stock Exchange. We're still majority family owned, but I report to a board of executives, as well as to our shareholders. We also have a number of significant projects in progress, including a joint venture to mine manganese in the Pilbara, which is reaching final negotiations. It is also widely known that I will take over Molyneux Mining next year, and that we are already in a period of comprehensive change management.'

'So you're worried that a baby will impact your share price?'

Ivy's eyes narrowed. 'No, not the baby. No one had better think that a baby will impact my professional performance.'

Oh, how she *hoped* that was true. She ignored Angus's mildly incredulous raised eyebrows.

'It's all about how the baby came to be here, that's the problem. My whole career has led to my next birthday. Everything I have done, every decision I have made, has been with this succession in the front of my mind. I am known for being meticulous in my planning. For never making a snap decision, for never being reactive in my actions. Even my boyfriends have been chosen with some consideration for my career—I always do background checks. I never take anything or anyone on face value.'

Except she'd never done a background check on Angus. The only thing she'd cared about that night was how good Angus had made her feel.

'So a baby is okay. But hot, crazy sex on a beach with a stranger isn't.'

Ivy recoiled a little, and felt her cheeks grow warm.

Now her gaze dipped to her fingers. With some effort she untangled them, laying her palms flat on the table to force them still.

'I wouldn't have put it quite like that,' she said. 'But yes. Ivy Molyneux would *never* be that reckless.'

There was that word again. Reckless.

This time it triggered a remembered snatch of conversation, the echo of her mother's voice from a time for ever ago: *How could you, Ivy? How could you be so reckless?*

'But you were,' Angus said. 'We both were. I was there.'

His low words snapped Ivy's attention back from a better-forgotten memory. And something flickered in his eyes. Despite all this, despite this situation, despite this conversation, she recognised it.

Heat. Not like in Bali, but still there. Despite everything.

She knew her already warm cheeks were now scarlet, but all she could do was ignore that. And, as she should've at the wedding, ignore this *thing* between them.

Or at least try to.

'I know,' she said, very softly. 'That's what I'm trying to fix.'

The shocking warmth of his hand covering hers drew her attention downwards again, and she realised belatedly she must've been wringing her hands.

She'd trained herself out of all her fidgeting and step counting years ago, but right now this unexpected regression managed barely a blip amongst everything else that whirled inside her.

As in Bali, his touch impacted everything. She knew her heart had accelerated, and her whole body now seemed focused on where their fingers overlapped. Completely inappropriate warmth pooled low in her belly, and for long seconds Ivy wished like anything that this were a very real date.

But then Angus spoke.

'I get what you're trying to do, Ivy,' he said.

Instantly hope began to blossom inside her, delicate and beautiful. But then his fingers tightened gently on hers, and Ivy knew.

'My answer is still no.'

And for the second time today awful, unwelcome tears filled her vision.

Ivy never cried.

But then, Ivy never did a lot of things she'd been doing lately.

She snatched her hands away from beneath his, and for the briefest moment Angus reconsidered his decision.

He'd never be this close again to the fortune she'd offered him. Would he regret it some day? Was living a lie for twelve months really all that bad given such a massive payday?

And a second consideration snuck into his subconscious. *Or maybe he should just do this for Ivy?*

Angus straightened in his chair, subtly putting further distance between them.

No. He wouldn't regret passing on the money. His parents had taught him the value of hard work and, in every aspect of his life, he'd never been one to take shortcuts.

And for Ivy?

No. That was a slippery slope he did not want to get

on. When he was deployed, he never allowed himself to clutter his mind with those he left behind. It was why he would never marry, and it was why he had never meant to have children. It wasn't fair to anyone to be shoved aside in that manner. But it was what he did. It was, quite simply, who he was.

So no, he wasn't going to do this for Ivy.

'I'm sorry, I don't feel like eating,' Ivy said, breaking the silence. She pushed her chair backwards a little quickly, and steadied it with one hand as she stood.

Angus followed her lead and pulled himself to his feet, more than keen to get out of the bar. Around them, other couples and small groups appeared to be enjoying their meals. A man reached out to stroke the cheek of his date. Four well-dressed young women suddenly cackled with laughter and clinked their wine glasses together.

Everyone else's lives appeared to be carrying on beautifully, and normally, and yet Angus's life had just irrevocably changed for ever.

It still didn't seem possible. Didn't seem real.

Ivy was already negotiating all the happy diners, and Angus needed to take several large strides to catch up with her. Automatically, he reached out and rested his hand in the small of her back.

At his touch, she went still, her chin shooting up as she met his gaze.

She'd done a poor job hiding the sheen to her eyes back at the table, and she was far less successful now. Again her gaze was more than wobbly, and he was reminded that he wasn't alone in his shock and disbelief.

He felt he should say something. Something reassuring and supportive.

But he didn't have any experience in this kind of thing. Hell, his ex-girlfriends had made it clear he was a complete failure at even the most simple of relationships—let alone what to say to the woman who had just announced she was carrying his child.

So he said nothing at all, and Ivy's gaze just kept on wobbling.

'Ivy!'

Against his palm, Angus felt Ivy tense.

At the bar, only a few metres away, sat a seriously glamorous blonde. Her hair tumbled in generous waves over one shoulder, and beside her was a significantly less glamorous man.

Ivy appeared struck dumb, and didn't move a millimetre as the pair approached them.

'It's been months!' the blonde exclaimed. 'How are you?'

'I—uh—' Ivy began, and then went silent, simply sending him a panicky glance. Her body was moving now. She was trembling.

Immediately Angus slid his hand from her back to her waist, and tugged her gently against him. Even now, when he shouldn't, he noticed how naturally she fitted against him. And how soft and warm her body felt.

'I'm Angus Barlow,' he said to the couple, offering his free hand.

Then for the next three minutes he scrounged every last ounce of charm he possessed to conduct the most trivial of conversations, while Ivy managed the occasional nod and single-word response. And then he politely excused them, and escorted Ivy outside as quickly as their legs would carry them.

Outside, the night was cool against his skin. His arm was still around Ivy, and in the cold it seemed illogical to remove it, given the flimsiness of her dress.

He was still walking briskly, keen to put as much space between himself and the bar, when Ivy came to an abrupt stop and disentangled herself from him.

'Where are you going?' she said.

Angus paused. His car was parked in the opposite direction.

'I have no idea,' he said.

And amongst all that had happened tonight, those four little words were suddenly hilarious, and he burst into a harsh bark of laughter.

A moment later, Ivy joined in, and they both stood together on the footpath, cackling away just like those women having dinner.

When they both fell silent, Ivy looked up at him again.

No wobbles this time, just direct, real Ivy.

'Thank you,' she said.

CHAPTER FOUR

Ivy listened half-heartedly to her sisters' enthusiastic gossip. They sat across from her, their finished breakfast plates pushed aside. To her left sat Ivy's mother, nursing a mug full of cappuccino.

Around them, Sunday morning at the exclusive beach-side café was a buzz of activity. Ivy found herself picking up random snippets of conversation: the waiter two tables to her right repeating an order; an older man complaining at the lateness of his grandson; and from somewhere behind her a high-pitched: *Really?* followed by raucous laughter.

Their table abutted a wall of bi-fold windows, their louvred glass panes opened to welcome the salty breeze. Beneath them, keen sunbathers lay on brightly coloured towels in an irregular patchwork. It was an unusually warm October day, and Cottesloe Beach was, it seemed, the place to be.

It had worked out perfectly, really. Her family—just Mila, April and her mother—had dinner every second Sunday. But this weekend she'd suggested breakfast instead, so here they were.

The weather would be perfect for it! she'd said.

And everyone agreed.

As lies went, it was very much the whitest of them, but it still sat so uncomfortably. All to avoid refusing a glass of wine.

She was so close to her sisters, as different as they were. Mila, with her chocolate-brown curls and brilliant smile, was the baby, and the family artist. Never much interested in study, she'd barely finished high school before beginning a string of courses at TAFE—jewellery design, dress making, and a few others that Ivy had long forgotten. But then she'd started—and this time finished—a pottery course, and that was it. Mila had found her calling. Now she had her own studio, with a shop front for her work out the front, and space for her to teach out the back. Quiet, but opinionated and wise, Mila could always be counted on to see through the crap in any situation.

Then there was April. Beautiful, clever but flighty, she'd been the real rebel. She'd partied through uni, and still partied now. She'd completed her Environmental Science degree—chosen for its not so subtle dig at the way her family had made their fortune—but, apart from a few internships, hadn't settled into full-time work. April brought sunshine wherever she went—always the first to smile and the first with a kind word.

And there she was. Ivy. The eldest by three years, she'd followed the script exactly as her mother had hoped: a diligent student throughout school. A top student at university, all the way through to her masters. Then straight to work for the family company, working her way up, just as her mother had, with, of course, a healthy dose of expected nepotism.

But Ivy knew she deserved her position at Molyneux Mining. She'd worked her butt off to get there.

So, yes. In contrast to her arty sister, and her partying sister, there she was: studious, perfect daughter Ivy. Mila and April even gave her well-deserved needling for it.

But, of course, it had never been entirely true.

Ivy knew that. Her mother knew that. But no one else did.

Her mother had fixed her mistakes of more than a decade ago.

Unfortunately, Ivy was no closer to fixing her latest mistake.

She just needed time.

She *would* tell them about her pregnancy. Soon.

Just not today.

'Earth to Ivy?' April was grinning at her, fun sparkling in her gaze. 'You still with us?'

Ivy blinked, and forced a smile. 'Sorry. Just thinking about an email I have to write when I get home for the Bullah Bullah Downs project.'

In unison, her sisters groaned.

'I was just saying that I saw Holly at the shops yesterday,' April said, with a grin. 'She had some *very* interesting news.'

Ivy went perfectly still, pasting on a faux smile. She had the fleeting, horrifying thought that somehow she'd forgotten blurting out the news of her pregnancy to Holly as she'd exited the bar on Thursday night.

'*Apparently*,' April continued, 'you were with a rather hot guy?'

So Evan hadn't told April she'd asked for Angus's number. She could barely remember the vague, somehow work-related excuse she'd given her brother in law, but apparently it had been plausible.

'Oh, he was a blind date,' Ivy said, with a dismissive smile. 'He was nice enough, but it was a bit of a disaster, really.' That was true, in a way. 'No spark, you know?'

Definitely a lie.

The conversation moved on, her mum and sisters familiar enough with her occasional forays into dating to accept what she'd said.

But Ivy remained silent, quietly furious with herself.

She couldn't have news of her pregnancy leaked until she was one hundred per cent prepared, and gossipy speculation about her and Angus would not help that cause.

She needed to be more careful.

And more importantly, she really needed to fix this. Soon.

'Gus! How are you, mate?'

Angus finished the last two repetitions of the set, then swivelled on the seat of the leg press to grab his towel. Cam Dunstall wore his own towel hung over his shoulders, but he clearly hadn't begun his workout as he was the only person in the crowded barracks gym not coated in a layer of sweat.

'Good,' Angus said automatically.

Cam's attention darted to his still-bandaged right wrist. 'Going okay?'

Angus smiled at his friend's obvious concern. They both knew if his wrist was busted, so was his SAS career. He wasn't much use if he couldn't use a firearm.

'Nah, it's no big deal,' he said, truthfully. 'I met with the specialist today. He's happy with my progress. He sees no reason why I shouldn't be back on deck within the month.'

Cam's smile was broad and relieved. 'Awesome news, mate. Hey, you missed out on some fun last week—middle of the night hanging out of a Black Hawk chopper. Good times.'

Cam then went into great detail about the training exercise, while Angus mopped his face and arms of sweat. He'd finished today's workout. In fact he'd been here for the couple of hours since his doctor's appointment.

The good news about his wrist was not unexpected. To be honest, his hand felt very near to normal now—if the doctor had let him he'd already be back at work.

So his workout was supposed to be the highlight of his day. It was Monday, four days since Ivy had dropped her bombshell.

On Friday he'd gone for a run instead, needing to be outside.

Then on the weekend he'd stayed at home, deciding that

cutting back two huge branches from the towering blue gum in what was once his mother's back garden was the best use of his time. But even two days wielding a chainsaw hadn't helped.

And today hadn't helped either.

He still didn't feel normal. The exercise high he craved eluded him.

It wasn't fair.

That made him smile. Out of all that had happened, the incredible bad luck that had plonked him and Ivy in this situation—*that* was what was unfair?

'Mate?' Cam was looking at him strangely. 'I was just asking if you'd heard that Patrick has been moved. To *training*.'

Ah. A smile was certainly not appropriate here. That was no promotion.

'He's still not right, then?' Angus asked, knowing that was probably the wrong way to phrase his question, but at a loss to come up with something better.

'Yeah. That post-traumatic crap. Like Tom, I guess.'

Like Tom.

Guilt lowered Angus's gaze momentarily. How long since he'd called him? They'd come through SAS selection together seven years ago. Tom—strong, confident, supportive, *brave* Tom. His closest mate. The best soldier he knew.

Or at least, he had been.

'Some of the boys are going out for a beer tonight. Want to come?'

Cam was clearly keen to move the conversation on.

Angus got that.

But he shook his head. No. Ivy had texted him earlier, and he was meeting her for a coffee.

Not that he told Cam that, but the other man jumped to

the approximately right conclusion anyway, giving him crap about choosing a girl over his mates.

So Angus laughed and let the words roll off him, wishing like hell they were true.

'Thanks for meeting me.'

Angus raised an eyebrow as he slid into the fifties-style café booth. 'This isn't a business meeting, Ivy.'

She shook her head. 'No, of course not.'

It was just easier for her to think of it like that. She'd even prepared for this *meeting*, in a way. Mentally determining an agenda of items to cover, so that this could be over as efficiently as possible.

She was sure Angus would appreciate that, too.

Quick, efficient and over quickly. A good plan.

'So, I've got a couple of points I'd like to discuss, and I'll start with the most important. Do you intend to be a part of our child's life, and if so, to what extent?'

Angus didn't even blink at her directness. 'I intend to be the best father I can be,' he said. 'Which means I want to be a huge part of their life.'

Ivy nodded sharply. It was the answer she'd expected, although she couldn't exactly say why. She was pleased, though. She'd never been close to her own father. 'Excellent. Okay, so the next point is—'

'Hold it there.' Angus glanced at the coffee she'd downed in the few minutes she'd been waiting for him. 'Now the big question is out of the way, how about I go get us both a coffee, and some cake, and we relax a bit?'

'Relax?'

He grinned. 'Honey, the way I see it we just agreed to another eighteen-odd years to talk about this baby. Why rush things now?'

And with that he stood, and headed for the counter.

Ivy just watched him in somewhat stunned silence as he

made his order, and returned to the table with a number on a chrome stick, which he placed between them.

'I just asked for whatever you had again, plus a selection of cakes as I have no idea what you like. Okay?'

Ivy nodded numbly.

'Great!' he said. 'So, tell me something about yourself.'

'Pardon me?'

He shrugged. 'You heard me.'

Ivy bristled. 'Look, it's great that you're all so fine and relaxed and cool with this, but I don't think you understand how—'

'Ivy,' he said, so firmly that her words froze on her tongue. 'I promise you that I *understand* exactly what is going on here. It's all I've thought about for *four days*. I dreamt about it, even, although I can't say I've spent much time sleeping. I am exhausted, and stressed out of my mind. And frankly, I'm over it. I'm over feeling like that, but I can't do anything about it. Neither can you.'

Ivy's gaze travelled across his face, for the first time noticing the dark circles beneath his eyes and the spidery lines of red in his stare.

He'd just described her weekend, and beneath a thick layer of concealer she even had the matching blackened eyes.

'But we've both decided to do this, so we might as well get to know each other. So again—tell me something about yourself.'

Tell him something?

I'm scared? I don't know what I'm doing? I have *no idea* what to do with you?

'I think that Aussie Rules football is the best game in the whole entire universe.'

And then Angus smiled. A gorgeous smile, an amazing smile.

'So now we have two things in common,' he said.

* * *

A selection of cakes later, Ivy stood with Angus outside the café. It was dark between the street lights, and only the occasional car swished past.

'Where'd you park?' Angus asked.

Ivy shook her head. 'I didn't. I just need to call my driver and he'll come pick me up.'

A sudden gust of wind made her shiver, and Ivy wrapped her arms around herself tightly.

Angus took a step towards her—and for a moment Ivy thought he might put his arm around her again, as he had at the wine bar. But then he didn't, and Ivy took a little longer than she would've liked to decide she was relieved.

Tonight hadn't been as she'd planned. They'd talked about all things unimportant—the favourite football team they shared, the latest movies they'd seen, and even the weather. It *had* been kind of like a date.

Or rather exactly like one. Except it hadn't had that early-date awkwardness. The overenthusiastic laughter or the well-rehearsed anecdotes.

It had been...nice. Better than nice.

'I don't remember—did you ask me to tell you something about myself?'

'No,' Ivy said, smiling. Then added in an obedient sing-song voice: 'So, Angus, tell me something about yourself.'

'I don't leave ladies waiting on the street in the dark. Come on, I'll drive you home.'

Ivy raised her eyebrows. 'What if I live on the other side of the city?'

Angus had already walked a few steps, and looked surprised she hadn't already followed. 'Do you?'

She lived a five-minute drive away. 'No.'

He smiled. 'Well, there you go. But it wouldn't have mattered. I like driving.'

He waited another moment. 'So am I waiting here while you call your driver, or are you letting me drive you home?'

It would take longer to call Simon and wait for him than for Angus to drive her home, and she could think of no good reason to refuse. So she found herself walking beside Angus the short distance to his car, parked around the corner.

It was exactly the type of car she'd expect him to drive: big and black and foreboding. Although its vast size didn't assist with the unexpected sensation of intimacy when the doors were shut and they both sank into the lush leather seats.

Angus didn't switch the radio on, and they sat in silence after she gave him the brief directions to her house.

Now it did feel like a first date. As if they'd just been out for a romantic dinner and Angus were driving her home and they were both wondering if there'd be a kiss on her doorstep.

How sweet. How quaint. How *backwards* given how she and Angus had met.

Ivy dug her nails into her palms, needing to force herself to face reality.

She couldn't let her thoughts wander like this. She needed to focus, to remember what this *really* was.

'I have an estimated due date,' she said, the words sounding brittle in the silence. 'July the second.'

Instantly the atmosphere in the car shifted.

There. Romantic notions *gone.*

'Okay,' Angus said. And Ivy supposed he couldn't say much else.

'That was what we were supposed to talk about today,' she said. 'That's why I wanted to meet. To tell you that I had a scan today, and the baby has measured at five weeks and one day and that it's due on July the second.'

Her words were more jumbled than brittle, now.

'Thank you,' Angus said, and Ivy couldn't interpret his tone at all.

He slowed the car to turn into her driveway. The entrance was gated, but Ivy reached into her handbag for the small remote that swung the gates open.

Angus nosed the car up the long curved driveway and came to a stop before the limestone steps that led to the front door of her rambling nineteen-thirties double-storey home.

An automatic porch light flicked on, but otherwise the house was in darkness.

'No butler to meet you?' Angus asked, although his tone was not pointed, but curious.

Ivy laughed. 'Do you think I have someone feed me grapes as I bathe, too?'

He shrugged. 'You have a driver, so I assumed you had other staff.'

'No,' Ivy said. 'I mean, because of the hours I work I have a weekly cleaner and a regular gardener, but that's it. My home is my sanctuary, and I value my privacy.'

It already felt a little too private in the car, so Ivy opened her door and slid her feet out onto the driveway. She turned to thank Angus for the lift, but he'd climbed out of his seat too, and in a few strides stood beside her at the bottom of the steps.

Ivy didn't know what to do now. Why had he done that? Why hadn't he driven off and escaped while he could?

'So I'm confused. If you value your privacy, why have your driver ferry you to meet me, twice? Where did you tell him you were going?'

'Simon would never intrude on my personal life,' Ivy said.

Although it had taken considerable subterfuge to attend her dating scan today without Simon knowing. In the end, she'd had him drop her off some distance away, and she'd walked to her appointment.

He never would've commented if she'd asked him to drop her off right outside the ultrasound clinic. But really? April and Mila didn't even know yet. She couldn't have her driver find out first, no matter how discreet he might be.

'But regardless,' Angus said, 'wouldn't it just be easier to drive five minutes from your house to meet me?'

He appeared genuinely flummoxed, and Ivy couldn't help but smile. 'Easier, yes—if I had a licence.'

At this he went from flummoxed to stunned. 'How is that possible?'

'I never learnt,' Ivy said. 'Long story.'

And it was. Long and best forgotten.

Ivy turned slightly towards her house. 'So, thanks for the lift, Angus.'

She spoke a little softer than she'd planned, and his name sounded unexpectedly intimate on her lips.

'My pleasure, Ivy,' he said, but totally normally, as if he were talking to the waitress back at the café.

Ivy gave her head a little shake. She was being very, very silly with all these thoughts of dates and doorsteps and softly spoken names.

He'd already started to walk back to the driver's side of the car, so Ivy quickly raced up the steps, the heels of her boots clicking against the stone, and her hand already in her bag, searching for her keys.

But then she heard heavier footsteps on the steps behind her.

'Ivy, wait.'

So she did, key in hand. 'Yes?'

Angus took the steps two at a time and soon stood before her. The porch light's glow was soft, but the angles of his face seemed sharper in the mix of light and shadows.

'Were you okay today?' he asked. 'At the scan?'

Ivy blinked, and her throat felt suddenly tight.

'Uh, yes,' she said. 'Of course. It was fine. I was fine.'

She'd been beyond nervous. Scared and clueless, but still okay. More okay than she'd expected, actually.

'Good,' he said, with a sharp nod. And with that, he was off back down the steps.

Ivy put her key in the lock, but then found herself turning back to face him. He wasn't in his seat yet; instead he stood inside his opened door, as if he'd been watching her.

'I saw him,' she said. 'Or her. Just a spot at the moment. Or a blob. A cute blob, though.'

Angus nodded, and his lips quirked upwards.

'Goodnight, Ivy.'

'Goodnight, Angus.'

And then he climbed into his car and drove away.

CHAPTER FIVE

IVY HAD JUST broken into the secret stash of dry crackers in her desk's bottom drawer, when her phone rang.

Angus.

When he'd driven away from her place last week, they'd had no further plans to meet. So she'd decided she'd just call him occasionally with details of the baby's progress; after all, it was wise to keep her distance until she'd worked things out.

Yes, she knew at some point she'd need to organise some formal access arrangement or similar. But again, that could take place between their lawyers.

So there was definitely no real need to see him again.

Which was a relief, unquestionably.

Then why was her stomach doing all sorts of odd things?

'Hello?' she said, finally picking up the phone.

'You hungry?'

'Starving,' she said, honestly. 'I'm always starving now.'

Ah. That was what the stomach thing was. She clearly hadn't eaten enough crackers.

'Great. Meet me downstairs in five minutes. I know a great burger place we can go to.'

She had a meeting in twenty minutes, so she couldn't, even if meeting Angus in public again wasn't a terrible idea, anyway.

'Sure,' she said, instead.

Then Angus ended the call, and Ivy called her assistant into her office to rearrange her meeting. Ivy chose to ignore

Sarah's incredulous expression—people shifted meetings for frivolous reasons all the time.

Just not Ivy.

Even so, just over five minutes later her heels were click-ing across the terrazzo floor of the Molyneux Tower's foyer. Angus stood against one of the mammoth round pillars that dotted the vast space, and also stopped the thirty-three-floor building from collapsing into St Georges Terrace.

Around him men and women in suits and smart coats flowed past, hurrying to lunch, or coffee or meetings. In contrast, nothing about Angus was hurried.

He'd propped his shoulder against the pillar, his arms crossed loosely before him. He wore jeans that might have once been black, but now were faded to a steel grey. His navy T-shirt fitted snugly, highlighting his width and the muscular strength of his arms, while one booted foot was crossed casually over the other. Every line of his body looked one hundred per cent comfortable. As if, despite the marked difference in his attire from every other per-son in the building, he fitted here perfectly.

But he didn't.

Here, in contrast to the gloss and shine that was Moly-neux Mining, Angus looked *raw*. Strong, and hard and... virile.

Here, he was juxtaposed against Ivy's real life—her re-ality. It should have been a shock, and it certainly should've bothered her.

It definitely would've if she'd allowed herself to think about it. Or if, in fact, she'd been able to think at all.

But she couldn't. As soon as she'd heard his voice she'd apparently lost all common sense. And the instant she'd stepped out of the lift she'd known he was watching her.

Just like in Bali the weight of his attention was remark-able. Remarkable enough that she wobbled a little on her heels when her gaze met his.

He studied her as she walked towards him. She sensed, rather than saw, his gaze travel along her body, taking in her heels, her charcoal pencil skirt, and the pale pink of her silk blouse. She wore a short, three-quarter-sleeved cream wool coat, but it wasn't because of the cold that she shivered when she came to a stop.

That would be because he'd smiled.

'I have a meeting in forty-five minutes,' she said, instead of smiling back.

Her voice was more prickly than the professional she'd hoped for. An attempt to regain control, maybe.

When had she ever been in control around Angus?

He shook his head, his smile now even broader. 'Ivy, Ivy, Ivy...'

She didn't know what that meant, and her eyes narrowed.

But he didn't give her a chance to speak, instead reaching out to wrap his large hand around hers.

'Come on,' he said. 'We'd better hurry up, then.'

Angus considered letting go of Ivy's hand once they'd stepped outside onto the gusty, skyscraper-lined street.

But then he just didn't. What was the harm, really, of holding a gorgeous woman's hand for a minute?

None he could think of. At least none that bested the satisfaction he was getting from Ivy's rather stupefied, and also rather un-Ivy-like acquiescence.

As much as he liked driven, determined, controlled Ivy, there was something to be said about how she reacted to him. He hadn't forgotten a moment about what had happened between them in Bali, and certainly not the way she had responded to him. It was as if *all* her nerve endings had become focused on where he'd touched her. As if how she felt, and how he made her feel, were all that had mattered.

It had given him a sense of control—but not. Because there was no doubt that everything Ivy had done was what she'd wanted to do—it was just that instead of focusing on work or responsibilities, she'd been focusing on what felt good. What felt *really* good.

So it had felt natural to grab her hand today. To stop her beginning another unnecessarily professional and awkward conversation between them. Because he'd known his touch would shut her up.

What he'd forgotten was the impact of her touch on *him*.

Which was why he'd considered dropping her hand as they'd stepped outside.

Considered, then dismissed.

Because touching Ivy felt pretty damn good.

And triggered some pretty damn *amazing* memories. Of naked skin that glowed in the moonlight. Of the glide of her body against his. The sound she'd made when he'd finally slid inside her...

They were at the burger bar.

Angus dropped her hand, and Ivy put space between them, not meeting his gaze.

'There's a table free at the back,' he said, spotting it amongst the lunch-time rush.

With barely a nod, Ivy walked over while Angus grabbed a couple of menus.

Soon after they'd ordered, and Ivy sat with her water glass cupped in both hands, waiting.

She might just as well have spoken: *Get to the point, Angus.*

It was tempting to do the opposite, as he had in that café. To force her to slow down. To just talk without purpose for a minute or as long as they liked.

But his body was still heated from the simple touch of her hand and those not so simple memories.

And seeing Ivy today was about the future, not the past.

'Have you told anyone?' he asked.

'No,' she said, studying him almost cautiously. 'Why?'

'Because I'd like to tell someone.'

Her eyes widened. *'Why?'* And then, *'Who?'*

She looked so shocked he had to smile. 'My mother, and for the usual reason I tell her things—I'd like her to know.'

'Oh,' she said. 'I suppose I hadn't thought you'd want to tell anyone now. It's still so early.'

Yes. His late-night Googling had taught him a lot more than he'd ever thought he'd need to know about pregnancy.

Ivy's gaze had dropped to the table. She'd abandoned her water to fiddle with a napkin, weaving the paper between her fingers. 'Can you wait?' she said. 'I…' a long, long pause '…I need more time.'

Angus almost told her why it didn't really matter when he told his mother. He could've told her yesterday and it was almost impossible she'd remember today. Most weeks, he was lucky if she remembered his name, let alone that he was her son.

But then Ivy would wonder why he'd asked her permission at all.

Angus wasn't entirely sure himself, beyond a sense that it was the right thing to do.

Ivy had raised her gaze again, and she met his, waiting impatiently for his response.

'Okay,' he said, with some reluctance.

When he visited his mother—at least a couple of times a week whenever he was home—he talked. Talked more than he'd talked all week, about anything and everything.

Because that was how he remembered his mother: talking. Once she could've talked the ear off anything and anyone, revelling in her ability to draw remarkable stories out of the most random of people: the girl at the checkout, the elderly man at the park, the parking officer issuing her a ticket…

So silence in her presence made Angus excruciatingly uncomfortable. And while, like his father, he was *not* one

to ever talk for the sake of it, when he visited his mother,
he did.

And he told her everything. Partly because he did actually want to tell her, but mainly because he desperately
needed to fill the space around them both with words.

He'd visited her yesterday, and omitting Ivy and the baby
from his monologue had felt like a lie of omission.

Stupid, really, given she'd never know. Really stupid.

Lunch arrived, and for a few minutes they both ate in as
much silence as was possible when eating burgers stacked
high with gourmet ingredients.

Ivy had been visibly relieved when he'd agreed with her,
but the atmosphere between them had changed.

'I thought that after the twelve-week scan would be a
good time for us to formalise arrangements,' she said suddenly, a tomato-sauce-tipped chip in her hand. 'Then we
can both be free to share the news appropriately.'

Formalise? Appropriately?

Angus gritted his teeth. *Really? This again?*

'Haven't we got beyond this, Ivy? This isn't a business
deal. This is our child.'

Ivy put the chip back down on her plate, untouched.

'Of course,' she said. 'But I find it's easier if everything's
in writing. Then we won't have any more misunderstand-
ings like today.'

'I wouldn't call today a misunderstanding,' Angus said.
'I'd call it a conversation.'

Ivy raised an eyebrow. 'Hmm.'

She pushed her plate away, although it still held half
her lunch.

'I thought you were starving?' he asked.

'I was wrong,' she said. 'I need to get back to that meeting.'

Angus checked his watch. 'You still have fifteen minutes.'

She hooked her handbag over her shoulder, the motions rushed and tense.

'I have to make a phone call I forgot about.' A pause while her gaze flicked out towards the busy street. 'Sorry.'

She was clearly running away, and Angus was not about to chase after her. She reached into her handbag, but Angus stopped the movement with a pointed look.

'I'll cover it,' he said.

Ivy nodded, another agitated movement.

Then she was gone, walking as fast as she could in those towering heels.

And Angus sank back in his chair, leisurely enjoyed the rest of his lunch and wondered what on earth to do with Ivy.

It's better this way.

Ivy nodded sharply to herself as she sat alone in the VIP Lounge at the Perth Airport charter terminal.

It is.

Simple. Uncomplicated. Straightforward.

Sensible.

Why she hadn't thought of it in the first place was beyond her.

Her lawyer had couriered the contract to Angus this morning. Its intent was simple: from now on, all communications between them would be via their lawyers, and they both agreed to keep the pregnancy secret until mutually agreed to in writing. Plus, of course, Angus would receive a generous lump sum on signing.

Now she really didn't need to see Angus again.

Which was *such* a relief.

And necessary.

Because what had she been thinking when he'd called a few days ago? In the same breath that she'd acknowledged to herself that meeting with him so publicly was a terrible idea, she'd cancelled a meeting to do just that.

And of *course* Angus had been noticed in the Moly-neux Tower foyer, but she'd been too swept up in...in whatever stupid hormonal thing that Angus did to her that she hadn't cared.

By the time she'd returned from lunch the office had been full of gossipy murmurs. No one was silly enough to ask her about Angus directly, of course—not that that made any difference.

Why had she let him hold her hand?

And how did she fail to consider that Angus may want to tell people?

Her behaviour when it came to Angus Barlow made no sense, and more importantly—it was dangerous. She needed to protect herself, and her child. Hadn't she learnt all those years ago how foolish it was to allow how she felt to guide her decisions?

Back then, she'd lost herself amongst her silly, fanciful ideas about love, and she'd vowed never to let that happen again.

Now she dated appropriate men. Men who were a good match for her life and her career.

Certainly not men who made her skin tingle and her heart race.

If, after the tragic events of all those years ago, she needed a reminder that her decision was for the best—well, this was it.

From the moment Angus had watched her walk down that aisle, she'd got just about everything wrong.

Today, that fat contract with Angus had put things right.

Angus might not like it, but it was for the best.

Ivy stood up, walking over to the small coffee station in the corner of the room. Two walls of the lounge were almost entirely windows, offering her a floor-to-ceiling view of the runways. She was at the northern end of the airport, but the main public domestic and international terminals were close by, so large passenger jets dotted the landscape—both on the tarmac and in the cerulean sky.

The Molyneux Mining jet sat patiently in front of her, and Ivy expected one of the flight attendants would come and collect her shortly.

This trip to Bullah Bullah Downs was just what she needed. It had meant a bit of schedule reshuffling, but it would be worth it. Maybe there, amongst the million-odd acres of space the station stretched across, she'd feel more like herself again.

Her stomach growled, and Ivy glanced downwards, surprised to see her hand resting on her still-flat stomach.

'Ivy.'

Ivy spun around, recognising that deep voice instantly.

'What are you doing here?'

She'd tried to keep her voice calm, but failed miserably, her words all high pitched.

Angus stood in front of the closed door to the lounge, a backpack slung over his shoulder. He wasn't leaning against anything this time, but he still managed that lackadaisical *thing* he did, every inch of his lean frame all easy and relaxed.

Except for his jaw. That had a harder line than usual.

And his eyes.

His eyes… Ivy didn't know how to describe them, she just knew that as he walked—casually—towards her, they were all that she could look at.

Today they didn't have that sexy sparkle of green amongst the hazel…they were just…*flat*.

Even when she'd told him she was pregnant, he hadn't looked like this.

'So, where are we off to, today, Ivy?'

'Pardon me?'

Angus folded himself into the chair Ivy had been sitting in earlier, casually leaning backwards and crossing his feet at the ankles.

'You heard me,' he said. 'I made an educated guess of our destination, so I suspect I've packed appropriately regardless. But still. I'm just plain curious.'

'Packed?'

He nodded, raising his eyebrows. 'Now, this is one thing I haven't read about in early pregnancy: hearing loss. Interesting.'

Ivy's gaze narrowed, her brain rapidly recovering from the shock of Angus's sudden appearance.

'You're not coming with me,' she said.

While she might have worked that out, she had no clue why on earth he would want to. *What was going on?*

'Of course I am,' he said. 'Your very helpful assistant advised that you would be unavailable for the next three days, which is unacceptable to me. So here I am.'

'Nothing I do needs to be acceptable, or otherwise, to you,' Ivy said, with some venom.

He nodded again, the action utterly infuriating. 'Oh, yes, it does, Ivy. I think that's the bit you forgot when you spoke to your lawyer. Your disregard for our agreement *not to tell anybody* is remarkable.'

Ivy crossed her arms in front of herself. 'I had to tell my lawyer.'

'No,' Angus said, softer now. 'You didn't.'

Ivy bit her lip. He was right, and she wasn't sure the fact that she really hadn't wanted to would make Angus any happier.

'I've realised that it would be better to formalise things sooner rather than later. Neither of us meant this to happen, and although I appreciate how nice you've been so far—' Angus raised an eyebrow when she said *nice* '—there really is no need for it. I can keep you updated on the baby's progress via my lawyer, and we can organise an access arrangement for after the baby's birth.'

'Yes,' Angus said. 'I noticed that part in the contract—organised between our lawyers, of course.'

Ivy nodded. 'Yes. That way we have everything in writing. Nice and clear.'

'And you don't have to see me.'

Angus stood up, and in three large strides was right in front of her. Close enough that it took everything in Ivy not to take a step backwards.

'We don't have to see *each other*,' Ivy clarified. She held Angus's gaze as he looked at her, but it was hard. It was as if he was attempting to look beyond her eyes—to work out what she was thinking.

Unfortunately with Angus so close, what she was thinking was nothing particularly coherent at all. Which was, of course, the problem. She just couldn't allow this—this pointless, hormone-triggered *reaction* to him.

'But what if I like seeing you, Ivy?' he said. Deliberately he swept his gaze along her body, from her hair to her toes, and slowly back up again. She was dressed for the flight in skinny jeans and a fine wool long-line jumper. Hardly her most glamorous outfit, and yet she still felt the appreciation in his gaze. Felt that *weight*.

'I—' Ivy began, but really had no idea what she was trying to say.

'Ms Molyneux?'

The voice came from the doorway. A male flight attendant in his perfectly ironed uniform waited patiently, his expression curious.

'We'll just be a minute,' said Angus, and Ivy glared at him.

'We?' the attendant asked. 'Ms Molyneux, should we have the paperwork for your guest?'

Ivy shook her head, but said nothing.

Angus leaned close, so only Ivy could hear him. 'I am going to be a part of this child's life, Ivy, and that means being a part of yours—and *not* through a lawyer. This is the second time this week you've run away from me, Ivy, and I don't like it.'

'I don't run away from things,' Ivy said, low but firm.

'Don't you?' he said, taking a step back. 'What would you call this?'

'*Work,*' she said. 'Besides, how would I explain who you are?'

Angus's lips quirked into a smile of triumph.

Ivy closed her eyes and counted to ten. Slowly. More than once.

'Fine,' she said, when she looked at him again. She turned to the still-waiting attendant. 'Louis—please organise the appropriate paperwork with Mr Barlow.'

Then, with a resigned sigh, she went to collect her laptop and handbag from the coffee table as Angus left the room.

Alone again, Ivy looked back out to the runway. Her plane still waited patiently for her, but the sky beyond had turned from a perfect blue to an ominous grey. Appropriate.

Her stomach growled, but the platter of plastic-wrapped cookies at the tea and coffee station suddenly held no appeal. Instead she watched the trajectory of a passenger jet across the gloomy sky as she struggled to get her thoughts back in order and work out what on earth she was going to do next.

But it was a pretty impossible task.

As with everything that had happened with Angus until now, Ivy had absolutely no idea what she was doing.

CHAPTER SIX

Two hours later the plane touched down at Paraburdoo airport.

For the entire flight, Ivy had sat stiffly across from Angus, appearing remarkably uncomfortable despite her luxurious leather seat. She'd spent much of her time busily typing away on her laptop, only occasionally taking a break to stare out of the window.

It was quite a view, too. In Perth, the landscape had been in shades of green, but as they'd travelled north it had transformed into a world of browns and ochres, patterned with deep cuts and ridges—some the ancient gorges of Karijini National Park and others the brutal gash of an iron ore mine.

Unlike Ivy, Angus had enjoyed his time aboard the Cessna. He'd chosen a European beer from the extensive bar, and worked his way through a good portion of the cheese platter placed before them.

The silence hadn't bothered him; he knew—with the pilot and Louis nearby—it had not been the time to talk.

At the airport, the heat buffeted them the moment they exited the jet. Perth in October was quite mild, still a good few months from summer. But here in the Pilbara it never really got cold—at least not during the day—and today the temperature was well into the thirties.

The airport was busy—a hub for all of the iron-ore companies ferrying their fly-in/fly-out workers from the city. Even with only a single runway, it had a decent terminal, today filled with men and women in high-visibility clothing and steel-capped work boots.

Outside, a car waited for them. A hulking white four-wheel drive with a substantial bull bar, an oversized aerial and an air snorkel, it was far from a limousine—and yet there he was, the driver, waiting beside the front wheel for them.

'Do you know how to get where we're going?' Angus asked Ivy as they walked to the car.

'Of course,' she said. 'I've been coming here my whole life.'

'Then tell him he's not needed.'

Ivy stopped dead. 'Pardon me?'

'There it is again, that early pregnancy hearing loss.'

Ivy's lush lips formed into a very thin line.

Angus sighed. 'We don't need a driver. I can drive.'

Her mouth opened and closed a few times, as if she was searching for the perfect argument.

'If he drives, I'll talk about the baby all the way there.'

Ivy's eyes widened. 'That's blackmail.'

Angus shrugged. But then, Ivy had stopped playing nice when she'd had that contract couriered to him.

He wasn't surprised when Ivy walked ahead to speak to the driver. Minutes later, the other man was gone, and Angus was in the driver's seat, Ivy belted in beside him.

She tapped away at the GPS embedded in the dashboard.

'There,' she said. 'Follow this. I'm going to take a nap.'

Then she turned slightly away from him in her seat, and firmly closed her eyes.

Angus didn't believe for a second that she was actually going to sleep, but he didn't argue.

They had two days ahead of them to talk, if necessary. He was in no hurry.

* * *

'Ivy?'

Ivy blinked sleepily. A large hand cupped her shoulder, shaking her gently.

'We're here. But it doesn't look much like an iron-ore mine.'

Slowly her eyes focused. The car's windows were coated in a thin layer of red dust, thanks to the kilometres of unsealed roads they'd travelled along to arrive at their destination. Fifty-seven kilometres north east of Paraburdoo, Bullah Bullah Downs homestead sat silently against a backdrop of yellow-flowering cassias and acacia trees and amongst a tufty carpet of spinifex in greens and blueish grey. The building was old, originally built in the early nineteen-twenties, but renovated extensively on the inside by Ivy's mother multiple times over the past thirty years.

The homestead's red tin roof was exactly the same shade as the soil it was built upon, reaching out to create a veranda to encircle itself. The walls were solid stone, the mortar rough and ready.

It was remote, it was arid, and it was *home*. In many ways more like home than the mansion in Dalkeith where Ivy had grown up.

Ivy loved it here. Despite everything, and despite having Angus Barlow beside her, she smiled.

She'd slumped against the side of the car as she'd slept, and Ivy now straightened up, stretching out her legs.

The road out here was mostly dirt and studded with pot holes. How she'd slept was beyond her, and it hadn't been intentional. She'd planned to just close her eyes and buy some time before she and Angus spoke.

Buy some time to do what, she wasn't exactly sure.

'Where are we?' Angus asked.

'The homestead,' Ivy said as she opened her door and

pivoted in her seat to climb out. 'Come on, I'll give you a tour.'

Keen to get inside, Ivy jumped from the car, but the instant her feet touched red dirt she knew something was very, very wrong.

Patches of white flashed into her vision, blocking the homestead, and blocking Angus when she instinctively turned to him.

'Angus?' she began, but that was all she could manage before everything went black.

'Ivy?'

Everything was still black. Something coated her lips, so Ivy took an experimental lick.

Dirt.

Yuk.

Her eyes sprung open. Immediately in front of her was the deeply corrugated tread of a four-wheel drive tyre. She was on her side, her legs bent, her arms laid out in front of her.

Ivy knew enough from basic first-aid training to know she was in the recovery position.

'I fainted,' she said.

'Just for a few seconds,' Angus said from where he knelt behind her. 'Enough time to freak me out.'

The remnants of that sudden dizziness remained, so for now Ivy didn't move.

'Freak you out?' Ivy said. 'Surely a simple faint isn't going to ruffle a soldier?'

Angus's laugh was low. 'I suppose you'd expect a soldier to catch you, too.'

'You didn't?' she asked, surprised, although now she registered a dull ache in her hip and she could see a few grazes on her arms, tiny pinpricks of blood decorating her skin. 'You're right,' she said with a smile, 'I am disappointed.'

'One moment you were there, then I heard the thud as you hit the ground. Thank God you didn't hit the car or a rock.' He paused. 'Has this happened before?'

'No,' she said. 'Although I have felt a bit nauseous if I don't eat regularly.'

'You didn't eat on the plane,' Angus said. 'So it's been at least three hours.'

'Yeah,' Ivy said. 'I was too grumpy during the flight to eat.'

She must still be dizzy; it wasn't like her to be quite so candid.

Angus laughed out loud. 'Grumpy with me or not, promise me you won't go so long between eating again.'

Ivy's automatic reaction was to tell Angus she was a grown woman perfectly capable of feeding herself. In fact, she rolled onto her back to tell him exactly that—but then met his gaze.

And it wasn't flat any more. It wasn't anything like it had been back in the VIP Lounge, or on the plane, and definitely not the ruthless stare he'd maintained when he had demanded she send her driver away.

The flecks of green were back in his eyes, and all she could see was concern.

Big, bad, brave soldier or not, she had scared him.

So those sharp words stuck in her throat.

'When we get inside, I want you to call your doctor.'

Ivy nodded obediently.

'Feeling faint is common in early pregnancy, but even so I'd feel better if you discussed this with a professional.'

She nodded again. 'You've done more research than me,' Ivy said.

He shrugged. 'I believe in being prepared.'

'Except when making love on the beach,' she teased.

Ivy had absolutely no idea where that came from, and instantly her cheeks went scalding hot.

But Angus laughed again. 'Maybe a bit too early for that joke, Ivy?'

'Probably,' she agreed, but her blush was fading.

Fainting was almost worth it to hear him laugh. To see that sparkle back in his gaze.

'How you doing now?' Angus said. 'Do you think you'll be able to walk to the house?'

'Of course,' she said, levering her upper body off the ground.

'Not so fast,' he said, and then in a smooth, effortless motion, he scooped her up. With a powerful, warm arm beneath her knees, and another encircling her back, it was momentarily impossible to talk. He held her close, her head nestled against his shoulder. He smelt fantastic: clean and strong. Instinctively she curled closer, wanting to be as close as possible to all that heat and strength.

In the shade of the veranda, finally Ivy's voice returned.

'Why did you ask if I could walk if you were always going to carry me?'

'Because I like it when things don't go the way you expect.'

She had a feeling she should be offended, but a combination of sun, dizziness and Angus's befuddling proximity meant she was in no position to mount a defence.

And with that, he carefully placed her back on her feet, a supportive arm remaining around her waist.

With his free arm he gave Ivy her handbag, liberally covered in dust.

In silence she found the key, unlocked the front door, and, with Angus's arm still close around her, led them inside.

The homestead's lounge room was something else. Angus couldn't imagine the room had even a passing resemblance to the decorating of the early nineteen-hundreds, but it was certainly beautiful. The floors were polished jarrah, the leather couches oversized and comfortable. Above the cast-iron fireplace a huge mirror reflected the view—although now it was dusk the undulating landscape's shades of red and splashes of green were muted. Elaborately patterned curtains edged the windows, and a thick-pile rug lay beneath their feet.

Air conditioning ensured the temperature inside was perfect, which Angus was grateful for as he studied Ivy.

She lay stretched out on the couch, her gaze trained at the ceiling. She'd had a shower to wash away all that red dust, and now she wore a loose singlet and yoga pants, her wet hair looped into a ponytail.

She insisted she was fine, but still—he worried.

He didn't think he'd ever forget the sound of Ivy's body thudding against the red earth.

Amongst so many—objectively far worse—memories that crammed his head, it was strange that he was so sure of that fact. But he was.

And he couldn't even say it was just about their baby. In fact, it wasn't until she finally opened her eyes—and it had felt like hours, not seconds—that he even thought about him or her.

Was that bad?

He propped his elbows on his knees, rubbing his hand against his forehead.

Probably.

Slowly, Ivy pulled herself to a seated position.

'Careful!' he said, automatically.

She responded with a glare. 'I am not an invalid. Even my doctor gave me the all-clear.'

'As long as it doesn't happen again.'

She sighed. 'It won't.' She gestured at the half-eaten box

of crackers and the remaining wedge of Cheddar cheese on the coffee table. 'I am suitably fortified, I promise.'

But still, he watched warily as she crossed the room to the adjacent kitchen. She walked slowly—he suspected mostly for his benefit—and made it to the fridge in one piece.

On cue, she threw her arms out with a flourish, and took a theatrical bow in his direction. 'Waa-*lah*! Behold! The amazing walking woman!'

Angus didn't even bother to raise an eyebrow, although he couldn't help his halfway smile.

Somehow they had fallen into a truce. A demilitarised zone of sorts.

But this wasn't what he had planned—this rather cosy scene in such a luxurious setting.

But then, he'd expected they would talk in a meeting room at a mine site. As it turned out, the three Bullah Bullah Downs mines were located many, many kilometres away from the homestead, and when he'd asked Ivy said she'd had no plans to visit them.

So he had been right. Ivy had run away to Bullah Bullah Downs. She'd quite literally sent the contract, and run.

And while a big portion of him was incredibly angry at her behaviour, all he saw as Ivy walked towards him with an overflowing platter in her arms was how she'd looked, crumpled on the ground beside the car.

Fragile. Vulnerable.

Not that she'd appreciate him thinking that. And Angus didn't really think it was true. Ivy was strong, Ivy was independent.

But she was also pregnant, and for reasons he didn't fully comprehend—she was scared.

'I may have gone overboard in my attempt to divert any hint of a rumour,' Ivy said, putting the platter down on the coffee table. 'So please enjoy your sushi and selection of soft cheeses. There's also a *lot* of wine in the fridge.'

Angus leant forward to study the feast. 'And I see you aren't about to starve, though.'

'No,' Ivy said with a smile. 'Hard cheeses, bread and nuts seem to be my thing at the moment. And apples. And cake. There are actually quite a few cakes in the fridge. I may have been a little overenthusiastic when I made my catering order, too.' She paused. 'I suspect any rumours will instead be in relation to my new-found gluttony.'

For a while they both ate quietly, picking at the decadent food before them.

Tension still simmered between them, but now it wasn't tinged with anger.

Pity he'd have to change that.

'Why did you send me that contract, Ivy?'

Ivy's head jerked up. She put her plate back on the coffee table, and then rearranged her legs from underneath her so she sat primly on the edge of the sofa, rather than comfortably cross-legged amongst the pillows.

'I should've done it to start with.'

'That doesn't answer my question.'

She looked away, staring out through the now darkened window at nothing.

'I felt it was my only option.'

'That doesn't answer it either. Why?'

Her gaze snapped back to meet his, and it was immediately obvious that their truce was over. 'You just don't get it, do you?' she said, jumping to her feet. 'This is so easy for you, while *everything* in my life has to change. It's not fair.'

Just like that, Angus was angry, too.

'This is life-changing for me too, Ivy.'

But she shook her head. 'Don't be ridiculous. I told you what's at stake here. My entire professional career hangs in the balance. Nothing has to change for you.'

Nothing had to change for him?

But before he had a chance to set her straight, Ivy continued, oblivious to his clenched jaw and the frustration running through his veins. 'I don't think you understand that I *have* to fix this. I can't just carry on like it's all okay, and that we'll work it out, because we *won't*. We can't have coffee and lunch and talk about football and cancel meetings and just hope that magically it will all work out. Because it *won't*.'

She was pacing the room, crossing from the couch to the kitchen and back. Her arms were wrapped tight around her, and she didn't look at Angus at all.

He stood up, deliberately blocking her path, needing her to look at him.

Needing the Ivy he knew to be looking him straight in the eye when she spoke.

But she instead stared at a spot somewhere on his chest, her jaw in a stubborn line.

'How does not seeing me at all fix anything, Ivy? That was all I saw in the contract, nothing about your career. Or about how you'll erase what happened between us in Bali.'

Her gaze shot upwards to cling with his. 'I don't want to erase what happened in Bali,' she said softly, then shook her head as if she'd only just realised what she'd said, her cheeks a deep pink. 'I mean, just the bit where I forgot to take my pill that day.' Then her gaze dropped down to her belly, which she covered with her hands. 'Oh, I don't think I meant that either, which makes no sense at all.'

Her fingers rubbed at her eyes, smudging make-up he hadn't even realised she'd put on after her shower.

'Ivy, tell me how the contract fixes anything.'

Her hands fell away. 'It doesn't fix everything,' she said. 'But it fixes *you*.'

'What does that even mean?'

She threw her arms in the air, taking a step backwards

so she could gesture between them. 'It fixes *this*. It fixes me having to see you, having to deal with you being all strong and nice and sexy and *confusing*. I'm not myself when I'm with you. I make poor decisions; I don't think straight; I don't do *anything* right. I can't control anything right now. I can't stop my stupid body fainting. I can't stop eating crackers. I can't stop the fact that my whole world is going to collapse around me once I finally get the guts to *tell* anyone but my lawyer that I'm pregnant.' She took a step towards him, tilting her chin upwards to meet his gaze. 'But I can control *this*. I can stop *this*. It's a start, anyway.'

Then her shoulders slumped, and she went to walk away.

But Angus's hand shot out, wrapping around her upper arm.

'You can't control me, Ivy. You can't control everything, no matter how badly you want to.'

He stepped even closer. Ivy's chest was moving up and down as she took deep breaths, as if trying to pull herself together.

Angus loosened his grip on her arm, letting his hand run down past her elbow to her wrist. Beneath his fingertips, she shivered.

'Are you okay?' he said, suddenly worried. 'Are you cold?'

She laughed, but without humour. 'No, Angus. That's just yet another thing I apparently can't control.'

Ivy's heart felt as if it were beating a billion miles an hour. That seemed to be what it did when Angus was so close to her, doing that strong and sexy thing he did so well.

And her skin shivered too, of course, when he touched her.

He'd gone completely still, which was good. It gave Ivy some chance of pulling herself together. Mortification was attempting to distract her from the immediate sensation of

Angus's touch. Because mortified she should be, for pacing around the homestead, ranting to Angus about things he certainly didn't need to know.

But then his fingers began to move again, and the only thing Ivy could possibly think about was the man standing right in front of her.

'I didn't need to carry you inside today,' he said, his voice low and like velvet.

'You were making a point,' she said. 'About expectations.'

She'd barely needed the prompt. Today had confirmed that Angus Barlow was never going to behave the way she expected—or wanted.

But he shook his head. 'No,' he said. 'At least that was a far secondary consideration. Mostly I just wanted to touch you.'

Ivy closed her eyes as warmth pooled low in her belly.

He was still touching her, his fingers having traced their way back up along her arm, across her shoulder to lightly brush against her exposed collarbone.

His touch was so light Ivy found herself swaying towards him, wanting him to be firmer, wanting to feel more than a hint of his strength and his heat.

She jumped at the sudden weight of his other hand on her hip, and his hand went still, as if allowing her a moment to adjust.

And then that hand was moving too, his thumb exploring the shape of her hipbone, his fingers flaring out to caress the upper slope of her backside.

Then the hand curled around further, to splay across the small of her back. Firm. Hard.

Her eyes still closed, she could suddenly feel his breath against her cheek, then her ear.

'You lose control when you're near me,' he said, so softly.

It was pointless to argue, even if she was capable of it. Instead she simply sighed.

'Ivy, I don't want to be in control around you.'

Her eyes snapped open at the feel of those words against her lips. If she moved even a centimetre, their mouths would touch.

But she didn't have to. The hand on her back pulled her firmly against him, his other hand sliding up to tangle in her still-damp hair.

And then his mouth took hers, and he was kissing her.

Hard and hot and all-consuming.

Out of control. But then, that was hardly unexpected.

Her own arms had managed to make their way to his shoulders, to cling and to wrap behind his neck. He didn't really need her to pull him closer, but she gave it a go, wanting to feel every inch of him plastered against her body.

She kissed him back without restraint, far more so than in Bali. She tasted his tongue, explored his mouth, licked and sucked his lips.

And, *God*, how he kissed her back. He was right, she was never in control around him, but as they kissed he gave her the illusion of control, letting her take the lead, letting her press smaller kisses along his jaw, or break away to change the angle of their lips or choose to take things slow or fast.

But it wasn't real. The moment Angus lost patience with her playfulness she found herself in the air for the second time today, being carried to the couch, and pushed deep into the pillows beneath his delicious weight.

And he kissed her then with intent, his hands inching beneath her singlet, her skin aching for his touch.

Her fingers slid along his spine, digging into the heavy muscles as they explored his breadth and shape. But then they found what they were really after—the hem of his T-shirt—and she got to work pulling the fabric upwards, desperate to feel his naked skin against hers.

She cradled him between her thighs, and it was impossible not to rub her body against that hardness.

Then his fingers made it to her bra, cupping her through the satin and lace, his thumb perfectly rough against her nipple.

But then he went still. Completely still.

'Is it okay for the baby for me to be on top of you? Should we swap?'

He might as well have thrown a bucket of water over them both.

Ivy had frozen when Angus went still, but now she felt as cold as ice, the mention of their baby plunging her back into reality.

How had she let this happen?

She pulled his shirt back down, and shoved both her hands against his shoulders.

'Get off me.'

Instantly he was on his feet. 'Are you okay?'

There they were again, those lovely concerned eyes.

Ivy sat up, pulling her bra and singlet back to where they were supposed to be. She knew she was blushing, could feel it covering pretty much every square inch of her skin.

'I'm going to bed,' she said. 'Take any of the other rooms. They all have fresh linen.'

Then she noticed all the food still out. She grabbed at a random serving platter. 'I'll just put this away first. You can go to bed, though.'

She just wanted him away from her.

'Ivy,' he said. 'What just happened?'

She shook her head. 'I think it's better if we both agree nothing happened, don't you?' She remembered his words from that first coffee. 'You know, we've got eighteen years ahead of us and all that?'

Eighteen years with yet another meaningless night of

sex to try not to think about…which of course, would be all this would've been. No, not a good idea.

Finally she managed to look at him.

He nodded sharply. 'You're right,' he said. 'I'll help you tidy up.'

Then together they put the food away and cleaned up the kitchen.

Very politely, very awkwardly.

Then, just as Ivy began walking up the hallway to her room, Angus spoke.

'I'm not going to sign that contract, Ivy. I'm going to be part of our baby's life, and that means I'm going to be a part of yours. Like it or not.'

She didn't bother turning around. 'I know.'

CHAPTER SEVEN

ANGUS LAY IN his incredibly comfortable king-size bed and stared up at the elaborate ceiling rose above the guest room's elegant chandelier without really seeing it.

He'd had a really good night's sleep.

He'd always been good at sleeping anywhere, and at any time—an essential skill in his career. And he certainly didn't need air conditioning, a fluffy doona and fancy sheets.

There were only two times in his life he remembered being unable to sleep: a couple of weeks ago, when Ivy told him she was pregnant. And the night his father died.

That was it.

He also didn't really dream. He just lay his head on the pillow—or in his swag, or on the ground—and slept. *Boom.* And he slept for however long, and woke up. That was it.

Tom had asked him once if he had bad dreams.

Bad dreams about what they'd seen. What they'd done. What had happened to them. What could've happened to them. What could still happen to them.

Because it turned out Tom had really bad dreams. The type of bad dreams where he woke up soaked in sweat, or where his wife needed to shake him awake.

The type of dreams where sometimes he didn't want to go to sleep.

Sometimes, Angus had said. *Sometimes I have bad dreams.*

And Tom had nodded, and swallowed, and looked so

damn relieved that his mate understood what he was going through that Angus had been glad he'd lied.

But it had been a lie.

Because he didn't have those dreams.

He didn't come home from combat and then feel unsafe in his own home. He wasn't alert to every sound, to every movement.

He didn't sometimes sleep in his lounge room with all the lights on. Or drive all night so he didn't have to sleep at all.

He didn't gamble or drink or do drugs to dull painful memories.

He debriefed, he came home, and he was fine.

But not everyone came home fine. Tom hadn't come home fine. The guy that Cam had told him about—Patrick—he was messed up too.

And Angus knew some of the guys saw psychs at times. It made sense. Most guys seemed to work their way through it, and they'd all been told enough times about normal reactions to trauma that he knew it was just that: *normal*.

Although some guys didn't work through it. Tom hadn't.

But how about him? How about Angus?

How could he be so unaffected? How could he blissfully sleep like a log when he'd experienced so much, *knew* so much?

When your work dealt directly with life and death—and the pendulum could so easily swing one way or the other—*of course* that would mess you up, at least a little?

At some point—before Tom's diagnosis with post-traumatic stress disorder—Angus had been quietly rather proud of his resilience.

He'd thought he was particularly tough. Thought he was particularly strong.

But Tom had been tough, as tough as Angus. Tougher. Stronger.

So now…now he didn't think he should be proud.

Now he wondered what it was he lacked.

Of course it wasn't the same, but wasn't it at least a little unusual that he could have the most explosive kiss of his life with a woman who'd literally turned his life upside down, and then sleep in a strange bed for—he rolled over to check his phone—almost eight hours straight?

Shouldn't he have tossed and turned, just a little?

Yesterday Ivy had tried so desperately to control him—to pack him away into a neat little lawyer-lined box. She didn't like the undeniable pull of attraction between them, that was clear. To be honest, Angus wasn't a big fan, either.

It *did* complicate things.

Last night Ivy had told him she lost control around him, and he'd openly told her that he found it pretty hard to stay in control around her, too.

And that did surprise him. He'd followed Ivy up here because that contract had made him so damn angry—and because he wasn't going to let Ivy manipulate him.

He certainly hadn't intended to kiss her.

He wanted a relationship with his child, and he wanted a cordial relationship with Ivy. Nothing more.

There was a reason he was single now, and his previous girlfriends had all eventually become fed up with him.

He'd begun to join the dots years ago, beginning to see the similarities between his ability to process and shrug off the impacts of war and his ability to distance himself so effortlessly within a relationship.

The thing was, in his job, it was a good thing. In day-to-day life, not so much.

So it was better, he'd decided, simply not to have relationships. That way he didn't hurt anyone. And he certainly didn't want to hurt Ivy.

Angus levered himself up and swung his legs off the

bed. He'd slept in only his boxers, and the air conditioning was cool against his skin.

Last night, when Ivy had yanked up his T-shirt, the air conditioning had been shockingly cold against his heated body—for a moment. But he'd immediately forgotten that when he'd been so absorbed in Ivy and the soft skin of her hips, and belly and breasts...

Angus smiled.

So no, he might not have dreamed of Ivy, or tossed and turned all night.

But it couldn't hurt to think about her now: how she felt, how she'd looked.

The flush to her cheeks, the pink of her lips, how she'd felt so perfect beneath him, even if separated by too many layers of clothes...

The house was silent as Angus walked to the en-suite bathroom for a shower.

He wasn't usually one to daydream, either.

But for Ivy, it would seem he'd made an exception.

Ivy woke up to the smell of cooking bacon.

Mmm. Bacon.

Bacon?

Ivy's eyes popped open. Sun was streaming in through the curtains she'd left open all night, and it was clearly a long time past dawn.

Angus.

She squeezed her eyes shut again.

Angus.

He'd filled her dreams—not for the first time—and he was still here now that she'd woken up.

Not that he could've left. It wasn't as if he could easily flag down a taxi.

But that would've been nice, though. To wake up, and for Angus to have magically disappeared.

That way this weekend could've been what it was supposed to be. A break. A *proper* break, not like every other holiday she could remember.

No work. No nothing. Just—herself, and Bullah Bullah Downs.

Perfect.

But that really wasn't working out, was it?

Nothing was working out right now. *Nothing.*

Not her supposed holiday, not the contract, and not that kiss.

How had she let that happen?

Ivy noticed she'd brought her fingers to her lips and snatched them away. Why had she done that? To test if they felt different? Bruised? Ravished? Special?

They didn't, of course. Because nothing had changed, not really.

What was yet another awkward memory between them?

She climbed out of bed and got dressed. It would be hot today—it always was this time of year. She'd planned to head out to one of the gorges at Karijini today, but without a driver that wouldn't happen. She'd had Martin booked all weekend to come collect her as needed, but she'd been too flustered at the airport to think of only cancelling his initial task of driving her to the homestead.

Instead, she'd organise for the Molyneux jet to fly both Angus and herself home today. It wasn't as if she'd be able to relax this weekend, even once Angus left.

Besides, it would also give her all of Sunday to work.

Dressed in tailored navy-blue shorts and a cream linen tank-top, she headed for the kitchen.

Angus sat on one of the tall stools at the breakfast bar, a full plate of bacon and eggs piled up in front of him.

'I hope you don't mind,' he said, his back to her. 'I may have already started.'

He twisted on his seat, and then paused as he ran his gaze along her body.

'You have great legs,' he said, so matter-of-fact that Ivy blinked. 'I haven't seen that much of them before in daylight.'

At this, she blushed.

He grinned, and left his plate to walk to the other side of the bench. The gas cooktop sat in the middle of all that white-speckled granite, a couple of fry pans already in place.

'How do you like your eggs?'

Ivy still stood, frozen, in the door way. This wasn't what she had expected. She'd expected silence. Possibly antagonism.

Not this. Not a sexy smile, complete with matching sexy stubble.

He stood comfortably in her kitchen. As if he belonged, and as if he had nowhere else to be.

'Scrambled,' she said, eventually, then left the relative safety of the hall to slide onto the stool beside his.

She ate her breakfast almost warily, not at all sure what was going on.

'What are we doing today?' he asked, laying his knife and fork together on his now empty plate.

'I'll phone my office after breakfast and organise for the jet to come pick us up. With any luck we'll be home by late afternoon.'

'Why would you do that?'

Ivy looked up from her eggs, surprised. 'Because you want to go home, and I can't justify the cost of the jet flying up tomorrow as well.'

Angus leant against the low backrest of his stool, and crossed his arms. 'I never said that. I'm happy to stay.'

'You're happy to stay?' Ivy repeated. 'You mean, you're

happy to remain uninvited in my home with me—a woman you don't like very much?'

His lips quirked upwards. 'Oh, I think we both know that isn't true, Ivy.'

Ivy shook her head as her cheeks heated, ignoring him. 'No,' she said, 'I think it's best if we both go home. I was silly to fly up anyway. I have so much work to do—'

'Ivy,' he said firmly. 'I meant it last night. I'm going to be a part of our baby's life, and that does mean being part of yours. Given that, doesn't it make sense we get to know each other better?'

'Didn't we try this before, at the café?' she said. 'Besides, we can talk on the plane if you want. Play twenty questions with each other or something.'

'I'm not getting on a plane today, Ivy. I'm going to drive out to Karijini and explore. I've never been to the national park before—it would be crazy not to go this weekend when we're so close. And I was hoping you'd be my guide.'

His plans were so similar to what Ivy had originally intended, it would've been uncanny—if visiting Karijini and mining iron ore weren't basically the only two things you *could* do in the Pilbara.

Even so, it was tempting.

A big part of her—the stubborn part—wanted to stick to her guns, and insist she absolutely must fly home to work.

But another part of her—the bit that was tired of arguing, and also just plain *tired*—couldn't do it.

She could think of a lot worse things to do today than go swimming in a secluded waterhole amongst plunging gorges two and a half billion years old. And working all afternoon was certainly one of them.

Plus, reluctantly, she had to acknowledge that Angus had a point. If she was stuck dealing with Angus—and she was, now that he wouldn't sign her contract—maybe it would

help to spend more—platonic—time together. Maybe fa-
miliarity would even dilute the attraction between them.

She could hope, anyway.

'We'll go to Fern Pool,' she said, 'but we need to get
moving. It's a decent drive.'

Angus studied her for a long moment, and Ivy liked that
she'd clearly surprised him.

Then he smiled, and Ivy found she liked that even better—and couldn't bring herself to care that that probably
wasn't a good thing.

'Sounds like a plan,' Angus said. 'Let's go.'

Angus drove them out to Fortescue Falls. The forty-
minute drive took them from red gravel to smooth bitumen and back to red gravel again as they approached the
car park. October wasn't the best time of year to come to
Karijini, with the unrelenting, impossible heat of summer
only weeks away, but it did mean far fewer tourists, with
only two other cars parked amongst the dirt and the surrounding scrub-tufted hills.

But they were lucky—today was perfect: low thirties
with a glorious, cloudless blue sky. At a little hut, Ivy paid
the small entry fee, then smiled at Angus over her shoulder as she pointed towards the deep red sand track ahead of
them. He wore a black T-shirt, knee-length shorts, leather
work boots and a backpack slung over his shoulders—and
he looked one hundred per cent like the soldier he was,
complete with bulging biceps and muscular calves. Ivy
didn't think she'd ever admired a man's calves before. In
fact, until today, she wouldn't even have thought it possible
that they could be attractive.

But, it turned out, they could. Hair and everything.

It wasn't a long walk to Dales Gorge, less than half
a kilometre. Here it was perfectly flat and easy—a stark
contrast to the descent ahead of them. Ivy enjoyed the si-

lence as they walked, after Angus had taken her twenty questions dig to heart and they'd talked most of the way here. About nothing particularly important, mostly about the Pilbara and the sights of Karijini Park—which Ivy had appreciated, still feeling a little raw from the night before.

There was just something about this man that had her revealing more than she ever intended.

In more ways than one, actually.

That thought made her smile, and she must have giggled, as Angus went still beside her.

'What's the joke?' he asked.

Ivy forced her lips into a horizontal line, and shook her head. 'I don't know what you're talking about.'

Which was completely the wrong thing to say, as now she'd intrigued him.

'Oh, really?' he said, 'Because—'

'Why don't you have a girlfriend?' Ivy blurted out, cutting him off.

Slightly horrified and with no clue where the question had come from, Ivy charged on ahead, although, given they were almost at the start of the walk down to Fortescue Falls, she really didn't have very far to go. At the lookout she pointed down into the abrupt one-hundred-metre-deep gash in the landscape.

'This is Dale Gorge,' she said. 'You can see the falls all the way down there.'

Angus, who had easily kept pace beside her, laughed. 'Yes, I got that.'

Ivy nodded. 'Of course. Right—so—this way!'

She knew he was still smiling, but decided not to pay any attention. Instead, she thought it was better to focus on her surroundings. It had been a couple of years since she'd been into Karijini. As she took in the vivid red of the ruthless, tiered red-brown cliffs and the rumbling sound of the falls beneath them, it seemed impossible she'd left it so long.

'I don't have a girlfriend because of my job,' Angus said.

Ivy tensed at the words, wanting to wish back her question. She had to walk slowly now. The path was narrow and twisting.

Angus was directly behind her, his boots crunching far more loudly than her sneakers.

'I'm not a fan of emotional farewells.'

She'd meant to remain silent, hopeful the subject would change, but once again she'd lost control of her mouth. 'But wouldn't that be worth it for the equally emotional welcome home?'

'I'm told I'm not much good at those either,' Angus said. Ivy sensed his shrug, even though she couldn't see him. 'Besides, that's only if I do come home.'

Ivy slipped on some gravel, and threw her hands out for balance. Instantly Angus's hands were on her, catching her at the waist before she could fall.

He quickly righted her, but slid his hands away just a little more slowly than was necessary.

'Thank you,' Ivy said softly, but was quick to start walking again.

Stupidly, she hadn't really put a lot of thought into Angus's career. She'd been caught up in the sexiness of it—the idea of a soldier: the uniform, the weapons, the courage. Not the reality, and certainly not the brutality of war and of death.

Her stomach had plummeted at his casual words: *only if I do come home.*

For their child, of course. She'd lost her father—not through death but through distance and lack of interest— and that had been difficult enough.

And maybe it had plummeted just a tiny bit for her.

'How do you do it?' she asked. 'How can you risk so much?'

They were about halfway into the gorge now, and the

colours of the rocks led the way—changing from orange to red to purple as they descended. To their left, the falls, which had seemed barely more than a trickle from a distance, now revealed their true size. A tourist, clambering along the adjacent rocks, gave some scale to the sprawling, towering year-round falls.

'Because I love it. The teamwork, the tactics, the challenge. It's what I've wanted to do since I was seventeen, and I'll do it for as long as I can.'

'But what about—?' Ivy began, but didn't really know how to continue.

'The bad stuff? You mean like death and destruction? Living under constant threat? Killing people?' He rattled off his terrible list roughly, and didn't wait for her to clarify. 'Of course that isn't fun. At times it's awful, actually. Indescribably awful. But then I get to come home.'

If he came home.

'And then a few months later, go and do it again.'

That was what Ivy couldn't wrap her head around. To survive war, and then risk it all again.

'Yeah,' he said. 'Sometimes—' he began, then stopped.

'Sometimes what?'

They were deep within the gorge now. Down here they walked amongst greenery and paperbarks—an incredible contrast to the parched landscape above.

'Sometimes I wonder if maybe it should be harder for me to go back.'

There was enough space for Angus to walk beside her, and she looked up at him.

'What do you mean?'

But he wasn't looking at her. Instead he lengthened his stride, then looked back over his shoulder. 'Come on, I'm keen to get to this Fern Pool you were talking about.'

He clearly wasn't going to answer her question, but still

Ivy very nearly repeated it. Besides, wasn't she just trying to get to know him better? Just as she was supposed to?

But it was something she'd glimpsed, however briefly, that meant she kept on walking in silence. For the first time since she'd met him he'd looked...

Ivy wouldn't have said *vulnerable*, because that wasn't even close to true. But something like that, something she'd never expected to see in Angus Barlow.

Angus had made it to the top of the falls, and he stood there, waiting for her.

He studied her as she approached, his gaze sweeping over her, the motion not all that dissimilar to the water as it rushed across the ancient, angular, straight-edged rocks, tracing the shape and lines of her.

But Ivy forgot to be annoyed or embarrassed by his attention, because she'd just worked it out—worked out what she'd seen.

Just for a moment, the shortest of moments, Angus had looked *exposed*.

Fortescue Falls was unusual. When Angus thought of waterfalls, he thought of a sheer pane of water, tumbling from a cliff. But here, the falls surged along a gradual series of steps and benches—like an elegantly curved stairway from amongst the trees down to the clear green pool below.

Ivy was playing tour guide, telling him that the waterfall flowed—miraculously—year round. She pointed out some of the vegetation and talked of local birds and bats. She was nervous, although Angus wasn't entirely sure why.

One moment she was so, so self-assured, the next self-conscious and talking too quickly, her gaze skittering away.

He didn't know what to make of her questioning his single status. Part of him liked it—liked that she'd wondered, liked that she'd been so appalled that she'd actually voiced the question. But another part of him—a big part—shied away from even such an oblique reference to a relationship between them. Ivy had been absolutely right to stop them both last night. Another night in bed together was not going to aid the relaxed, shared—and lawyer-free—parenting arrangement he kept telling Ivy he wanted.

Although of course it didn't mean he had to stop checking her out. She'd stepped away from him now to head down the track to Fern Pool, their true destination today. So of course he took the opportunity to have a good old look at her very nice view from behind.

It wasn't as if he hadn't noticed Ivy have a pretty thorough look at him at times.

Sex might be unwise. But looking didn't hurt anyone.

CHAPTER EIGHT

EXACTLY WHAT A terrible idea this had been only became clear to Ivy when she stepped onto the man-made wooden boardwalk that provided the only access to Fern Pool.

No one else was here, of course. Ivy had been here dozens of time with her family over the years, and *not once* had they had the pool to themselves. Even out here, more than a five-hour drive from the nearest major regional centre, tourists made sure they got to the Karijini. And they certainly made sure they got to Fern Pool.

Just not today.

Angus dumped his backpack onto the wooden boards, and Ivy looked determinedly across the crystal-clear water as he tugged off his T-shirt. Above them stretched a remarkable fig tree, and, of course, ferns were everywhere. It was lush, it was green, it was *wet*—everything that the desert-like Pilbara shouldn't be.

But it was also supposed to be full of tourists—a handful of lily-white British backpackers, a posse of raucous kids up here camping with their parents, or at least a pair of retired grey nomads.

Someone. *Anyone.*

Because without them, this place—this place with its mirror-flat water; its pair of tumbling waterfalls; its surrounding, towering layers and slabs of rock in reds and browns and purples was just...was just...

Undeniably, terribly and completely...romantic.

Dammit.

'You coming in?'

Angus stood directly in front of her, so of course she had to look at him. She made an attempt to stare only at his face, but almost immediately failed, her attention sliding rapidly downwards.

She'd felt that chest beneath her fingertips, felt it pressed hard against her.

But she hadn't had a chance to look at it—the moonlight in Bali had certainly not been as generous as the Karijini sun.

So she'd known he was broad, and hard, and ridiculously strong. But seeing him made it all new again. He was muscular, of course, but not in a stupid, body-builder way. There was still a leanness to him, a practicality—this man didn't just lift weights, he was fit, agile, supple.

He had a smattering of black hairs along his chest, but otherwise his skin was smooth. The occasional freckle dotted his lovely olive skin. His nipples were somehow darker than she expected. The ridges of his abdominal muscles deeper.

His board shorts sat low on his hips. He had that muscular V thing going on, and her eyes followed in the direction it was pointing...

Before she finally came to her senses and snapped her gaze back to his.

His grin was broad, and his eyes sparkled.

'So, Ivy—are you coming in?'

It was the same question, but also different. Was his voice lower? More intimate?

She took a deliberate step backwards, and promptly stepped onto his backpack, and the beach towels that Angus had pulled out for them.

It was the pool. The damned pool's fault for being so intimate and dreamily secluded.

Still grinning, Angus walked to the metal ladder that

provided access to the pool, although Ivy finally managed to drag her gaze away as he climbed in.

Instead she turned her back, as pointless as that was, to pull off her top and shorts. She liked that Angus had bothered to read the sign beside the pool, and he hadn't jumped in, as many others did. Ivy hadn't read it today, but she knew what the first line said: *Fern Pool is a special place.*

A place where you didn't make loud noises or jump off the waterfalls. Where you respected your surroundings and the traditional owners of the land.

It certainly shouldn't be a place where she ogled a half-naked man.

Her clothes neatly folded on top of Angus's backpack, Ivy rolled her shoulders back, and took a handful of long, deep breaths.

She told herself not to be self-conscious, although of course that was pointless. She could've been underwear-model thin and she *still* would've felt insecure around all of Angus's bronzed perfection.

And she certainly wasn't underwear-model thin. But she *was* in her favourite black and white striped bikini, and if she breathed in her stomach was almost flat.

Her hand rested on her still-normal-sized tummy.

She'd forgotten again.

Although this time, remembering that she was pregnant didn't trigger a spiralling panic, or make her want to squeeze her eyes shut and wish just about *everything* away if she could just find a way to fix what she'd done.

In fact, all it did was cause her to turn around, and to search for Angus in the water.

The pool wasn't large, but Ivy didn't have to search far anyway. His forearms rested on the edge of the boardwalk as he floated in the water, watching her.

'How long until the baby starts to move?' he asked.

'Ages,' Ivy said. 'Eighteen to twenty weeks, I think?'

Her lips quirked upwards. 'I thought you were full bottle on all this pregnancy stuff?'

He pushed away from the boardwalk, his eyes still on her. 'Haven't got to that chapter yet,' he said. He flicked his hand through the water, sending a light spray of water in her direction. 'I've noticed you're still not swimming.'

The drops of water that now decorated her feet were surprisingly cool, given the heat of the day. But then, down here, beneath the shade of the great fig, the light was diluted.

'Although I'm not really complaining,' Angus continued. He was treading water only metres from the ladder. Close enough that Ivy knew he was—and had been—checking her out.

She blushed, which was just about her default reaction to Angus it seemed, but also found herself smiling. Almost as if she was enjoying his attention.

Fern Pool romanticism *was* getting to her.

That was enough to get her into the water quick smart.

And it *was* cold. Cold enough that she gasped.

But just as she had as a kid, she immediately ducked beneath the water to soak her hair.

Better to get it over with quickly.

Ivy and Mila had always agreed on that approach. While April had swum around shrieking about not getting her hair wet *yet*, which had been pretty much an engraved invitation for her sisters to splash her with as much water as possible.

'What are you smiling about?' Angus asked, treading water beside her as she tucked her hair behind her ears.

'A nice memory,' she said, and then filled him in.

Angus rolled onto his back as she spoke, so he floated, staring up at the sky. 'It doesn't surprise me at all that you've always got straight to the point,' he said.

Except around Angus. Somehow, and sometimes, around

Angus, being direct seemed impossible. Her words escaped her. Her *brain* seemed to escape her.

'Do you have any brothers or sisters?' Ivy asked.

'No,' Angus said. 'Just Dad, and Mum, and me. We didn't really travel as a family all that much. You're lucky.'

Ivy laughed. 'We didn't always think that coming up here was all that great. But Mum was all for multitasking on a holiday—coming up here meant a business trip *and* a family getaway. Although my sisters and I did go to the US a few times to visit my dad.'

'The actor?'

'Yeah,' Ivy said, not surprised Angus knew that detail. Most people in Western Australia did—but then, a mining heiress didn't elope with a handsome, if small-time, Hollywood actor and have nobody notice. 'He left when I was pretty young, and we've never been close. He calls me on my birthday.'

She followed Angus's lead and stuck her legs and arms out so she could float on her back. Water lapped against her ears and she closed her eyes, enjoying the sensation of weightlessness.

'Are you close to your parents?' Ivy asked.

'Yes,' Angus said. 'And no. I mean—'

Ivy tilted her head so she could see him. He floated so close to her that if she reached out just a little bit further, their fingers would touch.

'I was very close to my father, but he…died. And my mother has early-onset dementia, which is pretty awful really.'

'Oh, that *is* awful,' Ivy said, jackknifing from her back to swim to him. 'I'm so sorry.'

He'd done the same thing, but he didn't wait for Ivy. Instead he swam away, in big, generous breast strokes, to the pair of tumbling waterfalls.

But he stopped just short of where the falls hit the pool,

and turned as he treaded water. 'I wish we had travelled together as a family more. But my dad worked too hard. Every weekend he was at the shop. He *had* to be at the shop—at the furniture shop we owned. Even when he didn't really need to be, he still thought he had to.'

Angus wasn't looking at her. His chin was tilted upwards, as if he was examining the thick, ropey branches of the fig tree that stretched towards the sky.

'My mum's like that,' Ivy said.

Now he looked at her. '*You're* like that,' he said.

'I am not!'

He simply raised an eyebrow.

Ivy opened her mouth to argue, but realised it was pointless. The fact was she wasn't very good at holidays. When she did go away, she kept one eye on her smartphone, and made damn sure she always had access to a Wi-Fi network.

But she'd hated how her mother had never truly been present on family holidays. She couldn't do that to her own child.

'I'd like to take our baby on holidays when he or she is older,' Angus said.

'Me too,' Ivy said. Then quickly added, 'Not with you, of course.'

'Of course,' he said, glancing at her with a smile. But there was a sadness to it, as if he was thinking of the family holidays he never had. Or the father he had lost.

'How old were you?' Ivy asked, 'I mean, when your dad died?'

'Seventeen,' he said. 'It was very sudden. I'd always thought I'd follow in his footsteps, continuing to run the family business or something. Although to be honest I hadn't worried too much about it. I was at an age where all I cared about was playing footy on the weekend. Or hanging out with my mates. I'd never had to deal with the future before.'

'So the army wasn't a lifelong dream?'

Another smile, but still without humour. 'No,' he said. 'Part of it was the physical aspect of the job. When dad died, I started to really get into my weights, and fitness. It was a distraction, I guess. A focus. As mum started to get unwell not long after. So the sense of achievement from lifting heavier weights or running further, or faster…it was… I don't know. Something. Something that wasn't thinking about what I'd lost, and what I was losing.' Angus wasn't looking at Ivy now, his gaze again focused somewhere in the giant fig's branches. 'But now I think it was a lot about the structure. The formality. With my dad gone and mum not really my mum any more—it was kind of a relief to have a schedule and orders to work to. Later, I fell in love with the job, with the mateship, the teamwork, the tactics. But early on the job was like an anchor for me, something I could rely on.'

'That's a heck of a lot for a young man to deal with,' Ivy said, her heart aching for a lost and grieving teenage Angus.

He nodded. 'Yeah,' he agreed. 'It was. Sometimes I wonder if—' But his words trailed off, and he turned back to the cascading water. 'Did you ever climb up behind the waterfall?'

Ivy blinked at the abrupt change of subject, but didn't push. Somehow she knew that Angus didn't share that story easily. If at all. 'All the time,' Ivy said, her tone consciously upbeat. 'It's slippery, though.'

He threw her an amused look, that sadness erased from his gaze.

'Oh, I'm sorry,' Ivy said, deadpan, as she swam up to the rocks. 'I should've realised you did slippery-rock training in the SAS.'

'Honey, you'd be amazed at what I can do,' he replied, and then, right on cue, slipped a little as he hoisted his legs onto the lowest, moss-slick rocks.

Ivy giggled, and Angus glared—but couldn't hide his grin.

The falls here were delicate in comparison to Fortescue, falling gently only about three metres from the protruding ledge of red rock above where they swam. Beyond the curtain of water, slabs of rock provided tiered seating of sorts, decorated with clumps of ferns.

It had been a while, but Ivy remembered which rocks provided the best grip, and it only took her a few seconds to clamber past Angus and to settle into her favourite spot—directly behind the waterfall, the tumbling water blurring and distorting the world around her into indistinct reds, blues and greens.

It didn't take long for Angus to join her, seated to her right. He stretched his longer legs out in front of him, just as Ivy had, although his toes also touched the falls. The sound of the water echoed back here, but it would still be easy to hold a conversation.

But they didn't say a word.

Instead, they both just sat silently together, not quite touching, looking through the waterfall.

At first, Ivy itched to speak. To say something. Anything.

But she couldn't.

Back here, on the other side of a blurry world, Ivy somehow knew that to talk would break this. Would break this moment, would destroy this unexpected sanctuary.

So while at first she'd wanted to shatter the silence, to pop the bubble of this special place, in the end she couldn't.

All she could do was sit here, and breathe in the scent of ferns and moss, and lick drops of water from her lips.

She'd propped her hands behind her, to balance herself on the rocks. Angus had done the same, but now he twisted slightly. Ivy turned to look at him, and his gaze locked with hers.

The light was different back here, and his eyes seemed different too. The flecks of green more emerald, the hazel base more gold.

As he looked at her he reached across his body, and skimmed the side of her thigh with his fingertips. His touch was impossibly, tinglingly light—and then it was gone.

There wasn't so much a question in his gaze. It was more he was simply waiting.

Because he knew, as she knew, where this was going to end.

But he needed to wait, because Ivy needed to wait.

Ivy needed to hold onto whatever tatty remnants of control she might still have when it came to Angus for as long as possible. He'd said, last night, that she couldn't control him.

Well, she couldn't control anything around Angus.

And now, just like last night, she really didn't want to. Despite everything.

She let go of a breath she'd been unaware she was holding, and something in Angus's expression shifted.

His gaze dropped to her lips, and his hand went back to her thigh.

But again, his touch was light.

Ivy didn't move. She couldn't really, without the possibility of sliding back into the pool. But again, she really didn't want to.

Her gaze followed the trail of his fingers.

Along the outside edge of her thigh, leaving a smattering of goose bumps.

Up, over her hip, and around the knot on the side of her bikini bottoms.

She was leaning back against her hands, so she was looking down her own body as his hand slid from her hip to lie, momentarily, flat against her belly.

Her gaze darted to his face, but his attention remained on her stomach, his expression unreadable.

Then he was on the move again, moving even more slowly now, tracing loops and circles along her ribs, beneath her breasts.

Her breath was coming more quickly now; she could see her chest rising up and down as warmth and need swirled within her.

Then, too quickly, his fingers moved up and over her bikini top, only brushing the swell of her breasts with the most frustratingly light movement.

But she couldn't protest, because words would end this.

Ivy didn't ever want this to end.

Everything she had was focused on his touch. Her eyes fluttered shut.

Over her collarbone. Across her shoulders. Up against the delicate, shivery cords of her neck.

Along her jaw, tilting her chin. Slowly, slowly, upwards.

His breath against her mouth. His hand sliding backwards and amongst her tangled hair.

Then, finally, his lips on her lips. His mouth on her mouth.

Cool, and firm, and tasting of the waterfall. Fresh, and perfect, and magical.

It was the most tantalising of any of their kisses. The most delicate, the most careful, the least carnal.

But it fitted this place.

And Ivy was lost amongst their kiss. She touched him only with her mouth but it was more than enough. She kissed him slowly, he kissed her leisurely, as if they had for ever.

Here, it felt as if they did.

Then a splash tore them apart.

A blokey laugh and then a yell: *'Cannonball!'*

Through the waterfall heads bobbed in the water, and then a shape flew through the air.

Another splash. More laughter.

They had company.

Angus was already on the move, and he turned to offer her his hand.

She shook her head, and smiled. 'No, I've got this.'

As she swam towards the boardwalk, Ivy knew that now was about when she should be feeling that familiar cloak of regret.

But she didn't.

She couldn't.

Angus did help her climb up the ladder, and gave her hand a little tug when she stood on the boardwalk, to pull her close so he could kiss her quickly—but firmly—on the lips.

Ivy knew what that was.

A promise.

And she shivered, despite the heat of the sun.

CHAPTER NINE

IVY FELL ASLEEP on the drive back to the homestead.

A combination of hours in the sun and early pregnancy fatigue.

And also, probably, that delicious lethargy from being so very thoroughly kissed.

She dreamed of that kiss, and of that place behind the waterfall.

When Angus shook her gently awake after he'd brought the car to a stop, it felt only natural to reach for him. To curl her hands behind his neck and to pull his lips down to hers.

But this was a totally different kiss from before.

This kiss wasn't slow, or gentle or restrained.

And neither was Angus.

There was a *click* as he released her seat belt, and then he was pulling her towards him, and then on top of him as he leant back in the driver's seat. Ivy smiled as she straddled him, rising up on her knees so she could reach his mouth.

His hands slid up to grip her butt, and then one slid upwards to reach beneath her top.

She still wore her bikini, dry now after the walk back from Fern Pool. It only took one tug on the string at the back to loosen the top half, and Angus just shoved the fabric away as he filled his hands with her breasts.

Ivy sighed into his mouth.

Their kiss before had been unforgettable, but this—this rawness, this lack of restraint—she *needed*.

And that need superseded any other emotion that did

its best to wave manically at Ivy from somewhere within her subconscious.

Because frankly Ivy knew that this was a bad idea.

The same way it had been a bad idea in Bali, and it had been a bad idea last night.

But that hadn't been enough to stop her then, and it certainly wasn't going to stop her now.

She needed this. Her structured, controlled, *planned* life had plummeted into a chaos that she had no idea how to fix. Maybe she couldn't fix it, and if she thought about that too long it terrified her.

But *this* felt good. *This,* at this moment, felt right.

Even if it wouldn't feel right tomorrow.

It didn't matter.

Angus's lips coasted along her jaw, pressing hard kisses along her neck.

'You good?' he said, deep and low, against her ear.

She nodded firmly *yes*. And as if that might not be clear enough, she said it aloud, too.

She felt his smile against her skin.

Ivy's hands had shoved his T-shirt up as much as was possible, her fingernails grazing his chest and those lovely muscles of his stomach, before she explored lower, sliding just beneath the top of his shorts.

Then Angus pushed her top up, and his mouth quickly covered her nipple, and Ivy went perfectly still.

His tongue was hot, gentle, rough, all at once. He took his time, licking, kissing—waiting for her reaction before doing again what made her sigh.

His big hands were flat on her back, holding her still. She sank down onto him as her head fell backwards, loving the feel of his hardness beneath her.

She impatiently shifted her hips, and Angus used his teeth, so, so gently, against her breast. *Later.*

But it already felt as if she'd been waiting far too long.

Since the waterfall. Since Bali.

Her hands had lain, useless and forgotten, on her lap, but now she put them to use, feeling for the snap closure on his shorts, as his head and shoulders blocked her view.

For a moment, she did go still, though. To watch him kiss her breasts. She had the same realisation every time she was close to him: he was *so* big, *so* broad, *so* overwhelming.

But right now, so careful. So focused.

On her.

It was a heady sensation. Sexy.

And she didn't just get to look at him, she got to feel him. Got to explore his strength, and experience how incredible all that controlled, amazing, coiled strength made her feel.

Finally she pulled the snap open, and it was easy to rip apart the Velcro fly on the board shorts.

He wore nothing beneath, and she shimmied backwards on his thighs so she could see what she'd just revealed.

Angus leaned back against the chair, and then, with a cheeky grin, reached down to adjust the chair so he reclined back further.

He looked so pleased with himself, Ivy grinned back, but then he reached for the button of her own shorts, and she formed her lips into a stern line.

Later.

She gripped his length in her hand, running her fingers from base to tip.

His breath had quickened, and he studied her from beneath half-lidded eyes.

She moved her hand again, enjoying the feel of him, the warmth and the sensation that he was growing even harder as she touched him.

'Ivy.'

The roughly spoken word dragged her attention back to his lips. She rose to her knees, desperately needing to kiss him again.

And when they did kiss, it was rough and messy and desperate.

Between them they unzipped her shorts, and somehow she managed to wiggle her way out of them, along with her bikini bottoms, twisting this way and that on Angus's lap.

'You're killing me here, Ivy.'

But finally she was free to straddle him again, and his hands cupped bare skin, gliding around to slide through her wetness, and to circle her where she needed it most.

She groaned, and kissed him again. Hard.

She reached for him, but then his lips were at her ear.

'I'm clean. There's been no one else since Bali.'

It shouldn't have been the perfect thing to say, but somehow it was. 'Me too,' she whispered.

And then she couldn't wait even a moment longer.

She wrapped her hand around him again, then slid, not slowly at all, downwards.

She sucked in a breath, the sensation of having him inside her, stretching her, filling her, almost *too* good.

But then she moved, and that was even better.

His fingers gripped her bottom, but she didn't need him to guide her. They fell instantly into the perfect rhythm, and his mouth found hers, kissing her again and again.

And the tension built inside her, growing and tightening low in her belly with every stroke and slide and sigh.

Then his clever fingers touched her where they were joined, and that was all it took to push her over an edge she'd felt she'd been teetering on for ever.

And fall she did, into wave after wave of sensation.

Then Angus was moving her hips harder, and faster, and the waves just kept on coming, overwhelming her in a way she'd never, ever experienced.

Then he was groaning into her ear, and finally, finally Ivy began to float back down to earth.

She lay there, sprawled on top of him, the four-wheel drive loud with their heavy, laboured breathing.

'Would it be wrong if I asked you to carry me inside again?' Ivy asked.

Her legs felt as substantial as fairy floss.

She sensed his smile, even though her face was pressed against his chest. 'No problem, just give me a minute. Right now, I just about need someone to carry me.'

And Ivy just smiled against his still-heated skin.

'So I have a theory,' Ivy said, a few hours later.

On Ivy's king-size bed, Angus rolled onto his side to face her. She stood in the en-suite doorway, wrapped in a pure white bathrobe, and with a towel twisted around her hair.

'Yeah?'

She nodded. 'A theory that makes this weekend okay.'

'This weekend is better than okay, Ivy.'

She narrowed her cool blue eyes. 'You know what I mean.'

She crossed the wide floorboards to perch primly on the edge of the bed. Angus sat up, the sheet puddled around his waist.

'Well, my theory is that you'd already seen me naked in Bali, so it isn't like this weekend makes any difference.'

'Because I would've been thinking of you naked whenever I saw you to pick up or drop off our kid, anyway.'

'No!' she said, swatting at his legs beneath the sheets. Then, 'Really?'

He shrugged. 'Of course. On the plus side, now I can imagine you in daylight.'

Ivy flopped onto her back on the bed and stared up at the ceiling. 'Oh, no.'

Angus grinned. 'Look, we both knew in Bali that we were just having fun. We both know now that we're just having fun. I'm sure we're both mature enough to behave like grown-ups in the future.'

'Except for the imagining me naked bit.'

'If it makes you feel better, I don't mind if you imagine me naked, too.'

Ivy tilted her head to glare at him.

'Do you want to hear my theory?' Angus said.

'Only if it doesn't involve nudity.'

'Done,' he said. He reached for the tie of Ivy's bathrobe, and tugged it open, just because he could. Ivy watched him, but didn't move, the hint of a smile on her lips. The terry towelling of the robe didn't move a lot, but it did reveal a lovely slither of skin. Not enough, though. 'Okay, so my theory is that this weekend is a great idea because clearly we needed more than Bali to get this thing out of our systems. If we *hadn't* slept together again, we would've had all this unresolved tension between us. This way we clear the air.'

'So having sex now will be good for our parenting in the future.'

'Exactly.'

'You should be in the Molyneux Mining marketing department,' Ivy commented.

'*You* shouldn't be wearing so many clothes.'

He moved so he was leaning across her, one hand on either side of her face.

'Well,' she said, very softly, 'technically I'm not wearing any clothes.'

Angus reached between them, pulling her robe completely open. He levered himself upwards, to survey what he'd revealed.

'You know what?' he said, after a very long while. 'I think you're right.'

He leant down, kissing her gently before pulling away to look at her again.

'Although, maybe I'll just check one more time.'

Ivy laughed, then tugged him down for another kiss.

Angus made breakfast again the next morning.

He'd woken beside Ivy after—as standard—another excellent night's sleep.

It had been a very long time since he'd last woken up in a woman's bed. A year, at least. Maybe two.

It was a slightly uncomfortable realisation.

He'd had girlfriends, of course. Nothing too long-term—a few months, maybe.

What he'd told Ivy yesterday had been partially true. He didn't like emotional farewells.

But not because *he* found them emotional.

It was stupid really, that the tears always surprised him. There he was, thinking everything was fine, that both he and the woman he was seeing were happy casually dating. And then the tears came. The earnest requests to keep in touch whenever he could.

Yet he never felt that way. He had no problem at all leaving. And if he was honest, it was more that he didn't make time—rather than that he forgot—to reply to emails or to video call home when he could.

So those farewells simply exposed a disconnect. Between the type of relationship he wanted—with no tears and no expectations—and the starkly, starkly different relationship his girlfriends had expected.

Eventually a pattern even he couldn't fail to miss had arisen amongst his ex-girlfriends' angry, parting words.

Thoughtless. Selfish. Cold. Distant.

And he'd realised, maybe around the time that Tom had left the regiment, that it was better if he didn't do relationships at all—even the most casual. So he might go out on the occasional date. But he'd never stay the night.

No expectations. No hurt feelings. No confusion.

He'd determined he simply wasn't wired for long-term relationships. For marriage. For commitment.

But everything had changed with Ivy's pregnancy. Now he, like it or not, had a permanent commitment—to his child. He'd have a child who might, once old enough, want to come and wave goodbye. Who would expect him to email or video call and would maybe even make one of those welcome home signs to hold on his return.

He hadn't planned this, but it was his new reality.

But what if he fell into his old habits? He'd been no good at maintaining a romantic relationship—what if the same applied to his child?

He remembered how much it had hurt when his dad had chosen hours in his office over his son. He'd adored his father, and deep down he'd known he was loved. But sometimes he had felt like an afterthought. Forgotten amongst the importance of work.

He didn't want to be that type of father. It was why he'd never intended to have children, to avoid the risk altogether.

So he needed to do everything he could to prevent that happening. To prevent his child being hurt.

It was why he was so persistent that he would be part of Ivy's life. They hadn't yet talked about how they would manage their co-parenting, how they would share custody—how they'd do anything. He knew, instinctively, that Ivy wasn't ready for that discussion yet.

But what he *did* know was that he needed to do this right.

Lawyers, obviously, wouldn't work. Neither would unresolved tension with Ivy.

'Morning.'

Ivy padded into the kitchen, rubbing her eyes. She wore a pale pink singlet and neat white underwear, and Angus honestly didn't think she'd ever looked more beautiful.

She hardly looked at him as she climbed onto the bar

stool. A hand reached up to pat ineffectually at her less than sleek hair.

'I couldn't bear to look in the mirror,' she said, looking at him with a half-lidded sleepy gaze. 'But I still suspect I should apologise for the state of my hair.'

No, last night she'd been a bit too distracted after her shower to think about drying it.

'You look stunning,' he said, meaning it.

She stuck out her tongue. 'Ha-ha.' Then she grinned. 'But I forgive you, because you've made me breakfast again.'

'Pancakes, bacon, bananas and maple syrup,' he said.

'Bacon?'

'It's a taste sensation,' he said. 'Trust me.'

She raised a sceptical eyebrow, but tucked into her breakfast, none the less.

Later, she helped him load the dishwasher.

'I wouldn't have picked you as a cook,' she said.

'Don't get too excited—breakfast is my speciality.' He could've left it at that, but then found himself still talking. 'My mum was an incredible cook. I guess I picked up a few things from her. I do a mean lasagne.'

'I'd love to try it one—' Ivy began, then stopped abruptly.

She took an already clean plate to the stainless-steel bin, and scraped at it with a knife to remove non-existent scraps.

I'd love to try it one day.

The atmosphere in the kitchen had shifted.

Before it had been all light, and flirtatious, with everything they said and did touched by the afterglow of the night they'd shared.

But with that one short sentence, this wasn't the casual, one-off weekend they'd agreed to last night.

Sun still streamed through the huge sliding doors, but now it seemed *too* bright. As if it were shining a light on all that was wrong with this image, rather than all that was superficially right.

He should have returned to his own bed last night.

Maybe it was just a slip of the tongue. Maybe Ivy wanted nothing more, either.

But it had been unwise to persist with this faux cosiness, this illusion of a sexy weekend away between a loved-up couple—complete with a home-cooked breakfast.

He didn't want this.

He didn't want any of this.

But more importantly, he wasn't capable of it, either.

CHAPTER TEN

THE DRIVE TO Paraburdoo could only be described as awkward.

As was the flight home.

They spoke, but it was terribly, terribly polite.

Everything had changed so quickly. One moment all was well, and Angus had been all warm and sexy; the next it was clear—*so clear*—that it was over.

But what was *it*?

It was dangerous. As dangerous as how she'd felt when she'd woken to the smell of pancakes, or when Angus had kept touching her so subtly as they'd cleaned the kitchen. A hand on her hip, here. A deliberate brush of her fingers, there.

So, so dangerous.

She should be grateful she'd made that silly comment. And logically, she was.

She'd known that it would end, and soon. Was it wrong that she'd hoped it to last even a few hours longer? Could it really hurt if they'd pretended until they arrived back in Perth?

Or at least until they'd left the homestead?

Well, of course it could. Because what would it have achieved? Really?

A few more kisses. Maybe more, if they'd been quick.

No. Stop it.

Ivy had her hands rested neatly on her lap as she sat in the back seat of her car. It took everything she had not to twist them into knots. Because Angus sat beside her.

That had been another brilliantly awkward conversation:
'*I'll get a taxi home.*'
'*Don't be stupid. I insist.*'
'*Ivy—*'
'*Please just let me drive you home.*'
And however she'd said that last bit had finally con-
vinced him. That bothered her, too.

What had she revealed for him suddenly to agree? Why
had she even cared?

Why couldn't he have just signed the bloody contract?
Why? Why? Why?

The car rolled to a stop on a quiet, tree-lined street in
Swanbourne. Ivy didn't know what she'd expected, but the
lovely federation cottage with its neat box hedges and generous sprays of lavender was definitely not it.

'It was my mum's,' Angus said, reading her mind. 'But
I like it.'

She liked that he did, not that it mattered.

'I'd imagined something more…macho,' she said.

'And what does that mean?'

Something modern and concrete and angular?

No. That didn't fit Angus.

'I don't know,' she said. 'Maybe a log hut where you drag
the food you've hunted with your bare hands?'

Angus barked a surprised laugh, the sharp sound unexpected amongst the still-simmering tension. 'You're unique,
Ivy,' he said.

She liked that he'd said that too.

He grabbed his backpack, and climbed out of the car.

He didn't say goodbye. He didn't look back, either; he
just walked up the recycled brick path to his front door.

'We going straight to your place, Ms Molyneux?' her
driver asked, looking in his rear-view mirror.

Ivy realised she was staring at the now-closed cottage door.

She gave her head a little shake.

'Yes,' she said. 'Thank you.'

The weekend was over.

'Ivy? Are you listening?'

Ivy blinked. She was at April's place, a lovely house perched on the beach in North Cottesloe. She held a mug of hot chocolate in her hands, and she'd been watching April as she'd talked, but, as hard as she tried, she hadn't really been listening.

It was three days since she'd arrived back from Bullah Bullah Downs, and yet Angus still crowded her thoughts.

She tried to tell herself that was normal; after all, she'd never had such a casual—uh—*relationship* before, so it probably made sense that the experience would linger.

It was just that the lingering had been at *the* most inappropriate times. Like during an important conference call today when she'd completely lost her train of thought, or now—when clearly April had just told her something important.

'I'm sorry. Something's on my mind.'

'I know, I know,' April said, with the air of the long suffering, '*work*.'

Ivy opened her mouth to correct her sister, but then snapped it shut. No. It was impossible to tell April only part of the story, and she still wasn't ready.

'Well,' April said, dragging out the word theatrically, 'I know it's a bit earlier than I've always said, but Evan and I have decided to try for a baby!'

Ivy went completely still.

April was beaming. 'I know it's kind of weird to tell you—I mean, basically I'm telling you that Evan and I are having lots of unprotected sex—but, you know, I just *had* to tell somebody.'

It took some effort, but Ivy arranged her lips into a smile. 'That's brilliant, April, how exciting.'

April tilted her head, studying Ivy. 'You okay?'

Ivy nodded vigorously. 'I'm fine. And I'm *thrilled* for you.'

And she was. Just the secret that she was keeping from everyone now felt a million times larger.

'I'm going to tell Mila too. *Not* Mum though.' Her sister paused. 'I'd rather keep it a big surprise for her and tell her when we fall pregnant. She'll be over the moon!'

'You think?' Ivy asked, surprised. 'She wasn't all that maternal with us.'

They'd had a team of wonderful nannies to look after them while their mother worked her incredibly long hours. She still worked those hours, now.

'Of course. Who wouldn't want to be a grandmother?'

'I suppose,' Ivy said, but didn't really agree.

But then, her relationship with her mother had always been different from that of Mila and April. Her mother had always been tougher on her, always held her to a higher standard of achievement, always pushed her harder. Because—her mother said—*you're just like me.*

Now would be the perfect time to tell April of her pregnancy.

Right *now*.

Because now she didn't just feel as if she were omitting something, she felt as if she was outright lying.

But April would shriek with excitement and ask a million questions and be all joyful and just plain *happy*, and she wouldn't understand when Ivy tried to explain why she was so damn terrified about it all. So. Now wasn't the right time.

But she did have to tell her. And Mila, and her mother.

Soon. Very soon, because she couldn't keep hoping she'd miraculously come up with a better plan.

It wasn't going to happen.

And as nice as it would be to tell only April and Mila, and to bask in their excitement before they started to connect the dots and work out what it actually meant for Molyneux Mining, the better way was to tell them all together.

Because her mother would connect the dots immediately. She'd leap right to the point, because that was what she did. As in business, it would be better that way.

April had left the room, and came back now with a small pile of pregnancy magazines, which she placed carefully on the coffee table in front of Ivy.

'Look, I know this is totally jumping the gun, but honestly, I don't know *anything*, and none of my friends have had kids yet, and...'

Yes. She'd tell them all at dinner on Sunday.

That evening, Angus pushed the buzzer on the stainless-steel panel bolted to Ivy's limestone fence, and waited.

After a minute, Ivy's voice came through the speaker. 'Yes?'

'It's Angus,' he said.

He'd then fully expected to have to explain why he was here, but instead the gate immediately began to open.

Surprised, he climbed back into his car, and drove up the neat driveway.

Ivy stood with her arms folded at the base of the steps that led to her front door, dressed in jeans and a loose T-shirt, waiting for him.

He jumped out of his car, and slammed the door behind him. 'I expected that to be more difficult.'

'I expect that people call before visiting,' Ivy said, one eyebrow raised. Her hair was loose, and a few tendrils blew across her cheeks in the evening breeze.

He shrugged. 'I was concerned that warning you may have resulted in another contract on arrival.'

'I let you in because I didn't want you to pull another stunt like at the airport.'

Angus grinned. 'I like that. Now I'm a stuntman, *and* a soldier.'

Ivy rolled her eyes, but his comment had the desired effect as she couldn't hide a subtle smile. 'I suppose you want to come in?'

'Up to you,' he said. 'I'm mainly here for a delivery.'

He held out a small brown paper bag.

Now he'd intrigued her. 'For me?'

'Don't get too excited.'

She took the bag, and he could see her warring with her inherent politeness.

'It's dark,' she said, eventually. 'Come inside, I'll open it in there.'

He followed her into the house. They walked past a broad, curving staircase and elaborate leadlight doors to the open-plan kitchen and living area.

While the kitchen was modern, the house seemed to have retained most of its original features—with detailed ceiling mouldings, a high plate rail on the walls and wide polished jarrah floorboards. The furniture was a mix of old and new, and it felt as if Ivy had decorated it, rather than some fancy interior designer.

He liked it, and he told her so.

Ivy smiled. 'Thanks. I used to walk past this house on the way to school. I always wanted to live here when I was a kid. I thought it was magical with all its arches and curves, and the Juliet balcony upstairs. My mum bought it for me after...' Her words trailed off as she walked over to the fridge. 'Would you like a drink?'

'That's quite a gift.'

'Well,' Ivy said, 'at the time my mum wanted to make quite the gesture.'

'About what?'

Ivy held open the fridge door and pointed at the shelves.
'Juice? Wine? Beer? Water?'

'Beer,' he said. He hadn't planned to stay, but now he
couldn't remember why.

He watched her as she carried the beer to the bench, and
then located a bottle opener in her cutlery draw.

Her jeans were faded and loose, as if they were her old
favourites—and he imagined her taking off her tailored
work clothes to slide into them.

Which wasn't the greatest idea.

He immediately wondered if she'd worn the same style
of underwear today as she'd worn in the Pilbara: plain and
simple but incredibly—incredibly—sexy. Or if she'd worn a
skirt to work today like the one she'd worn when they'd had
lunch. Prim, and fitted and—yep—incredibly sexy as well.

'Let's just say,' Ivy said, 'that my mother was keen to
end what she considered my *rebellious* phase.'

It took him a moment to remember what they'd been
talking about.

'Aren't you going to ask me when *I* was ever rebellious?'
she prompted.

He shook his head. 'It doesn't surprise me at all.'

Ivy pushed the now-opened bottle across the kitchen
bench towards him. She leant one hip against the granite,
a glass of juice in her hand.

'Really?' she said, and seemed pleased. 'I don't think
anyone has ever thought me capable of being a rebel.'

'But you just said you were.'

This wasn't making a lot of sense.

Her gaze darted downwards, as if she now found her
juice endlessly fascinating. 'I wasn't, not really.'

'Just enough for your mum to buy you a house so you'd
stop being one.'

'No, it wasn't like that,' Ivy said to the flecks of stone
in the bench top. 'I mean, yes, I did say that, but...' Then

she looked up and caught Angus's gaze. 'Really, it doesn't matter, does it? My mum bought me a house, which probably fits every spoilt-little-rich-girl stereotype ever, and that's the end of it.'

She'd left the bag he'd handed her on the corner of the bench, near where Angus stood, and now she strode over to pick it up, clearly hoping to change the subject.

Her movements were rushed and awkward, and it took some effort for Angus not to reach out for her—but to do what, he wasn't sure.

'Ivy, you go after what you want, and what you think is right,' Angus said, deciding if he couldn't reassure with his touch, he'd try something else. 'I might not always agree with you, but I can still respect your drive, your focus. So yes, if what you wanted wasn't the "right" thing to do, I have no trouble imagining you rebelling.'

Ivy studied him for a moment, with wariness in her eyes—as if waiting for a punchline.

But after a while, her lips curved into half a smile. 'Thank you,' she said. 'That was a nice thing to say.'

'And for what it's worth,' he added, 'I don't think anything about you is stereotypical. Of anything, or anyone.'

Her smile broadened. 'Are you saying I'm a bit weird?'

He grinned, too. 'You know I'm not.'

Her gaze dropped again.

He tapped at the bag she was still holding. 'Can you hurry up and have a look?'

When she looked up her gaze was teasing again. 'Goodness, you're pushy!'

'You're surprised?'

Then she laughed, and it was as if all that awkwardness—and whatever it was she'd almost told him—had never happened.

She dumped the contents of the bag onto the bench.

A couple of thick, glossy booklets; an application form; and a few other bits and pieces he'd printed off the Internet.

'A learner's permit application?' Ivy asked, picking up the offending piece of paper as if it had a disease. 'Why would you think I'd want this?'

'Because I think it's crazy that a woman your age, in a city like Perth with less than stellar public transport, *doesn't* have a licence.'

Ivy shrugged. 'I'm not going to get a licence just to make you feel better.'

'No, although I'm surprised you'd be comfortable being the only mum in your mothers' group being dropped off with bub in a limo. Now, *then* you'd be fitting every spoilt-little-rich-girl stereotype in the book.'

Her eyes narrowed. 'Did you come across mothers' groups in all your researching?'

No, actually. Tom had told him, years ago, after a 'swarm of babies' had descended on his home a few months after he'd had his first.

'I can come up with other similarly awkward scenarios, especially as our baby grows up. I don't know about you, but I would've hated being dropped off at footy training in the family Rolls Royce with a driver in a silly hat in the front seat.'

'I don't own a Rolls, or a silly hat for my driver to wear,' Ivy said, but the bite had gone from her words.

'I've hit a nerve?'

Ivy ran her hands through her hair, absently piling it up on top of her head before letting it tumble back down to her shoulders. 'You can be very annoying, you know that?' she said, then sighed. 'I used to get crap at school because I had a driver drop me off, not my mum. Everyone thought I was a snob—which is saying something given I went to a very posh school. My sisters were good at dealing with that sort of teasing, but I was just rubbish at it. I tend to think of clever things to say half an hour after it would've been useful.' She looked down at her tummy. 'What if this little bub takes after me in that way, and not you?'

'True,' he said, with a completely straight face, 'that would be tragic.'

Ivy reached out to gently shove him on the shoulder. 'Ha-ha. Let me guess—you were the most popular boy in school?'

'Close,' he said. 'Maybe third most popular is more accurate.'

He was only partly teasing. School had been a lot of fun for him—until his father's sudden death had ripped it all away.

Ivy was looking at him curiously. 'You okay?'

Angus deliberately smiled, annoyed that he'd revealed something in his expression.

'Of course. So—you're going to get your licence, then?'

Slowly, Ivy nodded. 'Yeah,' she said. 'It would seem so.'

'Great!' he said, with a little more enthusiasm than was necessary. 'I'll come over on Sunday for your first lesson.'

'Pardon me?'

Angus took a long sip of his beer. 'I'll teach you,' he said. 'We still have a lot to work out before the baby arrives—and we'll need to come to some sort of parenting arrangement so access, financial issues and so on are clear between us. And I still think it's important we continue to get to know each other better.' He paused, then added, 'Clothed.'

As he'd intended, Ivy blushed a deep scarlet.

'Are you sure that's the best idea?' she asked. 'We can have those discussions in a meeting room at the Molyneux Tower. Or my lawyer's office. Keep it more formal. And surely they can wait a few months, anyway?'

'I can't see any benefit in a delay,' Angus said. 'Especially as I could be deployed at any time once I return to work.' He raised an eyebrow. 'But what are you worried about? Am I that irresistible?'

Ivy glared at him. 'I know that *I'm* clear that we can't… um—'

'Have sex?' he prompted helpfully.

'Yes,' she said. 'We can't do that again. It's too complicated.'

'Agreed,' he said.

But still it took some effort to leave his half-drunk beer with a comment that he needed to drive home, and to make his exit only a few minutes later.

It would've been far too easy to stay.

CHAPTER ELEVEN

'You bought a new car?'

Angus stood in front of Ivy on her driveway, dressed in faded jeans and a T-shirt, squinting—somehow attractively—just a little in the bright early afternoon sun.

Ivy smiled, running a hand along the neat Volkswagen hatchback's glossy silver hood. 'Yes. I thought it was better to learn in a smaller car, rather than your giant four-wheel drive. Also, apparently it's better to learn to drive a manual.'

'So you bought a new car,' Angus repeated, shaking his head.

She shrugged. 'I don't think it's that big a deal.'

Ivy had embraced this 'learn to drive' project a little more zealously than was necessary, she knew. She'd read the books Angus had left her, done a couple of online mock learner's quizzes, then gone in to sit her learner's test at the local licensing centre during her lunch break the very next day.

Buying the car had been surprisingly fun. She'd never really given any car a second thought, but suddenly she was reading motoring reviews, going out for test drives with her assistant, and picking out her favourite colour.

She was enjoying the distraction; it meant she had something else to think about whenever her day wasn't wall-to-wall Molyneux Mining that wasn't her pregnancy, or Angus.

And cars were a lot less scary to think about than what on earth she was going to tell her mother and sisters that night at dinner.

Or so she'd thought.

It was one thing to agree with Angus's irritatingly accurate logic and to get her learner's permit. But quite another to actually, physically drive.

Angus theatrically opened the driver's door for her. 'After you, m'lady.'

With a deep breath, Ivy slid into her seat. Once seated and strapped in, she focused on her breathing.

One in, two out, three in, four out, five in, six out...

It was the first time in weeks she'd counted anything, although it wasn't all that surprising.

The breathing had helped when she'd first got in a car again when she was nineteen. So had the counting.

In fact, that was when the counting had started. All those years ago, as she shook with nerves in the passenger seat of her mother's car.

Seven in, eight out, nine in...

Angus was explaining something. 'So from left to right it goes clutch, brake, accelerator,' Angus said, pointing at the pedals at her feet. 'Remember it's just ABC, in reverse.'

Ivy nodded, although it was a bit difficult to focus on what he was saying beyond her mental counting.

He then talked her through how to use her mirrors, and Ivy managed to follow his instructions well enough to adjust both the rear-view and side mirrors sufficiently.

Then she fussed around quite a bit adjusting her seat.

Too far forwards. Too far back. Too far forwards again.

Seat-back was too upright. Too reclined.

Then she found she could lift the seat up and down. So she did that a bit too, the little motor whirring away as she pushed the up and down buttons.

But eventually she'd adjusted as much as was possible, so had to sit still.

'Don't be nervous,' Angus said. 'You'll be fine.'

It was lucky Ivy was wearing sunglasses, because otherwise Angus wouldn't be so sure. She'd tried this once before, years ago.

She remembered how she'd looked then, in that mirror behind the sun visor. She'd flipped it down and stared into her own eyes as she'd given herself a little lecture:

You can do this, Ivy. Everyone learns how to drive. Don't be so pathetic.

It hadn't worked then, but surely now—twelve years later—she would've got over it all?

Surely?

'Ivy?' Angus asked gently. 'Can you start the car? Foot on clutch, gear in first. The handbrake is still on, so we won't go anywhere.'

Ivy guessed he'd given her these instructions more than once, but they might as well have been gobbledegook.

Regardless, she put her left hand on the gear stick, and shoved her left foot down hard on the clutch. With a wiggle that was probably too rough, she put the car into first gear.

There.

A ghost of a smile curved her lips. *Maybe she would do it this time?*

Hand back on the wheel, she reached with her right hand for the keys.

All she had to do was twist the key forward and…

She couldn't do it.

She snatched her hand away—why she wasn't sure— and the key dropped to the ground, landing with a thud on the soft carpeted floor.

'Ivy?'

But she didn't wait; instead Ivy threw open her door and leapt from the car, running up her front steps two at a time.

At her door she realised she'd left her handbag—and house keys—in the back seat of her new car.

When she pivoted back to the car, Angus was right

there—only a metre or two away. He'd taken his sunglasses off, and concern was obvious in his gaze.

Ivy kept hers on, despite the shade of the veranda.

'You're not just nervous,' Angus said.

'No,' she said.

'And the reason you don't have a licence is nothing to do with being a spoilt little rich girl who couldn't be bothered.'

'No.'

'Can you tell me the real reason?'

No.

'I was in a car accident when I was nineteen.'

That was more than she'd told anyone, ever. More than anyone else, but her mother, knew.

Oddly, even though she hadn't meant to say the words, it felt good to say them.

'Were you hurt?'

Ivy shook her head. She didn't want to say this bit. This bit wouldn't feel good to say.

'A few bruises, a big one from the seat belt,' she said. 'But nothing, not really.'

She'd often felt it would've been better if she had been injured. A gash to her face that everyone noticed. A scar on her skin, and not just on her insides.

'You were the passenger?'

Angus had stepped closer. His hand moved, and for a second Ivy thought he was reaching for her, but then the moment was gone.

'My boyfriend was driving us home. He'd taken me to this club, a pretty seedy private one, upstairs somewhere in Northbridge. He'd been drinking, a lot, but he insisted on driving home.' Now she'd started talking, the words wouldn't stop. 'I'd only been seeing him for a few weeks. He was really tall, with overlong brown hair and an eye-brow ring. He had tattoo sleeves up both arms, but one was only half inked in. I thought it *so* cool. I thought he was *so* cool. He wasn't like any guy I'd met before. He wasn't rich. He wasn't poor, either, but I kind of pretended he was—like he was the kid from the wrong side of the tracks and I was the sweet rich girl he was going to corrupt.'

'He was your rebellious phase,' Angus said.

'Oh, yes,' Ivy said. 'I wanted to rebel so badly that I grabbed the first vaguely disreputable guy I could find and held on tight. We barely knew each other, really. All we did was go out drinking and clubbing. But I thought I was in love, you know? I'd spent my whole life being the perfect firstborn daughter, and now I wasn't. Although I wasn't all that brave. I told my family I was with girlfriends. So I was kind of rebelling on the sly.'

Ivy smiled without humour. She knew she was saying too much, and all jumbled in the incorrect order—but she couldn't stop.

'So Toby drove me home. I knew he'd had too much to drink, and I told him I'd call one of the family drivers to come pick us up. Or I'd pay for a taxi. And honestly, he looked at me like I'd just suggested we take ballroom-dancing classes.' She shook her head. 'I knew he shouldn't drive. I mean, I didn't even have a *sip* of alcohol until I turned eighteen. I'm that person. I'm the annoyingly sensible one. But that night I decided I wasn't. That I was cool and relaxed. But I wasn't. I couldn't relax. I basically held onto my seat for dear life, and Toby noticed, and got angry, and told me I had to trust him.' Ivy kept entwining and untwining her fingers, again and again. 'And he drove faster. And faster. And I told him not to, at first I tried to sound relaxed but then I was literally screaming at him as he thundered down the street.' A long pause. 'Then he lost control, hit a tree, and was killed instantly.'

The simple words, in a way, reflected that night. In the end, it was so simple. One moment Toby was there, beside her: loud and arrogant and drunk. Then—gone. Just like that.

'What an idiot,' Angus said.

'He paid a high price for his mistake,' Ivy pointed out.

'But he almost took you with him.'

Ivy couldn't argue with that. 'The whole driver's side of the car caved in. I had to be cut out of the wreckage, but I was okay. Totally okay. I walked away.'

That night was still mostly a blur. She'd had a few drinks herself, although she'd been far from drunk.

Her memories were more little snapshots from the night: Toby's smile when she'd walked into the bar and he'd checked out her too-short skirt; putting her mobile phone back into her bag, without making that call for a driver; the click of her seat belt when she strapped herself in; Toby's frenzied, ugly, manic expression when she'd pleaded with him to slow down, to stop, to let her out...

Then the impossible arrangement of Toby's seat and the steering wheel after impact. The feel of his pulseless wrist beneath her fingertips.

Ivy hadn't realised she'd closed her eyes until she felt her sunglasses being lifted from her face.

She blinked up at Angus. He was very close, but not touching her.

'But you weren't okay,' Angus said. 'No one is okay after something like that.'

Ivy bit her lip, and ignored him. 'When the police arrived, they found drugs in the car. I was so stupid and naïve I'd had no idea. I didn't even know what drugs they were. I still don't. And the worst bit is that even if I had known, I was so caught up in Toby and his tattoos and being an edgier version of myself it probably would've only added to Toby's mystique. The police questioned me at the hospital, but then my mum arrived, and it all went away.'

'What does that mean?' he asked. He still stood close. Too close, probably, but Ivy didn't mind. It helped, actually.

'It means what I said. My mum made it all go away. I don't know what she did. I didn't ask. Maybe I wouldn't have been in trouble, anyway? Who knows? All I know is that when I went home, my sisters didn't know I'd been in a car accident. When I read about the crash in the papers the next day, there was no mention of me. It's like I was erased from the whole incident.' She paused, thinking. 'It wouldn't be all that hard. I know the right people to call, now, should I want a story pulled. For Molyneux Mining, it's important to have a close relationship with the media. Bad publicity can be so damaging.'

'But what about the damage to a teenager?' Angus asked, his words harsh.

Ivy had been staring at the print on the front of his T-shirt, but now her gaze shot up to meet with his. 'I would've been a lot more damaged if the story had got out,' she said. 'It would've followed me for ever. It was difficult at the time, but I'm grateful for what my mum did. It turned me around, set me back on track.'

'On track to take over Molyneux Mining next year.'

Ivy nodded sharply. 'Yes.'

'And you never made another mistake again.'

'Yes,' Ivy said, automatically. 'I mean, no, of course I've made mistakes. I make mistakes all the time.'

'But nothing big. Nothing that would ever have anyone question Ivy Molyneux's competence, or business sense, or suitability to take over the company.'

'No one would *dare* do that,' Ivy said, getting annoyed. 'I would never do *anything* to jeopardise Molyneux Mining. I learnt my lesson.'

Angus studied her, his gaze tracing her eyes, nose and lips, then returning to meet her gaze. 'I get it now,' he said.

'The marriage proposal, the contract. Your rabid need to fix everything, to control everything.'

Ivy bristled, but he didn't let her speak.

'It's because you actually think it's possible, don't you? That you can do what your mother did all those years ago, and sweep it up—make everything uncomfortable, messy and awkward just disappear. Just go away without any consequences.'

'It is possible,' Ivy said, stubborn enough to argue. 'And there are *always* consequences. Like how I can't drive.'

That poor attempt at a joke received only a look of derision.

'It's about minimising damage,' she continued. 'About controlling the...'

But she heard what she was saying and knew she was going around in circles.

Suddenly she *was* standing too close to Angus. She stepped around him, intended to go and get her bag out of the car. There wasn't going to be a driving lesson today.

She should get inside. Get some work done.

But Angus grabbed her hand.

Ivy spun around to face him, snatching her hand away. 'But *you* won't go away, will you?' she said. 'No matter how I ask you, or what I say, or what I offer...'

'No,' he said.

One simple word, but it made her want to scream.

But scream at what?

That, as he'd told her before, she couldn't control him?

Or scream at the fact that she didn't really want him to go away at all?

Ivy's shoulders slumped.

She couldn't pretend any more. She wasn't miraculously going to come up with a plan. She wasn't going to fix this. This wasn't going to go away.

'I'm telling my family tonight,' she said, very quietly.

'I'll come with you.'

'I didn't ask you to come,' she said.

'You never would,' he said, stepping closer to her again. 'But I'd like to be there. Maybe it would help.'

Ivy was absolutely sure it wouldn't. He would only complicate the most complicated of situations.

And yet…

'Okay,' she said.

She'd told herself she didn't want him to come, but couldn't quite make herself believe it.

He took another step closer, and she tilted her chin upwards. Then, before she really knew what was happening, he kissed her.

A soft kiss, a gentle kiss.

'It'll be okay,' he said, against her lips.

She stood stock-still as he skirted around her and walked to his car.

'What time should I pick you up?' he asked.

'Six-thirty,' she said.

And then he was gone.

Of course, it wasn't a surprise that Ivy's mother lived in a palatial mansion. Angus had expected nothing less.

The dining room was very grand. The table was long enough to allow space for two chandeliers above it, and the table was set like something from a magazine, with white flowers everywhere.

Ivy's sisters sat at the table. The pair had been chattering loudly as they'd walked into the room, but when they saw him they instantly fell silent.

Through another door, Ivy's mother entered the room with a bottle of champagne.

'Oh,' she said, her gaze flicking over him. 'I'd better get another table setting.'

Then she turned on her heel, and walked out.

Ivy was incredibly tense beside him. Very, very softly, she was counting under her breath.

His instinct was to put his arm around her, but he knew that wouldn't help.

Although, in fact, his true instinct was not to be here at all.

He hadn't done this before—this 'meeting the family' thing. So far, he wasn't much of a fan.

'Thirty-seven...thirty-eight...'

He reached out and wrapped his hand around Ivy's.

Maybe it wouldn't help, but maybe it would.

Ivy glanced up at him, and attempted a smile.

There was a clink and clatter at the table as Ivy's mum returned and set a place for Angus.

She walked to him, holding out her hand. 'I'm Irene.'

He needed to drop Ivy's hand to shake Irene's, and instantly Ivy stepped away. She rushed to the table, and dropped into her seat as if they'd been playing musical chairs.

'Angus Barlow,' he said.

Irene's handshake was firm, but that was no surprise. She studied him with care, distrust flickering in her blue eyes.

This also was no surprise. He'd bet his house that Ivy hadn't brought another man to Sunday dinner before.

A minute later they were all seated. Irene's personal chef came out to talk them through the upcoming courses, and shortly afterwards their entrées arrived. A tiny stack of vegetables and salmon, with a sauce smeared theatrically across the plate.

April and Mila remained silent, seated across from them, as if waiting for Ivy to speak. They snuck curious glances in his direction, and the tiniest of encouraging smiles.

Irene sat at the head of the table, to Angus's right. Her lips were formed into a perfectly flat line.

But she was waiting, too.

No one touched their cutlery. No one picked up their glass of champagne.

And the tension just continued, and continued to build.

Ivy took a long, deep breath.

Then she shifted in her chair so that she faced her mother.

Another long, deep breath.

'I'm pregnant,' she said.

Silence.

'I'm the father,' Angus said, because he couldn't let Ivy do this alone.

But Irene didn't pay any attention to him. Instead she surged from her seat and went to one of the room's huge windows, staring out into the night.

'Oh, my *God*!' April shrieked, clapping her hands together. 'Ivy! That's amazing! Congratulations!'

Ivy picked up her water glass, then put it back down again, untouched.

Mila's reaction was more subdued. Her gaze flicked between Angus and Ivy. 'Was this planned?'

Ivy shook her head, but didn't seem capable of speech.

'No,' Angus said, unnecessarily, but needing to say something.

'You kept *this* on the down low, Ivy,' April said, indicating the two of them—and seemingly oblivious to Ivy's discomfort. 'When did you start going out?' She paused, then laughed. 'Goodness, I was so distracted at the wedding I didn't notice *anything* between you. Can you believe it?'

April turned to her younger sister, but Mila was watching Ivy.

'We're not—' Ivy began.

'Going to bore you all with how we met,' Angus finished for her.

Ivy's eyes widened in surprise, but she didn't correct him.

'What will you do next year?' Mila asked, and at her question Irene turned from the window, crossing her arms in front of her chest.

'Yes,' the older woman said, her gaze steely. 'What are we going to do?'

Not 'you', but 'we'.

'Well,' Ivy said, 'around about July, *I'll* be having a baby.'

There. There was a bit of the bite and sass he was used to.

'Don't be facetious, Ivy,' Irene said. 'I think you understand what is at stake here.'

'Of course I understand what's at stake here, Mum,' Ivy said. She pushed back her chair, and stood up, gripping the edge of the table. 'I'd like to negotiate a period of maternity leave, and a delay to me taking over your position. I do apologise for that, but it's unavoidable.'

'Unavoidable?' Irene zeroed in on Angus now. 'I have no idea who you are, but I'm sure you've heard of condoms?'

April and Mila both looked mildly scandalised that their mother had said *condoms*.

Angus leant back in his chair, deliberately relaxing his body, knowing that would infuriate Irene. He shrugged. 'Accidents happen.'

'They do,' Ivy said. 'Everyone makes mistakes sometimes.'

She glanced down at him, her lips shaping into the tiniest hint of a smile.

'This isn't just a *mistake*, Ivy! Your *recklessness* has ramifications for the entire company. I don't think you do fully understand the gravity of the situation, and frankly I'm disappointed that you don't. I—'

'Mum,' Ivy said, cutting her off. 'I think you need time

to digest this news. I think we should go. I'll see you at the office, tomorrow.'

This was Angus's cue. He casually rose to his feet, then took his time saying goodbye to Ivy's sisters.

They didn't rush as they left the house. Ivy just walked with purpose, without saying a word, until they stepped out onto the terraced entrance to the Molyneux mansion.

The heavy door clicked shut behind them.

'Ivy—'

But then Ivy halted his words with her lips.

She kissed him as she hadn't kissed him before. It was more intense, more thorough—more *confident*.

She wrapped her hands behind his neck, tugging him as close as possible. Her body was plastered against his, chest to breast, hip to hip.

She kissed him, and he kissed her, until they were both breathing heavily, until Angus *needed* to drag her to the car, and then home, as quickly as possible.

But then Ivy took a step back, and ran her hands through her hair.

'Wow,' she said. 'I haven't pashed a boy on my mum's front doorstep before.'

Angus laughed. 'I always knew you were a rebel.'

CHAPTER TWELVE

Ivy wasn't sure how she felt.

She wasn't sure how she was supposed to feel.

She hadn't expected to feel like this.

She felt...

Okay, mostly.

Not great. But okay. She'd spent so much time imagining what it would be like to tell her mother about her pregnancy that she hadn't really thought about what would happen *after*.

But she'd known it would be bad.

But it wasn't. It was...okay.

Ivy leant back against the headrest as Angus drove her home.

'I'm starving,' she said. 'I can order some takeaway when we get home if you like?'

The question sounded like something she'd say if she and Angus were the couple he'd implied they were, and inwardly Ivy cringed a little.

But although Angus slanted a look in her direction, he nodded.

'You're not going to faint on me before then?' he asked.

She smiled. 'No. I had a pretty good idea we wouldn't be eating dinner at my mum's, so I had a snack before we left.'

A fortifying most of a block of chocolate, actually.

But by the time Angus stopped the car at her place, the atmosphere between them had shifted.

At her mother's house, it had seemed almost like they

were a team—banded together against anything her mum could throw at them.

Afterwards, she hadn't thought twice when she'd flung herself into Angus's arms. It had just been the right thing to do, her way of releasing some of that tension. And, *wow*, it had felt good.

But really, her pregnancy announcement hadn't solved anything. She was over the first hurdle, but there were a whole crap load of hurdles still to come.

It had felt like a victory, but really it wasn't. Her bravado had been false.

Kind of like she and Angus were a team—but really, they weren't.

At the front door, in the pool of porch light, she paused as she fished for her keys in her bag.

'Why did you let my family think we were a couple?' she asked. She sounded more defensive than she'd intended.

'I figured it was one less thing you had to deal with tonight,' he said.

'Okay,' she said. 'But what happens now?'

'Nothing happens,' he said. 'One day you'll just tell them we've broken up.'

He made it sound so easy.

She'd found her keys, and stabbed at the lock, taking a couple of goes before the key slid in.

Then she shoved the door open, her movements stiff.

'Isn't that what you wanted?' Angus said, remaining on the porch while she stepped inside. 'Even right at the beginning? A fake boyfriend, to avoid the so-called scandal?'

Ivy wasn't sure why she was angry, but she definitely was.

'A fake boyfriend who kisses me sometimes,' she said.

'You kissed me, tonight.'

'I know,' she said, with a sigh. 'This is confusing.'

'Ivy, I can't offer you any more than—'

She held up her hands, her cheeks turning pink. '*No*. Stop. I don't want this either, so no need to let me down gently.'

No. She'd made this mistake before, with Toby—getting caught up in attraction and hormones. Letting her emotions lead her, rather than logic and common sense. A relationship with Angus was not a good idea. The way she lost control around him... No. She couldn't risk losing herself in some crazy idea about love, again.

But still...even if allowing anything serious—if allowing the hint of love—was not acceptable, maybe there was still an alternative?

'Maybe what I want,' Ivy began, searching for what she was trying to say, 'is a fake boyfriend, with benefits.'

A way to, once and for all, sate this *thing* between them. To get it over with. But with no false expectations. No risk.

There was a long, long pause.

'A fake girlfriend, with benefits,' Angus said, as if testing the concept out on his tongue. His grin was wicked. 'I think I can work with that.'

This time, Angus kissed her.

And Ivy kissed him right back.

For the first time in as long as she could remember, Ivy was late to work on Monday. She'd had no excuse—Angus had left before dawn for the barracks as he was back at work now that his wrist was fully healed. He'd woken her when he'd left, and kissed her gently on the forehead.

Not long after, her alarm had gone off.

But she hadn't been ready to get up yet, so she simply hadn't. She'd curled up beneath her doona and fallen asleep to the vague idea that she should probably reset her alarm— and fortunately the arrival of her driver at seven-thirty had later served as a sufficient alarm replacement.

In the end, she wasn't that late, not really. It wasn't even nine a.m., but even so her staff seemed not quite to know what to do with her.

Ivy didn't know quite what to do, either.

She wasn't as bothered by her lateness as she would've liked, which concerned her a little.

But then, today she was doing all sorts of unfamiliar things—confronting her mother being number one on that list. So yes, maybe tardiness was the least of her worries.

Later that morning, Ivy took the lift to her mother's office.

It was on the very top floor, a floor above Ivy's offices, and was a hive of activity. Ivy weaved her way past the network of open-plan workstations and glass-walled meeting rooms to reach Irene's suite, separated from the rest of the floor by heavy, jarrah doors.

But her mother's assistant looked confused by Ivy's appearance.

'I have a meeting booked with Irene,' Ivy said.

Theresa shook her head. 'No,' she said, 'Irene has cancelled all her meetings for the rest of the week. She's flown to a conference in Berlin.'

'Oh,' said Ivy. 'Of course!' She shook her head, as if she'd just made a silly mistake.

But this had never happened before.

Ivy would never have described her relationship with her mother as perfect.

For all they were the same, they were also very different—despite her mother's insistence that Ivy was just like her.

But in business, they *were* in sync. Together they'd run Molyneux Mining for nearly a decade, with Ivy's role growing year by year.

The conference in Berlin did exist, but they'd decided, together, that another senior executive could attend in their place.

Irene's sudden change of mind was not a business decision.

It was extremely personal.

For all her bravado last night in the face of her mother's disappointment, it had been incredibly hard for Ivy.

But, she realised now, some part of her had hoped for something different today. That after a night to sleep on Ivy's revelation, Irene's reaction would be different.

After all, Irene had three children—*surely* she should understand?

Surely some part of her would be excited to meet her first grandchild? Just as April had said?

But no.

Ivy had, for the first time in her life, put her own needs ahead of Molyneux Mining.

Her mother didn't like it. She would never like it.

And that hurt.

'You're counting again,' Angus said.

Ivy's gaze shot up to tangle with his, her lips now pressed firmly together.

Then she sighed. 'I do that sometimes. Despite my best efforts.'

They walked together from the car park to the front of the nursing home.

'Nerves,' she continued. 'Stupid nerves. I used to do it all the time, and I thought I'd grown out of it, but apparently not.' A pause, then a pointed look. 'I blame you.'

'Me?' he asked, innocently. 'I don't make you nervous. Hot and bothered, maybe?'

She glared at him.

'But you don't need to be nervous tonight. My mum will love you.'

'And that's the problem,' she said. 'I always *know* I shouldn't be nervous. That's the frustrating thing.'

They stood outside the glass door of Reception. Ivy rolled her shoulders a few times, and took a deep breath.

She was still dressed for work, in fitted trousers and a spotted silky blouse.

Angus leant close. 'You look gorgeous. You won't say the wrong thing. And if you do, don't worry—she probably won't remember anyway.'

Ivy's jaw dropped open. 'Isn't that in terribly bad taste?'

Angus grinned. 'Trust me, my mum would've been the first to make that joke. Come on, let's do this. I *promise* my mum won't bite.'

The nursing home was a small, boutique facility, made up of a collection of detached villas and a larger single-level building for the high-dependency patients, like his mum. Once through Reception, Angus led Ivy through the communal living and dining rooms to his mum's room. It was spacious, like a generous hotel room, with a bed, a small seating area, and a separate en-suite bathroom.

His mum sat on the couch, watching the ABC news.

'Angus!' she said, smiling at him as they entered the room.

This was a good start. On the very worst days—for both of them—Angus needed to remind her who he was.

'Mum,' he said, 'this is my friend, Ivy Molyneux. Ivy, this is my mum, Hillary.'

'Nice to meet you,' Ivy said. She held out her hand, which Hillary shook firmly.

Hillary glanced between the two of them. 'And?'

'We have some news,' Angus said. 'Can we grab a drink, first?'

Soon they were all settled with cups of tea, seated around the small coffee table.

Ivy was fidgeting. Subtly—by twisting her fingers in her lap—but fidgeting none the less. It made Angus smile.

Such a powerful, polished, woman.

Yet so…*Ivy*.

'So, Mum,' Angus said. 'Ivy and I are having a baby.'

Ivy's eyes widened, as did Hillary's.

Then his mum's eyes squeezed shut. The older woman twisted to face Ivy. 'I've forgotten you, haven't I?' she said. 'I'm so sorry. I do that a lot, now.'

'Oh, no!' Ivy said. 'You haven't met me before.' When Hillary raised an eyebrow, she added, 'I promise.'

Hillary's gaze zipped back to Angus. 'I feel I've missed something here.'

Angus smiled, and then—briefly, and significantly censored—told his mother how he and Ivy had met.

She smiled, and nodded, as he spoke.

Angus was relieved. He'd asked Ivy to come tonight because when he'd called the nursing home earlier, he'd been told his mum was having a good day. But that was never a guarantee.

And it was important to him that Ivy met his mum. Stupid really, but somehow, given he was beside her when she told her family, he felt it should be the same with his.

His mum would never be as she had been—the woman who would've put Ivy instantly at ease and talked her ear off about all manner of random things.

But at least tonight she was a reasonable-strength version of his mum—not a version so diluted by dementia that he felt as if he was interacting with the disease, and not the mother he loved.

Now Hillary asked Ivy a bit about herself, but Ivy was talking too much, and over-explaining. Not Ivy's fault—he should've warned her—but he saw Hillary's eyes lose focus as all the words began to overwhelm her.

Ivy noticed too, and her sentence trickled out to nothing. She looked stricken, and Angus reached out to squeeze her hand briefly. 'You're doing good,' he said, softly.

Then he asked his mum about her day. Hillary launched

into a detailed explanation, which might have been a true reflection of today, or an amalgamation of the last week or month—or have never happened at all—but regardless, his mum was animated again, her eyes full of life.

Ivy slowly began to relax back into her chair, her tea cradled in her hands.

'How is Scott?' Hillary asked Ivy, suddenly.

Ivy's body instantly stiffened, and her gaze flicked to Angus.

'Pardon me?'

'Scott is Carise and Tom's son,' Angus said. 'This is Ivy.'

But his mum shook her head firmly. 'No, no. I remember her. Long brown hair. Pretty blue eyes. Baby boy with a pink blanket because she believed in gender neutrality in colour schemes.'

This was the frustrating, awful bit. That a snippet of conversation from years ago could be remembered, but not the person his mother was talking to right now.

Ivy leant forward, placing her teacup carefully back in its saucer. 'My name's Ivy,' she said. 'I don't have a baby yet. But when I do, we'll bring him or her to visit you.'

Another agitated shake of the head. '*No,*' Hillary said. 'I haven't forgotten. I saw the wedding photos. Your husband is very, very handsome. Almost as handsome as my son.' She paused, looking thoughtful. 'But he got sick, didn't he?' Hillary balled up her fists, rubbing them into her eyes. 'Why can't I remember?'

'Mum,' Angus said gently, 'it doesn't matter.'

His mum turned back to Ivy. 'So, Carise, how is Scott?'

Ivy sent Angus another panicked glance. 'I'm not—'

'Scott is well,' Angus interrupted. 'He's walking now! Getting into everything. Tom is having to baby proof everything.' He forced a laugh. 'I guess I'll find out all about that soon enough.'

Hillary blinked. 'What do you mean?'

Hell.

It *still* hurt, every time.

'I'm going over to help Tom out with installing latches,' Angus said, improvising.

He had, actually. Three years ago, when Scott had started walking.

His mum seemed happy with that.

She also looked tired. Impossibly tired.

For the next few minutes he filled the silence, just as he always did. With bits and pieces about work, about things that happened years ago, things that happened today.

Hillary soon finished her tea, and Angus called a nurse to help her get ready for bed.

He kissed her on the cheek, and her hand reached up to curl into his hair and pull him close, just as she always had.

'I love you,' she said into his ear, as clearly and as firmly as ever.

A few minutes later, as they stepped outside the building, Ivy once again threw herself into his arms.

But this time it wasn't a kiss. There was nothing frantic or desperate in her action.

She simply hugged him. And held him.

'Who is Scott?' Ivy asked. 'And Carise and her husband?'

She'd propped herself up against her pillows, the sheet pulled up over her legs. She wore a faded navy singlet and her underwear, while Angus wore only boxers. Tonight was the first night they'd climbed into bed even partially dressed.

It was dark in Ivy's room, the only light glowing from a bedside lamp.

'Carise is the wife of an old friend, Tom,' Angus said. 'Scott is their eldest son, although they have a daughter now, too. Maybe more.'

It had been too long since he'd been in touch. Appallingly long.

'Were they close to your mum?'

Angus shook his head. 'No. They visited once to support me. I needed someone else who'd experienced my mum like that, you know? I had no family to come with me. To talk to about how I felt. I thought maybe if...' Another shake of his head. 'A stupid idea. It didn't help.'

'What happened to Tom?' she said gently. 'Your mum said he was sick?'

There was sympathy in her eyes, and Angus realised what that meant.

'He's not dead,' he said, very quickly. 'He wasn't that type of sick. I mean, he isn't that type of sick—cancer type of sick. He had PTSD.'

'Post-traumatic stress disorder.'

'Yeah. We worked together.'

Ivy nodded her head, as if that explained everything. 'Ah. That doesn't surprise me. You must deal with such awful, awful things.'

This bothered Angus.

'Why shouldn't it surprise you?' Angus said. 'It's what we train for. It's what we're *built* for. It's what we do. Why should it be such a shock that we manage to deal with it okay?'

His words were harsh, and far louder than he'd intended.

'I didn't say that,' she said. 'I just said I'm not surprised that some soldiers are impacted by PTSD.'

'And what does that make the rest of us? Robots?'

Ivy looked taken aback. She reached out for him, but he shifted a little so her hand fell to the sheet without touching him.

He knew he was being unfair. This wasn't about Ivy and what she'd said.

It was about his guilt. For a lot of things.

He slid from the bed, the thick rug beneath Ivy's bed soft under his bare feet. Despite how little he wore, Ivy's state-of-the-art climate-control system meant he wasn't at all cold.

Even that irritated him for some reason.

'It doesn't make you a robot,' Ivy said, very softly.

He had his back to her, but he could see her in the reflection of her ornate dresser mirror. She'd pushed herself up from the pillows, as if she'd been about to follow him, but had changed her mind.

'This is what you meant,' she said, after a while. 'At the gorge. You said that maybe it should be harder for you to go back. To go to war, to leave your loved ones behind. I didn't understand at the time.'

He shook his head. 'You wouldn't understand now.'

Why had he done this? He'd only needed to tell her enough to explain who his mum had been asking about. Ivy didn't need to hear any of this. He didn't need to answer any questions to do with this.

'No,' Ivy said. 'I'd never truly understand. But I can listen to you.'

Angus still watched her in the mirror. She hadn't moved. She looked beautiful, her hair loose, her face freshly scrubbed of make-up.

And she carried his child.

The scene was so domestic. They could be a married couple, thrilled at the impending birth of their first child.

Was this what had happened to Tom? Had he started to realise how much he had, and how much he had to lose?

Angus wanted to leave. He wanted out of this room and this domesticity.

But what would that achieve? If he went home, Ivy would still be pregnant. They were tied together for ever.

'When I go away,' Angus said, 'I won't be able to tell you where I'm going. Or what I'll be doing, or when I'll be back. Sometimes I'll get no warning at all, so neither will you. Sometimes I might be able to contact you when I'm away, sometimes I won't.'

Ivy's reflection nodded.

'I'll probably miss some special occasions,' he continued. 'Like birthdays. School assemblies, that type of thing.'

'How do you feel about that?' she asked.

'Not good,' he said. 'But not bad enough to quit my job.'

Ivy's eyes widened. 'It never occurred to me that you would.'

'Really?' he said. He turned to face her now. 'You think it's normal to still want to risk my life and to want to be away from home for indefinite periods of time now that I'm going to be a father?'

'I don't think what you do is normal,' Ivy said carefully. 'But that's why people like me do jobs like mine, and people like you are in the SAS. We're lucky there are incredibly brave, strong people like you. Australia is lucky.'

'How patriotic,' Angus said, his tone completely flat.

'Hey,' Ivy said. She pushed herself onto her knees, crawling to the edge of the bed so she was close to him. 'Don't dismiss what you do. What you do is important.'

'What a lucky kid we'll have,' Angus said. 'A mum who works seventy-hour weeks and a dad disappearing for months overseas.'

'I won't be like my mum,' Ivy said. 'I *won't*.'

'I know. You'll hire the very best nannies. And I'm hardly in a position to expect you to stay at home. I—'

She'd jumped to her feet, and laid her hand flat against his chest—although her push didn't move him an inch.

'Yes, I *will* hire a nanny, but not the way you think. I've already had preliminary designs drawn up for a nursery and play room on my floor at the Molyneux Tower. That way I can spend all my breaks, and lunch, with the baby. Plus I've been reading about breastfeeding, so this way I'll

be able to continue after I return to work after six months.'
She sighed, rubbing her forehead. 'I know it's not perfect.
I've thought about maybe working part time, but I just
can't, not right now. Maybe in a few years, once the company is more established under my leadership. So you're
right, I won't win any mum of the year awards...but it's all
I can do for now. I can't give up all I've worked for—' she
snapped her fingers '—just like that.'

Her hand still rested on his chest, but it was gentle.

'I can't understand what you do,' Ivy said, 'but I *do* understand loving what you do. My sisters honestly believe
I've been somehow forced into my role at Molyneux Mining, as if Mum managed to indoctrinate me into her mining
executive regime, but it's not true. I love it. I love the challenge, the pressure, the responsibility. And maybe it makes
me selfish not to give it all up, given I don't need to work
at all. I could be a lady of leisure for every day of my life,
and still have more money than I know what to do with.'

Now she took her hand away, so she could wring her
fingers together.

'I don't think you're selfish for wanting to do what
makes you happy,' Angus said.

'Ditto,' Ivy said.

But it wasn't the same.

'Tom used to be like me,' Angus said, unsure why he was
trying to explain. 'We even look kind of the same, about
the same height, weight, brown hair—that kind of thing.
We did the selection course together and then the eighteen-
month reinforcement cycle. We were even assigned to the
same squadron and deployed together. Tom was great. I
thought I was an insane trainer, but Tom sometimes out-
did me. We pushed each other, we competed against each
other—we were both just so proud to have made it. We
loved the training—honestly, when you get paid to jump
out of a helicopter, to storm a passenger ferry or to abseil

down a skyscraper, you can't really believe it. We couldn't wait for our first mission.'

He paused, rubbing absently at his bare belly.

'He was fine, at first. Or I thought he was. He asked me, once, whether I ever had bad dreams about what we'd done, and seen, but I hadn't. I lied though, told him I had. Then he got married, had Scott. Maybe that made it worse? I don't know. He started seeing one of the psychs at work. He never told me—he never told any of us. But I started hearing rumours, you know?'

'Did you talk to him about it?'

Angus shook his head. 'No. I didn't really want to know. To believe it.' Which made him a pretty rubbish friend. 'Shortly after, he was seconded to a non-combat role. And we gradually drifted apart.'

'Why?'

'I don't know,' he said.

But that wasn't true. He just hadn't let himself think about it. So he tried again.

'I think,' he said, 'that it made me look at what I do, at what soldiers do, differently. It made me start to think that if someone as strong, as brave and as elite as Tom could be affected in that way, that maybe it might happen to me. At first, it was almost like I thought it could be contagious or something.'

He laughed without humour.

'But really, it wasn't that. I wasn't worried about it happening to me, because I know it wouldn't. It's been years now. I've been on many more missions. I've seen a hell of a lot. And I'm exactly the same. *Exactly.* I come back home, I debrief, and I carry on with my life. There's this other guy at work, now, who has just been diagnosed with PTSD. There has been at least one other I know of, too. I've read a bit about it. About guys who can't switch it off when they come home. Who patrol their home, who drive all night, who jump at every little unexpected sound. Yet I'm completely, completely fine.'

'So you think there's something wrong with you.'

'*No,*' he said. 'I know there are crazies in the army. People who get a kick out of death and destruction. But that's not me. For me it's a job. It's about doing what I've been trained to do: protecting my mates and achieving the mission.'

Ivy touched him again, and he realised he'd turned from her, and was staring at the bedspread.

Her fingers brushed his arm, then fell away.

'You think there is something wrong with you because you're not Tom. Because you are capable of doing your job, and also living your life.'

He rubbed at his eyes. He knew she was right; he'd had the same thoughts himself, many times.

But to agree, to voice it…

'I'm lacking something,' he said. 'I shouldn't be able to leave so easily—to walk away from my mum, my girl-friends and now from my child, and risk everything…for what? At the end of the day it's a job. A pay packet, no matter how anyone wraps it up in patriotic propaganda.'

'I think you're wrong,' Ivy said.

He faced her. She was wrong.

She'd asked why he didn't have a girlfriend at Karijini. He knew why—he didn't want a wife, a family that he'd leave again and again without issue. It wasn't fair to them.

It couldn't be normal to be like he was, to be so intrinsically a soldier that nothing seemed to impact him.

Maybe he was a robot. A machine.

Ivy was looking at him with so much emotion in her eyes. She wanted to help him, he knew. But he couldn't be helped.

This was who he was.

And right now, he didn't want any help. He didn't want

words, or reassurances, or all those things that he supposed a wife or partner would offer.

But he still wanted Ivy.

So he reached for her, pulling her roughly against him.

Her eyes widened, but then her hands crept up to his shoulders.

He kissed her, and he wanted it to *just* be a kiss. A physical thing, a carnal thing.

So he wasn't gentle with her.

He held her hard against him, but she just gripped him harder back, kissing him with lips and teeth and tongue.

His hands gripped her bottom, and she wrapped her legs around his waist, rubbing herself against him.

'Angus,' she breathed against his lips.

But he didn't want that, he didn't want any more talking, any more words.

He turned, practically tossing her on the bed, then following her immediately, covering her with his body.

He kept half expecting her to push him away, to say this was too fast, too much...

But she didn't. Her hands were everywhere. Skimming the muscles of his chest. Her nails scraping far from gently down his back.

Somehow he got her singlet off over her head, and she helped him push down her underwear and throw it somewhere over his shoulders.

In between crazy, passionate kisses he tugged off his boxers. Immediately her fingers wrapped around his hardness, and he sucked in a breath, going still. Her mouth was at his shoulders, and she bit him gently.

He knew what that meant: *Don't stop.*

So he didn't. She was wet, hot, perfect.

And then he was inside her, and it was *more* perfect, more intense, more everything.

It was hard, it was fast, and all it took was Ivy moaning in his ear to push him over the edge.

He groaned, and he was gone.

For long minutes he lay collapsed partly on top of her, their heavy breathing gradually, gradually slowing.

But still, neither of them spoke.

For the second time tonight, Angus considered leaving.

But this time, because he couldn't see any point in staying.

And yet, when Ivy slid out of bed to go to the bathroom, he didn't move.

He saw the questions in her eyes when she returned. She'd expected a rapid escape as well.

But she didn't ask him to leave.

Instead, still without a word, she climbed back into bed. He reached for her, pulling her against him, her back to his chest.

And like that, they fell asleep.

CHAPTER THIRTEEN

'YOU'RE SURE YOU want to do this?' Angus asked on Saturday morning.

'One hundred per cent,' Ivy said, her attention on her feet as she pushed down the clutch.

She sat in the driver's seat of her little silver hatchback. Not relaxed, of course, but surprisingly okay.

And *very* determined.

She wasn't going to let a mistake from her past have such an impact on her present, or her child's future, any more. She *needed* to do this.

'So I put the car into gear,' she said, moving the gear stick into first, 'then I turn on the ignition...'

This was the bit that had derailed her last time, and she tensed as she twisted the key.

But...*there*. The engine came to life. Not as loud and scary as she'd imagined.

But still. It wasn't exactly reassuring, either.

'Good job,' Angus said. 'Now—'

'I've got this,' Ivy interrupted. She had to do this herself. 'I release the handbrake, but my foot is still on the brake pedal, so I'm not going anywhere.'

Why did this have to be so complicated?

'And now I just need to gently press on the accelerator, while releasing the clutch...'

Hmm. This part was most definitely easier said than done.

'All I need to do is take my foot *off* the brake pedal, and put it *on* the accelerator, and the car will move forward.

And I have heaps of space ahead of me, so I needn't worry about flying into my front fence.'

Beside her, she knew Angus was smiling.

'So yes, start to release clutch, foot *off* the brake and *on*...'

The car moved.

At about two kilometres an hour, but it had most definitely moved.

'Oh, my God, I'm actually *driving*!'

'You're driving, Ivy!'

They were approaching her front gate at a snail's pace, but the road beyond it was still far too close.

'Turn left at the gate, Ivy. There's a school car park you can practise in only a short distance away.'

Very firmly Ivy pressed on the brake, and as she forgot all about the clutch the poor little Volkswagen jerked to an inelegant halt.

She patted the leather steering wheel in apology.

'Nope,' Ivy said. 'No roads today. How about you show me how to reverse back the way I've come, and we call it a day?'

'This will be the shortest driving lesson in history,' Angus commented.

'Or the longest, if you count the twelve years it took to get to this point.'

He nodded. 'Understood. Great job, Ivy.'

She grinned at him across the centre console. 'I know,' she said. 'Thank you.'

The next day, Angus drove her to that school car park.

It wasn't exactly vast, but the stretch of bitumen still gave Ivy a relatively reassuring margin of error.

He'd even brought along a couple of traffic cones, which he set up as a mock intersection.

Slowly—too slowly, according to Angus—Ivy practised starting, and stopping, and turning, and parking.

And after a lot of encouragement, going fast enough to make it into second gear.

That was met with raucous applause from the passenger seat.

When safely stopped, Ivy glared at him.

'You're not being particularly sensitive.' She sniffed. 'This is very difficult for me.'

Angus clearly knew she was being—maybe—just the slightest bit dramatic, and laughed rather dismissively.

'There isn't a lot of use in learning how to drive if you never go fast enough to actually *get* anywhere.'

Ivy glared at him. But this time, when they did a lap of the car park, she made it into third.

That afternoon, Ivy drove Angus, very cautiously, to the café where she'd met him for coffee. It felt as if it had been for ever ago, but it had only been a few weeks.

She was doing well. Really well.

A yellow square with a big black *L* on both the front and rear windscreen of the little Volkswagen proclaimed to all around them that Ivy was a learner driver. Although the way she crept along the street made that pretty clear, anyway.

He'd kept her on side streets, not wanting to frustrate other drivers, but now, at the café, there was only one parking space left, between two of the mammoth, European-badged SUVs that were standard for this area.

When Ivy realised this, she slowed so much that the car stalled, jolting them both forward in their seats.

'Dammit!' she said, smacking the steering wheel. 'I haven't stalled all day.' She glanced at Angus. 'Maybe you should park the car this time. That looks a bit tight.'

He raised an eyebrow. 'Ivy Molyneux is backing down from a challenge?'

Her gaze narrowed. 'Of course not. It's just...' A long pause. 'Of course not,' she repeated. And then restarted the car.

Just to increase the degree of difficulty, another car had driven up behind them. Unfortunately it was impossible for the driver to pass until Ivy had parked, with a concrete median strip keeping the other car immediately behind them.

Ivy had noticed, but she said nothing, her jaw clenched in concentration. The car rolled slowly forward, the indicator ticking loudly.

'Don't cut the corner,' Angus said. 'Remember to follow a wide arc, like we practised, so you are driving into the space straight.'

She nodded tightly.

She turned, but too abruptly. 'Too close,' Angus said, 'reverse a bit and try again.'

Second attempt was closer, but still not quite right.

With a sigh, Ivy reversed yet again.

The other driver was losing patience, and revved his engine.

Ivy was tense. Her gaze kept flicking to her rear-view mirror.

'Don't worry about him,' Angus said. 'You're doing fine.'

She bit down on her lip as she tried for a third time.

'That's it,' he said. 'Now straighten up.'

And that was it. She was parked.

The impatient driver sped off behind them, wheels squealing.

Ivy calmly clicked the handbrake into place, and turned off the ignition.

'I don't think that guy realised what he just witnessed,' she said.

'Or what a momentous occasion this is.'

'Exactly,' she said, with a wide smile. 'That was awesome. Let's go have a celebratory latte.'

Ivy practically bounced out of the car.

On the footpath, she turned to face him. 'I just *drove somewhere*, and *parked*,' she breathed.

She stood on her tiptoes, brushing her lips against his.

'I think that deserves a celebratory kiss, too,' she whispered.

Because he agreed—but that didn't meet Angus's definition of a kiss—he reached for Ivy again.

But he'd barely kissed her, when they were interrupted.

'*Eeeeeuuuuwwwwwwww!* Kissing!'

They broke apart. A small boy, maybe four, stood at their feet, pointing at Angus.

'That's gross.'

Angus grinned.

'Sorry, mate, but one day—'

'Scott!'

Both Angus and the boy turned at the deep male voice.

The man, the boy's father he assumed, was shadowed by the café awning. But he was tall, and familiar.

Angus froze.

Tom?

Then the man stepped out of the shadows, crossing the short distance to retrieve his son.

He had blond hair, like his son. It wasn't Tom.

'Sorry, guys,' he said. He nodded at Scott. 'He's got some pretty strong opinions at the moment.'

Then they were gone, continuing their walk down the street.

'Angus?' Ivy asked, curiosity in her eyes.

He gave a little shake of his head, needing to refocus.

'Do you know them?'

'No,' he said, his voice cracking slightly. He cleared his throat. 'Let's get that coffee.'

But something had shifted.

After coffee, Ivy drove them cautiously home, but for the first night that week he didn't stay.

When he walked in his front door, before it had even slammed shut behind him, he had his phone in his hand, scrolling down his list of contacts.

If Ivy could work past her fear of driving, he could do this.

But he still paused before dialling the familiar number. *For heaven's sake.*

He could go to war without even a single bad dream, and he couldn't make a damn phone call?

Angrily, he stabbed at the green dial icon, and pressed the phone too firmly against his ear.

It rang.

Almost immediately, it was answered.

'Angus?'

He needed to clear his throat.

'Tom,' he said. 'I'm sorry.'

Irene Molyneux was back.

Ivy stood alone in the elevator as she travelled from the ground floor of the tower direct to her mum's offices. No mucking around today—her first order of business was to talk to her mother.

The elevator walls were mirrored, and she stared at her own reflection.

Did she look different?

She knew about the whole pregnancy glow thing, but did it happen this early?

She was seven weeks now. Seven weeks and...two days?

Her tummy looked the same, anyway. Although that would change soon, if her appetite carried on as it had been.

She smiled. On Saturday night, she'd eaten almost an entire pizza.

Angus had seemed rather impressed. Ivy had been mildly horrified.

It had been fun, though, sitting cross-legged in front of some random Saturday night movie, eating pizza out of cardboard boxes, and garlic bread from amongst infinite layers of aluminium foil.

Ivy didn't remember ever feeling so relaxed with her other boyfriends. Angus made her laugh so easily, and he was quick to laugh himself. He...

He's not my boyfriend.

She dug her nails into the palms of her hands.

And, after last night's abrupt disappearance after she'd driven them home from the café, that *he's not my boyfriend* reality had only been underlined.

The elevator dinged as it came to a stop.

This wasn't the time to be worrying about glowing, or pizza, or non-boyfriends, anyway.

The doors slid open, revealing the organised chaos of Irene's floor.

Ivy wore her favourite suit today. A charcoal-grey pencil skirt and a short fitted matching jacket.

Her hair was up, looped into a neat bun, and she wore the pearl stud earrings her mother had given her the day she started work at the family business.

She wore them to work every day, but today—as she'd pressed the backs of the earrings into place—they had felt significant.

Silly, really.

She hadn't booked a meeting, but when her mother's assistant immediately ushered her into her office it was clear Irene had been expecting her.

Of course she had.

In so many ways, they were *so* similar.

'Ivy.'

Her mum pushed back her high-backed leather chair, stood and stepped around her desk.

Good. She hadn't wanted to talk across that wide expanse of marri.

Because this *wasn't* business. Whatever her mother might think.

'Mum,' she began, ignoring her mother's gesture to take a seat. This wouldn't take long. 'I'm not going to apologise for being pregnant. I'm sincerely sorry for the inconvenience this will cause the company, but I'm not sorry I've decided to proceed with this pregnancy.'

Irene remained silent.

'All senior executive appointments at Molyneux Mining offer three months' full maternity pay, with the opportunity to take up to nine months' subsequent unpaid leave with your position held for you. I see no reason why this would not apply to me.'

Still complete, unreadable silence.

Her mother's gaze was steady, revealing nothing.

'Given the unfortunate timing,' Ivy continued, 'I'd like to take only six months' total leave. I know you only took six weeks with each of us, but I just don't think I can do that—'

Irene's gaze had dropped, and Ivy realised she'd laid her hands on her stomach.

Despite everything, Ivy's mouth curved into a smile.

She always smiled, now, when she thought of her baby.

She met her mum's gaze, trying to remember where she'd got to in her well-practised speech. But she couldn't find those words, when she realised her mother was smiling, too.

'I think that's a good idea,' Irene said. 'Six weeks wasn't long enough with any of you.'

Ivy blinked. 'Pardon me?'

'I'm comfortable maintaining my position throughout the period of your leave,' Irene said. 'Although I assume you will be returning full-time after that?'

The pointed question was almost reassuring—Irene was still very much her mother, not some strange transplanted alien.

Ivy nodded. 'Yes.'

A sharp nod. 'Good. I have heard about your plans for a nursery downstairs.' She sniffed. 'Such options weren't considered thirty years ago. I'm sure you'll find it incredibly distracting.'

Ivy opened her mouth—but was stopped with a glare.

'Although I'm sure if anyone can juggle such an arrangement, you can.'

Ivy was so stunned, that she simply mutely nodded.

'It occurred to me,' Irene said, 'on the flight home from Europe, that things have changed considerably in the past three decades. A woman in my role was unusual back then. I couldn't afford to be the mother I wanted to be, *and* the businesswoman I knew I could be.' She shrugged. 'Life is all about choices.'

And for the first time, ever, Ivy wondered if her mother questioned hers.

'Thank you,' Ivy said, because it seemed like the only appropriate thing to say.

'However,' Irene said, marching back behind her desk. She slid open a drawer on silent runners, and emerged with a thick white envelope. 'The circumstances of your pregnancy are less than ideal.'

She remained on the far side of the desk. The softness that had intermittently lightened her gaze had gone.

Right now, Irene Molyneux was all business.

'I've had our lawyers draft a contract for your...' she waved her hands in a dismissive gesture '...*boyfriend*.'

'He's not my boyfriend,' Ivy said. She wasn't interested in pretending any more.

But Irene barely blinked.

'Regardless, you're not married, or known by the public or our shareholders to be in a long-term relationship. When announced, particularly given the timing, it will be clear that this pregnancy is unplanned. Which is not what the public expects of *Ivy Molyneux*.'

Her mum made her name sound like a brand.

'However I feel it is somewhat realistic that you would keep a long-term relationship secretive. Hence I'd like our story to be that—'

'*No,*' Ivy said, as firmly as she'd ever said the word.

'Pardon me?' Irene said, her eyes narrowing.

'There will be no contract,' Ivy said. 'I'm embarrassed to say that I had exactly the same plan, myself.' She laughed dryly.

'Mr Barlow wouldn't sign?'

'He never will, no matter what we offer him,' Ivy said, 'but that's not the point.'

'Don't be ridiculous,' Irene said. 'Everyone has a price.'

Ivy actually snorted. 'Angus doesn't.'

Using his first name was a mistake.

Irene's expression became probing.

'You love him,' she said, dismissively.

'I *don't,*' Ivy said, but not quite immediately.

Love wasn't something you were allowed to consider when your relationship was based around sex and an accidental pregnancy, was it?

She squeezed her eyes shut for a long second.

'This isn't about Angus,' she said, deliberately saying his name again. 'This is about *me.* I'm not prepared to lie about this, to anyone.' She shrugged. 'I thought like you, a few weeks ago. A few days ago, even. That this was a disaster. That this could ruin my reputation. People would lose faith in me. Our stock price would crash. Our new magnesium deal would be in jeopardy. The world would end.'

It sounded ridiculous now. Yet she'd been so earnest when she'd said it all to Angus.

'I'm allowed to make a mistake, Mum,' she said. '*We're* allowed to make mistakes. Even someone like you, who never, ever does. It's not healthy to cover everything up. To pretend we're always perfect.'

'Mila said you're learning to drive,' Irene said abruptly.

'Yes,' Ivy said.

'I suppose you think I was wrong to do that.'

She meant what she'd done that night Toby had died. She didn't need to elaborate.

'I was protecting you,' Irene said. 'I knew what you were capable of. I couldn't let you destroy your future.'

'But I don't think I would've,' Ivy said. 'That night changed my life. But I never got to process it like a normal person. To deal with it. I should've learnt that I needed to trust my instincts, to be strong, to do what I knew was right. But do you know what I learnt instead? That it's not okay to make mistakes. *Ever.*'

'I've never said that,' Irene said. 'I would never tell you that.'

Ivy shook her head sadly. 'You didn't have to.'

She walked towards her mother. The room was absolutely silent now, and her heels echoed loudly on the polished wooden floor.

She reached for the large white envelope, tugging it from Irene's hands. Then turned, and dropped it into the recycling bin beside the desk.

'Mum,' she said. 'I love you. Thank you for delaying the handover of Molyneux Mining to me, and for understanding my need to take maternity leave. I love Molyneux Mining, and I'm incredibly proud that you have entrusted me with it. But I need you to also trust that it's okay that

I made a mistake and I can't fix it, or control it. That it's okay I had a one-night stand and ended up with a baby.'

At this, Irene sucked in a sharp breath.

Ivy smiled.

Irene didn't. But she did speak.

'I do trust you,' she said. 'I wouldn't be handing you the company, otherwise.' Then she reached out, grabbing Ivy's hand. 'But please be careful.' She met her gaze, and now it was her mum looking at her, not a powerful mining magnate. 'I don't know this Mr Barlow, or what type of man he is. But I do know it can be very, very difficult falling in love with the wrong man.'

'I'm not—' she began.

But Irene simply shook her head.

'I need to get back to work,' her mother said, all brisk and businesslike. 'So do you.'

'Of course,' Ivy replied.

And left.

CHAPTER FOURTEEN

THIS HAD BEEN a mistake.

Angus had an inkling as he opened his front door to let Ivy in.

And was absolutely sure by the time she stood in his kitchen and took in the two neat table settings at his dining table.

No, it was hardly white linen and candles—but it *was* a bit of an effort. Matching place mats. A jug of water. Cutlery in all the correct places.

It looked…romantic.

Which wasn't what he'd meant.

'Don't freak out,' he said, attempting to explain. 'This is supposed to be an apology for being a bit weird yesterday after we bumped into that guy and his son. Nothing more.'

Ivy's expression gave away little. 'Nothing more,' she repeated.

Great, so she understood.

Maybe.

He invited her to take a seat, anyway. She ignored the table, and slid onto one of the tall stools at the breakfast bar.

'Is that—' she asked, peering behind him and through the oven window '—*lasagne*?'

Angus shrugged. 'Possibly a bad joke,' he said. The awkwardness back at the homestead that day hadn't been all that dissimilar to right now.

But Ivy smiled. 'I like bad jokes,' she said. 'Besides, I genuinely want to try your mum's famous lasagne.'

He grinned. As Ivy relaxed, so did the tense atmosphere.

Mostly.

As they talked about favourite meals Ivy still wasn't quite *right*. She was fidgeting, for one thing.

She'd put her hands on her lap to hide that familiar twisting and untangling of her fingers, but he knew she was doing it.

Her attention was also erratic. She seemed reluctant to meet his gaze, her own flittering off in random directions.

Yes. This was stupid.

Had she even cared that he'd rushed off last night?

Maybe she'd been relieved. They'd been spending so much time together.

More time than he could remember spending with any other woman.

That realisation made him a little uncomfortable, too.

'I called Tom last night,' he said, abruptly, keen to take his thoughts in a different direction.

'Really?' Ivy smiled. 'That's brilliant. Did you talk long?'

'No,' he said. Ivy's face fell. Angus smiled. 'But that's normal. I don't think I've ever had a long conversation on the phone with a mate. I rang him, I apologised for being a useless friend and asked if he'd like to catch up for a drink. He said yes.'

'That's good,' Ivy said. 'It was pretty obvious what happened yesterday. I'm glad you did something about it.'

He wasn't sure what would happen when he saw Tom, but at least he'd tried. If it was too little, too late, then he'd just have to deal with it.

'I should've said something last night,' he said. 'Rather than rushing off.'

Ivy nodded, but then stilled that subtle movement. 'Why?' she said. She wasn't looking at him; instead she appeared to be studying the bubbling lasagne. 'It wasn't any of my business.'

Angus walked to the fridge, grabbing the salad he'd made earlier.

He walked over to the dining table, plonking the bowl down between his two neat place settings.

He knew what Ivy was doing.

Hadn't he done this himself, many, many times?

When physical intimacy had begun to merge into even a hint of more?

It was just different with Ivy, of course.

Her pregnancy had added a complexity, a depth to their relationship that wouldn't have existed, otherwise.

Wouldn't it?

No.

'I told my sisters today that we weren't really a couple,' Ivy said, twisting on the stool to face him. 'I'm not much good at subterfuge, I've decided.' She paused. 'And I hated lying to them. I spoke to my mum, too. She's approved my six-month maternity leave.'

'That's good,' he said.

Their conversation was almost formal, now. It reminded Angus of that very first coffee, which Ivy had attempted to run like a business meeting.

It remained that way when they took their seats at the table and as Angus served the lasagne; their knives and forks scraping noisily against their plates.

Ivy discussed the obstetrician she'd selected, but didn't invite him to her first appointment in a few weeks' time. She'd keep him informed, of course.

Of course.

He was relieved. This *thing* had always had an end date.

He'd known, hadn't he, that tonight was a mistake? That he'd inadvertently set up a scene that could be misinterpreted? That Ivy might think meant more?

So it was good that Ivy had come to her own conclusion. That together they could end this amicably.

If part of him was disappointed, it was because he was still just as attracted to Ivy as he'd been when he'd seen her walk down that aisle in Bali. Even tonight, dressed in jeans, a T-shirt and an oversized cardigan, she was beautiful.

Of course he'd regret that he wouldn't get to touch her again. Kiss her again.

He'd thought he'd have longer.

But not too long. Too long would just confuse an already overcomplicated situation.

'Angus?'

He blinked. Clearly Ivy had been talking to him, but he had no idea what about.

But he smiled, and she repeated her question, and their formal, just slightly uncomfortable conversation continued.

At least the lasagne was delicious.

You love him.

Her mother's words still bounced about in her brain. It had been almost twelve hours since their meeting, and yet she still couldn't shake her mother's erroneous assumption.

Telling her sisters had helped.

It was good to lay it out so brutally: we met for the first time at April's wedding. We had sex. Now we're having a baby. The End.

April had been her usual starry-eyed self: *'Are you sure there's not something between you both? You seemed so natural together. So right.'*

But Ivy had laughed, and made absolutely no mention of their…affair? Fling? Thing?

It was irrelevant, anyway. Something short term based purely on physical attraction. No more substantial than what had happened on the beach in Nusa Dua.

Except for what you've told him. What he's shared with you.

Mila had been pragmatic. *'Maybe it's good you're not*

in a relationship. At least that way you don't need to worry about what happens when you break up.'

Ivy stared at her dinner.

True to form, she'd made her way through a mammoth slice of lasagne. Remnants of white sauce and a lone champignon were all that remained on her plate.

Conversation had spluttered out, although they'd both made a good go at it.

But the atmosphere was just *wrong*. None of the ease and the fun of before.

Which made sense, of course.

When she'd walked into Angus's kitchen and seen all the effort he'd put in—and *then* the abject horror on his face when he seemed to realise what all of that could imply...

Well, it had made a decision she'd already made just that much easier.

This had to end. But now it would end, tonight.

She didn't want this, this faux intimacy, this illusion of something more.

Angus *clearly* didn't.

She offered to help him tidy up, but she knew he'd refuse. It was best she left as soon as possible.

At the open door, Ivy's hand stilled before pushing open the flyscreen.

She turned to face Angus.

He was close, very close. She needed to tilt her chin upwards to meet his gaze.

His front room was dark, and the light that spilled from the kitchen threw Angus's face into shadows.

'It was fun while it lasted,' Ivy said, then cringed. 'Oh, God, that sounded lame.'

Angus laughed, his teeth bright in the darkness.

Ivy rushed to make her exit, yanking hard on the flyscreen handle.

But Angus reached out, pressing his hand against the small of her back and turning her to face him.

How many times had he done that? Touched her there? Both firm and gentle?

He stepped even closer.

'This is probably not the done thing,' he said, 'but how do you feel about one last goodbye kiss?'

She should feel it was pointless. A stupid idea.

Instead, she stood on tiptoes, reaching for him.

His kiss was gentle. Without demand.

And still not familiar. Even now, when they'd kissed so many times, it was *still* exciting, *still* different. Still special.

Her fingers curled up into his close-cropped hair, pulling him closer, inviting him to deepen their kiss.

And he did, but she felt the shape of his smile the second before his tongue brushed against hers.

Oh, God.

He was so good at this. Maybe she was good at this too, because his hands were now firmer at her back, drawing her closer.

She smiled now as her body pressed against his. So strong, and tall, and broad.

The tone of the kiss was now far from gentle.

But it wasn't desperate, either. This might be their last kiss, but there was no need to rush.

Then he lifted her just off her feet, moving her to her left until her back was flat against the wall.

His hands slid around to sit at her waist.

His mouth broke from hers to trail along her jaw. His breath was hot against her ear.

'I know technically I said a goodbye kiss, but how would you feel about…?'

And Ivy giggled, and nodded her head, and pulled his mouth back to hers as his warm hands slid beneath her T-shirt.

There was no question this was unwise, and unnecessary—but then, couldn't the same be said for nearly everything that had happened between them?

And she just *couldn't* regret any of it. Any of it.

She knew she wouldn't regret tonight.

Soon Angus led her down the hall to his bedroom. He flicked on the light, and she was glad; she needed to see him.

She'd never been inside his house before tonight, but she barely glanced at anything but the bed.

She just wanted to get there as soon as possible. Wanted to feel Angus against her as soon as possible.

But then he was on top of her as she sank into the mattress, and that was all that mattered.

How he felt, how he made her feel.

So good.

Somehow their clothes were gone, and her fingers drew patterns on Angus's gorgeous bare skin.

She felt the need to remember this. To savour this.

Angus had slowed too. His hands traced her curves, sliding from thigh, to hip, to waist, to breast.

She'd thought before that every kiss they'd had was different.

But *this* was different again. *This* was almost reverent, as if the two of them were etching this moment in their memories.

As if it were special.

Angus kissed the hollow beneath her hip. Then her belly, working upwards.

She shivered, her hands now still on his shoulders. Enjoying this.

It wasn't *as if* this were special. *It was* special.

Or at least, it was special to her.

I love him.

Her hands gripped his shoulders as she finally admitted the truth to herself.

That truth was why she'd needed to end this tonight, why she'd decided she no longer had time for pretending and fake anything. Not because it was dangerous, and because she needed to protect herself—but because it was already too late.

She had a choice now. To push him away. To tell him this was a mistake and escape into the night.

That would've been the right choice. The smart choice. A last-gasp attempt at protecting herself. Protecting her heart.

He lifted his head, questions in his gaze.

But she didn't shove him away. Instead she slid her hands to his arms, as if she were capable of tugging him back up to her.

Although he still understood what she wanted, and slid his body upwards.

And he kissed her again. Again, and again, and it was exactly what Ivy wanted.

She wanted all of this; she wanted him here, close against her, inside her.

Afterwards, she knew she'd been right.

She wouldn't regret this. This last time together.

But she could certainly regret loving him.

Angus considered leaving a note.

Ivy was still asleep, curled on her side in his bed.

He was showered and dressed, and he'd packed yesterday before she'd arrived. He was flying out today—on a mission that he couldn't tell her about.

So yes, a note would be easier.

Instead, he sat on the bed beside her, and reached for her—shaking her shoulder gently.

It was still dark outside, and Ivy blinked as her eyes adjusted to the glow of his bedside lamp.

She stretched, reaching her hands above her head so they bumped against the headboard.

'Hey,' she said, all sleepy.

'Good morning,' he said. 'I'm off to work.'

'What time is it?'

'Early,' he said. 'Sleep some more. There's no rush to leave. I just wanted to let you know I'll be gone for a while.'

'How long?' she asked, suddenly appearing more awake.

His lips quirked. 'I can't tell you that. Or where I'm going.'

She nodded in understanding. 'Okay. But I'm not going to see you any time soon.'

He didn't quite know what to make of her expression, but he felt he needed to say something more.

'Last night was fun…' he began. Then realised what he'd said.

'Hey, that's my lame line,' she said. Then her gaze fell downwards. Her fingers tangled in the white bed sheet. 'But yes, it was fun.'

He went to stand, needing to go.

But she laid her hand on his thigh, and he went still.

'Angus—' she said. Then sighed. She lifted her gaze, meeting his head-on. 'Look,' she said, 'I know what we said. About this being the last time. I know what I said, about that stuff with Tom not being any of my business.' She paused, but her gaze didn't waver. 'But honestly, I did care. I did want to know. And last night I wanted to tell you all about what happened when I spoke to my mum yesterday. But I didn't, because I'd decided that this had to end.'

'Why?' he asked.

'Because if I didn't end it now, I was worried I'd never be able to end it.'

Angus remained silent.

'I know this isn't what we planned. I know this isn't what either of us wanted. And it's endlessly, impossibly complicated. We need to work together for another eighteen years at least, and we need to be civil. So ending it now *is* smarter. While we can walk away without hurt feelings and anger and disappointment.' For a moment, she looked down at her fingers, but only to pull them free of the fabric and lay them flat against her stomach. 'But what if I don't want to be smart? What if I'm not quite so scared of making mistakes any more?'

Not quite so scared.

But she *was* still scared. He knew what she was offering him. What she was revealing to him.

Her gaze was raw. Open. Emotional.

It was…

Overwhelming.

He didn't know what to think.

Last night he'd been so worried about her feelings that he'd made her dinner.

And that *had* been a mistake.

That was something he'd do for his partner. His wife.

That was why it had felt wrong. Because Ivy wasn't those things.

No one would ever be those things.

She was a woman who, through circumstance, he was having a baby with.

She was smart, and brilliant and beautiful—but that didn't matter.

He wasn't built for more than what they'd had.

He just wasn't wired that way.

Ivy had pulled back subtly, her body no longer leaning towards him.

'I can't,' he said, finally.

For a long while, there was silence.

'You're wrong,' Ivy said, eventually. 'You *can*. I know you think you're missing something. I know you think of yourself as some flawed, fighting machine.'

He wanted to argue, but he met her strong, determined gaze and knew he needed to let her speak.

Besides—hadn't he used the same words? To her, that one time, and to himself, many more?

'But, Angus,' she said, softly, 'you *do* care. You *do* feel. And you do those things so, so deeply.' She sighed, her lips curving into a sad smile. 'When I told you my plan, all those weeks ago, I'd been so sure you'd accept. I mean, who would pass up the chance to be an instant millionaire? But now I know exactly who can't be bought with money. The type of person who believes in honesty, and hard work, and doing things the right way, regardless of the cost.' She paused. 'A *good* man. A very good man. A man who wants to know the mother of his child, who insists on being a part of her life for the sake of his child—because he wants the very, very best for his son or daughter. A man who loves his mum, loves his friends, and—yes, I know you'll roll your eyes when I say this—loves the country he fights for.'

Her hand was still on his thigh, and she pressed her weight against him, as if to punctuate her point. 'You don't lack *anything*, Angus. You're capable of anything you want. Even love.'

It was only now Ivy's gaze wobbled, and then eventually drifted downwards.

He didn't know what to say. He hadn't expected this.

But then, he hadn't expected any of what he'd experienced with Ivy.

Her words continued to reverberate around his head, but they were too unfamiliar and too new for him to grab onto.

He'd taken far, far too long to say anything.

'I can't,' he said again. It was all he could say.

'Okay,' she said, and her hand fell away.

CHAPTER FIFTEEN

Five weeks later

APRIL WAS A *lot* more excited than Ivy was.

Her sister had grabbed a brochure from the ultrasound clinic's reception desk, and opened it up on Ivy's lap. They sat together in the waiting room, one other couple also waiting patiently in the corner.

'*See,*' she said. 'You can have your 3D scan etched into a *glass cube.*'

Ivy raised an eyebrow. 'How about we wait until we know that I have a healthy baby before we start ordering keepsakes?'

April bumped her shoulder against Ivy's. 'You'll be fine,' she said. 'I know it.'

It probably wasn't fair to think that April was more excited than Ivy was. Of course Ivy was excited. After all, today she'd get to *really* see her baby for the first time. It was just she was also nervous.

So nervous.

Silly, really. She'd visited her obstetrician only a few weeks earlier, and everything had been fine. Her baby's heartbeat was strong.

She'd tried to explain how she was feeling to her sisters, and they'd said the right things, but…

The thing was, it wasn't the same for them. It wasn't *their* baby.

Angus would understand.

Ivy tilted her head backwards until it bumped against the wall, staring up at the ceiling.

He'd emailed her a couple of times while he'd been gone, when he'd been at camp. She hadn't really expected that, although she supposed she should've. He'd never just disappeared, even when she'd wanted him to.

He'd been polite, asked how she was going, how the baby was. That was it—nothing else. Certainly no mention of their last conversation.

Despite everything, she hoped he'd be home soon.

Yes, a huge part of her cringed at what she'd said when she'd last seen him. When she'd so haphazardly laid her heart on the line.

It was *embarrassing*.

Mortifying. And a lot of other things.

But—she couldn't regret it.

She looked down at her tummy, at where the best mistake of her life was growing.

No. She had no regrets.

And so she did wish he were here. So he could tell her his latest titbit of baby development he'd gleaned from his research. So she could voice her concerns time and time again and not feel as if she were being a crazy person, because Angus would *get* it. He'd understand. He'd be all strong and reassuring and he would probably even hold her hand—just because she needed him to.

Of course even if that morning all those weeks ago had ended differently, he still wouldn't be here.

He'd warned her of the realities of his work, and she'd understood—but it was still hard.

She didn't have any right to miss him, not really. But their baby would.

She laid her hand on her stomach.

But she reckoned this baby would be pretty tough. This

would be their reality—Daddy away for weeks or months at a time. But back for long stretches, also.

And this baby would be *loved*. So loved. Angus would love this baby with all he had. He already did, Ivy was sure.

And wasn't that what mattered, really? Love?

The sonographer walked into the reception room, and called out Ivy's name.

April grinned, immediately jumping to her feet, and Ivy followed behind her.

Minutes later she lay on her back, her still-pretty-flat tummy exposed and smeared in gel.

The sonographer explained what she was doing, and directed Ivy's gaze to a screen mounted above her and to the right. 'You'll be able to see everything there.'

And then she could see everything.

A baby. An actual tiny baby with arms and legs and a fluttering, healthy heart.

Tears stung her eyes and crept their way down her cheeks.

April gripped her hand, and smiled, with tears making her own eyes glisten.

Ivy loved this baby with absolutely everything she had. With an intensity she hadn't thought possible.

Her whole life had been about her career. Every day she'd woken up to thoughts about work and gone to sleep after checking her email. Her weekends had simply interrupted her business hours—and, while she'd had some vague, future plan of maybe, maybe one day getting married, it was always to the most sensible, the most appropriate of men. Certainly not men that made her skin tingle or who took her breath away.

She used to think she was being wise in her dating choices. That she'd learnt from the mistakes of her past, and was ensuring that she'd never again fall in love as recklessly as she had with Toby. She'd believed she needed to protect herself from the loss of control that love seemed inevitably to bring.

But now, now that all these years later she'd fallen in love again, she knew how wrong she'd been.

She hadn't put up barriers to protect her career, or to retain control—not really. She'd put up barriers because Toby had been her first love—and, however misguided, losing him had *hurt*.

She hadn't wanted to feel that way again.

But despite her best efforts, here she was.

Desperately in love with a man who didn't love her.

And it hurt. So much.

She knew what she'd told Angus had been right—that he was capable of loving her.

The problem was, he didn't.

But this baby in front of her, wide awake and rolling unhelpfully for the smiling sonographer, he or she *would* love her.

And, for now, that would be enough.

The Friday he arrived home, after just over five weeks away, Angus visited Tom.

The days were getting longer now, and Tom and Angus sat on the edge of Tom's timber decking as Tom's two kids ran about the backyard in the fading sunlight.

Carise had hugged him, hard, when he'd arrived, but said barely a word.

She was clearly glad he was here, which surprised him.

Being invited here had surprised him, too.

Surely deserting your friend in his time of need nixed any future dinner invitations? It would seem not.

Although Tom was, understandably, cautious, and far from the jovial, loud man that Angus remembered. Was that the PTSD? Maybe. But Angus guessed that, tonight, it was mostly his fault.

Tom didn't know what to expect of his supposed mate who'd just so randomly dropped back into his world.

Angus didn't blame him.

For a while, they both quietly sipped their beers as they watched the kids.

'Scott is getting tall,' Angus said, just to say something.

'Yeah. Amber will be tall, too, I reckon,' Tom replied.

Then that was that.

'Mate,' Angus said, trying again. 'I'm so sorry for—'

'Yeah,' Tom said, cutting him off. 'That was pretty low.'

'I'm sorry,' he repeated, because—if nothing else—he could at least just keep saying that again and again.

His friend sighed. 'I know,' he said. 'I know it wasn't like I told you what was going on, not really, but I'd kind of hoped you'd ask. You know?'

Angus nodded. Yes, he knew.

'I was—' he began, but that wasn't right. 'I thought—' But that wasn't right either. 'I didn't understand,' he went with, eventually. 'I didn't understand at all.'

Tom smiled, squinting a little now that the sun was low, peeking between the trees along his back fence.

'You still don't understand,' he said.

'No,' he agreed. 'I'm sorry, I don't.'

Tom slanted him a pointed look. 'Stop apologising or I'll have to ask you to leave.'

And that comment was *so* much like the Tom that Angus remembered that Angus grinned, holding his glass and spare hand up in mock defence. 'Okay, you get that I'm sorry.'

Tom nodded.

'It was hard for me to tell you,' Tom said. 'Especially you. We'd been along this SAS journey together, and I'd just seriously derailed. You were still strong, and I was weak. A failure.'

'No, Tom—'

Now his friend held up his hand. 'Nah, I know. I'm not a failure for having a mental-health issue—and I have a se-

riously brilliant therapist who has helped me realise that.'
He paused. 'She's helped me with a lot of things, actually.
Reprogramming my thoughts and reactions in certain situations, that type of thing. I still have the occasional bad
dream, but mostly I'm all good.'

Angus smiled. 'I can see that.' And he could. There was
an ease to Tom that was new, and a calmness. 'But do you
ever miss it?'

The challenge of what they did. The adrenalin rush.

Tom smiled. 'I knew you'd ask. But the answer is simple:
no. I have a new career now. I've just got my builder's ticket,
and my business is going well. I choose my own hours, I get
to spend more time with my kids...it's great.' He downed
the last of his beer. 'But then, it was always different for you,
wasn't it? The regiment is more than a career for you. It's your
life. It's who you are.'

It's who you are.

But was it?

He thought of the past five weeks, and the complex international training exercise with a close Australian ally
he'd just completed. It had been tough, it had been chal-
lenging, and he'd learnt a hell of a lot.

And he'd loved it. Loved every last second of it.

So yes, the SAS was who he was. Since his father's death
it had been all that he'd wanted, and now he'd made it, it
was all he ever wanted to do.

But for the first time maybe he needed to ask a different
question. Was the regiment *all* he was? Was it *all* he wanted?

A familiar musical jingle jolted Ivy out of her lovely deep
sleep.

She blinked, staring up at her ceiling. Light streamed
in through her lounge-room window—but then, that was
to be expected in the middle of an almost summer Sunday afternoon.

Ivy swung her legs off her couch, and padded on bare feet down the hall to the intercom panel near her front door.

'Hello?'

'It's Angus.' His voice was just as delicious as she remembered. 'Are you okay?'

'Of course,' she said, surprised. 'Why wouldn't I be?'

'You didn't answer your phone,' he said. 'Can I come in for a bit?'

She pushed the button that would let him in, then unlocked and opened her front door, before heading into the kitchen.

She grabbed the CD she'd had copied for Angus at the ultrasound clinic, and checked her phone. Three missed calls from Angus while her phone had been on silent during her nap.

For some reason that made her smile.

Angus's heavy footsteps approached down the hallway.

When he stepped into the room, he seemed bigger than she'd remembered. Even taller.

He was dressed casually, a white T-shirt, dark shorts and flip-flops. It had become warm while he'd been gone, and today it really did feel like summer. Especially for Ivy, given her body's thermostat seemed permanently set about five degrees hotter than before she was pregnant.

As always, the weight of Angus's attention did all sorts of things to Ivy's tummy. She'd need to work on that reaction; it was hardly helpful.

She was dressed in the girly version of his outfit—white shorts, red singlet, no shoes. She hadn't expected any visitors today, and she knew she was all creased from her nap, but Angus *still* made her feel as if she were the most stunning woman he'd ever seen.

Maybe that was just how he looked at all women? Regardless, it wasn't helpful, either.

'Any bump yet?' he asked.

He crossed the room, but he seemed…different. He always seemed so relaxed, so confident, so comfortable—but not today.

She shook her head. 'Not yet. A few extra kilos, but I can't blame the bub for that.' Ivy held out the CD. 'Here, so your visit to make sure I'm still breathing isn't wasted. I'm not sure if you saw that photo I emailed you, but here are the rest. Personally, I think the 3D images are a little creepy.'

'Thanks,' he said. He rotated the CD case in his hands a few times. 'I didn't just come to check on you. I called because I wanted to talk to you.'

'Okay,' Ivy said. She gestured vaguely at the couch, and then her bar stools. 'Take a seat?'

He shook his head. 'No, I—' He flipped the CD case a few more times. 'Ivy,' he said. 'I want to talk to you about my dad.'

That was about the last thing she'd expected him to say, but she simply nodded.

'I told you that my dad died when I was seventeen,' Angus said. 'But I didn't tell you what happened.'

'You said it was sudden,' Ivy said, remembering.

'Yeah. Although it wasn't an accident, or an illness—he stepped in front of a train the day he realised he'd lost the family business.'

'Oh, Angus—' Ivy began, instinctively stepping towards him.

But he shook his head. 'I used to be so proud of him. He started with only one furniture shop, and ended up with thirty. He took us from a ramshackle house to a mansion. But that was the problem, in the end—he overexpanded. Took one too many risks.' Angus shrugged. 'That's what I don't get though. I *know* he could've started again. He'd had nothing before, and Mum and I didn't care about the flash house, school and car. I'm still angry at him about that.' He paused for a long time.

He took a step towards her now, but then seemed to change his mind, and remained where he was. 'Anyway—

the point of all this, and I promise there is one, is that when my dad died, I couldn't sleep.'

'That makes sense,' Ivy said, but she was completely confused.

Angus's lips curved upwards without humour. 'I'm not very good at this. Maybe we should sit down.'

He led her to her couch, and they sat, side by side—but with a good-sized polite gap between them.

'I've always been a great sleeper,' Angus said. 'But when dad died, I just couldn't. Which I'm sure is normal. It went on for months—months of tossing and turning and snatches of sleep, and it certainly didn't get any better as Mum started to get sick. Then one night, I slept, and I was back to normal. And that only happened once I'd finished school and joined the army. It was like my subconscious could finally rest again amongst the rigidity and structure the armed forces gave me.'

He leant forward, putting the CD on her coffee table with a clatter. He remained leaning forward, his elbows resting on his knees as he looked at Ivy.

'The night you told me you were pregnant, I couldn't sleep,' he said. 'That was the first time since Dad died that's happened. But then, once I got my head around the idea and even feeling good about it—everything went back to normal.'

He sat up properly now, turning slightly so he faced her.

'Until two days ago. I had an awful night's sleep on Friday. And an even worse one last night.'

Ivy had no idea where this was going. 'I'm sorry?'

His smile was subtle. 'You should be, given it's your fault.'

'I'm lost,' she said. She'd never seen Angus like this. There was an uncertainty in his gaze she was completely unfamiliar with.

'I used to think there was something wrong with me because I didn't have Tom's nightmares, or that I was some robot because I enjoy the challenge of combat. I thought because I could walk away so easily from my girlfriends to go to war, because I never missed them—and because I was never that excited to see them when I returned—that I had to be lacking something. As if when my dad died and my mum got sick that my ability to love had gone with them. I thought that all I was was my job, and that, yes—maybe I was just a fighting machine incapable of emotion.'

Had he shifted on the couch? Or maybe she had, because now their knees were almost touching.

'But I worked out that I'm not sleeping because my life has been knocked off kilter, and until I set it right again it's not going to get any better. And the reason I'm floundering so badly—both right now and when I try to get some sleep—is because of you, Ivy. Meeting you has changed everything.'

'So you want me back in your life so you can get some sleep?' she asked, only half joking.

'No, I want you back in my life because I love you.'

And Ivy was so stunned she said absolutely nothing at all.

'I've realised I was wrong. It isn't that I'm not capable of emotion, or of falling in love—I just wasn't prepared to take that risk. And before you, I certainly hadn't met someone where that risk even seemed an option. I know how devastating it is to lose the people you love, and for the past fifteen or so years it's been a hell of a lot easier just to distance myself from all of that. If I don't love someone, it's easy when I'm deployed. It's easy to walk away.' He caught her gaze. 'You were right the other night, you know, but I wasn't ready to hear it. I had too many years of believing what I'd been telling myself, that I couldn't comprehend anything different.'

They'd both moved closer now, their knees bumping together.

'I used to think...*love* was dangerous,' Ivy said. The word was still hard to say, even if the echoes of Angus's declaration still rang in her ears. 'I thought love would cause me to lose control. To make poor decisions. To lose myself.' Her lips quirked. 'And, well—I was right about the control bit. I'm not quite myself when I'm with you, and that scared me. But the thing is, I've realised I'm *not* nineteen any more. I'm an adult, and my own person, and I'm not about to get swept up in silly delusions and daydreams. And yes—maybe it doesn't hurt if I lose control, now and again. You've even helped me learn that it's okay if I make mistakes.'

Angus reached out to still the hands that she barely realised she was twisting and untwisting together. He held them between his, his touch warm and reassuring—but, even now, shooting shivers along her skin.

'You're amazing, Ivy Molyneux,' he said. 'Amazing, and strong, and smart, and beautiful. I made the worst mistake of my life that morning, but I hope like hell I'm not too late to fix it now.'

Ivy looked down at their hands. At first she'd kept her hands still, but slowly she shifted her fingers, until their hands were linked together.

She leant closer, then lifted her gaze until it tangled with his.

'I love you,' she whispered against his mouth. 'You and our baby weren't part of any of my plans, but you've turned everything upside down in the most wonderful, perfect way. I guess that's how love is supposed to work? Without any plans.'

'Yeah,' Angus agreed, his breath warm against her skin. 'No plans. But lots of risks and probably more mistakes along the way. Are you okay with that?'

Ivy nodded as she smiled. 'Oh, yes,' she said.

She closed the infinitesimal gap between their mouths with a soft kiss.

'We all make mistakes, Angus,' she said, 'but I know I'm not making one now.'

EPILOGUE

IT WAS A beautiful day for a wedding.

Once again, an aisle stretched before Ivy. Once again, guests twisted on their white wooden chairs to look in her direction.

But today, it wasn't beach sand that she walked upon.

Instead, her path was a dusty red, her destination the dappled shade of a boab tree.

It was late October in the Pilbara, the sun warm—but not harsh—against her skin. Ivy walked to the gentle sounds of an acoustic guitar duo, the only sound amongst the surrounding silent landscape of Bullah Bullah Downs.

Until Nate began to cry.

Instantly, every guest's attention shifted to the pram that Irene Molyneux pushed back and forth, just to the left of the rest of the bridal party. Ivy's sisters, in their emerald-green dresses, abandoned their posts beside the swollen trunk of the Boab to coo somewhat helpfully—but it was Angus, in tailored shorts and an untucked white shirt, that immediately took action.

By the time Ivy stood beside him, her son was cradled against Angus's shoulder, and his cries had quietened to a half-hearted whine before spluttering out to a contented sigh. Angus smiled at Ivy, then kissed Nate's dark head.

Irene gestured to take Nate back, but Ivy shook her head.

Nate was happiest in his dad's arms, anyway.

A moment later Mila, April and Tom were all back in place, and Ivy, Angus and Nate stood before the celebrant.

A year ago, in Nusa Dua, Ivy never would've imagined any of this. A son, a soon-to-be-husband, a wedding.

Her whole life had been her career, her entire focus on Molyneux Mining.

But now—everything had changed.

Her career was still important, but it could wait a few more months.

Since Nate's birth, life had been a blur—but a different type of blur from before. Rather than meetings and emails and negotiations it was all about feeding, and nappies and—if she was lucky—sleep.

She couldn't say she loved every aspect of motherhood so far—especially not those three a.m. feeds—but she definitely, definitely loved Nate.

'You okay?' Angus asked, softly, as the celebrant introduced herself to the guests.

He was so handsome in the dappled light. His hazel eyes were gorgeous, and even now they made her heart leap whenever he looked in her direction. And he was a wonderful father. He'd been home for Nate's birth, and then gone for eight weeks. It had been hard, for both of them, but now he was back for a few months and was making every moment with his son count.

Yes, she definitely, definitely loved Angus, too.

Ivy nodded.

'No step counting?'

Ivy shook her head, surprised at the question. 'No, not in months.'

Angus's gaze had knocked Ivy off her axis all those months ago, but her world had realigned now. Different, but better than she ever could've imagined.

'I did,' Angus whispered.

'Really?'

'I counted your steps,' he said, with a smile. 'As you walked down that aisle.'

'Why? Do I make you nervous?' she teased.

'No,' he said. 'I was counting backwards, counting down until you become my wife.'

'That's very romantic,' Ivy said, with a smile. Angus's gaze traced every line of her face, as if she were the most beautiful thing he'd ever seen. She'd never felt more loved. More happy.

He shrugged. 'Seemed the time for it.'

Ivy laughed. 'But—how did you know what number to start counting at?'

'Would you believe I had special SAS training?'

'I'd believe you got it totally wrong and ran out of numbers too early.'

Angus grinned as their son burrowed tighter against his shoulder. 'If I did, it was only because Nate distracted me.'

He leant closer, to whisper against her ear. 'I love you.'

'I love you too.'

Together, smiling, they finally turned towards the celebrant, and the ceremony began.

And as the words washed over Ivy she wasn't worried about counting her steps, or work, or what anyone thought—or expected—of Ivy Molyneux.

As she stood here beneath the Pilbara sun, surrounded by the people she loved, all that mattered was *this* moment, *this* man, and this amazing baby they'd made together.

She'd wasted so much time terrified she'd made the worst mistake of her life that night in Nusa Dua.

But instead she'd got everything—absolutely everything—spectacularly right.

* * * * *

HARRY ST CLAIR: ROGUE OR DOCTOR?

FIONA MCARTHUR

To Lesley, who makes me smile, Vicki, who smiles as well, and Margo, from all those years ago. All friends who shared Bali with me. And my son, Andrew, who changed that tyre in the desert on the way to Ayers Rock and shared the magic of the red centre with me. And always Ian, my own rock. Happy thirtieth anniversary, my love.

CHAPTER ONE

SUNSET. Glorious Bali Island.

Harry St Clair glanced around the hotel swimming pool and grimaced. His usual calm deserted him just thinking of going back to Australia and the practice of medicine. To make it worse he was half an hour early to tell them it wasn't happening.

The pool chairs were littered with tourists sipping cocktails while waiting for sunset and he was careful not to catch the eye of any of them, especially the women, as he scanned for the man who'd arranged to meet him. Now was not the time for dalliance.

Bonnie McKenzie watched him arrive. All the women did. When he approached the pool the ladies' necks stretched like those of inquisitive turtles to follow his broad shoulders, and she rolled her eyes. She could hear Sacha, in the chair next to her, whisper to Jacinta, and she hoped the words didn't carry to where he stood.

'They call him the package. 'Cause he looks good, talks good and I'll bet my new black bikini he feels good. But he's a heartbreaker. Tells all the women he's not into relationships.' Jacinta sighed dreamily as her friend went on. 'He's not staying at the hotel. I asked the waitress. He's here to see someone.'

To Bonnie the man didn't look like a package. He looked like an isolated lighthouse off the coast of Wales that she'd once seen on television.

Alone, surrounded by jagged rocks, immovable in any storm as he waited, protected by a wall of sceptical disinterest in everyone until an older woman in a ceremonial sarong tapped him on the arm and he smiled. Then everything changed.

Then there was something about the tilt of his head and warm greeting as he responded to the Balinese lady with such kindness, such honest charm, it called even to Bonnie—which surprised her, because since selling her engagement ring she'd vowed she'd never be that receptive to a man again.

Good genes, her gran would have said. Bonnie found herself thinking, *Good jeans*, and she looked away and pressed her lips together to hold the smile in. These young midwives she'd travelled with from Darwin were a bad influence.

She looked back, fairly sure he couldn't see her under the shadow of her umbrella'd deckchair. He was talking to a man now, shaking his head at the elderly sunburnt tourist she'd seen around the hotel, but her eyes were drawn back to the younger one.

There, good lighthouse, a beam of radiance as the man beside him made him smile, and again, when he lifted one strong hand and shook the other man's hand. So he could soften and, yes, Bonnie could see why the girls felt the need to discuss him.

Now he looked casual and relaxed, lazily footloose in his cut-off blue jeans, his long brown legs testament to some sporting pursuit that kept him fit. Being footloose and declaring it seemed imminently sensible for him, and much better than stomping on hearts to scale the heights of a profession, like some Bonnie knew.

She could see this man's loosely buttoned sports shirt fought a losing battle if it wanted to disguise the width of his shoulders or the leanly muscular biceps that peeked out of the short sleeves. Not something that usually fascinated her, leanly muscular men, but those arms teased her now, corded with strength and generous with leashed power. She glanced down at the sudden swish of goose bumps across her own skin and lifted her face to find the breeze that caused it.

Hopefully there was a breeze...

Bonnie shifted back further under the umbrella in case her malady was too much sun. She glanced around and saw she wasn't the only woman still sneaking a peek. So, thankfully, she wasn't the only basket case because it seemed he called to every person with two X chromosomes.

No doubt being such a woman magnet could be a trial for him after a while and she wasn't about to join the party.

The thought settled her. Good. At least she had her common sense back, though she had to admit there was something shadowed and intriguing in his persona that begged the question of his past. Well, there was stuff in her own past, plenty of baggage for the unwary, and he could keep his load because she had enough of her own.

Bonnie looked away to the reds and golds of the Balinese sunset leaking colour into the waves. When Sacha actually nudged her to admire him again, Bonnie shook her head and whispered, 'Not interested in packages. I'm here to enjoy the sunset without discussing men.'

Sacha rolled her eyes. 'As you like. You watch the pretty ball in the sky and I'll watch my own view.' The girl winked and Bonnie shook her head and pressed her lips together again. She had to. The incorrigible young midwives had been making her smile since she'd unexpectedly joined their holiday.

Pushed into a short vacation by her friends in Darwin, this break had been designed to put a spring back in Bonnie's step before she started the new job at Ayers Rock, or Uluru now, she reminded herself, the ancient Aboriginal name for their sacred place. And, in fact, although her mouth still felt a bit stiff, she was finding more to smile about every day.

The last sliver of molten fire disappeared into the sea with an audible sigh, though, strictly speaking, the noise came from the collective breath of appreciation from the watchers as they turned and began to meander back to their rooms before the tropical night encroached.

'So what are we doing for dinner?' The girls lived for action and Bonnie searched in her head for a skerrick of enthusiasm. Nope. None there.

She'd floated quietly in the deep end of the pool last night and avoided them because she'd spent the first three days with a plastered-on smile. Now she just wanted to soak in the calmness that she had to admit had unexpectedly filtered back into her soul by Balinese osmosis.

'Think I might curl up on one of the lounges and

stare at the colours as they fade. Then maybe dinner in my room.'

'Okay.' The girls jumped up now. The nature show was over and youth needed diversion. 'Maybe we'll catch up with you later at the club.' They grinned, waved and took off like they'd miss the chance of a lifetime if they didn't run.

Harry St Clair watched the scantily clad nymphs hurry away but his eyes were drawn back to the quietly restful woman in the chair. He'd noticed her while he'd been talking to Bob. Allowed himself to be distracted from Bob's attempt at persuasion, though it hadn't been a hardship scoping her out. And here he was, still loitering when he could have gone.

He hesitated, conscious of his own aversion to disruption by people when he wished to be alone, and very aware of the 'don't bother me' signals that flew above her like those Balinese kites you'd see any afternoon here—happy doing their own thing.

But she intrigued him, attracted him ridiculously with a little flick of her hair and the stretch of her fingers when she put her glass down, and suddenly he didn't want to eat dinner in peace.

A little harmless weather conversation with an intriguing little sun-lover would chase away the demons the job offer had left him with. And he'd had a beer already so he wasn't driving back to Ubud until tomorrow.

She looked nothing like the usual women he flirted with. She looked more like someone he'd actually converse with. Like his housekeeper's sister, he'd just seen, or any woman safely married and motherly and therefore not interested in him as a fling, but this young woman seemed someone he could briefly connect with, which in itself was strange. Connection hadn't been on his agenda—especially in the last two years.

Serene, that was what she was, though serenity over sadness? Maybe it was just his ego because she hadn't looked his way at all and she obviously didn't feel any of the vibes he was getting.

Harry gave up the struggle and crossed to her umbrella. 'I wondered if they'd leave you alone,' he said, and as an opening remark it was pretty lame, but she looked even better up close. He was right. Her eyes did hold a background of darkness, or maybe green-toned memories that made him want to ask why. Maybe that was why he'd felt drawn to her.

She wore a cheap silk dress that looked incredibly cute on her, unlike the flaunting swimwear the others had worn, as if she wasn't confident displaying her body.

Shame, that.

The concept of conversation grew even more attractive. If he could convince her, that was, because she looked like he was the last person she needed to see, and usually that was enough deterrent when he just didn't care enough.

She took her time to tilt her firm little chin to a ridiculous angle so she could look up at his face. 'Actually, they're my friends.'

'Sorry. Didn't mean to be rude.'

Bonnie was in a dilemma. The palpitations had come from nowhere and his proximity was making it hard not to blush. The lighthouse offered her the five-star smile free of charge. Dazzling sweep of light. Then his words sank in. And even an apology. Not something Bonnie was used to getting from men. Nice of him, Bonnie thought, but she wished he hadn't because she didn't need more reasons to be attracted.

'I'm not judging,' he said. 'I remember being young.'

In years he was nowhere near old but there was a wealth of experience, possibly not all good, behind those dazzling eyes of his. Some days she felt decrepit too but didn't know this guy well enough to agree.

'Poor you.' Though he didn't look poor in any sense of the word. She wondered what had happened to make him feel aged but that was probably all part of his pick-up plan. He had to be somewhere between thirty and thirty-five, which put him five years older than her at least.

Up close he was even more impressive in a gut-wrenching, tear-the-breath-from-your-throat kind of way she didn't like to admit, but thankfully she could now call on months of training in unattainability. 'Do I know you?'

More smile and the look he was giving suggested he'd like to move that way. She ignored the little buzz that grew with the idea. 'I don't know. Do you?' He held out one tanned hand and she looked at it. 'Harry St Clair,' she heard him say.

Such beautiful hands. Long fingers, square-clipped nails, fine hairs across a strong back—and a wedding band. She hadn't noticed that before and she didn't know why she'd be shocked. Maybe because the way he was smiling at her had nothing to do with fidelity. It was a strange old world when people could act like this.

Bonnie uncurled herself from the chair and stood up next to him. She was tall but he was taller by a fair margin and that only made her more annoyed. She couldn't hide the contempt in her eyes but then, that was what happened when you smelled a rat when you expected aftershave.

She raised her eyebrows and then her chin. 'I don't know you.' She shook her head. 'Do I know your wife?'

His hand dropped and his other came over the ring and hid it from view. 'I doubt that. She's been gone for more than two years.'

Bonnie closed her eyes. He was a widower? Hell. 'I'm sorry.' But it was too late now. She'd jumped to the conclusion he was just like Jeremy, Dr Sleaze, with the harem of women in the wings and their joint bank account he'd emptied.

Infidelity brought back the memories she'd thought she'd zippered away in a sealed compartment, like she'd packed her suitcase to fly into Denpasar. But that was no excuse for accusing him.

She could feel her fingers against her side, twitching a little as if hoping he'd put his hand out again and give her another shot. But her hand wouldn't make the journey by itself. Her barriers were secure. That was a good thing. 'I'm sorry. I have to go.'

Harry wasn't ready for that. Hadn't expected it because it didn't happen to him often. In fact, he couldn't remember the last time he'd been given the flick so smoothly. He followed her. 'I didn't catch your name.'

She kept walking and obviously she didn't care if he heard her or not. 'I didn't throw it,' she muttered.

So this was how it felt, Harry reminded himself. Unpleasant, but more interesting. Maybe he was a masochist? The wall around her was higher than the one around the Royal Palace in Ubud and twice as fascinating. He knew all about walls to keep people out. Suddenly it became imperative he have more than a brief chat with her about the weather.

He took two big steps and caught up with her. 'But you threw an insult. I'm only looking for a nice platonic dinner partner to share Jimbaran Bay with. Maybe we could talk about that?'

At least she'd stopped. Turned to look at him. But she wasn't saying anything. He could feel those liquid eyes assessing him, and he felt as if he were posing, like in a passport photograph, with that frozen, trying-not-to-look-like-a-psychopath expression on his face.

It was as if she didn't know what to say so she didn't say anything at all. More people should try that. It was attractive. And at least it wasn't no.

He went on because he knew he had seconds before she disappeared. Make it count, old boy. 'I really am Harry St Clair. They know me here. I'm reluctant to ask someone else.' He glanced around as if there were loads of women he could ask. 'All those candles and tables in the sand at Jimbaran are just too romantic.' He shrugged. 'I can tell you loathe me. I'd feel safe with you.'

He felt like groaning. What the heck was falling out of his mouth? He was an idiot and he wouldn't blame her if she ran away. Where had that come from?

'I think you've tickets on yourself,' she said, and her

eyes suddenly looked as lush as the local jungle and just as dangerous. Maybe this wasn't such a good idea because this woman had weapons he wasn't that sure he could hold out against if she used them all.

'I apologise. I was insensitive about your wife.' She looked away and he thought he heard her sigh. 'I don't know you enough to loathe you but I guess I could think about trying.'

Bonnie glanced over her shoulder at the pinking horizon. Was she mad? Was it too late to squirm out? 'The sun's gone. Why go to Jimbaran now?' She'd heard of the bay past the airport. 'Everything I've heard's about the sunset.'

He slanted a quick look at her as he followed her towards the main building of the resort. 'I enjoy eating seafood on the beach. But not alone. My treat?'

'Wow. A big spender. I might choose lobster.' Even to her it sounded like a yes. She didn't know the man. But then, the girls had implied he wasn't a serial killer. Most men who looked like him usually weren't. No doubt some women would do their own dying to attract his attention.

But there was that tiny worrying buzz that hummed somewhere near her stomach when she looked at him. The last time she'd been attracted this noticeably to a man it had ended in major disaster and she'd decided she truly enjoyed being single.

Which would be why her friends had practically forced her onto the plane to Denpasar. Hmm. Maybe she didn't enjoy total isolation from all men all the time. Maybe she just needed a holiday flirtation to restore her self-esteem and a sense of balance?

'I'm good for the bill.' He glanced at his watch, a flash one, and she wondered if it was real or one of the ten-dollar fakes that were sold on every corner in Kuta. It looked real but then, so did he and she didn't believe in him. And this hotel was nice but not expensive. Not a place for watches like his. Lots of things didn't make sense.

He went on. 'I'm starving. You look great. Don't suppose you'd come as you are?'

He was way too pushy but she was hungry now, not sure where that appetite had come from. She glanced down at the halter-necked silk dress she'd picked up at the markets. It was cool, comfortable and matched the sequined slides she'd bought with it. Why change for a man she barely knew?

'I'll leave a note under the girls' door.' It didn't hurt to pretend somebody cared where she went and with whom.

He nodded. 'Great idea. In case we're late.'

Cool green eyes met blue. 'We won't be late.'

Harry looked across at her and tried to figure it out. Every time he looked into her eyes he fell more deeply under her spell. And she was determined. It was her way or the highway and he respected that. But it would be good to settle why he'd been so affected by her and then get her out of his head. Note to self: not into his bed. Good plan.

Harry hoped she couldn't see how amazed he was she'd agreed at all. He'd thought they'd imploded after she'd mentioned Clara but they'd come around again. He was ridiculously pleased about that. Maybe it was just the fact he could talk to her and not feel he had to be someone he wasn't. Not sure why that was either.

'I'll get a taxi, then, shall I?'

CHAPTER TWO

IT SEEMED Jimbaran Bay had become an institution like Kuta with a long strip of restaurants.

The beach lay stretched to the north of them with choose-your-fish and lobster tanks, flame-leaping barbecues and the biggest array of fresh seafood Bonnie had seen for years.

Then there were the hundreds of wooden tables spread across the sand almost down to the lapping water, each restaurant's tables abutting each other as they squeezed side by side.

A pall of barbecue smoke lay over the parking area when the taxi dropped them off, people coming and going, taxis and private cars and even limousines jostling for space. And, of course, hundreds of motorbikes parked in orderly rows.

Bonnie gazed in awe at the confusion and choice. 'How do you know which restaurant to eat in?'

'Been before. I have my favourite and they'll save a good table for me.' Harry watched her drink it in. Her pleasure made him look again, inhale the smoke, hear the chatter between the competing restaurants, and recognise some of the reasons he seemed to end up here when he came down to this end of Bali.

But most of his unusual lightness of heart seemed to be emanating from being with the woman at his side. Strange, that.

She walked with him down the concrete passage between two vying shopfronts and he could feel her presence near his hip like a little force-field of energy reacting with him. Swirls of awareness prickled like the sprays of loose sand that flicked off their shoes as they walked.

When they hit the beach the sun had well and truly gone, a darkening silhouette of a fishing boat glided out on the waves as the candles flared into life along the tables. Darkness fell softly, like one of those cashmere pashminas the women wore here. He heard her sigh out a little more tension from those militant shoulders and it made him feel good.

Bonnie felt herself relax as she looked around. This was different. Time out of the real world, maybe because of the semidarkness. She could get used to eating in the dark on a beach too. It was so unlike her to come with a stranger but there were enough people to keep her safe here and she could always catch her own taxi home. And suddenly it felt fun to be out with a good-looking man for an uncomplicated dinner. Her friends would be very proud of her.

They crunched through the sand all the way down to the water's edge. Bonnie glanced at couples and families and noisy groups of tourists all munching and laughing in groups as they passed.

To her delight every table had at least one person sucking milk from a coconut through a straw. The cheerful mood lifted her spirits even higher. She used to be a happy person and it was nice to glimpse a little joy again.

Finally their waiter stopped at a table. It wasn't quite in the water but there was no one in front to obscure the last of the glow on the horizon. She stood for a moment and just gazed out over the waves. Definitely a cool place to have dinner.

Harry beat the waiter to her chair and pulled it out for her. 'Your throne, madam.'

She could feel the hairs on her arms respond to his nearness. Visceral response. Pheromones. This wasn't good. She wanted flirtation, not irreversible fascination. Please, not that sort of happy. Her eyes met his and she didn't smile. 'I'm your dinner partner, not your date.'

Snap. Reality bit. Harry was silent as he sat down and then picked up his fork to examine it. Carefully—while he let her words sink in. Nice fork. Silver with three tines. Not much of interest there. 'Got it. No chairs held. And I'll have no deep and meaningful conversations from you either,' he joked, but there was an underlying truth in his words.

He glanced up and caught the fiercely guarded expression on her face. She was as bad as him. Funny how he'd never realised how bad he was. 'What about car doors? Did that offend you?' He saw her face tighten even more.

She closed her eyes and held up her hands and he could foresee the moment when she'd say she shouldn't have come.

Panic flared in her eyes and he cursed his stupidity.

Some bloke had done a doozy on her. Oops, he thought, but didn't say it out loud. He accepted the message and tapped the table so she looked at him. He tried selling his smile again. 'I'm sorry.'

That was when he realised he didn't know her name. Pleasant and non-threatening dinner conversation coming up. 'I really don't want to eat alone. But what shall I call you?'

Bonnie forced herself to calm down. Panic weakened defences and that was the last thing she wanted. Her name? Now, there was a dilemma. She had this stupid urge to make up a name, something wildly outrageous that he'd know wasn't real, so it didn't cause problems but would maintain distance in case she needed more space than he was willing to give.

Brain vacuum didn't help. 'Bonnie.'

'So tell me, Bonnie...' He paused and she smiled to herself because it was plain he didn't believe that really was her name. Delicious.

'Are you in Bali long?' He sat back in his chair with a little smile curving his lips. Good grief, he had gorgeous lips.

She blinked. 'A week. Then I start a new job.'

'So what's your new job?' When he leaned back his shirt stretched over his chest and her mouth dried.

She tried to unobtrusively rustle up some saliva so she could answer. 'Outreach nursing, at Ayers Rock. I'm a registered nurse and midwife and do short stints in isolated places.'

A strange expression crossed his face so fast she couldn't guess the cause. Interesting but he didn't explain it. Just nodded.

Blimey. Talk about danger, Harry thought. The same place as the job he'd declined. And too close to a town he wanted to forget. His wife had been a midwife, they'd met at Katherine when he'd worked for the RFDS. Fate was out to smack him apparently.

When he changed the subject she didn't seem to notice. Thank goodness. He'd already said he only wanted a dinner partner, which apparently suited her fine.

Back to discussing her might be safer. 'So what have you done here in paradise you wouldn't have done at home?'

She gestured to the beach in front of them. 'Apart from dining with a man I don't know, you mean?'

He wasn't silly enough to fall into the trap. 'Hmm.'

She shrugged. 'Nothing, really. Swam, but I did that in Darwin, shopped at markets and watched the sunset over the ocean, but we do that at Mindil on Thursdays and Sundays in Darwin too.'

He watched her think about it. Her thoughts may as well have been typed up on a screen. It was amusing how transparent she was and he found it delightfully refreshing. 'While I'm here I'd like to see some of the countryside. The terraced rice fields and a volcano— none of those where I come from.'

He nodded. He'd found a topic. 'So you should do the bike ride from Agung.'

He could tell she'd vaguely heard of it but couldn't place it. 'And that would be…?'

He gestured loosely in the direction of Kuta. 'Up in the mountains, a couple of hours' drive, well worth it. The bike ride's about twenty-five kilometres long.'

'Probably not happening, then.' She shrugged. 'I haven't ridden a bike for ten years.' She laughed at the thought. 'That'd be a sight. I wouldn't be able to stand up after.'

Bonnie tried not to get sucked under his spell but his smile was infecting her. Flashing like a beam over the waves when she least expected to see it in the gloom and made her think of the lighthouse again. He sat forward a little, leaning towards her in an effort to enthuse her. 'The ride's all downhill. Through villages, rice fields, over a river. You'd love it.'

She only had a few days left. She doubted she'd organise herself enough for that. 'I don't think bike riding's on my list.'

She watched him frown. 'Sure it is. If you're up for it, let me know. I have great contacts.'

She'd love it but she didn't need his help. Or his company. One night of exposure and flirtation was enough to start with and this guy was just too potent for a bruised heart like hers. 'I'll see what the girls say.' They'd probably ask how many men were going. But she wasn't debunking the myth that she had protection.

Thankfully it seemed he'd accepted she wouldn't be pinned to a decision. 'So what else would you like to do while on beautiful Bali?'

Well, she knew she didn't want to talk about herself. Never had really. 'How about you tell me what you're going to do. How long you're here for?'

He raised his dark brows and smiled. 'So bossy,' he said. She wished.

Then, as if vaguely surprised at himself, he did answer her. 'I'm here indefinitely. There's a house up in Ubud. My mother lived there a few months every year. I've been visiting for a while.'

Real watch evidently. 'Wow. And I'm guessing you have servants and everything.' Even she could hear the reverse snobbery in her voice. Where had that come from?

He tilted his head and she guessed he'd heard it too. 'There's a family that maintain the buildings, yes. Have done for fifty years. Ketut and his wife have looked after my mother and she looked after them. But like family—not servants. You have a problem with that?'

Of course she didn't. And the idea of extra family was a sweet one. She'd be happy to have a distant aunt, let alone a Balinese family looking after her. No reason on earth why she should mind except to wonder why he wanted to waste his time with her. 'No. I'm sorry. I keep putting my foot in it with you—not sure why. It's not common for me.'

'Maybe it's because I keep you off balance.' He grinned. 'But, then, that's not nice for a platonic friend so I'll apologise too.' He glanced down at the menu. 'We'd better order before it's too dark for you to see what you're eating.'

Now her hunger seemed to have soaked into the sand under her feet and she wished she could follow it. Who was out of practice as a relaxed dinner companion? 'What are you having?'

He put the menu back on the table. 'I'll do the set plate with lots of seafood and a side salad.'

She couldn't even read the menu in the dark. 'Sounds good.'

He sat straighter and glanced around. 'You get a drink with it. Have you tried the local beer? It's very light.'

She'd seen it advertised everywhere. 'No, but bought the T-shirt.'

He grinned and signalled the waiter, who appeared like magic. 'We'll have two Jimbaran specials, two beers and a coconut drink, please.'

Obviously she'd been blatant with her curiosity about the coconuts. But it was nice he'd seen her interest. Or was it? She'd need to watch this man. He was unobtrusively delightful.

The waiter produced two beers from his passing friend, set them down and departed with a big white smile. Harry handed one over to her. Then he carried on the conversation as if there'd been no break.

'Those T-shirts are the most common exports with tourists. Hope you didn't pay more than twenty thousand rupees for it.'

So he was focused. She'd need to watch that too, but she'd been dying to talk to someone about this.

She tapped her glass with her fingernail. 'I have issues with bartering. I can see the Balinese enjoy it, but I'd prefer just to buy the darn thing without the hassle. I find it very stressful to pretend I'm offended at the price.'

He took a sip and when he didn't answer, she decided to copy him. A tentative sip. The drink was light, still beery and she wasn't that much of a fan, but it was cold and wet and felt wonderful going down.

Then he said, 'Wimp,' and she nearly choked. He grinned and went on. 'Barter is fun. It's part of Balinese culture, like mental gymnastics. Good bargaining can make a huge difference to a family wage if they're lucky.

But the experience should never be unpleasant or too pushy.'

'Yeah, well. I'm such a sucker.' She sighed. 'What do you do when people look sad and you feel guilty you haven't bought anything?'

'You smile.' He grinned and showed her how. If he smiled at someone like that they'd probably give him the thing, she thought. Free.

He went on. 'It's the secret of Bali. Smile and mean it. For bargaining, if they start at fifty thousand rupees, you offer twenty-five. They'll look horrified, you smile and they'll smile and counter with forty. Then you say thirty and they'll take thirty-five. It's always good to aim for about five thousand under what you want to pay so the seller wins. It's good luck for the seller and we can all do with that.'

Not an accurate picture of barter when she was involved. She tended to wilt at the first horror and fake accusation. 'Forty-nine thousand would be a good barter for me. That sounds easy but it's not.'

The light from the candle flickered across his face. He shook his head and she decided he didn't have a bad angle she could concentrate on. 'That's because you're thinking personal. It's not personal. When it all boils down to it, if you want something, think about what you'd pay for it and be happy. Then change what they're asking into your currency and you'll see you still have a bargain. Carry a printed version of your dollar versus their currency. It's simpler to remember that way.'

She wasn't sure she was ever going to enjoy bargaining but maybe she'd give it a go with a little more enthusiasm. She could write out a conversion table. 'Okay.'

Or maybe she hadn't sounded as convinced as she'd thought because he said, 'Or look for fixed-price shops. There's always one around and then you'll get a fair price, not quite as cheap but they'll take out the wild swings when someone really good reels you in.'

She glanced at his confident face. 'I bet you don't get reeled in.'

'Not often. By the Balinese anyway.' There was an added nuance she didn't want to identify and thankfully their food arrived.

By this time it was darker, and even though her eyes had adjusted, the candle gave off small circles of light that didn't include the platter beside her. The waiter brought two more tiny candlelights but she still couldn't see what she was eating. 'So this is a taste sensation, not a visual one?'

He laughed, deep and amused, and she felt like a trickle of that cool sand under her feet had slid down her back and along her arms. Well, she was on a beach. It was okay. But she had a strong premonition there was more trickling sand to come.

'Want to see your dinner?' She watched him shift his body and reach into his pocket and then suddenly there was a blinding flash.

She rubbed her eyes. He laughed again. 'Sorry. Should've warned you.' His smile beamed in the night as her vision began to recover and he handed her his camera. 'It looks like this.'

Bonnie's meal was captured for posterity and illuminated clearly on the camera screen. 'You're really a do-now-think-later kinda guy, aren't you?' But she could see a long barbecued fish, brown and crunchy, and one gruesome eye. She wished she hadn't seen that but at least she wouldn't accidentally eat it in the dark. She shuddered.

'The less thinking the better,' he said cryptically, then went on. 'The ones in the shells are mussels, and despite the thought if you're not a shellfish eater, they taste wonderful. King prawns, calamari on skewers, crab and lobster meat piled on the side. And the green salad.'

It was all recognisable now. Actually, quite a neat trick to take the photo, she acknowledged, at least to herself. 'Obviously you've used this in the dark before.'

He tucked the camera away in his pocket. 'Too many times on my own. I'm glad you came.'

'So am I.' She was. And feeling more relaxed. Bonnie didn't think it was the beer, though maybe it had more of a kick than he was letting on, but the atmosphere here would make anyone feel good.

Smiling Balinese waiters, the muted wash of the waves just a few feet away, candles all around them and brighter lights in the distance. Every now and then a plane took off or landed at Ngurah Rai airport across the water and the stars had started to shine more brightly as the night deepened. 'This is pretty cool. Thank you for bringing me.'

'You're welcome.' Her coconut drink arrived and even in the dark it looked huge. 'Do you want me to take a photo of that so you can see it?'

She thought of the brightness of the flash and the disruption of the mood. 'I can guess. It's not worth the eye pain.' She picked it up and the milk inside sloshed. 'I'll never finish this.'

'That's why I only bought one. Drink what you fancy and leave the rest. I'll finish it so you don't feel guilty.'

There was something disturbing about the thought of him drinking from her straw, too easy to picture and not without sensory ramifications. She turned the conversation.

'The stars are amazing.'

'Bit too much light here to do them justice.'

'I love stars but wish I knew more about them.'

'I'm not much better,' he said, and they both glanced up then down at each other and for some reason they both laughed. The beginnings of a dangerous rapport. They both sobered.

Bonnie broke the silence. 'So what do you do while you're over here?' She took a sip and the strong flavour of coconut overlaid the beer.

He attacked his meal as if he wanted distance from that moment too. 'Nothing.'

He paused as if waiting for her to say how terrible to drift between jobs, but she wasn't going to.

For a short time, *nothing* would be great. And that pastime would be as far away from Jeremy as possible. Her ex didn't know anything about cultivating stillness. The longer they were parted the better she was feeling, except she'd learned a very valuable lesson about people who lied.

'So you don't get bored?' She took another bite and chewed while she waited. The fish melted in her mouth and the tang of lime made her sigh with bliss.

He put down his fork. 'Not yet. I do a bit of diving up at Lovina, some surfing.'

She picked up the coconut again. This meal was a symphony of different flavours and she was glad she hadn't chickened out. Surfing, diving, eating on beaches. Sounded idyllic. For a while. 'Do you do anything constructive? What's your profession? Your job when you're not surfing?'

Anything worthwhile? His raised eyebrows noted the observation that lay unspoken between them, but still the question had popped out and mentally she shrugged. Well, she did want to know because surfing and scuba diving wasn't a lifestyle, especially if he was trained to do something useful, or had done in the past.

She'd been devastated by her love life bombing out but she hadn't given up her life to hide in a distant country. No. If she was honest, she'd hidden in work. Which was the reverse of what he'd done, she supposed.

He was silent for a few beats. 'Sometimes I build things, work in the fields every now and then. And I'm studying yoga.'

The last thing she would have connected with him but then, he did occasionally give off restful vibes. 'I can't quite see you and yoga together.' She thought about it some more. 'So you're going to be a yoga teacher? I guess both our professions are about health.'

'No. I'm studying it for myself.'

She laughed. He amused her, he really did. 'Selfish 'R' Us? Who will look after you if you don't?'

'That's right.' He sat back in his seat and smiled. If she wasn't mistaken, she'd say he was relieved by her amusement.

She couldn't imagine not having work to take her

mind off the rest. 'So what about your parents? What do they think of you growing old on an island?'

'They're both dead.'

Oops. 'I'm an orphan too. It sucks.' She really didn't want to talk about this and wasn't sure why she was except she felt somehow responsible for the conversation. 'My mum died when I was twelve. Never knew my father and my gran brought me up. She died three months ago. I nursed her at home.' *And my sleazy fiancé slept with his ex and stole all my money while I was busy.* But she was getting over that. Really.

'Tough, but special. So you normally work as a midwife?'

'Mostly. I trained in Darwin, did a little time in ICU, but mostly a midwife. I love working remote in short stints but you miss out on the births mostly that way.'

She speared another succulent piece of fish. 'And you, before you came here?'

'Different things. None of them useful.' Slam. She felt the whoosh from the shutting door. Now she wished she'd shut her mouth. She kept it closed in case something else came out that she'd regret and ate another piece of fish and left him with the silence. He'd caused it.

Harry had a pretty good idea what she was thinking. Well, what could he say? She wasn't getting the truth. Oh, did medicine, fell in love, lost wife and child because I was stupid, now have abdicated from world.

By the time she'd finished her fish he could see she was full. Not a big eater, he gathered. In fact, she seemed a little on the thin side.

When the waiter returned he shook his head at

the proffered menus. 'I'm guessing you don't need sweets.'

'No, thank you.'

'Any chance of a quick stroll along the beach before we leave?'

She opened her mouth to say no but he kept talking and successfully forestalled her. Another win to him. 'Just to let the food settle. Only as far as the tables go and it's in plain view of everyone.'

He could see she hated the thought of giving in to him again. Her independence amused him and only made him more determined to conquer her reserve. He wanted to win! Now how long since he'd felt that?

Bonnie didn't know where this competitiveness had come from but probably she should listen to it as a warning signal. She was her own woman. Then her mouth said, 'Maybe for a few minutes and then I must get back to my friends.'

'Sure.' He stood up and despite their initial conversation he helped pull out her chair. 'It gets a little tricky in the sand when the chairs sink in a bit.'

Bonnie felt him beside her. Her arms did that hair-waving thing again and this time the shiver went right down to her toes. To break the mood she said the first thing that came into her head. 'Are you saying I'm so heavy I bogged my chair?'

His teeth flashed as he glanced at her figure. 'No.'

He nodded at the waiter to say they'd be back and they took the few steps to the water's edge and began walking along towards the airport in the distance. They didn't speak but strangely it wasn't as awkward as she'd thought it would be.

The waves lapped politely, no big chasers in the occasional wash up like happened at home, just gentle lapping that never threatened her light slides, or her concentration at maintaining a safe distance.

The sand crunched firmly beneath their feet and the stars overhead twinkled benignly down on them. She could feel her annoyance from his refusal to discuss his life recede like the water beside her and she let it go.

It didn't matter. Really it didn't. She didn't know him. Probably wouldn't see him again and it had been a very pleasant meal.

Then he ruined it. 'Any chance of meeting up tomorrow?'

She fought back the overreaction she wanted to make, like a full-throated scream of *Yes*, and impressed herself by the way her answer slid out quite lightly. 'No.'

'The day after?'

She wanted a flirtation, not an affair. Already she was too aware of every facial expression, every shrug of those lovely shoulders and the strength in those powerful legs that walked beside her. Sensory overload. She glanced at him. 'Thanks for dinner. Can we go back now?'

Harry felt her pull away, even though her body didn't move. It was a subtle stiffening and leaning to increase the distance between them. Unmistakable. Well, he'd blown that. Not something he was used to doing but he was just out of practice. Funny how he could be smooth with someone he didn't care how it went with and a bumbling idiot with someone he wanted to impress.

Now, why was he trying to impress her? He slanted a glance at Bonnie of the determined chin and wondered why as they walked back to their table. He liked it that she was taller than most women, though she was a little frail. He could easily imagine being able to span her waist with his hands, and maybe he should insist on dessert to fatten her up.

She seemed too fragile to him. Maybe nursing her gran had really taken it out of her. He could feel the swell of empathy pulling bricks out of the walls he'd built over the last two years, snapping mortar and the solid pattern of layers like a berserk tradesman. Now, how had he left himself open to that?

His sensible side began a mental slurry of cement on the cracks and crumbles and hardened his heart. Then the words came easily.

'I'll pay the bill and take you home, then.'

CHAPTER THREE

In the early hours of the morning Harry lay on his side and gazed out over the beach. He watched the stars inch their way across the sky. He'd tried turning his back on them but he knew they were there. Laughing at him. He couldn't remember the last time he'd tossed and turned over a woman. Well, he could but he didn't want to remember that disaster.

But Bonnie was different, softer, like a calm place to sit and enjoy situations and surroundings he'd forgotten how to enjoy. And that tinge of sadness around her sat like a mist he wanted to wave away. Problem was that voice in his head had burnt him before. He squeezed his pillow again and buried his ear into the packed softness of feathers. Softness was a pain.

Next morning, he found himself standing beside her breakfast table. Just in case she'd changed her mind. 'Good morning, Bonnie.'

Bonnie shook her head. Obviously Harry didn't understand no. Which for an intelligent man seemed a little bizarre.

She took a careful sip of her tea, savoured the honey—

Bali had lovely black tea—and ignored the little glow that wasn't leaf-related. 'Good morning, Harry.'

'You must be Bonnie's friends.' He glanced at the girls as if to check their response to her fake name. Bonnie's smile kicked. Now, that was gold.

'May I join you?' His open-necked shirt exposed a strong brown throat and the buttons strained as he leaned over the table. Her poor young friends nearly swallowed their spoons. Too much testosterone this early in the morning.

Sacha stuttered. 'O-of course.' With cheeks like fairy floss she practically offered him her own chair, then turned wondering eyes on Bonnie. 'You said it was a one-off.'

It was a six-seater table. Bonnie made a note to herself to insist on a table that would only seat three next time. 'He's obviously slow on the uptake.'

Sacha waved him into a bamboo chair and he sat down. 'I wondered if I could interest you ladies in a bike ride down Mt Agung. I have a friend who runs tours and he's got a couple of places left this morning.'

'Two or three?' Bonnie asked sweetly. It was a dare for him to be specific. He smiled sweetly at her.

'Three or four.'

'Even room for you?' Bonnie sighed. Before he could answer, Jacinta dropped her shoulders and Sacha did too. 'We're out. We booked that cooking class thing today.'

Harry attempted to look disappointed. 'And you?'

'It really is Bonnie, you know.' She smiled sweetly. Did she want to spend a whole day with this guy? Or would she spend it by herself, wishing she'd gone with him?

After the call last night this was her last full day and
the bike ride sounded ideal. She'd see the countryside
after all and she needed to break out of this cloud of
apathy she'd been in for the last few months. He was
certainly helping there.

It seemed unlikely he'd attempt to race her off in a
pack of cyclists. And she had some say in it. 'What time
is this ride and how do I know it really exists?'

'You do have a nastily suspicious mind.' He produced
a brochure and a mobile phone. 'But I expected that.
You could ring Wayan and ask him.'

She took the glossy pamphlet and turned it over in
her hands. The number stood out plainly and she was
very tempted to do it. He was daring her now and she
couldn't decide if he was real or fake. He'd be great at
poker.

He looked suspiciously ready to go in that open-
necked shirt that dared her to peek at the strong column
of his throat but she wasn't going to.

He wore different blue jeans and scuffed joggers that
might have been expensive in their heyday, and that
watch, which she'd decided was definitely not real. Like
him.

There, she'd made a decision. If the watch was fake,
he was fake. She'd buy one in the women's version and
this man would know the right vendor on the street.
'Where'd you buy your watch?'

'Geneva.'

She wrinkled her nose. There was no deception in
the answer. She'd been wrong. Again. 'What time is
pick-up?'

'Half an hour.' He was rushing her. He liked to do

that but she'd lost the bet with herself so she had to go. For an internal argument it was pretty thin. It was just so darned hard to say no to someone who made her smile. At least on the inside.

The bus had seen better days but the grins of the tour guides were shiny new. Typically Balinese, they oozed warmth and fun and pleasure at the company of tourists and the chance to show off their culture and country. Something a lot of countries could learn from, Bonnie mused as she was helped into the bus.

Four couples made up the bus passengers when they started again—two young female schoolteachers from Portugal, two chefs from France, a fitness instructor and his wife from the States, and Harry and Bonnie from Australia.

Bonnie was jammed against the window, which in itself was a good thing and not only for the view. It was a bit like choosing a window seat on the plane. You could create your own space if you needed. But she could still feel the warmth from Harry's jeans-clad leg against hers and that wasn't going away unless she broke the safety glass.

Harry laughed and joked with the others around them about accents and travel mishaps, a different person from the man she'd seen yesterday at the pool. Aloof and cynical seemed to have stayed home today. So why'd he been so threatened yesterday? Interesting.

Bonnie found herself relaxing back with a little proprietorial smile that said she was here—with him—as the little bus ground up the mountain. Until she realised her sin and it slipped from her face.

Then she frowned. Crazy. This was holiday, short-term, transient. Even more transient than she'd anticipated. Enjoy the moment, enjoy the company and most of all enjoy Harry. She was on vacation, for goodness' sake, and she'd soon be at the new job, wishing she had. This was safe.

Harry saw the moment Bonnie became a part of the group and suddenly the day seemed brighter. She smiled at him and for that moment the sadness he'd glimpsed in her eyes was gone. He felt his breath kick somewhere at the back of his throat and his chest expanded. He'd done that. He'd helped her feel better. And it felt good.

That was when he reminded himself to be careful.

He looked away from her profile, past the itching temptation to study the bones of her face and out the window towards the ancient volcano as it came into sight. Terraced rice fields skirted the mountains like layers on a brilliant green wedding cake and that thought made him shudder.

This wasn't him. Connecting with women was so not on his programme. He'd been there and the pain was so great he wasn't climbing that volcano so he could fall off again. He'd pulled himself away from all he knew, bolted home to Bali, the one place where he could drift and nobody would think it out of the ordinary. A place he could drown out the voice in his head that said he didn't want this empty life but he wasn't willing to risk more pain.

'Is that a volcano?' Bonnie turned towards him and her eyes were like the rice fields outside the window—iridescent with life.

He ran his hand down his face to clear any dumb

expression he might've been left with. 'Yes, Mt Agung. We'll be having morning tea at the restaurant above Mt Batur, at Kintamani—lots of old lava at the base of that one. Then we'll pick up the bikes at a village and ride downhill until we get to the river.' He shut his mouth. He was rambling.

'So how many times have you done this?'

He shrugged. 'A few.' Too many. 'Sometimes I help out when they're short of supervising riders, and it's always a great day.' Brainless, time consuming, just what he wanted.

She tilted her head. 'You said you were visiting. How long have you been here this time?'

'On and off, nine months this time.' She was studying him and he could feel his face freeze with the old barriers at giving anything away.

'A whole pregnancy,' she said, and he winced. Great timing. A good boot to the guts like he needed to stop the rot. Ironic.

He turned away and spoke to the Portuguese girl about surfing, blocking Bonnie out, and yet still he felt it when she withdrew her attention and looked back out the window. His breath eased out. The Portuguese girl batted her eyelashes at him but her interest didn't faze him like Bonnie's did. Funny, that.

Finally they made it to the first stop. He'd never noticed the trip taking so long before and he felt like shaking himself like a dog to get out of Bonnie's aura. He'd been mad to ask her out today. Not just mad. Dangerously insane.

For Bonnie, the view from the restaurant overlooking

the volcano at Kintamani took her breath, and thankfully her mind, off the puzzle of the man next to her.

From where she stood overlooking the valley, because the restaurant walkway hung over the cliff, the view presented the huge lake and black scarring of the lava across the valley floor. Great gaping inverted cones up the side of Mt Batur showed the force of the volcanic activity.

'When was the last eruption?' She asked the question without looking at him. She didn't have to turn to know he was right there. Her sensory receptors had warned her.

'Nineteen ninety-four. One of the earlier ones swallowed the temple at Kintamani village. The western slopes are closed at the moment. The seismological institute thinks there's risk of further eruptions. Pity. It's a great walk to the rim for sunrise.'

Bonnie looked through the window into the restaurant at the rice and crêpes waiting, very strange morning tea on offer, and glanced at the view again. 'What's the lava like up close?

'Hard and black. I rode across the whole field on a motorbike years ago and it was like jagged corrugated iron. The locals use it for building and you can see the areas where the lava's been quarried.'

As a guide he was knowledgeable, though distracting from the view, enthusiastic about local history, just not good at being consistently relaxing, and she couldn't see much of the yoga student this morning.

Then again, maybe it wasn't his fault because half an hour later, when she followed the others back to the bus and climbed in, it was Harry's leg alongside hers that she was waiting for. In fact, she could feel little waves of anticipation building as she sat down.

Disappointingly, this time they didn't touch. Interesting and a little unacceptable, and she wasn't quite sure how he managed it. As an experiment she allowed her knee to accidentally knock against his while she looked out the window and there was no doubt he shifted further away.

Definite reversal of the forces of attraction. She'd blotted her copybook somehow. Maybe it was the crack about pregnancy.

On her recent history of foot-in-mouth moments he'd probably lost a car full of children too. She sighed and then shrugged. This was why she didn't get involved with men. Too complicated and distracting. It was a beautiful day and she was going to enjoy it if it killed her. She smiled to herself. Or him.

Wayan, their guide, had spent the last five minutes of travel explaining about luwak coffee and the main export for the plantation they were about to visit, but Bonnie had faded out.

So when the bus trundled into a dusty car park alongside other decrepit buses all shaded by overhanging trees and vines, she wondered if this was where the bike ride started.

She was thinking about the last man she'd fallen for and how that whole fiasco had poisoned her life. How, foolishly, she'd thought they'd planned the whole wedding thing, the first two years of saving, agreed on children, she'd put her savings with his for the deposit on their dream home.

She'd come home shattered from nursing her gran,

vaguely aware she hadn't paid much attention to him for the last hard few weeks, and when she had come back for the comfort he'd promised—he'd been gone, along with her money. Not that she'd cared about that at that point.

'And it's the most expensive coffee in the world.'

Well, she couldn't afford that. Bonnie zoned in again and followed Wayan through the overhanging forest, listening as he identified coffee in various stages, tree types and fruit, aware of Harry at her shoulder not saying anything.

Finally they came to the cage where the luwak slept, incarcerated. Bonnie looked at Harry and whispered, 'What the heck is a luwak?' Harry gestured to Wayan and smiled and she tried to catch up.

'We leave them for one day in the cage,' Wayan told them, 'and then set them free again. It is only so you can see the actual animal. Asian palm civets—also known as luwaks here—normally sleep and hide at the time people visit the plantation.'

They all stared into the dark cage and tried to see the small furry animal, which looked a little like a cat-faced possum or smaller mongoose.

She whispered to Harry, 'I don't get it. How does it make coffee?'

He tilted his head and studied her genuine bafflement. A slow smile curved his lips. 'You weren't listening.'

'I might have missed a bit.' She shrugged.

Harry tilted his head and she could feel his scrutiny. Could feel the heat in her cheeks at his amusement. He was laughing at her—not with her—and she didn't like it.

'He's been talking about it for the last ten minutes.'

'So?' She held out her hands, frustrated by his teasing. 'Tell me now.'

Harry grinned. 'Luwaks are an alternative to conventional coffee processing. They process the beans internally.' He grinned again as she shrugged and shook her head, obviously not getting it. 'You don't pick the beans off the trees—you follow the luwaks around with a shovel.'

'They poo it?' Bonnie blinked. 'You're kidding me?'

Harry laughed out loud and suddenly the rapport between them was back in full force. 'I kid you not.'

He patted her shoulder. 'You get to try some soon. Luwaks only choose to eat the very best coffee beans, and they have a great internal processing unit that still leaves the coffee bean whole when they're...' he paused and grinned again '...finished with it.'

Bonnie shook her head. 'No way.' When had they discussed this? Had Wayan said that in the bus? How would this be the most expensive coffee in the world?

'They wash the beans,' Harry said blandly, but she could see the unholy amusement in his eyes. Just looking at him made her smile and boosted her fragile self-esteem that Jeremy had injured so badly. That was the point when she should have run away.

Bonnie screwed up her face and Harry laughed out loud. 'Double dare you.'

Drink second-hand coffee beans? 'I don't think so.'

'In the States it sells for more than a hundred bucks a pound. Not something you'll have a lot of chance to try again.'

True. But who'd want to? She followed Harry through to the coffee tables, where the rest of the group were ordering their coffee, and before she knew it she was sitting beside Harry with a steaming cup of black brew in front of her.

And everyone else seemed to be tasting it. *Ew.*

She looked around again and the Portuguese girls were chatting up the chefs as they sipped, and everyone still looked happy with their experience.

She was the only one not drinking. Even Harry had his cup.

Bonnie took a cautious sip. 'It tastes a bit like mocha.'

Harry raised his eyebrows. 'Is that what that is?'

He could tease. She put her cup down. 'Well, at least I tried it.'

Harry gave up his short-lived attempt to keep his distance with her. She delighted him with her honesty. She couldn't hide a single thought with those straightforward eyes of hers. Talk about windows to the soul. They telegraphed every thought and emotion like a green neon sign. Scary, and despite her antsy, prickly little exterior he could feel the need to protect her from the world like a growing seed inside him.

Hopefully that little weed of concern for her would die from lack of sunlight when she flew away. But for the moment he could give in to these crazy feelings because she'd only be there for a few days and he had no plans.

He could feel the chuckle in his chest as she manfully swallowed the coffee she didn't want. He reached across the table and scooped her hand into his, and she

let her fingers lie there. It felt good to have her warm
and protected by him. He tried not to see the grin of
Wayan, who'd never seen Harry so circumspect with a
young woman in all the time he'd known him.

Bonnie couldn't remember the last time she'd held
hands with a man. Her fiancé hadn't been into hand-
holding and it had almost been worth a taste of kopi
luwak coffee for the buzz of feeling a situation she
hadn't tried before.

Like she belonged with Harry for this minute anyway.
She was having a holiday fling, almost. Good grief. Her
girlfriends in Darwin would be whooping with joy.

'Come on, the bus is leaving, you can leave the last
bit. We get to find our bikes now and the real fun be-
gins.' They held hands all the way to the bus and it felt
'nice'.

Back on the bus, this time his hip returned to rest
against hers again and their knees bumped companion-
ably together as the bus ground down the hill. It was as
good as she'd remembered and she smiled secretly at
her own reflection in the window.

The village that housed the bikes seemed deserted
but Harry chose for her the least battered pushbike, no
doubt drawing on his experience of bike fallibility, and
the tread on the narrow tyres at least looked new.

'Have a little pedal around here while everyone gets
their bike,' he said, and she climbed on with a nervous
grimace. It had been years and she fought the tremble
in her knees as she took off.

At least she could touch the ground easily. The
Portuguese girl had a death wobble until Harry stopped

her and put her seat down for safety. Bonnie liked it that he cared.

Between Harry and the Balinese guides, everyone had their bikes set to go within ten minutes, bottles of water were handed out and then the lead rider took off with all his less confident ducklings behind him. Everyone except Harry and the fitness instructor rode stiffly. Bonnie and Harry brought up the rear, which seemed to set them apart in their own world.

The descent started out gradual. A bit like the way she'd little by little become relaxed around Harry, though he'd become slightly anxious when she'd nearly steered her bike into an unexpected drain at the side of the road.

'That ditch would have swallowed you. Stay nearer the centre,' Harry pleaded as she veered his way again suddenly to avert another catastrophe.

From then on he positioned his bike to keep her out of the gutter.

'Whew.' She took her hand off the handle to dry her sweaty palms on her used-to-be-white trousers. 'How embarrassing it would be to wipe out in the first kilometre.'

'Or worse,' he muttered, and glanced across at her. 'You can't just choose an orthopaedic surgeon here, you know.'

Bonnie laughed. 'I missed the hole. Nothing to worry about.' In fact, she felt remarkably relaxed now that the initial wobbles had disappeared.

The sun was shining, the road had the occasional country vehicle, but most of the time it was just the bike riders, fields and villages as they sailed past.

Harry pointed out features of different village temples, family buildings and the census plaques on top of the entry arches, which Bonnie had never noticed before.

'So each census tag has how many sons and their families, and how many adults and children live in the family compound.'

Bonnie slowed as they peddled past the entrance to another family compound and this time she could make out the little strokes denoting the family members. 'Cool. So there's five children in that compound.'

'Yep.' He looked quite pleased she was interested but it was no hardship. She found the insight into Balinese culture fascinating. And it was also attractive that Harry wanted to share his own interest with her.

Too many things were attractive about him. 'You care about these people, don't you? You're not just interested in them out of curiosity.'

He nodded. 'Of course. I've spent a lot of time here and anyone who does that comes to appreciate Bali and her people.'

'So why don't you work here?'

'I do a bit.' He didn't enlarge on it. Instead he said, 'My friend was born in a village near here. Sometimes the kids run out to wave as we ride by. They'll hold their hands out for a high five. It can give you a fright.'

The rest of the bike riders had stopped up ahead. There was a generalised wobble as they all put their feet down and Bonnie was no exception. She glanced at Harry's face as he tried to hide his grin. 'Don't even think about laughing.'

She pretended to frown at him and he held up his hands as if to say, 'Never.'

'We'll go through the village here, and then later on you'll be able to recognise the layout and functions of the buildings and compounds we still have to go past.'

She glanced down the discreet dirt track between the buildings and couldn't help feeling a little uncomfortable at the invasion of privacy. There seemed to be people at work in each section but none of them appeared fazed by the intrusion.

The whole compound looked sparse and basic. Not a place that was used to luxuries she took for granted every day. Happy children ran up and down with shrieks of merriment and a young father smiled at them as he plaited strips of thin bamboo with his tiny son.

Bonnie lowered her voice and leant closer to Harry. 'So what do they do for wages here?'

'Bamboo production.' He pointed to the huge stand of thick bamboo that grew at the bottom of the street. 'Dewi, here, is a skilled plaiter and his sheets of bamboo matting are used for the internal ceilings of most types of buildings. When you go back to your hotel you'll notice that the roof in your bedroom is made up of this plaited bamboo. It'll be from a village like this. Dewi's work is much sought after.'

Bonnie smiled at the young Balinese man and she couldn't help her wider grin when she realised his son was trying to plait a smaller version of his father's work. His little face was screwed up in concentration as he laboriously weaved.

The father spoke in Balinese and Harry laughed and answered him, then turned to Bonnie. 'He said his son looks perfect now but he'll get sick of it soon and start to cause mischief.'

'Where's his mother?'

Harry pointed to a covered work area ahead. 'She's stripping the bamboo with his grandmother, further down. Each villager does part of the process, from the man beside the bamboo who harvests to those that split it in half then quarters and pass it on to the next section, who keep thinning it down until Dewi has workable strips to weave with.'

They moved past the sections, the tourists snapping pictures and watching the villagers work, and all the time Harry spoke to the villagers in their own language, smiling and greeting them by name.

It was interesting to Bonnie how the people they met hailed Harry, patted him on the back, called out to him, considering he seemed transient, and she wondered if he ever thought of when he would leave and get on with his life.

But why should she care? She could feel a creeping sense of evangelistic purpose to save Harry's working soul and she stamped it down.

Stop it. He'd not thank her for it and it was none of her business. He was just a man she'd met. But a place inside her ached for the occasional glimpse of the caring, lost soul he tried to hide. She pulled her thoughts away and concentrated on village life.

She admired the one cow the family owned, the eldest son's pride and joy and, according to Harry, a huge investment. The cow chewed placidly and stared at them from a private sheltered bale, a long-lashed, happy cow, living in Utopia.

Pigs snorted in muddy pens and chickens darted underfoot, chased by a red-combed rooster, and Harry told her the wives cared for the other animals while the husbands cared for the cow.

Consistently, it seemed Harry picked up on her interest when the guide spoke of traditions and when he mentioned the ceremonies each family was responsible for.

Harry enlarged on the subject after Wayan had moved on. 'The cost of a burial sometimes take years for a family to save for—it can cost the same as their one cow. But the family are happy to ensure their relation is cremated with a full and proper celebration.

She looked around at the bare compound. 'What if the family can't afford a funeral when someone dies?'

'The person is temporarily buried, maybe a year or two, and exhumed when they can afford it. Or sometimes when another family is having a funeral they share the costs with several families who have members to bury. But it's a necessary expenditure for ancestor status.'

Harry waved at another man and as he stopped to talk Bonnie caught the eye of a young pregnant woman sitting quietly in the doorway of a building, slicing ginger.

There was something about the way she held her neck stiffly that attracted Bonnie's attention and she drifted over to say hello.

The young woman peeled the grey root swiftly and surely but every few minutes her face changed and she glanced down at her stomach. When she looked up she must have seen the concern in Bonnie's eyes because she shook her head as if to say it was nothing.

Bonnie allowed her own glance to drift down and tried to estimate the gestation of the pregnancy. Nearly full term, that was for sure, but not a big baby. Harry wandered off to talk to the Portuguese couple and Bonnie edged towards the doorway.

'Hello. I'm Bonnie. I'm afraid I don't speak much Balinese.'

'I am Mardi.' The young woman's voice was very soft and to Bonnie's relief quietly confident with her English. 'I worked in a restaurant before I married my husband and speak good English.'

'You're very clever. My Indonesian is bad apart from *hello* and *good morning*.' She smiled. 'Is your baby giving you pains?'

Mardi glanced down at her stomach with a gentle smile. 'A little. But he is not due until next month. It has happened for a little while each day this last week so I'm hoping my belly will go soon to sleep.'

CHAPTER FOUR

JUDGING from the changing expressions on the young woman's face, Bonnie doubted these pains would go away.

Bonnie waited for the strain to ease from Mardi's face again. Pretty decent contraction, she thought. When it had gone she said, 'Maybe she or he has decided to come today.'

Mardi looked down at the brown dust beneath her feet. 'Not today. My husband is away working to save money. We cannot afford the midwife yet.'

Bonnie wasn't sure how that worked when nature didn't play the game. 'What about the hospital?'

Calmly Mardi shook her head and her thick black hair barely moved in the coiled bun. 'The hospital costs are even greater.' She grimaced again and Bonnie frowned.

'Looks like labour to me,' Bonnie muttered under her breath. She'd seen quite a few. 'Have the pains been this close and strong before?'

Mardi shook her head and this time Bonnie saw the start of the glint of tears in her beautiful brown eyes. 'Perhaps I am a little fearful.'

Fear was the last thing a woman in labour needed. 'Is your husband's mother here?'

Mardi's coil shifted slightly again. 'She died at his birth. Which is why he wishes for me to have the midwife. His grandmother is here, but she cannot see well. His brother's wife is here and had one son in the hospital.'

Bonnie wanted to hug her but she also didn't want to intrude if she wasn't wanted. 'I'm a midwife in Australia. Can I help you?'

Bonnie glanced over her shoulder, hoping to catch the eye of Harry, but he was still laughing with the Portuguese girls.

She glared at him in frustration. As if she'd touched him, or thrown something at him, he stopped what he was saying and glanced her way. Without a word he crossed the road to her side.

He nodded at Mardi and lowered his voice as he looked at Bonnie. 'Is everything all right?'

Bonnie was thrown for a moment. Coincidence? Telepathy? She had no idea how that had worked. He'd been receptive and come quickly. The concept that she'd called him without words sent a trickle of unease through her. That was too much connection.

No. Just coincidence, that's all.

The thought was closely followed by the priorities she'd let slip as Mardi drew another sharp breath. 'We need to find Mardi's husband because she's going into labour.'

Bonnie had no doubt now. Just looking at Mardi, anyone would tell the time for false labour had passed and she'd bet her borrowed pushbike the baby would

come today. 'He's away to save money for the midwife.'

To her surprise Harry paled and then seemed to shake
himself into sense. His eyes narrowed and she could
almost see his mind weighing the options. For a carefree
surfer he was on the ball quickly. 'I'll take you to the
hospital. The backup vehicle for the bike ride is parked
outside.'

One lone tear slid down Mardi's cheek. 'I don't want
to go to the hospital without my husband. I will wait for
him.'

'Hospitals cost a lot,' Bonnie murmured quietly, as
if mentioning a common fact, and Harry looked at her
and nodded but he wasn't happy.

He rubbed his neck. 'But will that baby wait for you
both?' Harry said what Bonnie was thinking. Mardi bit
back a moan and Harry looked at Bonnie.

A glance akin to horror lurked in his eyes, again totally unexpected. But she guessed laypeople were often
fazed by the myths and misconceptions surrounding
childbirth.

'Birth's a normal event,' she couldn't help saying.
'Could you get Mardi's sister-in-law, please? And a doctor, if you can find one.' Bonnie rested her hand on
Mardi's arm. 'Perhaps we could go to your house and
you could collect what you would need to take with you,
for when your husband arrives?'

In fact, Bonnie wanted to see where they could have
this baby if it came more quickly than any of them
anticipated.

'We could do that,' Mardi whispered, and she stood
gingerly when the next contraction had passed. Bonnie

mentally rifled through the belongings she had on her that could be helpful, but she'd only carried a waist pack that held very little.

She gave herself a mental shake. Harry would sort something out if she asked him. The important thing was to get Mardi comfortable and semiprepared for her baby's possibly precipitous arrival.

This wasn't an unusual scenario in Outback Australia if a baby arrived early and one that didn't faze Bonnie too much. Though it would've been nice if there was a doctor around to share the load, in case of an emergency. She doubted she'd be legal to practise in a foreign country.

Harry strode off to search out Mardi's sister-in-law and as he walked he fumed at the cruelty of fate.

Why now, why here, why him? It was all very well for Bonnie to be blasé about birth, typical midwife, but she hadn't seen what he had. The last thing he wanted was a medical catastrophe in a Third World village. He'd have to be the doctor, get involved, and probably still not be able to improve the outcome.

He should never have come here with her. It was his own stupid fault. He'd known women were trouble he needed to avoid.

He caught sight of his quarry, Mardi's sister-in-law, and hastened his footsteps. Maybe if they found Mardi's husband quickly they could still get to the hospital in time. But if he'd interpreted Bonnie's face correctly, she had her doubts. He had his own.

Bonnie and Mardi had left the industrious centre of the village and moved into the narrow street of the family dwellings. Bonnie counted four buildings in a smaller compound and one stood higher than the rest, with steep steps leading up to the small veranda.

Mardi intercepted Bonnie's glance. 'My husband's grandparents' house. The grandparent house is higher than others as a mark of respect. As it should be.'

Mardi gestured down at a round shiny river rock to the left of the grandparent's steep steps. 'There lies the placenta of my husband's nephew. It is my husband's task to clean and bury our child's placenta below these steps.'

'So one stone, one grandchild?'

'That is correct. And should I have a girl it would be buried on the right side of the step.'

Bonnie grinned. She loved it. This was delicious food for a midwife's soul. Fabulous information, and she wondered if Harry was aware of it.

The next building they passed contained two sparse kitchens, side by side, and Mardi glanced inside. Despite her worries, Mardi smiled. 'This kitchen is mine, and the other belongs to my husband's brother's wife, Nyomen. It is said peace cannot exist if two women have to share a kitchen.'

'What a sensible arrangement.' Bonnie smiled with her. 'I can see that everyone lives very close together here.'

'Family is very important in Bali.' They both slipped off their shoes and Mardi gestured to Bonnie to precede her up the stairs to a room that shared a veranda with another room. 'This is my home. Everybody knows everyone else's business. We share all joys and sorrows. You cannot help but do so when we live this close.'

'And what is the other building that looks like a covered platform?'

'That is where we hold our ceremonies. Where my child will be blessed when three months old and can first touch the ground.'

Bonnie couldn't help a brief sidetrack. 'Three months before a baby can touch the ground?'

Mardi nodded. 'To touch the ground before then would allow the chance of evil spirits to enter a child.'

She'd bet some parents at home would disagree with that but she could see the warmth and benefit in a child knowing a pair of arms would always be there for them. No wonder the Balinese people smiled so much—they knew how much love and care was taken of them from the moment of birth.

Mardi stopped and leant against the doorframe. Bonnie waited quietly beside her and let her thoughts drift into that distant space she seemed to go to when she was waiting with a woman—not really a daydream when she thought of other things, more of a holding pattern that didn't use any energy or was distracting for the woman, that just 'was', while she waited.

The pain eased and Mardi moved inside the house just as her sister-in-law, Nyomen, arrived with Harry and glided up the stairs to help.

The two women embraced and Bonnie moved back to the edge of the veranda as Nyomen gathered several sarongs and a water bottle.

When the young mother-to-be stopped and leant against her sister-in-law again, Bonnie leant down to speak to Harry. 'Is her husband coming?'

Harry nodded stiffly, strain in every line of his body. 'He should be here soon.'

Good. But she doubted this baby would wait. 'So, ever been present for a birth, Harry?' His face closed and she could feel her own forehead crease. That looked bad.

So when he said, 'No,' she was almost surprised.

'Ah.' Pretending not to be surprised. 'That explains your nerves. Everything will be fine.'

'No, thanks. Let's get her out of here.' Harry's face held the granite stiffness she'd seen at the pool the day she'd first seen him. There were things going on here she couldn't fully fathom and unfortunately now wasn't the time to ask.

She rested her hand on his arm and he looked at her. 'We'll all be fine.' Bonnie actually felt sorry for him. 'She won't go to the hospital until her husband arrives. I'm afraid it's too late for that, anyway.'

She thought he'd heard her and accepted that, but then he shook his head as if waking from a trance. 'It's not too late. I'm not stupid. Let's grab her and go.'

She touched his arm again. 'Harry. Listen to me.' Her voice was very quiet so as not to disturb the labouring woman. 'And what? Have the baby in that old bus?'

She saw the moment when he really saw her, saw her logic, had to accept reality and the impending birth. He ran his hands through his hair and gradually his face softened, though there was no doubting his reluctance to face the inevitable. She saw the flash of pain that followed and was quickly hidden. 'You're right. I'm sorry. Lost it for a moment there.'

'It must have been a very bad experience,' she said

quietly. There was more history here than she'd anticipated. 'What can I do to help you, Harry?'

'Nothing.' He glanced at her and then away. Every
barrier in place shielding him from her empathy. 'Now,
what do you need?'

He was right. Maybe she had it wrong. This was
the response she'd expected from Harry. Thank goodness. She felt the pack around her waist and undid the
zipper.

'I don't imagine I'll be doing much. I just want to
be here to help keep Mardi and her baby safe. Maybe
good old-fashioned boiling water to sterilise some string
and a knife to cut the cord.' She patted the miniature
bottle of hand-sanitiser she always kept in her bag. 'Or
I could clean the knife with this.' She looked around.
'And maybe a dish of warm water to sponge Mardi with
afterwards.'

'What about the drugs you won't have?'

It seemed a strange thing to say but she shrugged it
off. 'She's healthy and we don't have any. She'll breast-
feed. This is what women are designed to do. Her body
will look after her. Why should she be unlucky?'

He held up his hands. 'Okay. Just thought I'd mention
it.'

'Maybe there is one thing. Will you reassure Mardi
and Nyomen I'm a midwife and I'd like to stay until
after the baby is born if her husband doesn't arrive in
time? The most important thing is for her not to be
frightened.'

He sighed. 'I can do that.' And more quietly so she
only just heard, 'That's about all I'm good for.'

When he'd finished speaking the two women nodded

their consent, and there was relief in both faces, relief that made Harry grimace as he turned back to her.

'I'll go see about the string and the water.'

Mardi made a small moaning noise, and Nyomen gestured to Bonnie to come inside the house. The women had made a small bed on the floor, and a neat pile of older sarongs had been placed beside her.

Bonnie washed her hands with the antiseptic, and offered it to the other women. Then she sat back a little and folded her hands. There was nothing she could do. She could see the baby moving under his mother's loosened sarong so that was a good sign. It was time to wait.

By the time Harry returned they'd set up a little screen with another sarong and the elderly grandmother was also in the room.

He wished himself anywhere but there. Even back out on the street. Back with the tourists. His nerves crawled with anxiety—not a normal reaction for a damn doctor, he told himself, but this was how things went wrong. This was what he'd decided he'd never get involved in again. Had told himself he didn't have to get involved with again because he could easily avoid becoming drawn in.

How Bonnie had stopped him from picking up Mardi and rushing her to the hospital he didn't know. But then, if she was as close as Bonnie said, the idea of the baby being born halfway down the mountain was no better anyway.

The sudden unmistakable sound of a baby's wail drifted from the room above him, and he looked up to hear the muted voices of happy women and even a laugh from the grandmother. His shoulders sagged and he felt like dropping his head into his hands as well.

Relief flooded over him. Waves of emotion he hadn't wanted. Overwhelming, and it was harrowing how close he'd been to inappropriate action. Maybe it was time to rationalise how much he needed to confront his issues.

He almost wished he hadn't met this pesky midwife, but couldn't quite convince himself that was true.

The relief inside expanded into unexpected pride— for clever Mardi, the unfazeable Bonnie, and the fact that he had trusted enough. Just.

The sound of running feet heralded the arrival of Mardi's stunned husband, and the poor man kicked his shoes off and bolted up the stairs to greet his wife and new daughter. Harry smiled at the voluble thanks that were being heaped on Bonnie's head. He let the sounds wash over him. He'd translate when they were on their own.

Finally Bonnie reappeared, a huge smile on her face, her eyes alight with the joy of the moment, and he could see how she revelled in her vocation. Lucky her. But he couldn't help that darker sliver of reality that said she'd been lucky.

Some people weren't that lucky.

Bonnie drifted out of the compound on a high, stunned again at the beauty and simplicity of childbirth, the pure blessing of a newborn baby and the luck of being a witness to it all.

Then she realised the bike ride had gone on without them.

'We'll catch them at lunch.' Harry smiled at her, but the strain hadn't been erased from his features and he looked far from carefree and relaxed. 'I thought it might be therapeutic to just keep rolling down the hill to soak in the morning rather than get a lift to catch up with the others.'

'Perfect.' He was right. She still had that smile on her face from the birth and everything seemed brighter and more precious as they cycled along.

'I gather there were no hitches to the birth?'

She heard him but it took her a couple of seconds to pull her brain back from euphoria. 'Baby's shoulders were a little tight but a change in position sorted that.' Joy bubbled and sang inside her and she wouldn't have given away this day for the world.

She watched Harry bounce airborne over a little hump in the road and she laughed out loud.

The birth had been incredible, Mardi a delight and the baby so gorgeous and big-eyed it brought the tears to her face again just remembering.

Harry felt like a heel. And a surly one at that. He wanted to share her joy but his mind kept returning to what could have gone wrong. To what had gone wrong in the past. He was so used to shutting people down he'd got out of practice at opening up. And there was something about Bonnie that made him want to share a little of himself for the first time in a long time.

She'd been so incredible at the village and he shuddered to think he might have been on his own and would have had to cope with that.

Though she was smiling when he looked back, he caught a glint of tears in her eyes and the sight nearly knocked him off his bike. He'd upset her. Harry veered closer. 'Are you all right?'

'Yes.' The smile she turned on him was even more of an assault than her tears. 'Just reliving the moment.'

The birth was making her emotional, not him. He'd forgotten how different women's thought processes were from men's.

The last thing he wanted to do was relive his trepidation during the birth. 'No, thanks,' Harry muttered, and she smiled again as if she understood. But how could she? She had no idea.

'Thanks for being there, Harry.'

He could feel those damn walls crumbling all over. 'Don't ask again.'

'Now who's the wimp?' she teased him. Something had changed for ever between them. They could never really be strangers again after this and they both knew it.

Was he a wimp? No doubt of that. He didn't say anything and she smiled again.

'This is so great. Thanks for finishing the ride. It would have been such an anticlimax to climb back into the bus and get dropped back at the hotel.'

'Hmm.' But then he looked across at her and couldn't help agreeing with her. The words came out before he realised what he'd been going to say. 'You're pretty amazing, you know.'

She shook her head and her ponytail wagged. 'Not me. It's birthing women who're amazing.'

'Spare me from the midwife.' He rolled his eyes.

Her face shifted to serious, the softness of laughter fading away, and he had the feeling she was going to say something he wouldn't like. 'Yes, I will. Spare you my presence. Tomorrow morning, when I fly back to Australia.'

'Tomorrow?' That hit him harder than he would have believed possible. 'I thought you had another couple of days?'

She shrugged her shoulders and the bike wobbled. He wished she wouldn't do that. 'I had a call last night, and they're short at my next posting.' She glanced at him. 'The fill-in medical officer isn't going to show and I'm flying back tomorrow to help cover.'

Too soon. Far too soon. But how ironic. She was going to Uluru early and it was his fault. 'It's not your problem until you start.'

She flicked a frown at him before looking back at the road.

She was going. Just when he'd dared to risk opening up. *See*, he told himself. *You are better pushing people away.*

Then she said, 'Have you always been like this?'

'Like what?'

'Egotistical, self-absorbed.' The words hit him like the splashes of mud he'd just pedalled through. Sticking to him. Was he? Or just plain scared?

They were passing through a village and two young boys ran out holding up their hands. Bonnie swerved because she wasn't concentrating and nearly collided with Harry, who took evasive action more easily than she had.

'Whoa, there,' Harry cautioned, though he still managed to high-five the two boys. Squeals of delight followed them down the road and he could feel a smile tug at his lips. He did enjoy seeing the village children.

She looked ahead to rice paddies and sighed. 'It must be hard work in there.' Just like that. She'd brushed him off. He'd asked her to but now he wasn't sure he liked the feeling she could do it so easily. It was darned good she was leaving tomorrow.

'Follow me,' Harry steered them onto a smaller track. 'This one comes out between the fields.'

They bumped down a rocky incline and suddenly the way was smooth again as they hit a concrete path that rose between the fields and separated one rice paddy from the next. Their bikes were at waist-level with the workers and several called out to Harry as they pedalled past.

Bonnie would have loved to have looked closer but she was too busy concentrating on not steering off the path into the water and reeds below. But it took her mind off Harry and she was glad of that. It wasn't her job to save the world. She plastered a smile on her face, determined to soak in the sun and the sensation of wind in her face and blow away the distractions of the man beside her.

Good. She looked happy again. Harry savoured Bonnie's uncomplicated enjoyment of the scenery and the people they passed, like a new-taste sensation. He rolled her spontaneity around in his mind like a sweet in his mouth. It had been too long since he'd felt those things and it swallowed the dark feelings he'd been left with.

But there was no escaping that through the course of today he'd begun to recognise that it wasn't healthy to stay as closed off from emotion as he'd been, so he noted her pleasure, learnt from it, and even began to question his isolation.

It hadn't all been escape here, though. A large part of Bali had been healing to his soul. He wished he could have shown her his mother's house. Let her feel the peace he always felt there. He wondered how she'd respond to that and to the different vibe of Ubud as a town.

He pedalled faster to catch her and when he was alongside he caught her eye. 'Will you have dinner with me tonight?' Funny how plans he formed for Bonnie were immediately acted on. Almost as if he acted before he could stop himself. Did he need more exposure when she was going? 'I'll drop you back at Kuta afterwards, and even take you to the airport tomorrow if you like.' The words just kept flying out. She was going. There was no offer of commitment in that.

Bonnie wanted to say yes. Knew she shouldn't because every minute she spent with this confusing and compelling guy meant he was going to be harder to leave behind when her plane took off.

She thought about Jimbaran, and the beach and all the people, and a secret place inside her whispered the urge to suggest somewhere more private, more amenable to intimacy, which should be the last thing she wanted. She was a fool. It was better to stay public. 'Tonight, yes, I'd like that. Not the airport tomorrow. I'll make my own way there.'

'As you wish,' he said, and she was glad. It was like a limit she'd set herself. So far but not all the way. Now, that had connotations she didn't want to think about.

'How about when the bus drops you off after the ride I'll pick you up in my car?' He glanced at her as if not sure how she'd react. 'Would you like to see Ubud? It's only an hour's run.'

She hesitated. She'd be agreeing to disappear into the middle of Bali with Harry. A man she hardly knew. But she was kidding herself if she thought she'd throw away the chance to spend a little more time with him before she had to leave.

And it seemed important to try to understand him before she left. Maybe even help him. 'Seems a long way to go for dinner.'

'Thought I'd show you my mother's house. We could catch a kekak dance or just have a quiet dinner overlooking the rice fields. I'd like you to see where I live and why I love it.'

She found herself agreeing, maybe foolishly, but the idea of being privy to a more personal side to Harry was too intriguing to resist. And she didn't want the day to end. This whole slice out of time would end soon enough, which was a good thing if she was going to get over being drawn to this often silent man, and why he was hiding here in Bali.

CHAPTER FIVE

LATER that afternoon, in Harry's car, Bonnie looked out the window as Harry drove.

Motorbikes were everywhere, swerving in and out of traffic, crazy loads piled on them, tooting politely to be let through. And nobody seemed cross.

Very different to Western cities she'd been to. She glanced at Harry as he slowed to allow a young biker to pass him, and he seemed lazily alert, not at all perturbed by the chaos. What was it about him that drew her to him? He was the opposite of her ex-fiancé, career-climbing Jeremy, which in the big picture should be a good thing.

Harry didn't seem driven by anything, footloose, fancy-free except for the ghost of a wife. Well, that was what she assumed. She hadn't actually asked him if he had a girlfriend but she didn't think so, he seemed content to just coast through life. He was unlike anyone she'd ever known or even been drawn to. Maybe that was the attraction.

The safety of him not being eligible in her eyes. And if she was honest, she was attracted to him despite her inner caution reminding her he was a man and men couldn't be trusted.

'Do you enjoy driving here?'

He grinned at her. Pure schoolboy without a care now. It must be nice to switch on and off like that. 'It's like the bargaining. Just smile and you'll be all right. Don't get worked up about anything and everything will run smoothly.'

Sounded like his life. 'Pleasantly detached in your bubble from the real world? Is that why you stay?'

He glanced at her and then away. 'Maybe.'

He changed the subject and she wasn't surprised. Right at the beginning he'd said there would be no deep and meaningful discussions. 'We're coming into Celuk. A village famous for silversmiths. I'd like to pick something up from a friend of mine.'

He slowed as they passed shopfronts and the occasional larger walled house, all proclaiming their trade in jewellery, and what woman didn't love jewellery? Bonnie was no exception as she turned her head from side to side to see the shopfronts.

When they parked, almost against the wall to get off the narrow street, there was barely enough room to open her door, but that wasn't going to stop her having a peek inside.

Harry grinned again and helped her squeeze out onto the little porch and up the steps into the shop. To her delight the inside exceeded her expectations. It seemed she'd found Aladdin's cave crammed to the ceiling with glass-fronted cupboards packed with all types and sizes of silver jewellery.

He introduced her to his friend, Putu, who reached under the counter and produced a small box filled with silver charms. Putu poked around in the box until he found what he was looking for and offered it to Harry.

She couldn't see what it was and at first thought it some sort of animal as Harry held it up to the light. She watched him clap his friend on the back and some money exchanged hands. And she looked away to control her inquisitiveness. There were trays and trays of all types of silver jewellery, plenty to distract a curious woman.

Harry strode across to her. 'Sorry to keep you in the dark but I wanted Putu to find the best one.' He opened his hand. 'I'd like you to have this, a keepsake of today.' Harry stopped beside her and held out his palm. 'As an apology for being so stressed.'

There in the middle of his strong brown hand lay a tiny silver baby, curled up and content, beautifully crafted and cleverly suspended on a finely intricate chain.

'She's gorgeous,' she breathed, and looked from Harry to the grinning shopkeeper. She could only marvel at the exquisite workmanship.

'In honour of your birth today.' He smiled and her legs wobbled in response. Good grief. She looked down at the shiny miniature again. Such dimpled cheeks and rounded limbs and something to remember Harry by. As if she'd forget him.

'Thank you, Harry.' She looked across at the silver-smith and smiled. 'You're very clever.'

Harry stepped closer and, typically, all the hairs on her arms recognised him and stood up. She might even miss that sensation when she went. 'Here. Let me put it on for you.'

She turned and lifted her hair so he could fasten the clasp, and his fingers on her neck lifted any other follicle that wasn't upright already. She stepped back, ostensibly to thank the silversmith but really to loosen the tightness in her chest and mentally fan her face.

The shopkeeper brought the mirror and she could see herself with Harry behind her, like a picture. A picture that would soon become a memory.

She turned and impulsively reached up to kiss his cheek. 'Thank you. She's beautiful. I love her.' He patted her shoulder and turned away to hide the expression in his eyes, and she sighed.

Well, that had been a mistake. Harry briefly closed his eyes. He'd thought by buying her a trinket he could lose the guilt he still carried by not telling her the truth. But it hadn't worked.

Actually, he felt worse, almost as though he was trying to buy her forgiveness, which was ridiculous when, in fact, he owed nothing to this woman he barely knew. So why did he feel he was deepening the deceit?

Because when it was all said and done she'd go on her way in good faith, blithely unaware he should have stood beside her at the birth and been there to support her in the responsibility. And he hadn't.

He'd lied by omission, run away from the risk of something going wrong, and pretended she had been the only person with the knowledge.

He helped her back into the car and ensured she had her seat belt on and wondered, as he climbed in himself, what the heck was he doing with her beside him at this moment?

Why hadn't he waved goodbye after the bike ride and

chalked the new insights she'd given him up for later thought or consigned them to the too-hard basket like he usually did? He had no idea but he had the sneaking suspicion he was going to regret this decision.

He eased his vehicle back into the mayhem of the traffic and decided his mind was as bad as the street. Chaotic.

Bonnie took one look at Harry's set face and chose to stare out the window. She suppressed another sigh. The man was like a roller-coaster—exhilarating on the downward loops but full of unexpected corners that threatened to derail her when she least expected it.

She'd just concentrate on the scenery and the bustling life all around her.

When they arrived in Ubud the main street was packed with shops. Windows were filled with hand-printed clothes, paintings, imitation designer luggage. There seemed to be dozens of restaurants, lots to distract her confusion from Harry's behaviour.

As they passed the stone-walled palace she began to see that the centre of town was built on a mountain, complete with rainforest and plunging gullies, and lush foliage everywhere. A town nestled in a jungle.

Ubud had a different feel to the beachside suburbs and Bonnie was glad she'd had the chance to experience the variation. It had nothing to do with more time with the enigmatic Harry.

Serene women in yellow sashes carried towering arrangements of offerings on their heads up stone steps, and everywhere were the welcoming smiles of Bali.

She wished she could concentrate on the colours and activity and sheer beauty around her, but despite her attempt at resistance her eyes were drawn to the man beside her.

Fascination lay in the way his brown hands moved confidently on the steering wheel, how easy he made it seem to navigate in the busyness and ordered confusion that was the main street, and how since they'd arrived in Ubud his shoulders seemed to have relaxed again into their more comfortable stance.

Her hand slid up to touch the baby around her neck. The gift had come from nowhere and she wasn't sure that he was happy now that he'd given it to her. But she couldn't read his face and maybe it would be better to let the distance grow between them again. She turned back to the window.

They crawled with the now-creeping traffic down a stone-banked incline then across an ancient bridge and suddenly the shops and traffic were gone and they were surrounded by rice fields again.

Harry bumped into a narrow lane and up another hill and the rice fields almost brushed the car. She assumed they must be getting closer to the time they'd arrive at his house and little waves of awareness bounced between them in the quiet of the car. Then he turned and smiled at her and it seemed it was connection time again.

The guy was such a light switch sometimes. On and off with the flick of a finger.

The suspense of their arrival became more momentous the longer it took to get there. She reminded herself he was a well-known entity here, and she wasn't really foolish sitting beside him going somewhere she didn't know how to get back from. The concept that Harry would force her into anything didn't enter her mind. She trusted him and she didn't know why. Just that she did.

Would anyone else be there? Was it only a peaceful dinner they were both thinking of or had thoughts of intimacy crossed his mind too? Should she keep reminding herself she was a paranoid woman with a poor track record in men?

She sneaked a look at his profile as he glanced to his right. Hopefully he was unaware of the mixed emotions she was hiding behind her sunglasses because she couldn't keep her thoughts sorted and orderly herself, let alone share them with him.

Field workers waved and Harry waved back, and Bonnie gazed around and pretended to be the tourist she was, but her eyes kept returning to Harry's hands. The very first time she'd seen him she'd felt a connection to those hands—until she'd seen his ring. How ridiculous. You couldn't fall in lust with someone's hands.

They finally arrived, as close as they could get anyway. Harry's house was on a rise, white-painted stone and many gabled, with a veranda on every side. He couldn't drive all the way to the door so they walked up a stone path along the edge of a rice field and she could see ducks playing in the water that lay beneath the rice plants.

When he opened the gate for her she felt her own shoulders drop because, magically, the peace and tranquillity wrapped around them both from the first footstep into the gardens.

It was as if she'd stepped into a lush green veil of peace. Unexpected and very welcome. Harry rested his hand on the small of her back as she stood there and drank in the serenity, and even his presence became a part of the whole.

'No wonder you love it,' she said quietly, and shook her head at perfection. Brushed grass, tiled edges around gardens, little waterfalls and fountains, and a myriad of tiny stone altars with incense and frangipani flowers artfully arranged.

Harry sighed with relief. It had been right to bring her. 'Come inside.' He could feel the swell of pleasure that she could see what drew him to stay.

He saw it through her eyes, re-examining the facets he loved with renewed appreciation.

Stone steps flanked by granite lions led up to a magnificently tiled veranda that peered over a sheer drop to the valley floor. A long way down, like a silver ribbon, a small stream meandered along under the lush rainforest that lay in pockets between the layered rice fields.

Further along the veranda, on what seemed like acres of tiles, cushioned cane furniture waited patiently for a casual visitor to drop and soak in the scene below.

A feeling of closeness grew as she shared Harry's vision of his home. Like a window into a part of him that could help her understand him. 'Thank you for bringing me here, Harry. It's wonderful.'

A smiling Balinese man, perhaps in his sixties, approached with welcoming hands held out towards her. Harry spoke from behind her shoulder. 'Ketut, this is Miss Bonnie. She is a midwife and flies back to Darwin tomorrow.'

Ketut inclined his head and smiled warmly. 'Welcome,

Miss Bonnie. It is with great pleasure I meet you. Come, sit, let me make you both tea after your journey.'

Well, that answered who else would be there, Bonnie thought, and stifled pathetic disappointment they wouldn't be alone. She remembered then that Harry had spoken of his mother's caretakers. She should have remembered.

'Hello, Ketut.' Bonnie settled into the luxurious cushions and raised her brows at Harry. She mouthed, *Wow* at the whole setting. 'Tea would be lovely. Thank you.' Ketut smiled and hurried away.

'I thought we'd have afternoon tea here.' Harry gestured to the view. 'You could look around after that and decide where you'd like to eat. If you'd rather come back here, we can let Ketut know in time for him to whip something up. He's a great cook.'

A busy restaurant was the last thing she wanted but she'd definitely be safer—from herself. Here, she knew she'd be tempted to peer through the cracks in the walls of Harry's isolation, to see why he affected her, why she worried about his inner sadness that he hid from the world but not from her, how she could help him. Every time she felt close to the answer in public he'd shut her out again and step back. Did she need that angst? Could she stop herself anyway? What if he did open up to her and they connected in a way that would hurt much more when she flew away tomorrow?

No, she didn't need that. 'We could go out. There's dozens of restaurants nearby. I'm easy.'

'No, you're not.' Harry watched her blink in surprise and her shock was ironic. He wasn't finding any of this girl/boy stuff easy when it concerned this woman. A notion all of his friends would find vastly amusing. 'But it's not your fault I find you difficult to fathom. Maybe I'm just out of practice.' He shrugged. 'But back to dinner. If you truly don't mind, let's eat here. We could walk the gardens. I'll show you the house and we can have drinks on the platform overlooking the valley. Ketut will be happy doing what he loves and we'll still drive through Ubud at night to show it to you when we leave to take you back to your hotel.'

She looked away to the river below as she tried to stay relaxed—or at least appear that way. Hard with her knee almost touching his as they sat side by side. Tension simmered like a pot of soup between them. Millions of tiny bubbles that surfaced beneath her skin as the heat of Harry increased. And there was the intimacy of the setting. His house. Foreign country. Alone except for the caretakers.

The mood settled when Ketut returned with fresh ginger tea and a gorgeous seed cake, but Bonnie laughed at them both when each rushed into speech as soon as Ketut left. 'You first...' Harry said.

Bonnie picked her cake up with forced enthusiasm, anything to break the awkwardness of the moment. 'I won't need dinner.'

Harry's glance warmed her. 'I want to feed you up before you go on the plane tomorrow.' That reminded them both she was going, until the direction of his gaze settled on her lips. She wished he wouldn't do that and she tried to concentrate on her imminent departure. His knee touched hers again, deliberately, and she felt more warmth sear through his jeans, the surge of intense awareness she would always associate with Harry. Not fair. Poor Jeremy had never been like this.

They looked at each other and it was as if invisible threads were looping and diving over each other in an intricate dance until she was encapsulated within a tapestry of secret knowledge they shared. Ridiculous. They shared nothing in common except today's experiences.

Her own gaze dropped to his mouth, those gorgeous lips she'd admired at Jimbaran, and she saw him smile, and just as quickly she blushed again. Harry stood up and she found herself beside him as he gathered her fingers into his hand and tugged her closer until her hip was touching his.

She moved into his arms as they stood together on his porch. Harry stared, unsmiling, down into her face and his eyes became deep royal blue, dark and promising, and she told herself it was because his pupils had dilated, a physiological event, not a revelation.

'I'd like to kiss you,' he murmured, his voice a physical caress.

Her heart tripped, stuttered and gathered speed. Her mouth dried. 'Why?'

He smiled with his eyes but still not his mouth. 'Because I think we'd both enjoy it.'

Lordy, yes. 'Oh.'

He leaned closer. At the last minute she closed her eyes, all the better to feel him with, and his mouth touched hers, gently. Homecoming—strange, when she'd never visited before. Like nothing she'd expected and much, much better.

He was the first man she'd kissed since Jeremy, and

instead of the masculine assertion that had always left her backpedalling away in confusion, Harry held the notion of mastery back. She could still taste the edges of his intent but it was infinitely subtle. Subdued by patience, imbibed with the same sense of peace she'd felt as she'd come through his garden gate. She felt like she belonged here. In Harry's arms. And kissing as he allowed her to choose the pace.

A novel idea, and tentatively she opened her mouth and tilted her tongue to his. Just a flutter. His arms tightened around her, he made a tiny sound in his throat as he pulled her closer into his body, and her other hand drifted to encircle his neck of its own free will.

And so the kiss gradually deepened, evolved, ripened into something tangibly alive and nourishing and enriching to her soul. To both their souls, she decided as she pushed closer, suddenly unable to be hard enough against his chest. She sighed with the rightness and connection and joy she hadn't experienced before.

Then, with a premonition she hadn't expected, like the dampness of a sun shower, she felt the tears in her eyes, a poignancy of devastation to come for when it must end, and that thought gave the connection a heart-rending simplicity she could barely endure.

It seemed Harry's arms were a place she'd been searching for and never known she'd missed, and when he gently withdrew, as warned, she was bereft.

How to hide what she'd just discovered? She stepped back and turned away and behind her back she could feel the wall rise between them—not surprising for two fort dwellers—and no doubt Harry's closed expression mirrored hers.

This was dangerous and foolhardy for a woman only just recovered from a broken heart. How could she have been so stupid?

'Maybe that wasn't such a good idea,' he murmured. She turned back, her face mostly under control, the tears wiped away surreptitiously. He smiled with his mouth this time, but not his eyes, no humour in his face. She knew just how he felt. 'Perhaps I should show you the house and grounds?'

She nodded, and they walked into the house, but again he captured her hand and she didn't want him to let her go.

The afternoon was surreal after that. The house seemed spread over many levels; because of the hillside, it floated up and down between rooms. Floated like the aura that floated between them.

Each window and landing gave space and light and vibrant exposure to the lime of the rice fields or the shininess of the tropical foliage. Each window beckoned like the heat that was building between them.

Furnishings, fountains and secluded benches in lush green nooks in the gardens all served as a backdrop for just one more kiss. Nothing more, no huge urgency, which in itself seemed surreal when they both knew their time together was ending.

One more lean into Harry's shoulder. One more stroke of his hand down her back. Both pretending the day wasn't going to end and talking of things not of the future and not of the past but of their inner thoughts. Music, books, morals.

As the afternoon lengthened, so did the kisses. The embraces became more intense, a slow build of fever was upon them like a tropical malady that had only one cure. And slowly, surely, inescapably, they finally drifted to the house and the master bedroom.

The huge four-poster with its snow-white mosquito net draped above seemed to smile at them. Dark, Balinese carved furniture stood like nodding sentries around them as he sat her down on the edge of the bed and stared into her eyes.

Bonnie knew she shouldn't be there, could see the risk of regret that tomorrow could bring her, the whisper of the voice of reason warning her she would lament her weakness, but this was all she could give. This wasn't weakness, this was strength. Her healing gift to Harry.

Bonnie couldn't leave him suspended, marking time, when he should move on. She didn't know why she felt she had the power to change that. That she was the one who could help battle his demons and ease his fear of more damage to his soul.

The tears tightened behind her eyes and her chest ached for him—this man who had broken through her defences with frightening ease—ached for his broken heart she wanted to mend.

But what about hers? This was crazy, and dangerous, and guaranteed to hurt later, but then, so would not being there with Harry. Not doing this. Harry had so many demons, and hers had flown—she wasn't sure when but she felt gloriously free.

Such was irony, that thought flitted away with the next kiss and the feel of him against her. Still he held her hand, as if he'd never let her go, and she allowed the fantasy its rein as they lay down fully clothed and began to kiss again. They could no more stop kissing than stop breathing. It was as if they both knew it was their last chance.

Kisses so tender, so sweet. Kisses that tugged at her very soul. She could feel the beat of his heart, thumping under the solid wall of his chest against hers, pumping faster as his kisses deepened, his need building, matching her own rising need until she too was breathless. Burning, aching, then suddenly afraid.

She should be afraid. The thought drifted in and out of her sensation-filled mind, afraid of him, afraid of herself and her own body she suddenly knew so little about, consequences, her body that was at the same time so innocent and yet so wanton.

Harry drew away, lifted his mouth from hers, stroked her cheek, and searched her face for a change of heart—again he'd read her mind and answered her unspoken plea like he had earlier that day—and she knew she had only to shake her head and he would hold her gently and be still.

And so the fear drifted away. Disappeared in the blue of his eyes and the understanding she could feel in her soul. How could this be wrong?

Now there was no fear. Only the knowledge that this was right. Nothing could be more right. And when they came together, their hearts beat in time, just as their bodies entwined like the vines outside the window.

Somehow it had become her goal to free him from his past. Her one focus to make him see how beautiful the world was and that he was allowing it to pass. She knew in her soul he was too good a man to leave like this and in that way she could never regret her gift to him—or his to her.

Afterwards he held her, dried her tears of joy, whispered his own amazement, kissed her eyelids and smoothed her hair.

Eventually, after much gentle teasing and quests of discovery, they showered together in the tiled room off the master bedroom with the window wide-open to the now empty fields. The workers would be home with their families; the birds too seemed to have settled.

The afternoon closed towards evening and they drifted toward the set table, 'Will you come back?' he asked, and the reality of her leaving eased between them like a third person.

'We'll see.' And they both knew that was a no. Yes, she was leaving. Tomorrow and a huge ocean and an even huger land mass would be between them. She'd glimpsed that spending more time with Harry would make her miss him more and she was almost glad she wouldn't have the chance. There was no future for them and she didn't want to regret what they'd had.

Perilously, they'd felt too right for people who would never fit their lives together, so no false promises had been made or exchanged. And that was right too. But he would always hold a place in her heart, as she hoped she would have in his.

Somewhere inside both of them peace remained.

Dinner was served on the veranda, two seats side by side, hips touching, and strangely there was no awkwardness between them to ruin the enjoyment of the colours of the approaching night and the last minutes of their time together.

Ketut had prepared a palate of ginger salad and garlic prawns with nasi goreng, everything redolent of the fresh coriander the Balinese loved. Everything tasted good. Shone brighter, smelt divine.

For Harry the last of the afternoon sun slipped away from an amazing day, a day of birth, warmth and approaching goodbyes from this woman who had tilted his world in a new direction. Perhaps because all those issues lay beneath their conversations they finally talked a little about the past and themselves. Though Bonnie found it easier to be open than he did.

She spoke of the nursing positions she'd held in the Outback. He'd seen the places, finally mentioned them but not in the context of the work he still kept from her, that he'd had flown in and out of them and for the first time in a long time a tiny stirring of regret for that life flickered in him.

He almost told her of Steve's offer. Confessed he was the medic who didn't show. His fault she had to leave early. But he didn't. Uluru was too close to the township of Katherine where Clara had died and already he'd compromised himself. The beginnings of shame for all he hadn't told her began to colour his evening.

'If you come to Bali again, I could show you more she has to offer.'

Bonnie narrowed her eyes at him. 'You never know the future but I hope you won't be here if I ever come back. I don't know what you're hiding from, Harry, but I hope you'll have decided to move on and do something kinder to yourself.'

Harry blinked. Nobody spoke to him like that. She was nothing if not forthright. 'Or you could come back,' he said.

'Or you could move on. Don't waste your life, Harry.'

He could have spoken of his mother's friend and how she'd started a birth centre for the women of the village. Those who couldn't afford to pay for a midwife in Ubud.

He knew she'd love that. How before his marriage he'd worked there several months a year, and loved it. How the ex-pats now used it as well because of the women-centred care they could have that so opposed the medically orientated care they would otherwise receive. But he'd not been back to the centre since Clara's death.

'Thank you for the day, Harry. It's been lovely.' She glanced at her watch, briefly touched his hand on the table and then stood up. Ketut appeared from the dimness.

Bonnie shook hands with Ketut. 'Thank you for a wonderful dinner.'

'You must come back.' Ketut slanted a glance at Harry who, to Bonnie's eyes, avoided the older man's suggestion.

'Maybe one day,' she said, and gathered her bag.

When they'd walked along the rice field path, she turned once more to look up at his house and it seemed so natural to have her hand in Harry's. 'It's been a magical afternoon and evening. Thank you.'

Harry helped her into the car. 'Thank you,' he said, but he was feeling more than a little battered. He wasn't sure what had possessed him to allow this woman as close as he had or why he'd broken his rule and brought her to his house. Let alone opened himself up and then kissed her like a hungry schoolboy and whisked her off to bed like a one-night stand. Of course, there had been an amazing connection he hadn't been prepared for. He'd been telling himself how dangerous she was since he had first laid eyes on her. Not a good choice. And ramifications he'd pay for later when he couldn't sleep.

Imagine if they hadn't been careful. He had a sudden vision of Bonnie with his child and the fear leapt into his throat like a rabid dog. He'd known her two days and pictures of disaster there were such that he knew he'd never recover from them. Thank goodness they'd been sensible there at least. Both of them.

It was deeply fortunate she was about to get on a plane and fly away. He'd never met anyone like her. Didn't understand how she could be so forthright, even hard on him, one minute and so giving the next. Perhaps it was the fact that she didn't think of herself when she gave and that shattered him. Her selfless generosity.

The drive to her hotel was accomplished with little of the usual traffic delay and all too soon she was turning to face him with her room key in her hand.

'Thank you for bringing me home, Harry.'

What could he say? She'd turned his life upside down in forty-eight hours. 'Thank you for spending your time with me.'

She stepped into his arms and it was his turn to close his eyes as he hugged her to him. He rested his chin on the top of her head for a moment and breathed in the vanilla scent of her hair that was already painfully familiar. Soaked in the feel of her against his chest, all soft, yet supple, a little too thin, and painfully dear already. He was mad, standing here ready to hurt as soon as she moved.

She pulled away and looked up into his face. Then she reached up and kissed him. Light and fleeting—like her. 'Goodnight, Harry. Look after yourself.' Then she turned round and walked quickly away.

'You too,' he said to her back.

The next morning Bonnie's suitcases needed only closing, and there were still two hours to go before her bus to the airport. Sweat trickled down her back as she sat by the pool in her sarong and swimmers with her book as she tried to block out the idea of any chance of seeing Harry. It would only be worse.

The tiny movement at the corner of her eye spun like a coin into a wishing well, a flicker of light as she turned the page of her novel. Bonnie blinked, looked around, not sure what she'd seen—maybe a thrown toy or the kick from an underwater swimmer—but the unease she felt made her drop her book and jog to the edge of the pool just to check.

A crescent of shadow lay on the bottom, one without movement and immeasurably gut-wrenching. Bonnie dived into the pool still wearing sarong and sunglasses just as a woman screamed.

By the time she surfaced with a limp toddler in her arms a crowd had gathered, and the child was lifted from her arms, then she too was pulled from the pool by willing hands.

'Someone, call an ambulance.' The woman who'd lifted the child from her glanced at the toddler's staring eyes and lack of movement and Bonnie saw panic flare in her face. Her face screwed up and she pushed the child into Bonnie's hands and walked away quickly— and left Bonnie to cope by herself.

Bonnie glanced around. For a moment she thought she saw Harry but then an old man stopped in front of her and she realised it was wishful thinking because nobody seemed willing to help her.

She sank to the ground with the child in her arms and jammed down the panic that would only make it harder. She didn't bother to check for a pulse before she puffed two small mouthfuls of air into the child's lungs. Then she shifted and began cardiac compressions, counting quietly as she strove to block out the people crowding to look but not to help.

The elderly gentleman knelt down beside her, his blue-veined hands shaking as he clasped them together. 'I don't know how to help. What do you want me to do?'

'Can you do mouth-to-mouth? Little puffs. I'll do the chest compressions, that's the most important. Watch me. I'll show you.' She shifted quickly and puffed two small puffs until the little chest rose and fell. Then she moved back to the side. 'Is anyone a doctor?' Bonnie said shortly, and glanced around at the bystanders.

'Anyone at all?' She began to count out loud again as her fingers found the child's sternum and began to compress on the little chest with cardiac massage. She shook her head when no one spoke.

'Twenty-eight, twenty-nine, thirty…' Bonnie paused,

shifted again to breathe twice. The little chest rose and fell, and Bonnie looked across at the older man. 'Can you do that?'

His eyes filled with tears. 'I don't think so.'

'Watch the clock for me, then, please.' She started again.

Harry's brain screamed to help but he couldn't move. He saw the old man shake his head and that was the moment Harry pushed his way through. He pushed not just through the people but the wall of fear that sucked the breath from his chest. Wrestled himself free from the giant steel claws that had held him back from the first moment he'd realised what was going on—the powerful memories of another dead baby he had worked on had been too strong.

His non-compliant feet hadn't moved, despite his brain urging them on, and his heart had thumped in his chest like it was going to explode. Then he'd felt relief as the older gentleman had joined her. He didn't need to get involved. They'd be fine.

But seconds later he'd seen the old man's shake of the head and Bonnie had looked up in desperation as she'd been left to her own resources again. Finally he'd been able to break the hold on his limbs and thrust himself forward. He hoped he wasn't too late.

Bonnie felt panic rising again as the little girl continued to lie flaccid beneath her. Then suddenly Harry, of all people, dropped down beside her to help. 'I'll do the compressions. I know what I'm doing.'

He compressed the toddler's chest. There was no hesitation, exactly a third in depth, no over- or under-compensation, which spoke of years of practice, and she shelved the questions that surfaced bitterly until she had time. Please, God, such precision would squeeze the little heart to force oxygen to the child's brain. In that captured moment, with the shock of the threat of death for this child a reality, for a split second in time as he cradled the child's chest Bonnie was struck by the snapshot of Harry's hands, hands she hoped she could trust with a child's life.

She breathed two breaths as the thirty-second mark came around again. 'Are you medical?'

'A doctor.' He didn't look at her. 'You must have seen her fall in. How long was she under for?'

'Twenty-eight, twenty-nine, thirty.' Bonnie paused, breathed twice, the little chest rose and fell, and Bonnie looked up at the old man. 'How's the time, please?' She started again.

'One and a half minutes.' How long had he been there? But that wasn't important. Why wasn't the little one responding?

The next half a minute dragged with aching slowness, thirty chest compressions, two breaths. Then another thirty seconds.

'Come on,' Harry muttered after Bonnie's next breaths and he compressed again, and as he finished speaking the tiny girl blinked slowly and finally screwed up her face before she coughed and began to cry weakly.

Bonnie felt a sob catch in her throat, the sudden heat of tears mixed with the swimming-pool water that still trickled down her face from her hair, and a huge shudder rippled down her back. She looked at Harry and no doubt her own relief was reflected in his eyes as he stared back at her.

Then raw ache at the back of her throat as she held back the sob continued to grow in size like a sharp rock in her neck and she pulled back out of the way as Harry rolled the little girl onto her side and into the recovery position.

She heard him say, 'Thank God,' as she inched further away. It had been him she'd seen. Why had he waited? Then the traumatised mother threw herself down beside her daughter and burst into tears. The sound of a distant ambulance siren drifted across the pool area.

Bonnie kept retreating until she could slip unnoticed back to her chair to retrieve her handbag. Her sarong had ripped, the wet fabric ungiving as she'd flung herself down, and she just wanted to hide somewhere and curl up after the near horror. She bit the skin of one hand to stop the chatter of her teeth as she felt shock well inside her.

A Balinese waitress approached diffidently and held out her wet sunglasses.

Bonnie met her eyes. There, too, huge tears trickled in mutual horror and dawning relief of the child regaining consciousness. 'Thank you.' The little waitress could barely make her words form. 'To lose a child would harm our souls for ever.'

Bonnie sucked in air. 'We're all very lucky.'

The little waitress inclined her head. 'Fortunate to have you, and the doctor.' They both looked across to where Harry's face was like granite as he stood with the little girl in his arms. He glanced up as if saying that had been too close.

The anguish in his face made the rock in her throat return. It had been him she'd glimpsed at the start. But surely not? However, when she replayed in her mind that image she knew it was true. Why hadn't he come straight away? Why had he left her alone when she'd needed him? Why had he not mentioned he was a doctor in the last two days? A man she'd shared special time with, a birth with, made love with. That was what liars did.

'I need to go to my room.' Bonnie tried to smile at the waitress but all she could think of was that she needed to get away before she broke down.

She saw him glance her way, saw him read the distress in her eyes. Harry was hurting too but she didn't care. He'd left her to cope on her own. He'd lied to her from the moment they'd met. The picture burned in her brain as she walked blindly to her room.

Like the last man she'd dared to care about.

Yes, she'd been very glad he'd been there at the end but would never understand his hesitation. He was a doctor and he'd lied over and over again to her.

By the time Harry walked out of the hospital in Denpasar an hour and a half later, the pain lashed him in a hundred places he'd forgotten—and none of them were physical.

He'd stayed fairly immune during the drive in the ambulance. The little girl, Ginger, had been awake and croakily stable but he'd been unable to leave her until she was safely in hospital and monitored by experienced personnel.

But walking out that hospital door into the stickiness of the Balinese heat, the memories hit him like a car full of tourists.

He'd done okay today, thanks mostly to Bonnie, but

how was he to live with the crushing guilt of his delay in response?

It had happened in his first emergency after Clara had died. His colleagues had told him it was only natural, to give himself time, but he'd backed away in horror. A man not to be trusted. A doctor unable to deal with emergencies. A man ashamed of a vocation that had been his life. So he had run to Bali.

Avoided any contact with medicine. And drifted. Drifted until a determined little midwife had dragged him into the very situation he'd been running from.

That was why he'd vowed he didn't want people's lives in his hands. Especially those of babies. Imagine if the little one had died.

That was why he stayed here. In the furore he hadn't apologised to Bonnie for not helping earlier. Being catatonic with fear, allowing others to do what he could have done better, was no excuse, and no doubt she despised him. Well, that was okay. He despised himself. He knew he was far from perfect. He just hadn't realised how far.

But there, in the back of his tortured mind, was the glimmer of a chance to explain. He could probably catch her at the airport if he left now but he didn't know what to say to her if he found her. But could he let her fly away without telling her why? And she'd need to debrief, if only a little. He was an expert in what happened if you didn't do that.

In the end it was Bonnie who found him. He'd been leaning up against a pylon in the departure hall when she'd walked past, dragging her suitcase.

She glanced sideways, saw him, jerked her bag a little as if to decide whether to stop or not, when Harry straightened.

'Hello, Bonnie.' Lord she was beautiful to him. She looked stressed, which wasn't surprising; she looked upset, which was his fault; and she looked confused about whether she was glad to see him or not. He supposed he could be thankful for that small mercy.

He met her eyes. 'I don't know what to say.'

She tightened her hand on the bag. 'Luckily that's your problem, not mine, Harry.'

He ran his hand through his hair and sighed. 'I'm sorry, Bonnie.'

She lifted her head. 'For which thing? Lying for the last two days or not helping me save a child's life until it was almost too late?'

He deserved that. 'All of it. And there are reasons for both.'

She shook her head. A physical denial. 'Well, don't try to explain because the excuse won't be good enough.' She glanced up at the clock. 'I have a plane to catch and I'm already late.' She put her hands up to her neck and undid the clasp on the necklace. 'I'd rather not keep this.' She dropped the little silver baby on a chain into his hand and jerked her bag. Then the words flew out as if she couldn't prevent them. 'How dare you lie to me? All this time.'

He closed his fingers over the charm and sighed. 'I lost my wife. My unborn child. I can't do medicine any more. I can't talk about it.'

She tossed her hair. 'Maybe you should because I can't see hiding it is doing you any good.'

'My choice.'

Brittle emerald, her eyes were like temple stones as she glared at him. 'I don't think you should have that choice. Lives are lost, Harry. Medicine isn't run by God. We do the best we can and sometimes our best isn't good enough.

'It's hard, but if every skilled doctor, every trained practitioner reared away from that reality, if they all turned their backs selfishly on their vocations like you have while you were buried here, how many more families have to feel that same sense of loss before you help?'

She tossed her hair and he could read the hurt in her face. 'There was almost another family today. How do you feel about that?'

He shouldn't have come. This wasn't doing either of them any good. 'It can't be my problem. I can't be calm like you were.'

That sobered the fury in her head. He saw it drain away and be replaced by pity. Pity he didn't want. 'You missed the nausea episode in my room that followed after I left the pool area. I wasn't so calm then.'

He heard her but it wasn't the same. She'd responded instantly to the situation. He didn't have that faith in himself. 'You were calm when it mattered and that's a big part of why that mother still has her child.'

Then he saw it in her eyes. Her own doubt and fear about a situation that wasn't so different from his— except she hadn't given in to it.

It was a lightning bolt of perception. Bonnie could choose not to admit the fear if she was unable to save the child, not give in to the helplessness of being alone in that emergency. The way he had. He never used to be like that. He'd been the first on the scene, the fastest with treatment. The golden boy of the Royal Flying Doctor Service. The bigger they are, the harder they fall.

Now he'd let her down. Continued to let himself down.

Then she lifted her head. 'Do you know how the little girl is?'

Her most important question. At least he could answer that for her. 'No ill effects so far. I just left the hospital.'

'Good!' She even smiled, not at him but into the air with relief, and he was glad about that. In itself it was validation of standing here feeling like hell. That smile made it worth it.

'Now I'm going,' she said, and he felt a slam of desolation he hadn't expected. At least he'd tried to explain. She pulled the bag forward a few inches and then stopped. 'You should give medicine another go, Harry. You might find salvation instead of hell. You never know. But if you ever want to talk about it, don't come and find me.'

Harry watched her disappear into the departure area and then turned away, but her accusations haunted him. Accusations he didn't want to think about. Was he egotistical and self-absorbed? He would have said self-protective. Or was it just the thought of practising medicine that jerked him into denial?

It was as well he hadn't had more time before her

flight left because he didn't know what he would have been capable of to try and talk her into staying just a little longer. To try to explain.

What was she saying? What did she mean? That someone else could have been there to help him when he'd lost his own baby? Someone like him, turning his back? Like Steve and that short-term job at the Rock and his own refusal to go?

He couldn't do it. Or could he? He'd managed with the baby but that had been a close thing. Could he go back to diagnoses and the mistakes that left him open to self-recrimination?

Then again, could he not? Life was looking pretty damn empty right at this moment.

During the drive back to Ubud, Harry noticed things he hadn't seen for a long time. Things Bonnie had pointed out to him with excitement.

He saw the families, crammed on motorbikes, children sitting on bags of grain behind their fathers, mums balancing their two-wheeled pick-ups as if it was the most normal thing in the world to carry a table on a motor bike.

It had always been this way as the motorcycle could be afforded and the car not, and suddenly to Harry it seemed incredibly alien to see babies, cradled by their precariously squashed mothers, jammed onto scooters between husbands and other children.

The small trucks packed with workers in the back; the Indonesian signage and waving palm trees were suddenly more visible. And here he was, pretending to be a part of it all when, in fact, he was really a bystander.

An isolated one too scared to be involved in his own world where he belonged.

Harry's world was in turmoil and Bonnie had done it. Bonnie and a little girl now safe in her mother's arms.

Bonnie had been there when he'd been screaming inside, *This baby's going to die too*, the scene fraught with emotion. An unwanted return to a situation he'd chosen to avoid, and now where was he? Apart from profoundly appreciative of her calm in an emergency, maybe it was the frailty of a toddler's breathing and the fact that he and Bonnie had skills to save a life that had him thinking.

Or maybe it was just Bonnie who was attracting these medical disasters. He'd managed to avoid them for the last year. He'd known her three days and they'd had two already.

He saw his life, drifting from one leisurely Balinese day to the next, focused on the small issues, never thinking of the large ones in case it made him aware of what he'd chosen to discard in his fear of being hurt again.

Maybe he did need a dose of Bonnie McKenzie's reality to kick him back into gear. Bonnie would certainly give him that but he couldn't face the thought of a hospital, even the slightly slower paced one in Darwin, impersonally rushing from one patient to the next. And he wasn't ready for the commitment of general practice.

The Royal Flying Doctor Service was always looking for staff but even in the state he was in he could see how frustrating it would be to fly everywhere wondering when next he'd get to Uluru and a certain straight-talking midwife.

That was the crunch. He needed to see if what he suspected was true. Needed to see if Bonnie was the key to a normal world. Nothing more than that because he wasn't doing the family thing again. Wasn't going there. But it still left a lot they could share. If she was interested.

But would she be happy to see him drop out of the central Australian sky into Uluru? He knew Steve would. If he hadn't found a replacement yet.

The acceleration as the wheels left the ground pushed Bonnie back in her seat. She closed her eyes then opened them again to watch the land fall away beneath her. Better to face reality after all her harsh words to Harry to do the same.

She looked out. That would be Jimbaran Bay there and she could almost smell the smoke from the barbecues on the beach.

Harry St Clair. Another liar. A doctor hiding from the world in a web of lies. She couldn't believe she'd allowed him into her heart.

And she'd done that for sure. How could it ever have seemed inevitable at the time? But she couldn't deny, at unexpected moments, there'd been a real connection between them. But she would not give her heart to a man she couldn't trust and he'd wiped out that possibility for ever. She'd have her heart back if it killed her.

The Harry St Clairs weren't ready for the world and she was.

Now she had to let their time recede like the island somewhere below the aircraft wing. Bali would always be a place of memories and moments of gold and a man who wasn't who she'd thought, and she doubted she'd ever forget him. But she'd never go back.

Enough. It was time to do what she was good at. Getting on with life.

CHAPTER SIX

BONNIE drove into Uluru an hour before darkness fell. All the other cars seemed to be heading out of the township in a mass exodus, off to see the sunset, like the tourists did when they hit the beach in Bali. Of course, thinking of sunset swamped her with the uncomfortable memory of a certain tall widower and that last sunset in Ubud. Had it only been two days ago?

She dragged her mind away from Indonesia and remembered her friend in Darwin telling her about the ritual of sunset at Uluru.

A motorbike pulled out in front of her and she swerved to miss the suspiciously young Aboriginal couple running late for nature's best show. The boy waved and grinned and she saw his girlfriend was pregnant, heavily so, and that too reminded her of Bali. A precariously loaded motorbike and cheekily happy faces.

'Slow down, buddy, or you'll miss more than the sunset,' she muttered, but her mind was stuck like a piece of grass stuck in a Balinese water buffalo's hide.

She'd promised herself she wouldn't regret immersing herself in the Harry St Clair experience but that hadn't happened. She'd been in way over her head and spent the flight back trying to place at what moment good sense had escaped her. Hadn't she learned her lesson? The men she seemed attracted to were not to be trusted. She must have a homing device that attracted compulsive liars.

On the positive side, she hadn't once felt that inertia and sadness she'd felt since Jeremy's desertion and deceit. She was too angry.

Even though she'd found another man to let her down, somewhere in the mix, maybe a little to do with the Balinese beliefs, she did feel alive. Angry, but alive.

Harry's main deceit was to himself and until he addressed that he'd never be whole. She couldn't help him and she needed to concentrate on helping herself.

Her car eased slowly along the curved road past the hotel and she slowed as her eye was drawn to the uninterrupted views across the red sand hills to the great monolith in the distance.

Like a sleeping dinosaur, but millions of years older, Uluru showed its age in wrinkles of stone that caught and held the last of the sun's rays in textured lines of light and dark orange, and she could feel the rise of goose flesh in an unexpectedly primitive response to nature's spiritual beauty.

She hadn't expected that.

It was as if she suddenly began to feel the earth beneath her feet again, to be able to enjoy the beauty of her first sunset and each new place in a way she'd been too stressed and rushed to do in the last year while she'd dealt with Gran's slow death.

She flicked her mind away from the pull of the past and soaked in the new territory that would be hers to watch over.

Bonnie picked up her speed a little as she drove past

a famous five-star resort with huge white sunshades soaring above the grand marble entry. The sort of place the Harrys of this world would stay.

Then she passed bungalows and an open-plan shopping centre and finally reached the neat and tidy medical centre nestled in its own block beside a small ambulance and police station, all the buildings lined up like a child's play village.

A lot of thought had gone into the planning of the township, the centre at the centre, she thought musingly as she pulled into the parking area out front.

Bonnie turned the car off and rolled her shoulders back into her seat. It had been a slow drive on the back way from Alice Springs, but she'd enjoyed the scenery. Taken her time, admired the meteor crater at Gosses Bluff, seen Kings Canyon and gazed in amazement at flat-topped Mount Conner in the distance.

She'd had a close shave with a couple of big kangaroos as the long day had shifted into late afternoon, and it was good to get her battered Jeep here safely.

When she pushed open the door to the office the blast of cold airconditioning washed over her face like a cool sponge and she couldn't help a further lift in her spirits.

New jobs were always a challenge but today it was a stimulation she was keen to relish. Especially today. Three months out here at the centre of Australia promised to be an intriguing addition to her portfolio and the perfect antidote to holiday disillusionment.

'Can I help you?' The small, impeccably made-up woman at the desk looked a little incongruous compared to the patients ranged around the room, mostly ebony-skinned Aboriginal men and women with a scattering of red-faced tourists.

The receptionist had a lacy blouse that showcased her trim arms and light tan, shirts like Bonnie had seen everywhere in Bali two days ago, like she herself had been wearing when she'd said goodbye to Harry on the way to her plane.

Bonnie shook off the thought. Okay already. She'd moved on. 'I'm Bonnie McKenzie, the new nurse practitioner. I start tomorrow.'

'Welcome. I'm Vicki.' She gestured to her badge. 'Receptionist.' Then she indicated a small doorway into a passage. 'My husband, Steve, is the practice manager here.'

She stood up. 'We're pleased to have you. Thanks for coming a couple of days early. Steve's still trying for a temporary doctor for the month we can't fill, and I'm starting to wonder if we'll ever get a permanent one.'

Vicki shrugged and then rolled her eyes. 'And the nurse you work with had to leave early because of an illness in her family. She'll be back next week, maybe.'

Vicki shrugged ruefully. 'Come through and I'll find Steve.'

Bonnie kept her face serene but her heart dipped a little. It didn't look like she'd be getting much of an orientation if the medical staff were all away. Still, at least the ambos were next door and the practice manager would have first-aid training. Think *challenge*, she told herself, and fixed her enthusiastic smile in place with a new determination.

'Steve. The new sister is here.' Vicki gestured to an athletic-looking man, probably a couple of years older than Harry, who had the kindest eyes Bonnie had seen for a long time. Suddenly she felt better.

Bonnie nodded, and she suddenly remembered that people in the Outback preferred to nod, unlike their city counterparts, who were used to brushing up against people in crowded streets. 'Pleased to meet you, Steve.'

'And you too, Bonnie.' He looked fondly at his wife. 'Has Vicki told you we're it at the moment?'

'So she said. As long as I can find everything, I'm sure I can help. There's always the option of shipping people out.'

'Spoken like a trouper.' He gestured for her to precede him further along the narrow hallway. 'I'll show you around.'

The building was small but efficient, two consultation rooms, a long nurse's desk in front of four beds with curtains, and a sterilising and stock room. The computers were state-of-the-art and the practice guidelines were on prominent display. It was starting to feel familiar already.

Bonnie had done postings at Kununurra and Broome in Western Australia, as well as two small Aboriginal community postings, and her last four months in Darwin had been mostly maternity.

'So how many ambulance officers next door?'

Steve and Vicki exchanged smiles. 'That would be zero. There's just you driving until the nurse comes back. And maybe our doc if we get one. If you need to be in the back for transport, then Steve and I can both drive out to meet you.'

Oh, goody, Bonnie thought ruefully. She could just

see herself haring off into the night in an ambulance to a car accident with the sirens blaring—out into the desert by herself. Now she wanted to ring her friends to come and play with her here.

'But hopefully you'll have backup, though we try only to work our doctors during office hours. It's so hard to get them here, we have to nurture them.'

Poor baby doctors. Bonnie fought to keep her eyebrows from scraping her hairline. She wasn't sure she succeeded. So nurses were more expendable. Mmm.

'So who are the people in the waiting room seeing?'

Vicki answered. 'Us. They're here for blood tests—people on heparin, insulin, stuff like that. Steve and I both take blood and we can do quick tests and send samples to be flown out on the afternoon plane for more complex results.'

'So these are all routine tests for regulars who have regimes printed out for them?'

'That's right. And the results are sent to the flying doctor, who changes any medications they need.'

That sounded efficient, and not something they needed her for. Maybe she would get to find her bed and settle in before she started tomorrow. 'So, where do I stay?'

'The staff from the hotels, the clinics and even the tourist companies like pilots and guides all stay in the staff village. If you keep on the road you came in on, the village is down the third road on the left. You're in the Desert Pea Villas, room two, and the doctor is next door. The other nurse, Cleo, is upstairs, and Steve and I are along the corridor a little in five.'

It all sounded pretty simple. And a little too close for someone who liked their privacy and space, but she'd cope.

It rained torrentially in the night. Not a common occurrence at Uluru, and the hollows in the rock filled with water from myriad waterfalls off the enormous face. The waterfalls made small puddles and not so tiny pools in undulations where the hollows occurred.

Bonnie woke before dawn and the first thing she saw, the gecko on the ceiling above her head, reminded her of Bali.

Great! She threw back the covers and sat up, forced herself to feel her feet on the cool floor and grounded herself in the present—away from the memories of dinner on the beach at Jimbaran and rides through the rice paddies with a smiling Harry.

A plan had formed last night when she hadn't been able to sleep to walk one of the base sections of Uluru before sunrise. Her phone would keep her in contact, and that would clear her head for the day. The plan sounded even better now. She pulled on her clothes.

The drive to Uluru parking area beside the rock was accompanied by a gradual lightening of the sky to grey and finally to a faint glow of orange that promised a spectacular sunrise on the other side. Not that she'd see that with this great hulking monolith between her and the sunrise when she parked her vehicle, but this morning she wanted to get closer and actually touch the face. She'd dreamt of it through the night and the thought promised an inner calm she looked forward to.

As she crossed the car park she gazed in awe at the

steepness of the actual climb to the top of the rock, steel posts and chains anchored to the almost vertical places on the accent face reached up to the pinkening sky above. Bonnie shook her head. No wonder some climbers had come to grief. It looked daunting and lonely, just her and none of the tourists still on the other side, awaiting the sun.

But it was awe-inspiringly beautiful. Wow. Her feet crunched in the sandy gravel as she crossed the deserted forecourt and followed the path to the base. It was cool beneath this giant shadow.

She kept left and finally the path snaked beside sheer cliffs and she could touch it. Lay her hand over the rough granules of time beneath her fingers and rest it there against the Rock's cool heartbeat. She had a sudden thought of Harry and whether he'd seen this. Felt this. What it would be like to share this with him.

The eerie sensation made her wonder whether the sight and feel and vibration of past eons would heal him too as she could feel the last of the walls inside her crumble and break into small particles of debris within her. Then she made him disappear like sand through her fingers because he threatened her new-found peace. She wandered alongside the sleeping beast for the next fifteen minutes before she turned back towards her car.

Shooting in and out amongst the scooped-out rock waterholes were pretty finches with scarlet upper feathers that were most noticeable when they were in flight. Firetails. She only recognised them because there was a shiny nature print above her bed with a close-up of the very same birds.

She wished she had someone—*like Harry, maybe,*

a dissident voice inside suggested—to share her new knowledge with. No—of course not. But it would be fun to recognise more than one of the species of bird around here and she promised herself she'd buy a book on local fauna. Who needed company for that?

Suddenly she wanted the distraction of work and hastened her footsteps towards her car.

By the time she'd driven back, showered and had breakfast it would be nearly time for work. It had been an eventful morning already and no doubt the day held more interest yet.

It turned out well. Her morning left her with barely time to think let alone be distracted by memories. Patients with heat stroke, and knee scrapes that needed washing and cleaning, a fractured wrist and an eye full of sand, and Bonnie's last patient for the morning, a pale lady, Iris Wilson, who'd apparently already fainted in the waiting room.

Iris wasn't happy with the conditions of the Outback.

'I'm not used to this heat. And I'm especially not used to the flies.' She shuddered delicately and looked ready to faint again. 'I'm terribly afraid I've swallowed one.'

Bonnie helped her to sit but before she could enquire, Iris rushed on. 'One of the dirty insects flew straight into my mouth and before I knew it, it was gone. All the way down. I feel so sick and weak. I can just imagine the disease that's starting in my poor stomach right now.'

'The flies are annoying,' Bonnie agreed, 'but I'm sure they have their place.'

'Not in my stomach,' Iris said crossly.

'No, of course not.' Bonnie battened down the urge to laugh with steely determination. 'Flies clean up refuse and even provide food for many other animals. And your stomach acid will make short work of any germs that went down with your fly if you did swallow it.'

She brought over the blood-pressure machine. 'But you look pale and I'd like to check your blood pressure. Are you sure you didn't hit your head when you fainted?'

'Hmph.' Still decidedly unimpressed, Iris shook her head. 'I don't want to see a nurse. I want to see a doctor.'

'That's harder. But certainly you can.' Bonnie smiled gently. 'But you'll have to go to Alice Springs for that. They have a very modern hospital there.'

'I think I will.' The little lady straightened her shoulders. 'How would I get there?'

Bonnie glanced at her watch. 'It's five hours by car but I've heard they've a scheduled bus that leaves from the mall.'

Iris swivelled her head and glared at Bonnie. 'What about an ambulance?'

Bonnie clamped down on her lips again. 'I'm afraid I'm the one who drives the ambulance and I have to be available here.'

The little lady visibly deflated and Bonnie wanted to pat her shoulder. Instead she soothed her. 'I swallowed a fly once and, apart from the thought, it didn't hurt me at all. I'm sure you'll be fine. But I'll check your blood pressure and get someone to help you back to your room so you can lie down until you feel better.'

Poor, unfortunate Iris nodded and sniffed and allowed Bonnie to fit the cuff and inflate it, but she wasn't happy.

When she'd finished, Bonnie patted Iris's arm. 'Your blood pressure's a bit low, so make sure you drink lots of fluids. It will go lower if you get dehydrated. Are you on any medications?'

'Won't take them.' Iris sighed. All of a sudden Iris seemed to shrink into the chair in front of her eyes and Bonnie felt her heart contract.

'I'm sorry.' Iris sniffed. 'I've been rude and ungrateful. I think I panicked a little.' She brushed her silver hair out of her eyes and sat up a little straighter. 'I used to be fearless you know, but after I lost my family, it seemed my nerves went at the same time.'

She sighed again, 'I always wanted to see the Rock but it's not as much fun as I thought, on my own.' She rolled her shoulders and gathered her bag, then gingerly stood up.

Bonnie came around to stand next to her. She didn't know why she did it but she held open her arms and to her relief the little lady crept in for a brief hug. 'Iris, I believe you used to be fearless, you're still quite frightening when you want to be.' They smiled at each other. 'But I think you'll feel better soon.'

When she pulled back Iris smiled tremulously, and Bonnie could feel a little lump in her own throat. Iris needed companionship. Everyone did.

'I did hear the Sounds Of Silence Dinner is a wonderful place to meet fellow travellers,' Bonnie said. 'Please think about it for tonight. I promise you'll enjoy it. Even on your own.'

Bonnie followed Iris out into the waiting room and

she was glad to see that, during the morning, between the efforts of Steve, Vicki and herself, all the chairs had finally become empty. 'Can you get someone to help Iris to her room for a lie-down, please, Vicki?'

'Of course.' She helped Iris to a waiting-room chair. 'And I'll make you a cup of tea while we wait.' She turned back to Bonnie. 'Can you see Steve, please, Sister? He has some news.'

When Bonnie entered the office Steve sat relaxed at the computer and sent a big grin Bonnie's way when she entered. 'We have a doc. He arrives this afternoon, the one I'd hoped for. Initially he cancelled but he's changed his mind.'

'That's great news.' Someone else to help with the ambulance, she thought thankfully. 'You know him?'

'He's a good friend, we grew up together, been out of circulation for a while. Lost his wife and child in a disastrous birth on his watch and he threw in the towel.'

Bonnie's palpitations hit her out of nowhere and her hand came up to her chest. She tried to keep her face from freezing and almost achieved it. She licked her lips to ask the question but Steve went on.

'Harry was always great at getting to the root of a problem, mandatory around here when there's only us and disaster. Especially with our Aboriginal patients. Except with himself, I guess. He's been keeping to himself for a while now. But I think we're all like that when things go wrong.'

This could not be happening. 'That would be Harry St Clair?' Well, she'd told him to break out. She just hadn't planned on it being so soon and close. 'I thought he was in Bali.'

Steve glanced up. 'That's right. Inherited a house there. We'd been corresponding for weeks since the last guy dropped out. A friend met up with him for me a couple of days ago in a last-ditch attempt. Thought I'd lost. But he rang last night.' Steve grinned at her. 'So you know him too. That's great.'

'Great,' Bonnie echoed, and she wondered if her face was as white as it felt.

Now it wasn't just an event to try to forget. There'd be the constant reminder of how stupid she'd been. It was a full-blown disaster and she could kill him for doing this to her.

CHAPTER SEVEN

HARRY could feel the tension mount as the arid red land-scape burned into his brain.

Memories of another flight, no premonition, the faces of those who waited for him, a tragedy that might never have happened if he'd ensured his wife had gone to the larger town when he'd said she should.

If he hadn't let himself be swayed by her wish to stay home a little longer.

Bonnie was right. He needed to face life and stop hiding from the past, though the pictures that clawed at him still scratched at his soul, though, just maybe, they seemed a little softer to him than before.

When they landed at Uluru Airport, the dry heat hit him like a hot newspaper in the face as he stepped off the plane, baked and arid—and he savoured the lack of humidity, so different from Bali.

It wasn't so bad being back—so far.

Steve waved from the gate and Harry lifted his hand in reply. Well, he'd have to perform now he was here. He'd hit the books since he'd booked his flight, hoping study would boost his confidence, maybe banish his ghosts, and he just had to trust it would all came back to him when that first obstetric crisis happened.

He really had no issues with emergency medicine— it was the babies and their mothers he didn't trust. No doubt Bonnie would be a whiz but he'd come to the conclusion she actually attracted maternal disasters, like a shiny lure on a fishing line.

He'd have none of that, thanks very much.

'So you made it.' Steve rubbed his hands together and Harry had to smile at his friend's enthusiasm.

'You don't have to baby me, Steve. I'll stay the month.'

Steve grabbed Harry's overnight case. 'Still got the old pack, I see. Vicki said hi. She's holding the fort with Bonnie.'

Harry kept his face impassive, he hoped, and it must have worked, because Steve went on, 'Our nurse. She said she's met you?'

Had he forgotten anything about her? He doubted it. 'Bonnie McKenzie. Tall, too thin, green eyes?'

'Don't know about the eyes…' Steve slanted him a glance '…but that's the one.'

Harry could see some serious questions and answers coming and tried diversion. 'So where's your car? I have to pick up the other box of stuff. I brought you some beer.'

'Cheers for that.' Steve rubbed his hands. 'Never enough beer in the desert. So when did you meet Bonnie?'

'Bali.' Nothing more. Hopefully they could leave it at that.

* * *

Bonnie was in the middle of suturing a triangular laceration on a young man's hand. She'd recognised the boy from the motorbike that first sunset.

'So, you came off your bike, Bernie?'

'Nah.' He grinned. 'Thumped a garbage bin 'cause my girlfriend got mad at me.'

Bonnie looked again and saw the way the scrape went from knuckle to knuckle and pictured it. Dumb kid. 'Make you feel better?'

A flash of white teeth in his ebony face. 'Yeah. Took me mind off me troubles.'

'What about the garbage bin?'

'Yeah. Came off better'n me.'

Bonnie shook her head. 'Men are strange.'

Harry walked in just as she said it. She glanced at him without a smile and tried to keep her face as neutral as possible. Not much else she could do. He looked disgustingly handsome and embarrassingly familiar.

Steve followed him in, beaming. 'Bonnie, Harry's here. You two know each other.' Steve was happy. Obviously. He had his doctor and it was his friend as well. His world was good. 'I'm off to find Vicki to let her know we're back.'

Bonnie had no one but herself to blame for Harry deciding to come out of his shell in her direction. And she needed to remember it was a good thing for him to have made that choice. But he'd sucked her in once and she wasn't falling for his new pack of lies.

'Hello, Bonnie.' Harry smiled that killer smile and she fought to hide her body's instinctive reaction that, no matter what her brain said, decreed it was physically good to see him.

'Harry.' She nodded briefly and glanced at a point on the wall past his head. 'Australia not big enough for the two of us?'

'Seems not.' Out of the corner of her eye she could see he did look ridiculously glad to see her. Did he have short-term memory loss or something? They'd left a long way from being on best terms and she wasn't pretending they hadn't. Obviously she seriously didn't understand men so she looked back at Bernie's hand in front of her.

Unfortunately she could feel the warmth of just being in the same room as Harry seep into her like warm rays at sunrise creeping up a wall.

He stepped closer and peered down at her neat work. 'So you suture great as well,' he said.

She finished up the last stitch and tied it off. 'No one else to do it at some of the places I've been.' She peeled a dressing and sealed it into place. 'Try and keep it dry, Bernie. Come back in five days. I'll have another look and take the stitches out.' She winked at the boy and smiled. 'That okay with you?'

'Yep, missus.' Bernie picked up his cowboy hat and jammed it on his head. 'I'm gonna go see that girl of mine.'

'Just remember you have to look after her. She's feeling big and clumsy. Tell her she looks beautiful to you.'

Bernie grinned. ''Course she's beautiful.' He winked. 'And so are you.'

'Yeah, right.' Bonnie accepted that with a grain of salt. 'And take it easy on that bike of yours. I don't want to have to scrape you off the road.'

Bernie bolted out and Harry laughed. 'You've made a conquest.' He looked her up and down with serious warmth in his eyes. 'Another one.'

Bonnie washed her hands and dried them for longer than she probably needed to. Anything to hold off the moment when she had to look at him again. 'So what made you decide to take this job in the end?'

'Someone told me I should try medicine again. So I'm here to see what happens.'

She let him have an exaggerated sigh. She was tired of holding it back. 'I wasn't thinking about a place next to me.'

He raised his brows. 'You have a problem with me being here?'

'Yes would be the short answer.' Did she regret he was there? My word, she did. Even more so because he looked so darned good and her shoulders itched with memory of the weight of Harry's arm around them. 'I might have made a few different decisions if I'd known we'd be working together so soon.' Like backing off straight after Jimbaran.

The silence lengthened while they both thought about that until finally Harry stated the obvious. 'I'm only here four weeks.'

'I know. I've mentioned that to myself a couple of times already today,' she said dryly. She steeled herself and met his eyes. 'I won't trust you again, Harry. You're not on a good wicket here.'

She wasn't sure what reaction she expected from him but his sympathetic look made her eyes prickle.

'Of course I understand that, Bonnie. What we shared

in Bali was based on my deceit, and I'm sorry for that. Maybe one day you'll see how that came about. But for now, what happened in Bali is left in Bali. I got it.'

All very well to say that now. But the reasons she'd given for allowing herself to sleep with this man came back and bit her. There hadn't been any good enough reasons. Even kissing and hand-holding would have made her skin heat with embarrassment. Let alone the fact that she knew every inch of his gorgeous body intimately.

This was ghastly.

So much for holiday flirtations not coming back to haunt you. She'd been such a fool and the heat still crept up her neck as she narrowed her eyes at him, trying to see if he meant it. She'd constantly underestimated his ability to con her. 'Okay.' Reluctantly her hand went out. 'Strictly platonic.'

'To platonicness.' Not a real word, so not a real vow, and a flippant comment that reminded her she was taking this more seriously than he was. What a surprise.

But when he took her fingers in his and gave them a quick shake, even with that fleeting contact, she knew anything to do with this man would have feelings and emotions attached to it.

Bonnie pulled away and turned her back. Damn. Damn and triple damn.

The rest of the day Harry spent with Steve and Vicki. Thankfully. It was good they worked out rosters, talked work, and despite Vicki's updates to Bonnie it seemed a lot of time was spent laughing over old times and Bonnie didn't feel excluded. Really. Honest.

By the end of the day Bonnie was drooping, exhausted, more from the nervous energy expended over coping with Harry's presence than the inconsistent workload. She could have done with a much busier workday to keep her mind occupied. Instead she'd been shoring up on her reasons not to fall under the spell Harry seemed to be able to weave over everyone. But not her. Certainly not her. She'd learnt her lesson.

There was a sticky moment when she remembered Harry's room was next door to hers but she didn't see him when she went to bed that night. He was still out with Steve and Vicki. By the time she'd reconciled herself to that it was after eleven and she was so exhausted she fell into a deep sleep when her head finally relaxed into the pillow.

When she woke in the morning, heavy-eyed and claustrophobic, she decided to return to the Rock for another dose of calmness.

Unfortunately when she pulled up Harry was just ahead of her and he saw her before she could turn around and drive away.

It was too late to avoid him now he'd stopped and was obviously waiting for her to catch up, and reluctantly she followed his footsteps in the red sand until she was standing beside him.

'Pleased I'm here, I see?' He didn't seem too perturbed and she wasn't in the mood to lie.

'No.'

He grinned at her. 'As soon as your plane left I missed your complimentary ways, you know that.'

'Don't tease me, Harry. My sense of humour is AWOL at the moment.'

'Okay. Let's enjoy the view.' He looked up at the monolith in front of them and raised his brows. The rock face above was in shadow still, and the darker areas seemed to have a life, a past life, and eons of stories to tell. 'Wow. Impressive.'

She glanced around and walked across until she could rest her hand on the granules of rock on the wall. She sighed. Cool and calm and having collected so much wisdom and experience. She could feel peace seep into her. 'Very.' He was right. She was there for healing, not for argument. And she guessed he was too. They did have to work together.

A peaceful walk sounded good. She buried her misgivings, tucked her hand in her jeans out of the way so she didn't swing her fingers into his, and set off.

A couple of hundred metres away, in the still coolness of the early morning, a toddler in a tracksuit wandered away from the visitor centre. She drifted further from her mum and her aunties and her grandmas cooking breakfast for the tourists to come, drifting across the sand like a floating grass seed, tiny footprints in the sand, a trail of flower imprints as she dawdled slowly, drawn towards the great monolith.

'Leila?' Her mother's voice also drifted towards the rock, and the little girl hesitated at the sound, but then a bird landed in front of her and she tottered after it.

When she came to the rock base a pool beckoned. The pool smiled at her and rippled with intriguing shifts of shadow and floating leaves and Leila reached down to capture a tiny twig that floated at the edge.

Bonnie and Harry nearly stumbled over the little girl as she peered into the grass beside one of the pools filled by last night's rain, and the memories of Bali slammed into both of them in the same instant. Not this time.

Bonnie's fingers reached down swiftly and gathered a handful of fabric from the little girl's jacket as a lifeline, and Harry was right beside her as they tried carefully not to startle the child or communicate the fear that had grabbed them both. Their eyes met. There was no way this poppet was falling in with them there.

Harry glanced around for the mother and suddenly in the still air she could hear a woman's frantic call. 'Leila?'

'Pretty,' said the little girl as she pointed to a lizard.

'Yes, it is pretty,' Bonnie said as she held out her hand. 'But you need to bring Mummy when you come here.' The little girl put her fingers in Bonnie's.

'Let's find Mummy, Leila.' Bonnie stood up and lifted the child into her arms as Harry cupped his hands over his mouth.

'She's here,' Harry called out. Their eyes met, and she knew they were both thinking of another little girl. She looked away as sudden tears stung her eyes at the memory of near tragedy. That was the only reason for the tears.

'She's fine,' Harry called out. 'On the path beside the base. With the nurse.'

Leila's mother burst from the bushes, her brow beaded with perspiration and the stress of dread, and Bonnie passed the little girl into her arms.

'She was sitting beside the rock pool,' Harry said.

The mother looked at both of them with such relief in her face Bonnie felt tears sting her eyes again. She could only imagine a mother's fear.

'Thank you. I don't know how she got out but I'll work it out before tomorrow.' The woman clutched Leila to her chest. 'Don't do that, baby. You frightened Mumma.' The woman looked at Bonnie again. 'She slipped away while we made breakfast.'

Bonnie nodded. 'They're so quick, I know. She was watching the lizard over there, I think.'

'So close to the pool.' The mother shuddered. They all saw the lizard trundle off and Leila's mum smiled at the reptile as if it was a friend. 'That ngiyari can drink with his feet, you know. Water moves from his feet to his mouth along grooves in his skin. Very clever lizard. But my baby should not be here.' The mother squeezed her daughter and the little girl wriggled with delight. 'Thank you, both. Again.'

Bonnie glanced up at the sky and guessed sunrise would have taken place on the other side of the Rock by now. They'd have to go soon. 'I'm Bonnie, the new nurse and midwife at the clinic, and this is Dr St Clair. Maybe we'll meet again.'

'I'm Shay. We'll see you soon. My baby's due for her needles.'

Bonnie grinned. 'I'll be gentle.'

When the mother had gone Bonnie and Harry walked another fifteen minutes around the base and tried to regain the peace of the Rock but it was gone. Lost in the memory of another child who'd nearly drowned and the lies of the man beside her, all Bonnie could think of was the way Harry had almost left her to cope on her own. How he'd lied.

She didn't need this. She turned away and walked quickly back towards her car. He knew why.

The day was fairly quiet. A few cases of sunburn and a fractured cheekbone from a fall. And Leila's immunisations.

Bonnie smiled when she saw mother and daughter. It made her feel almost like she belonged here to see them again so soon.

'I thought I'd come while I remembered,' Shay said quietly. 'My aunty said bring her in today.' Bonnie managed to keep Leila diverted while she slipped the needle in and Shay was smiling by the time they left. 'Not as bad as I thought it would be,' she said. 'I'll tell my friends you're good with the little ones.'

By the end of the shift Bonnie was tired. Tired of knowing every minute of the day what Harry was doing, where he was standing, who he was talking to. And when he caught her eye and smiled it was even worse. That night it took her ages to fall asleep and when she did it didn't last long enough.

A call came through at midnight. Bonnie dreamt her phone was ringing, persistently, annoyingly, until she woke and found it really was.

The night concierge at Reception apologised quickly and then dropped his bombshell. 'We've a call from a guest that her husband had severe chest pain and now he's blue. Security will pick you and the doctor up in the ambulance to save time. He'll only be a minute or two away to take you there.'

Bonnie threw the bedclothes off. 'Of course. Is someone doing cardiac massage?'

'The night porter's there. He's trained in first aid. And the man's wife is doing the ventilation.' Amazing.

'Great work. I'll be ready.' Bonnie tore off her nightgown and dragged on her loose trousers and jumper. It was cold in the desert at night, though she had no doubt she'd be warming up with the adrenalin that was rushing through her body already. By the time she was hopping to the door, pulling on her shoes, she heard Harry's door open. She threw hers open just as he raised his hand to knock.

'Good,' he said, and she followed his disappearing back down the hallway and out to the ambulance that pulled up as they arrived.

It seemed he was no slouch when he decided to attend. At least she didn't have to worry about that. They scooted off into the night, and as the security man drove them along the twists and turns of the side roads between the bungalows she glanced at Harry's face.

Straight into a code one on his first night. He seemed calm and focused despite this being his first official emergency since he'd left medicine and the moment reminded her again of their last, much smaller patient—when he'd finally decided to help. She banished the thought and crossed her fingers for a similar positive outcome for the sick man and his family.

The bungalow door stood open and Harry jogged ahead while Bonnie grabbed the defibrillator. Bonnie could see the porter on his knees as he gave cardiac massage and the slight blonde woman with the big resuscitation bag between her elbows as she held the mask

on her husband's face. She squeezed it twice after every
thirty chest compressions.

The light from the ceiling shone off the perspiration
on the porter's brow. Bonnie and Harry had come as
soon as possible but five minutes must have felt like an
hour for these poor people.

Harry slipped in beside the porter and took over the
compressions.

'You're doing great. I'll take that from you in a moment,' Bonnie said to his wife, and knelt down and
quickly undid the patient's pyjama jacket. Matted hair
on the man's chest would confound the pad, she saw, and
grabbed the razor to make two quick hairless areas to
place the pads of the defibrillator. 'Darned hairy men,'
Bonnie muttered under her breath.

When she had them attached in place she took the
resuscitation bag from his wife, who collapsed back
against the bed and watched as Harry ceased cardiac
massage to view the tiny screen. Bonnie saw her jam
her knuckles against her mouth and she nodded at her
in sympathy. 'Hang in there.'

'Don't touch patient. Press shock button,' the re-
corded voice in the machine said in a monotone.

Harry said, 'All clear,' and glanced around to check
before he pressed the shock button. The man's body
lifted slightly off the floor and then sagged back.

Bonnie heard the man's wife gasp and glanced back
over her shoulder with sympathy. 'He can't feel it. He's
unconscious.'

Unconsciousness was the best scenario. They recom-
menced cardiac massage for another two minutes until
the next ECG strip could be taken. The rhythm was

slightly improved but not enough to sustain life. The message was repeated and they shocked him again. After the next two minutes of CPR the man began to shift and moan and Bonnie allowed a glimmer of hope to settle in her chest.

This time the screen showed a more viable rhythm and the man's colour began to improve.

Bonnie slid the oxygen mask onto the patient's face and put down the bag and mask, then handed Harry supplies for inserting an intravenous cannula on his side of the patient while she did the same on her side.

Within five minutes of their arrival the man was stable, even rousing to consciousness while being manoeuvred onto the stretcher of the ambulance in preparation for transfer to the medical centre.

Harry had already arranged on his mobile for the arrival of the Royal Flying Doctor Service to fly the man to Alice Springs. Pretty slick even for the most experienced of practitioners.

She glanced across at Harry as he gave another injection. There was no doubt they'd worked well together in this situation, though as far as Bonnie was concerned most of the thanks should really go to those first on the scene.

When Bonnie drove the ambulance to the medical centre, she found the cumbersome vehicle surprisingly easy to manoeuvre. Harry monitored the patient in the back, and the man's wife sat with her hands clasped together tightly in her lap in the front with Bonnie.

Bonnie finally had a moment to spare the woman some attention. 'Are you all right?' She glanced across at Clint's wife. 'Your husband's very lucky you knew what to do.'

Donna, their patient's ashen-faced wife, a petite fifty-year-old blonde, twisted her hands and swallowed the tears in her throat. 'Yes. Thank you.' She looked over into the back, bright tears running down her cheeks. 'Thank you both. All of you. The wonderful porter who took over from me. Those compressions.' She shuddered. 'I was so exhausted by the time he got there.'

'He looked a little weary too by the time we arrived, but you both did an incredible job of keeping the blood and oxygen circulating.'

Donna ran her hand over her face to wipe away the tears. 'I never want to have to do that again. Thank goodness you came. Those portable defibrillators are incredible, aren't they?'

Bonnie could see Donna needed to talk. Needed to dump some of the nervous energy she'd been holding back so incredibly. She'd been amazing. What a heroine. 'They're very handy. And so quick to do the job.'

She thought of Donna's husband's hairy chest and smiled. 'I'm afraid Clint's going to have two shaved areas on his chest. Like two big eyes. Not very neat either.'

'He'll cope. I might wax the lot of him while he's unconscious,' Donna shakily joked, 'ready for next time.'

Bonnie took her hand off the wheel and patted Donna's shoulder. 'Hopefully he'll be sorted out by his doctor and there won't be a next time. But I think you're incredible, the way you're holding yourself together.'

Bonnie saw more tears spring into Donna's eyes.

Oops, sometimes sympathy wasn't helpful. She should have known that. Bonnie hastily changed the subject. 'The medical system here is very efficient. All the mod cons as well.' Bonnie pulled into the medical centre.

The next few minutes were taken up by transferring the patient to a ward bed and connecting him to the wall monitors. When they had Clint settled Bonnie went back to Donna, who'd been in contact with their grown-up children on the phone.

'The children are so appreciative. And impressed,' Donna said. 'I think he had more chance here than if he'd had the heart attack at home in Sydney.'

Bonnie smiled. 'You might be right. But a lot of the outcome depends on what other people do in those crucial first few minutes. You called for help and got on with it. You did everything right.' She smiled. 'I think you're marvellous. So it couldn't have been his time to go.'

'My word, it's not.' Donna glanced across at her husband as if to check he was still there. 'We've worked hard all our lives and he's not losing his retirement because of ill health. I'll make sure he eats the right things and does an exercise programme. In fact, I'll do it with him.'

Harry joined them. 'Sounds great. We all need to.'

Bonnie gestured with her hand. 'Harry. Dr St Clair. This is Donna, Clint's wife.'

'Hello, Donna. We didn't have much time to chat, did we? The night porter said you were terrific with the CPR before he arrived.'

'Thank you, Doctor. I hope I never have to do that again but as I said to Bonnie, I'm not losing him now.

We've got too much fun to have yet. Too many children together and too much history.' Donna's voice shook on the last word.

Bonnie felt tears sting her own eyes. History. Would she ever have that kind of history with a man in her life? Not just bad memories and brief emotional flings with liars and losers?

She saw the way Harry closed down, too. As if he didn't want to know about history, and children and wives losing husbands, or vice versa. Maybe she would understand more if she knew the circumstances of his loss but she refused to ask Steve or Vicki. It was Harry's story and if he didn't think she needed to know, she'd be fine with that. Either way, it wasn't her business. She'd keep it that way.

By the time Clint was flown out it was almost dawn. Harry and Bonnie saw Donna back to her room, which Housekeeping had tidied for her, and Bonnie tucked her in.

Harry waited at the door. 'Have a couple of hours' sleep, and Reception will help you get an early flight. It will truly take that long to get him settled into the ward and the tests will take up most of the morning until you get there. Try not worry too much.'

As they walked away, Harry captured Bonnie's hand and held it. 'Well done, Bonnie.'

She was not going there! Bonnie eased her hand free and kept her voice level. 'You should say, "Well done, team."'

'Actually…' Now that she thought about it, she stopped walking until he stopped too. 'Imagine if you hadn't decided to come and that was all on me and the porter?'

He frowned as if to say, 'So?'

She shook her head at his refusal to understand. 'This is exactly what I meant at the airport at Denpasar. I can't give some of those drugs, Harry. Not without medical orders. That all takes time and I really don't think Clint had time.'

She saw his comprehension settle. 'Maybe,' he said, still reluctant but aware of what she was getting at. Finally he nodded. 'Yes. I'm glad I was here for that. And for Clint.' He looked at her. 'And for you. I don't like to think of you having to cope with emergencies like that on your own, Bonnie.'

'People have to if the resources aren't there. Like you did before you gave up medicine.'

He frowned. They arrived back at the Desert Pea and Harry held the door for her. He didn't comment on her words.

And he wouldn't. Why should she be surprised? Bonnie yawned. 'Shame about a night's sleep.'

Harry glanced at the lightening sky. 'You go to bed. Stay there till lunchtime if you can. I won't sleep. I'll ring you if I need you. Maybe you can relieve me this afternoon when I crash.'

She glanced at him and she could tell he was wired. He wasn't shutting his eyes any time soon. She guessed he did have a lot to think about. And she was stuffed. 'Sounds very democratic. Goodnight.'

Harry watched her close her door and for a brief moment wished he could just follow her into her room and never come out, but he turned away. He'd burned his boats there. Best go for a walk around the grounds, let the morning air wash away the tension, and when he got back he could ring Alice Springs and see if Clint had arrived safely.

Harry flexed his shoulders. So he was a little unsettled by the last few hours but he was beginning to accept he just might be in the right place for him at this time. At least he wasn't dreading that first day on call any more.

Later that morning, Harry discovered he might not have offered to do the clinic if he'd realised it was antenatal clinic day. It was all very well to begin to feel more comfortable with medicine, but pregnant women were way too close to home.

By the time Bonnie surfaced about eleven he'd recovered his equilibrium, but his face lit up when she arrived. 'You could take over here, Bonnie.'

Bonnie smiled when she saw who the clients were. 'Hi, guys.'

Bernie's pearly white grin lit up the room and he nudged his girlfriend. 'She's the nurse I said about.'

Harry smiled at Bernie's delight. 'I was just saying to Tameeka that she should think about how long she stays in Alice Springs as she approaches her due date. In fact, she's only got five weeks to go she may as well go soon.'

Bonnie saw the frowns on both young people's faces and glanced between the three of them, feeling her way to diplomacy. 'Women usually wait until two weeks before their due date if they move into town.'

That didn't go down well with the medical officer. 'I

disagree.' Harry shook his head to underline it. 'We have no idea when that first baby is going to arrive and this isn't a safe place to have baby without the hospital.'

Bonnie tried not to telegraph her feelings but it was a battle she only just won. She wanted to frown like her patients were at this insensitive goose.

She tried another angle, hoping that Harry would get the hint. 'Do you have anyone you can stay with, Tameeka?'

Unhappily, the girl shook her head and rolled her eyes at Bernie. Bernie spoke for her. 'She's worried about bein' homesick 'cause I can't stay up there. I gotta job down here with the traditional owner tours. I work mornings from five till eleven. She don't need to go yet. It's only a five-hour drive.'

Bonnie lifted her brows and tried to lighten the mood of the conversation. 'Might be interesting, having contractions on a motorbike.'

'Nah.' Bernie grinned. 'My cuz has a car and he'll take us when she goes into labour.'

Harry shook his head. 'You can't wait until she's in labour.' He turned to Bonnie and mouthed, 'Talk some sense into them, please.' Out loud, he said. 'We'll see what we can arrange.' And left Bonnie to it.

'What's up his jumper?' Bernie said as Harry walked away.

'Apart from being up all night at an emergency, he wants what's best for Tameeka and your baby, that's all.' Inside, Bonnie was fuming. What a lot of angst for nothing.

If they sent Tameeka too early she'd get homesick and come home again anyway. Then they'd have a devil of a time getting her back to Alice Springs for the actual birth. Bonnie dealt with these issues all the time on outreach clinics. Heavy-handed tactics weren't helpful at all.

Didn't he realise it was a terrifying thing for the young woman to be sent to a large town on her own to give birth? Well, Bonnie would do what was necessary to smooth that path and hopefully it wouldn't all backfire in her face. Life might have more facets of frustration with Harry than she'd anticipated.

Harry walked away and he could feel the rigid set of his shoulders as he fought panic.

Everything had been going along fine until he'd realised Tameeka was exactly the same length of time into her pregnancy as his wife had been when she'd died. Thirty-five weeks.

That awful paralysing fear had grabbed him by the throat and he'd wanted to put the young woman on a plane and get her to safety. Get her off his hands. Away from his responsibility. Let Alice Springs deal with her birth and she and her baby could come home well.

Which was ridiculous. Tameeka might not go into labour for another four weeks. Bonnie was right. But he also knew a person who feared the natural process of birth should not be caring for pregnant women. And that included him.

Needless interventions, like sending pregnant women away too early, didn't help anyone. The inherent dangers if she came back and refused to leave again, increased risk of car accidents from multiple trips and postnatal depression from a lonely stint away from her family all had to be weighed up.

He didn't know what the answer was. Except now he was wishing he hadn't come.

CHAPTER EIGHT

AT THE end of the first week, Bonnie waited for the Sounds of Silence Dinner bus in the reception area with all the tourists. She doubted she'd have arranged it so soon except that when Clint had been flown out by the RFDS, Donna had given Harry and herself the tickets they couldn't use. And the porter loved the bottle of Scotch that Donna had said Clint wasn't going to open now.

It felt odd to be dressed up to eat on a sand dune but Vicki and Steve had been adamant it added to the ambiance of the evening. Even odder when she reminded herself who her dinner companion was.

When Harry arrived in dark trousers and a white shirt stark against his tan, the other women waiting swivelled to admire him, and Bonnie smiled wryly as she watched them compare the two of them. Just like in Bali.

'You look gorgeous,' Harry said, and the way his eyes lingered reminded her how accomplished he was at beaming light at her. She remembered how she'd thought of him as a lighthouse the first time she'd seen him.

Funny how she forgot about the competition in an instant and even forgot how well she knew this man. Actually, she forgot about everything except the powerful way he could draw her in like a merman to his ship-wrecking rocks. Watch those rocks, she told herself.

That day he'd come over to talk to her at the swimming pool seemed so long ago and such a convoluted dance they'd been in since then. So much for not being one of his harem of admirers.

At least he didn't turn it on at work.

Or maybe she had a force field when she was with a patient because after that first day or two she could separate the two then, helped immeasurably by that not-so-little issue of trust that she didn't have with him now.

But tonight she could feel herself weaken. Pathetic woman. 'Well, thank you, you're looking debonair yourself.'

Harry's fingers rested on her elbow as he steered her out to the arriving bus and the warmth of his possession ran up her arm. It was happening again. Waves of awareness tingling in her skin, heat, low and hard in her belly. Lordy, yes, this man made her know she was alive.

He leant down and spoke into her ear so the others couldn't hear. 'What's the chance you get through this night without a call out?'

It was hard to listen when she was feeling so intensely. It felt so good to be hip to hip again. Too good to have his hand on her skin and his face near hers.

She pulled back, needing to make a play for some distance. 'Fair to poor. But I'm going to enjoy the moments I do get. My friend in Darwin has been talking about this dinner since she did a stint here.' Now she was babbling. There had to be a happy medium.

He ushered her up the steps of the bus and into a window seat. His hip was against hers as the bus took off on the ride out to the dunes, the excited chatter of their dinner companions a hum around them.

Bonnie felt Harry's leg near hers, like on the bus on the day of the bike ride, but she was pretty sure she wasn't going to end up naked in his arms like she had that day. She blushed. She had better not. It would be a lot harder to hide the damage from a repeat performance of gullibility.

She looked desperately out the window towards the orange and red hues of near sunset. There was the Rock, she thought with relief, and hung on to that magnificent vision like a lifejacket.

Bonnie breathed in the sheer magic like an antidote. Slowly she gained a measure of stability. The sight filled her head until she could shift aside Harry for a moment and the issues they had, and just savour Mother Earth at her most majestic.

'Gorgeous,' she said as she turned back to Harry and found him watching her, studying her profile as if he couldn't understand something, and she felt her neck heat as she resisted the urge to give in and blush.

'Have I got a smut on my nose or something?'

He laughed without humour. 'Not that I can see.'

Bonnie frowned at him. They couldn't do this. Work together and continue the level of awareness they generated between them. She opened her mouth to broach the idea of strategies for managing that when she reminded herself they were surrounded by other people.

Funny how the world seemed to narrow down to just the two of them when she was with Harry.

In the end it didn't matter because the bus jerked to a halt, out in the middle of the desert between the two great icons of central Australia, the single massive of Uluru and Kata Tjuga, the huge collection of enormous boulders that made up the Olgas.

As she stepped off the bus Bonnie didn't know which way to turn, to watch the sun reflected against the rock or setting behind the Olgas, and the choice was an awe-inspiring dilemma.

Harry gestured to the silk rope and suggested she follow the guests up the incline to the top of the dune where a tuxedoed waiter stood with silver tray of champagne in crystal glasses.

The setting was beyond anything she'd expected. 'Thank you,' Bonnie said, and took a half-full glass from the man and slowly turned to admire the full view from the top of the dune. She crossed to the bar and at her request the waiter filled her glass with soda water. Harry did the same and she smiled at him. 'Trying to get into my good graces?'

'Not fair for just you to be on call.' She'd never said he wasn't thoughtful but she'd prefer if he made it easier to keep her distance and not harder.

They turned back to face the Rock. Neither spoke as the chiselled face of the massif grew more shadowed with wrinkled stone and signs of weathering in gold and different pinks that seemed to glow brighter. Too beautiful. As a backdrop, the dark velvet red of the desert, with sparse desert oaks interspersed up and down the rolling mini-dunes, blushed with its own radiance.

'Kangaroo, crocodile or Tasmanian salmon.' The

waitress offered tiny hors d'oeuvres with cress on crackers, and Bonnie blinked as the spell was broken.

She glanced at Harry, suddenly more composed. She did feel better. More grounded and relaxed with him. She could do this without making a fool of herself.

The idea of eating a wallaby wrinkled her nose, but crocodiles often ate humans so it seemed fair to return the favour. 'Thank you.' She glanced at Harry, darkly handsome as he watched her, and she pretended she wasn't perturbed by his study. Hers was a front but a fairly good one.

'After luwak coffee I'll try anything.' Bonnie took a serviette and biscuit with crocodile meat and nibbled at the edge of it. See, she could even allude to a previous time. She was strong. It was quite an act not to drop crumbs or her lass but her composure held.

Her juggling must have looked a little dangerous because Harry collected another serviette for her with a smile.

'Maybe we should take turns, and the other person can hold the glass, like an old married couple.'

Harry using the *M* word. Good grief. And he didn't look happy about it. She glanced away. 'There's a few of those here. Lucky things, to be travelling round together. Clint and Donna should be here. They'd fit right in.'

He didn't quite wrinkle his nose but he turned his shoulder to block out the concept of happily married couples. 'Let's move to a spot with a bench so we can sit and just relax to enjoy the view.'

Harry's aversion to marriage and happy couples was getting a bit old actually. Bonnie had no problem enjoying the history of the other couple. They found a spot on a rustically weathered log and as Bonnie emptied her hands she spotted Iris, her silver-haired, fly-swallowing lady from the first day, and waved.

Harry lifted one eyebrow as Iris bustled across, all chiffon and pearls, dragging a twinkle-eyed gentleman, and when she arrived she even kissed Bonnie's cheek.

'Hello, there, dear.' Iris was glowing. 'How lovely to see you.' She glanced over her shoulder at her beau. 'Fergus is a widower. We met last night. We had such a wonderful time that Fergus asked me to come with him again tonight.'

Bonnie shook the man's hand. 'That's lovely, Iris. Hello, Fergus. This is Harry, the doctor I work with.'

'Harry.' Fergus smiled and they shook hands too. Bonnie pointed to the tray as it went past held by a smiling waitress.

'Have you tried the crocodile?'

Iris giggled. 'I said to Fergus, if I can eat a fly I can eat a crocodile.' She glanced affectionately up at the elderly gentleman who looked down at her with an amused air. 'He thinks I'm silly.'

'Och, that's no' true. I think you're a sweet wee gas-bag and a lot of fun. Now, let's leave these young ones to enjoy their evening while I whisper sweet nothings in your ear.'

Iris waved and Bonnie couldn't help the grin on her face as she watched them walk away. 'That's great. A gorgeous Scotsman. She was so sad when I met her earlier in the week.'

'You're a softy. Care about each person, don't you?' Harry said. 'Really wish them well. Anyone and everyone.' He shook his head at the concept, pretended he didn't subscribe to it too. 'Not everyone is like that.'

She drained her glass. 'I know for a fact you care, so don't give me that. I've seen you in action in Bali. The kids on the bikes, that first night we met. Even the people here.' She stared at him. 'It's what we do, Harry. Why we do it. Coming back to medicine might help you find the large part of you that's missing.' She felt the wall go up.

'So I'm guessing you like it here.' Harry changed the subject and she mentally shrugged. It was still like being in a minefield, talking to him.

'I'm enjoying myself. I'd like more midwifery, but apart from the antenatal visits for the women from the settlement, as you've already said quite strongly, labours need to be shipped out. So I won't see much of that. But I'm enjoying the diversity.'

'Steve and Vicki do a good job.' They took two more hors d'oeuvres as they went past and conversation gave way to pleasure in the view.

She nodded and sighed happily over the sunset that grew more spectacular by the second, and without looking at him tried for some history that wouldn't upset him. 'So, tell me how you know Steve?'

He put his glass down. 'We grew up together, in Darwin. Went to the same schools, same group of friends, got married in the same year.'

He'd even mentioned his wife. That was a first. 'So your wife was from Darwin too?'

'No.' He stood up and looked at the bar. 'Do you want a soft drink? I think I'll get one.' Slam. End of conversation.

'Sure.' She stood up herself. 'I might go and chase the waitress for another one of those crocodile biscuits.'

Bonnie circulated among the other guests, Iris introduced her around, she spoke to the wait staff she'd seen in the Desert Pea accommodation and avoided looking for Harry.

When they were called through the silk rope again from the top of the dune down to where the tables were laid out in the desert below, he appeared beside her in time to be her dinner companion, along with six other people at their circular table.

She wasn't sure she'd have been so efficient. 'I thought you might have preferred to sit next to someone less nosy.'

He touched his own nose. 'You're not nosy. I'm just out of practice answering to anyone.'

'That's your right. Sorry if I upset you, Harry.' She chose her seat and tucked her bag under her chair.

He waited until she was seated, then sat down and they shared the sight of the vastness of the Olgas in front of them across the stretching desert. 'You haven't a mean bone in your body, Bonnie. Let's just enjoy the night.'

Bonnie chose to admire the snowy cloth and the silver cutlery and the glasses that shone in the candlelight. Much better than feeling patronised, and a little irritated, even isolated below the stars that slowly appeared out of the darkening night sky, which was ridiculous. Other people introduced themselves, so there were other people apart from Harry here, she must remember that. This was getting old too.

She joined in the introductions that followed, appreciated the revelry as the champagne the others were drinking, even if she wasn't, relaxed her dinner companions and loosened their tongues. It seemed they had a party of couples towing their caravans around Australia at their table.

'Been on the road for three months,' one of the husbands said with a grin, and his wife rolled her eyes. One of the other women giggled.

'We're in our fifth month,' another commented, and Bonnie listened in awe as they spoke of the places they'd seen and the unexpected adventures they'd found. She couldn't imagine being with one person for months on end in a vehicle. She certainly couldn't imagine Harry doing it, but by the end of a long dinner and their companions, at least, draining the replenished red and white wine, she could see the fun of it.

Later that night, when the bus dropped them off, even Harry found himself returning to the staff quarters more relaxed than he'd expected.

He heard Bonnie say, 'I had a ball.'

And it was actually easy to say, 'Me too.'

He could see Bonnie still smiling over the risqué comments that had followed them off the bus and suddenly he didn't want the night to end. Didn't want to lose the connection they'd built up over the evening. A connection he hadn't felt since Ubud, which, of course was his own fault.

'Fancy a pot of tea? Don't know about you but the evening seemed to end a bit suddenly for me.'

'Sounds good.' Bonnie looked up into the sky, searching for newly identified constellations, not so easy to see with all the lights around them. Out in the desert they'd extinguished the lights, the darkness had opened the whole sky to them, and it was a sight she'd never forget.

She spun around as she tried to identify the stars. 'It was much easier when the astronomer pointed them out.'

She sounded plaintive, and Harry smiled to himself. Her eyes had been brighter than any of the stars they'd seen tonight. She'd been so excited to learn the names of the constellations and individual celestial bodies when the stargazer had told stories and myths from the past. He remembered how she'd been interested in the stars that night at Jimbaran.

'Come inside before Security decides you're up to no good.'

Bonnie turned her head and waved at the man with his torch who was circling the building. 'I reckon he'd recognise us from the other night, but okay.'

They slipped in the front door and headed for the recreation room. 'You make the tea, I'll grab a box of chocolates from my room.' Bonnie was gone before he could answer.

Harry turned the lights on in the communal dining room and plugged in the jug. Maybe this wasn't such a good idea. Every moment he spent with Bonnie made it harder not to pull her into his arms and find that peace he knew was there. The feeling of rightness he hadn't lost since the magic of Ubud.

It had been like that with Clara too, he reminded himself. He didn't even want to think about the differences between Clara and Bonnie. He had enough guilt.

There'd been magic with Clara too, and then before

he'd known it he had been set up for heartbreak and disaster. No way was he going back. He had the horrors even imagining Bonnie in danger. And it wasn't fair for him to not make that fact plain to Bonnie. Tonight.

On her side she'd kept the relaxed rapport from the evening. He could see that when she arrived back clutching an unopened box of chocolates. 'My friends in Darwin gave me these. I'll never eat them on my own. Seems right for tonight.'

She ripped open the box. Delightfully exuberant. 'I had a great time.' Bonnie popped a white sweet into her mouth and sighed blissfully. She sank back into the chair with her eyes closed.

He reached across and chose a dark nutty one with a twisted curl on top. Serious decision-making while he edged his brain around how he was going to say this. 'Me too. Considering my behaviour earlier.'

She shrugged that away. 'You didn't want to talk about it.'

But he did now. 'I want to apologise, though.'

She didn't open her eyes. 'Okay. Done. Let's talk about something else.'

He supposed it was her turn to avoid unpleasantness but he needed Bonnie to understand how drawn he was to her, keen to spend time together if she was interested, but no strings and no future.

Not that she'd asked for any, and maybe the clarification was more for him than her, but he needed to say it. That he wasn't opening himself for that kind of pain again.

The jug boiled and he got up and poured the water in the pot and put the cups on the table. Neither of them took milk. He'd learned that at least since he'd arrived. He sat down. 'I'm guessing you haven't asked Steve what happened to my wife and I. I appreciate that.'

Bonnie sat up and pointedly stared down at the chocolate choice in the box. He wished she'd look at him so he could see what she was thinking. Her posture suggested she didn't want to hear and he was sorry about that.

After the relaxed evening it was probably a downer but she'd been happy to blast him at the airport and the sting lingered. She'd hear it and then they could both get on with their own lives.

She sighed and when she did look his way her eyes were the windows to the soul he'd expected. She'd accepted the conversation wasn't going to go away.

'Okay,' she said quietly. 'So you didn't meet your wife in Darwin.' She remembered his earlier statement. Of course she did. He'd bet she remembered a lot of things—some he wasn't proud of.

'I met Clara in Alice Springs. She did her training there and I met her again in Katherine when I started working for the RFDS.'

Bonnie so didn't want to do this now. 'Small planes make me sick. I could never nurse and fly at the same time.' It had been a pleasant evening, she'd been proud of herself as she'd made headway with her plans of distancing Harry by being friendly and concentrating on other people. Drinking tea late at night was not good for distance. She should have stayed in her room.

She'd begun to feel queasy just knowing he was going to talk about his loss.

Did he have to ruin a great night? Did she really need

to understand him? She was beginning to think the less she knew of Harry St Clair the better for her own sake, but she doubted she had a choice now he'd started.

Harry poured both teas. 'I never felt sick, flying. Usually too busy with a patient to think about my stomach.' His response came out lightly but she could see his mind was elsewhere.

Okay. Stop beating around the bush. Do it. Bonnie just wanted this over with. 'So how long were you married?' *How long before she died?* she really wanted to ask.

'A year. But probably came down to a few months by the time you took out the amount of time I was away. We should never have got married, or at least I wasn't keen on it until I had a less mobile job, but we did and very soon she fell pregnant, though we weren't planning on that either.'

This was it. The reason he was how he was. Her voice dropped. 'So what happened, Harry?'

'Amniotic fluid embolism. Early labour.'

Bonnie felt her heart sink. Not nice at all.

'We were in an outlying area. She should have gone to town at thirty-six weeks, been closer to the hospital. I wasn't even there till near the end. Didn't know what was happening. Nobody guessed. Everything should have been fine. No risk factors.'

Ouch. So he had no faith in natural labour. 'Rare and horrible,' Bonnie said quietly. 'We've had one in Darwin, though before my time, and I think I read that the incidence as one in about twenty-six thousand. You can't predict that. And not great odds if they do diagnose it when it happens.'

'Yeah. Usual diagnoses made at autopsy.' He grimaced. 'Clara was a previously healthy woman, healthy pregnancy, but they found her uterus had a small rupture during early labour, must have been congenital, and the amniotic fluid got into her bloodstream, caused an allergic reaction. She collapsed and even though we did an emergency caesarean we couldn't save her. I couldn't save her. Couldn't save my baby, though we tried. That resus nearly killed me. Certainly killed any desire to go back to medicine.'

'Until now.'

He lifted his head and his eyes narrowed. 'Who's fault is that?'

She wasn't taking the blame. No way. 'Not mine. Nobody forced you. You're your own man. But I'm glad you did. And I'm pretty sure Clint and Donna are too.'

His mind was still on Katherine with his own tragedy. No wonder she felt there was a part of him missing half the time. 'I don't know what I'd do if I came across it again.'

'Are you sure of that?' Bonnie didn't agree. 'Maybe you'd use what you learnt last time, pick it up way before anyone else, and give mother and child the chance they might not have had with the insight you gained. So that your wife and child's lives weren't wasted.'

He turned tortured eyes on her and Bonnie felt the squeeze in her heart that she was kidding herself if she thought she could stay immune to the hurt this man suffered. She was already too involved.

'It's the picture, Bonnie.' The words were barely a whisper. 'Her face as white as the hospital sheet.' He shook his head. 'My baby growing cold. It's engraved on my soul.'

Bonnie felt her own heart rip. She stood up, moved to his chair and crouched down to put her arm around him. She rested her cheek against his.

'It's incredibly sad. And so hard on you. But maybe you should try to see there's another side of the picture, Harry. Imagine it, because I can. It happened a minute or so later. Clara blowing you a kiss as she floated out the window, to heaven, with her baby. The two of them together, Harry, hand in hand. Sending you love for your pain but themselves at peace. Not bothered by pain or regret or fear.' She leaned over and kissed his mouth. Willing his pain to ease. 'There was nothing you could do.' Quietly and firmly she said the words he must have heard a hundred times before. Maybe this time he could allow himself to believe.

She believed it. It was the kind of image her gran had given her when her mum and dad had died, and the relief had been enormous. And healing. She wanted to share that with this man who'd inched his way into her heart, when a man in her heart was the last thing she wanted.

It was all in his face when he looked at her. Really stared her down while he thought about it, and she wondered if she'd gone too far. His face stayed unreadable, a pain-filled mask she couldn't see through, the huge wall between them bigger than it had ever been, like the Rock outside her window, but she couldn't take it back. Because she believed it true with all her heart.

Then he stood up and just walked away. Left her sitting there, staring after him, wondering, hoping, wishing she'd kept her mouth shut.

* * *

The next morning Bonnie woke early and lay in bed and watched the stars fade outside her window. Her head still spun from Harry's disclosures the night before and the picture of tragic disaster he'd painted.

It was a good premonition for what was to come.

CHAPTER NINE

TAMEEKA'S auntie wore a bright red football jumper and orange shorts. A big, rangy woman, she had square, bare feet still dusty from the road and she ushered the sheepish teens into the medical centre with an expansive wave of her hand.

It was late afternoon and Bonnie observed the young pregnant woman's apprehensive face and looked around for Harry. He was going to blow his top.

Her mind darted for answers as she waved them in. They could get the RFDS aircraft in if the plane wasn't half a world away, helping someone else, or they could take the ambulance and meet the Alice Springs ambulance two and a half hours up the road.

But getting to a hospital in time was the question. Damn not having a midwifery facility here.

She shook off her wishes and put them aside. 'Hello, there, you must be Tameeka's Auntie Dell. She said you'd be with her. I'm Bonnie.' She smiled at Tameeka and a nervous Bernie. 'Come through, honey. What happened to Bernie's cousin's car?'

Bernie shrugged. 'He went on walkabout two days ago and he's not back yet.'

Bonnie glanced at the clock on the wall. 'So what time did the pains start, Tameeka?'

'Not long ago.' The young girl wouldn't meet Bonnie's eyes, which wasn't that unusual, but Bonnie had her suspicions when the next contraction rolled around very firmly within the minute and lasted a good sixty seconds.

'I told her she 'ad to come.' Auntie Dell was born to be an authority figure and probably had a dozen nieces she'd be shepherding into labour. 'You're that nurse who picked up little Leila, aren't you?'

'Yes. Are you Shay's auntie too?' Bonnie smiled. She turned back to help Tameeka sit down. 'Thanks for bringing her in.'

It was a shame Tameeka hadn't seen her aunt a little earlier, Bonnie thought ruefully. That would have been good. But it didn't really matter when her labour had started. The past was the past, and it was what happened now that counted.

She had the sudden notion that concept should apply to Harry too, but she'd hear enough from him in a minute without pre-empting him.

'It's all good. You're here now. Do you mind if I have a feel of your tummy and listen to that gorgeous baby of yours, please, Tameeka?'

Tameeka lay down on the examination couch and Bonnie met her eyes before she attempted to feel. 'Okay if I feel the way baby is lying?' Tameeka nodded and Bonnie gently palpated the mound of ebony skin as she felt for the baby's back, bottom and head. She smiled. 'Your baby seems to know the way out. He or she's pointing the right way.'

Bonnie placed the nozzle of the little handheld foetal heart monitor on Tameeka's stomach and the sound of a baby's heartbeat filled the air.

'Love the sound of them babies.' Auntie Dell smiled beatifically. Bonnie nodded in agreement as she counted the beats.

'What if it's too late to go?' Bernie asked the question but it was there too, in Tameeka's eyes as plain as day.

Auntie Dell huffed, 'You'd be in trouble, bro.'

Bonnie softened the rebuke. 'Babies decide when and where they come. But we might get Tameeka to Alice Springs in time yet. At least she won't be sitting there by herself, waiting. It looks like it's going to happen today and I'm sure Bernie can miss one day off work.'

'Too right. I'm not leaving her.'

'I'm not leavin' either.' Auntie Dell planted her hands on her hips. Bonnie smiled to herself. She wasn't going to take on forcing Auntie Dell to stay behind so it was going to be tight in the ambulance if they had to drive.

'Who's not leaving?' Harry arrived with a measured tread and Bonnie's antenna picked up the underlying pressure in his voice. At least the face he showed the young couple was non-judgemental and she allowed herself to relax a little. Of course he'd be fine. Except Tameeka was in labour a long way from a hospital.

Tameeka's abdomen grew tight and she rolled her eyes as another strong contraction informed everyone it meant business.

'How long's this been going on?' Now Harry's eyes held a tiny hint of accusation when he looked at Bonnie. He'd have loved to blame her, she could see that. She guessed it helped to blame someone and she was the logical choice. Men!

'Not long. They've just arrived.' Bonnie's calmness eased the tension that had begun to tighten the room and Harry looked at the young couple.

Bonnie could almost see Harry's mind sorting options. He shot a look at Bonnie. 'Have you examined her yet?'

'Just felt her tummy. Head down, well engaged.'

He nodded. 'Tameeka, I'd like Bonnie to feel how far along in your labour you are. We have to tell the Flying Doctors when we ring them. Is that okay?'

Tameeka nodded and Bernie gulped and eyed the door. Bonnie could see he'd decided to leave this bit of women's business to the women and followed Harry out.

Bonnie heard him mutter to Harry as they shut the door. 'She said them pains didn't hurt too much and I thought it was them Baxtin Icks, practice pain things.'

The three women smiled at each other at the thought processes of men as Tameeka slipped her underwear off.

Bonnie folded the sheet back from the bottom of the bed. Tameeka closed her eyes and nodded for Bonnie to go ahead.

Bonnie pulled on her gloves and stared at the wall opposite as she concentrated on what she could feel. 'Okay. I can touch your baby's head a little way inside but not too far. The bottom of your uterus is very thin, pointing to the front, and opened enough for two finger widths. So that's nearly three centimetres dilated. The baby has his or her chin well tucked in so that's good.'

Bonnie stood back and removed her gloves. 'Your baby's head is right down so when you get a contraction it leans on the opening and makes the cervix a little bit wider each time. That's why the more regular the contractions, the quicker your labour.'

'What about them waters?' Auntie Dell had her hands on her hips again.

Bonnie turned back. She was getting to that but she had an idea Tameeka had a little more trouble following what she was talking about than Auntie Dell. She smiled at the older lady. 'The bag of waters is still there and Tameeka will probably still have a few hours of labour before her baby is born. Maybe enough to get to Alice Springs.'

Bonnie listened again briefly with the foetal heart Doppler to check the baby didn't mind somebody touching his or her head and then stepped back to wash her hands.

When she came back to the bed Auntie Dell had helped Tameeka up and to dress again. Bonnie looked at both of them. 'Any questions?'

'Can I stay here and have my baby with my auntie?'

Bonnie would have loved that but it wasn't an option they had with no backup. 'Unfortunately not. But we can try really hard to keep your auntie and Bernie with you until you have your baby.'

In the end, despite Harry's phone calls, the RFDS were away in Kakadu and Harry decided they'd use the road ambulance. He wasn't keen on the presence of Auntie Dell and refused to see the problem.

'There's not much room in an ambulance and she's

a big lady.' It seemed he wanted to be obtuse today and Bonnie was fast losing patience. 'I don't see how she can come,' he said.

They were outside the room and talking in low voices as they waited for Steve to bring the ambulance round. Bonnie almost laughed out loud. Fat chance of Auntie Dell staying behind.

'I'm interested, Harry. What do you need room for? Tameeka's a healthy woman, early in active labour, doing what she's designed to do. If you're sure we can't have her baby here, with the option of transfer out afterwards if anything isn't going smoothly, then you must be happy if we deliver this baby in the vehicle. In that case, we'll pull over anyway and can open the back door and let Dell out.'

Harry's eyes flared. 'We're not delivering this baby in the ambulance. She should have gone to Alice Springs two days ago.'

'She wasn't in labour then. And you couldn't predict this.' Bonnie's voice was very quiet and very calm. 'And there's not a lot we can do about that now, Doctor.' She didn't look at him or he'd have known she was ready to throw something at him for the misplaced tension in his face. She knew that he had issues but at the moment that was just tough.

'I'll get the ambulance if you want to ring Alice Springs and arrange for someone to meet us halfway.'

Harry wasn't finished. 'This is a prime example of you providing another episode I don't want to be a part of.'

'Whoa there, cowboy.' Bonnie didn't fancy the sound of that. 'Like what, Harry?' She felt like poking him in the chest but restrained herself. One of them needed to. 'What else have I forced you into? A brief fling in Bali? I didn't see you running away. In fact, I'd say you did the chasing. And I certainly didn't force you to come here and confront maternal medicine. But you are here so confront it.'

He didn't like that. 'We don't have time for this.'

'No, we don't, but you started it, and I'll be finished before Steve gets here so you can darned well listen.' She brushed the hair out of her eyes and fixed her eyes on his.

'You can't go on like this, Harry. Fear doesn't have a part of caring for pregnant women.'

He lifted his head. 'And we should have shipped her out because I'm not sure I can lose that factor.'

Stubborn, more than anything, she thought. 'Or maybe you don't want to because that would mean you're moving on? Why is it so hard to let go of the fear and guilt, Harry?'

He shook his head. 'It's not fear, it's caution.'

She felt like saying that was piffle. But she didn't. She really couldn't be bothered getting childish. 'Caution is fine, but we're guardians who stand at the side of nature, not the directors. Women have been doing this longer than we've been interfering.'

'From my perspective I can't trust things not to go wrong. You can't deny the mortality rate has fallen since we did start to interfere.'

'We're not talking penicillin here, Harry.' Bonnie sighed. 'The last thing Tameeka needs is a harbinger of doom draped around her neck.' She breathed out heavily and then glanced at the closed door to the consulting room.

'Doom happened to me. I can't forget that.'

'You told me you did everything possible. What makes you think I don't understand? It's not a new thing to lose a patient when the incident is greater than the resources. You were there and the resources weren't. Even in a major centre most mothers still die with what your wife had.'

'If they say I was negligent, I think I'll believe them.'

'I'm tempted to say "so what"? You hid away in Bali believing that anyway. Even when you did make a token return to medicine here in Ayers Rock you have so many rules and safeguards it's an escape anyway.' She shook her head and glanced at her watch. 'I can't help your insecurities but negative, fearful people should not be around birthing women. Now I'm busy. Let's get this girl to Alice Springs.'

Half an hour later they were thirty miles out of the township as Bonnie drove into the magnificence of the fading light. The sun had finished posing to the masses and it wasn't a great time to be on the road with the wildlife coming out to feed at dusk but Harry obviously thought it more dangerous to have a normal birth than risk hitting a roo. Bonnie ground her teeth and concentrated on the road.

Harry was in the back, which was lucky for him because Bonnie had a mind to tell him a few more home truths. She had Bernie up front with her and she didn't want the poor guy to feel her frustration. He'd already backed down when Auntie Dell had said she'd get in the back.

The next half an hour saw two near misses of kangaroos and a lucky wombat, and Tameeka's noisy breathing from the back sounded like a freight train. Serves you right, Harry, Bonnie thought grimly. We could have been in a nice pleasant room back at the medical centre with electric lights and equipment if we needed it.

At the end of yet another half-hour, outside the vehicle the light was restricted to the circular areas the headlights provided and the stars above. They still had an hour before they'd meet up with the other ambulance, and to make matters worse now a road train was bearing down on them from behind. Bonnie pulled over on a wide patch of dirt outside a rest area to let the monster truck go past.

'Bonnie?' Harry questioned from the back.

'I'm just letting the truck past.'

Then Tameeka's shaky voice. 'I gotta pee.'

Well, you can't wait another two hours, Bonnie thought silently, with a twitch of her lips. 'I'll just pull into this parking area.' Bonnie drove the few metres and reversed the vehicle so the back door was away from the road then turned the engine and headlights off. She jumped out and went around the back.

The night was quiet as the road train's engines faded into the distance and when she stepped away from the vehicle's cabin light the stars were brilliant and provided an amazing amount of gentle glow in the night sky.

Bernie was beside her and he lifted the back door up for her. Auntie Dell squeezed herself out like toothpaste from a tube and shook herself to stretch the bits that had been cramped in the back.

Then Harry helped Tameeka out and she leaned against Bernie when she could stand up. 'My back is killin' me when I lie down.'

'I know, sweetheart.' Bonnie looked around for some privacy for Tameeka. 'Come this way. I've got a torch in case we need it but there's some close scrub here, where you can go.'

'I don't need to do a wee,' Tameeka whispered. 'I just wanted to stop 'cause my back was killin' me.'

'That's okay.' Bonnie had her suspicions about the pressure the girl was getting now and wouldn't be surprised if this was it. 'You may as well go while you're here.'

Bonnie turned round to give her some privacy and she could see Harry walking up and down beside the truck like an expectant father.

Tameeka groaned and when Bonnie turned round she was on all fours with her head down.

As soon as the pain eased, Bonnie helped her up. 'You push a little then, honey?'

'Mmm-hmm. And all that water came out. It's still comin' out. Don't make me get in that truck.'

'Let's just get back to the light.' This was it. Bonnie shrugged fatalistically. So be it.

Harry came towards them and Bonnie said quietly, 'Her waters broke. She's going to have the baby now and she doesn't want to get back in the ambulance. She wants to have it under the stars. Is that okay with you, Harry?'

Harry sighed, hugely, and she watched his tight shoulders finally drop with the breath. He lifted his head. 'It's all coming true, isn't it? The more I try to stop things happening, the more they seem to go against me. You were right. We would have been safer at the centre.' He smiled without humour.

He glanced ruefully up at the heavens. 'But it's not about me. It's about Tameeka. As long as we have emergency light when we need it, let's make it as good as we can for her. We'll get some blankets in case she needs to be lifted into the back in an emergency. There's four of us, we can lift her with the blanket.' They'd still needed contingency plans.

Then he smiled at her and Bonnie felt the tension slip from her shoulders like a huge sack of potatoes as Harry stopped fighting against her. She hadn't realised how much stress she'd been carrying around.

Thank goodness, Harry. Excellent man. About time.

They set up a little bed on the ground, and dimmed the back lights but left the front cabin light on.

Harry unobtrusively rubbed his forehead with two fingers and finally allowed the moment to soak in. He glanced across to where Auntie Dell sat cross-legged on the ground with Bernie hunched a handswidth away as Tameeka breathed quietly now in the still evening air.

The stars flickered and shone above like a carpet of guardian angels and somehow, with each of Tameeka's breaths, he could feel the pinpricks of pain that had burred into his skin for so long flicker and then fade away. Even more slowly he allowed Bonnie's words of earlier that day to sink in.

Tameeka was healthy, her baby had grown normally,

and nothing had indicated there would be a problem. But he'd been determined to imagine every scenario that could go wrong.

He'd forced them onto the road and increased the risk when it would have been far safer to at least have facilities around them. He hadn't been smart, and his fear wasn't helpful to him, to the midwife and especially to the mother.

How far he'd come from the man who'd helped out at the birth centre in Ubud. How far from the joy and wonder he'd savoured with uncomplicated births just a few years ago.

Bonnie had tried to tell him that and he'd refused to listen. But still she sat with her hands clasped loosely in front of her. A towel lay across her lap, waiting to dry the baby.

She looked so calm, yet instantly attuned to every nuance of Tameeka's needs, and he envied her the faith he should have had, hoped he'd have again, thanks to nights like this and to Bonnie.

He'd had that faith once and after tonight he was determined to find it again. He'd lost the passion for well women doing what nature intended somewhere in his worry for himself.

Bonnie had sent him on the quest, and while it wasn't comfortable it had finally begun to feel right. This woman he'd been fated to meet, and who'd startled him out of his destructive stupor, shining brightly on the edge of his vision, then slowly lighting up his sky until she'd gradually warmed him from within.

She'd banished the darkness that even the brightness of Bali hadn't been able to penetrate.

Fifteen minutes later, with the night still warm and bright, with little breeze and just as Tameeka's baby's head crowned, a brilliant shooting star shot across the horizon like a smiling angel. Harry felt the magic as he glanced across at Bonnie and counted himself doubly fortunate to be there.

Harry leant across and rested his hand on the small of Bonnie's back as she lifted the mewling infant to her mother's breast.

'Now, that's what I call birthin',' Auntie Dell said.

CHAPTER TEN

OF COURSE mother and baby were well and they called off the Alice Springs ambulance. Harry drove back to Uluru. A beaming Bernie sat in the back with his family.

Tameeka slept with her baby stretched across her chest like a kitten and her baby's father keeping watch over them both.

When Harry broke the silence, it wasn't awkward—nothing could be while they all floated in post-birth euphoria—but the events of the day lay between them, waiting for the time he had to speak. 'I've been hard work, Bonnie.'

'This sounds familiar.' He could hear the smile in her voice. 'Like another birth.'

'Good grief.' Harry looked across at her and he could feel his mouth tilt. 'I think we're actually forming a bit of history.'

She widened her eyes theatrically. 'Not the *H* word, Harry? Oh, my goodness.'

It was okay. She understood. He had the impression she would always understand. 'You were right. Tameeka's birth was amazing. She was incredible.'

'Yes, she was. I think I mentioned she's designed to do it.'

'Okay, Miss Smarty Pants, you may have. But let's keep the births for the centre in Alice next time.'

'Yes, Doctor.' Demurely. He'd like to kiss that respectability away but he'd have to wait. But he could plan.

That was when it hit him. Splat, like the yellow smear on the windshield in front of him, drawn to the light, followed by a short, sharp blow as life as he knew it was wiped out. He loved her.

He'd fallen in love. He'd said he couldn't do it again and she'd made him. He'd lost his heart when he'd vowed he'd never risk that again.

He'd thought he'd been attracted, get back on the bike kind of attracted, which had drawn him here from Bali and suggested he needed to practise reconnecting with women without the drama of falling in love. Just rapport and teasing and maybe a little more of that lovely sex without strings.

But that hadn't happened. He was so stupid he could see it now like his own comet in the sky. That would be the comet that was going to wipe him out.

This was squeeze the heart, protect with your life, make babies and die together kind of falling in love— which was a whole different scenario and one he'd vowed never to be a part of ever, ever again.

He glanced out the window into the wall of darkness beside him and forcibly resisted the urge to slow the ambulance until it stopped, open the door and just walk away.

He was trapped. Trapped by his promise to Steve for

another week, trapped by internal walls he'd trusted to protect him, trapped by the woman beside him who had crumbled those walls with her straight talking and straight looks that flew straight to his heart, and now he was in deep trouble.

He couldn't help it. He went into defence mode. Couldn't stop it. If she hated him, good. He needed distance for the next few days until he could get himself away.

'If it happens again, I'll ask for a different midwife.'

Bonnie blinked and the curve of her lips dropped with shock. He was joking. Wasn't he? Her head swivelled to look at him and he was staring straight ahead with his mouth a grim line and cheeks stiff and stark in the reflected light. He wasn't joking. 'What did you just say?'

'I won't have my patients put at risk again. All pregnant women will be in Alice Springs a month before they're due.'

Bonnie's mind raced. What the heck had happened in the space of a minute? 'Certainly, Doctor. Perhaps we should send them when their pregnancy tests come up positive. At ten weeks.'

The stranger said, 'I don't want to discuss it any more. You know how I feel.'

Bonnie shook her head, still reeling but very close to telling him where to go. 'I know how the other doctor who was here five minutes ago felt, but this new guy is a pain.'

She would have said more, hadn't even started on what she felt like saying, but another road train had stopped at the side of the road and the driver waved them down.

Good. Anything to get her mind off the slow death she was planning for Harry.

Harry was pleased at the distraction too. He wasn't happy with the option his brain had chosen—to alienate Bonnie—but he guessed it had worked. She looked ready to jump out of the car herself.

This day was never going to end. He slowed and pulled up beside the truck driver as Bonnie wound down her window.

'You okay?' she asked, but he could see the man was holding his right arm tightly across his chest.

Trouble was confirmed when the man said, 'Got me fingers caught in the cattle gate.' He grimaced. 'Doesn't feel right.'

'Let's see.' Harry climbed out and Bonnie opened her door to get the bandages from the back, he guessed. Dell and Bernie climbed out and Harry could hear her rummaging through the drawers for the first-aid supplies.

By the time she'd returned to the truck driver Harry had him sitting on a log and was ready to bind the fingers.

He pretended to the world that everything was normal. He pretended to himself. 'Bonnie, this is Blue.'

Typically, Blue had a thatch of bright red hair that glowed even in the dark. His name was standard country humour about redheads, probably his nickname since school days.

Blue was in pain, Harry could see that, because his plastering of freckles stood out starkly across his nose and his pale face. Maybe not too much pain because his eyes lit up when he saw Bonnie, and Harry felt himself frown.

'G'day, there, Bonnie, you're a sight for sore eyes,' Blue drawled. He tipped his Akubra and the twinkle in his eyes was unmistakable. Blue was a larrikin, no doubt about it, and Bonnie didn't seem to mind.

Bonnie smiled at the man in a way that seemed just a little too friendly and made Harry realise just how far he'd sunk.

'Hello, there, Blue. Nice to meet you,' she said. 'I'll bet your fingers throb like blazes.'

Harry cut her off. 'Looks like you've broken two, and damaged the thumb badly.' He glanced at Blue's pale face, 'Lucky you didn't chop them off, judging by the slice here.'

Blue nodded, distracted from Bonnie, Harry was pleased to see, and much less amused. 'Yeah. Thought I did, happy to count 'em after I got 'em out of the gate.' He shrugged. 'At least the cattle didn't get out. One of the bolts worked loose and I'd fixed that first—bloody lucky—before I stuffed meself.'

Harry made short work of stabilising and binding Blue's fingers and then looked up at the truck. 'You'll need X-rays and suturing at the clinic at Uluru, we're the closest. Can you squeeze in the back with the others?'

Blue looked doubtfully at the ambulance and then at his truck. Harry correctly interpreted his concern. 'Sorry, I can't drive your rig. Can you phone someone to help?'

Blue scratched his head with his good hand. 'Might take a day or two and the cattle need to get to the sales.'

Bonnie stepped between them. 'If you sit in the cab with me, Blue, I can drive you to the medical centre, then you could take over once the doctor's fixed you up.' Bonnie turned her shoulder away from Harry to face the injured man and Harry saw Blue's eyes widen even further in admiration. Harry didn't miss that.

She went on, 'I worked out at Kununurra and drove a rig like this from Halls Creek six months ago when the driver had chest pain and we couldn't get help.' She glanced dismissively at Harry. 'The doctor has the ambulance covered.'

Of course she could drive a truck with three trailers on a dirt road. He probably could too, if he wanted to. She and Blue would have a lovely time. Harry felt like swearing but refrained. At least the man was injured. And he had no right to even think like that.

'You go ahead, Doctor,' Bonnie said firmly.

It was all good. He'd get space to get his head around how he was going to get out of Uluru without Bonnie finding out. And he'd bet Blue would look after her. Harry dug his toe into the dirt and then flicked a rock out towards the grass. It was great she could drive the rig. Really.

'Let's load up, then.' Harry glanced at Bernie, who obediently jumped into the back, and Dell paused as she surveyed the empty passenger seat. 'I'll come and sit beside you then, Doc.' Auntie Dell was happy. 'I reckon that'll be real comfy.'

'Lovely,' Harry said through his teeth. They all climbed in and Harry started the ambulance.

'Ya know…' Auntie Dell had been thinking. 'You and her should start a birth place for the women around here, Doc. Them girls don't wanna go away from their families to have their babies.'

Harry almost laughed out loud at the simplistic concept. 'It's a bit more complicated than that.'

'Nothing complicated about having a baby. It's getting the girls five hours' drive away at the right time that's complicated.'

The next day, Bonnie saw very little of Harry. If she entered a room he exited unless it was medically impossible, and at those times they were both too busy to worry about anything.

Even when Leila, the little girl they'd met at the Rock that first morning, came in with her mother and Auntie Dell with a nasty dose of gastro, Harry had eyes only for the toddler, and the way he cajoled the little one to a smile made the difference in his attitude to her even more noticeable, at least to Bonnie.

He stroked the child's fine hair as he looked at Shay. 'You might need to take Leila to the hospital at Alice Springs.' He shook his head at Leila's slightly sunken eyes and dull skin and erred on the side of caution, as usual.

Shay cast an agonised glance at Auntie Dell, who cast one at Bonnie—who suppressed a sigh. She was almost over going in to bat for everyone else.

That was what happened when a workplace lost equality between professionals. This was all Harry's fault. If she didn't know better, or try to believe better anyway, she'd say he was being as difficult as he possibly could just to incense her.

They both knew it was hard for the women to get to

Alice Springs and how unpleasant the journey would be with a sick child. Leila wasn't quite sick enough for the Flying Doctor to pick up and really just needed a watchful eye and some IV fluids.

'Shay wondered if we could try with IV fluids here,' Bonnie said steadily. 'Through today anyway. And see if Leila improves.' She glanced away from Harry's expressionless face to the mother, whom she smiled at to relieve the tension. 'Because that's what children can do.'

Shay smiled back with relief and Bonnie added, 'Then Leila could go home and get checked again in the morning.'

At least Harry considered it. 'And if she gets worse?'

'You'd check her before she went home and, of course, Shay would bring her back during the night if she was worried, wouldn't you, Shay?'

Shay nodded vigorously and Auntie Dell nodded once, firmly. Come on, Harry, Bonnie thought with a sigh. The little one is sick, but not critical, and was even starting to improve in front of their eyes. They could handle this here for the moment and maybe the family wouldn't have to be thrown into upheaval.

Thankfully he seemed to listen to her for a change, and even snap out of his mode enough to agree, albeit grudgingly. 'I'll check her later and decide then. Before three o'clock.'

Good. Bonnie threw in for good measure, 'Shay's Tameeka's older sister.'

'Really?' Harry's face twitched into a smile she didn't expect. 'How's Tameeka doing with her baby?' Harry asked.

'Real good,' Auntie Dell answered for her niece with a big white grin. 'Bernie's telling everyone how amazin' that birth was.'

'Great,' Harry said, and glanced at Bonnie. 'Hope we aren't going to have a rush of last-minute labours.'

Bonnie smiled grimly to herself. She'd asked for that. But he had seemed in a better mood. Though it was easier to hate him when he was a pain. Nice Harry was too hard to ignore.

She kept Leila until late in the afternoon, when, with the resilience of children and the extra fluids they'd infused, the little girl was ready to go home with her mum and Auntie Dell.

'I'll just get the doctor to check her one more time, Shay.'

Leila's mother nodded and Bonnie tracked Harry down in the records room, checking statistics. They looked like antenatal ones. Now what was his problem?

'Can you see Leila now, please? She looks much improved.'

He nodded and followed her out to the main assessment room. The little girl even smiled at him and Bonnie felt the tug of her heart at Harry's rapport with the little one.

'You were right, Bonnie,' he said after they left. 'She didn't need to go.'

He offered her a strangely whimsical smile she didn't know how to react to. 'I want to finish what I'm doing tonight and then I have something to show you. Probably tomorrow.'

He paused, then added, 'You'll be glad when I'm

gone and a reasonable doctor arrives that you can work with.' He didn't give her a chance to answer, just walked away, and Bonnie shook her head. Her heart might not agree but it was getting that way.

The next morning Bonnie felt unwell. She must have caught the bug Leila had because the thought of breakfast was not a pleasant one.

Her face paled and she rushed for the bathroom. Obviously the thought was enough.

Afterwards she fell back on her bed and wiped her face with the washer she'd grabbed from the sink. Whew. At least she felt a little better now.

She reached across to the night table and picked up the phone to ring Vicki and let her know she'd be late when someone knocked on the door. She groaned. She hoped it wasn't Harry. Today was not a good day.

'Go away,' she muttered into the empty room. The person knocked again and she sighed as she sat up gingerly and finally made her way over to the door.

She leant her head on the edge of the door as it opened. 'Not this morning, Harry. Not well.'

'What's wrong?'

'Haven't searched for a diagnosis, Doctor,' she said faintly, 'but I'm guessing I caught Leila's bug.'

'You look like death. Back to bed.' He pushed her back into the room gently and pulled back her covers. 'In you go.' She climbed in and he tucked her up like Gran used to do. Thankfully there was no sign of the grumpy doctor at all, and it felt weepily good.

When her head hit the pillow she closed her eyes, but she could hear a rattle in the corner of the room and

Harry reappeared with the metal wastepaper bin and a glass of water. 'Just in case.'

He grimaced in sympathy. 'Sip water. I'll be back in a while to check on you. I'll bring some lemonade or something.'

Bonnie heard the door close quietly and she sighed. At least she didn't have to try to go to work. She felt rotten.

By ten o'clock she felt fine. 'Shortest bug in history,' she said to Vicki when she walked in.

Harry's consulting-room door opened for him to show out a patient and he stopped when he saw her. 'What're you doing here?'

'I've recovered and I'm bored.'

Harry looked at his watch. 'It's morning tea time for me. Fancy some food, then?' He was looking at her strangely and she frowned at him.

'Only if you want some.'

His frown was heavy. 'I think so.'

He was acting oddly. Just an uneasy prickling that made her look at Vicki with a lift of her brows. Vicki shrugged in silent reply, as if to say, 'I don't know what's up with him.'

Bonnie had no choice but to duck under his arm as he held the door open for her.

'It's too far to the coffee shop. How about a cup of tea in the dining room?'

'Okay.' This was getting stranger by the minute.

He ushered her into the deserted dining room and plugged in the kettle. Then he sat her down. 'Steve's found a replacement for me and he flies in tomorrow. I fly out in the evening.'

Bonnie bit her lip. She hated fighting with him but she wasn't sure she wanted him to go. In fact, she was darned sure she didn't want him to go, which was weird when he drove her insane.

'Where are you going?'

'I'm heading to Katherine to finish something I should have finished a long time ago. Then I'm going on to Darwin. I'm meeting a few people who are interested in a proposal I might have.'

'That sounds good, Harry. Vague, but I'm glad for you.'

Then he said something totally off topic. 'It's five weeks since you left Bali.'

Time flew. Or did it? It felt like a year. 'So?'

He was peering at her. 'You were nauseated this morning.'

Horribly so. His point was? 'And?'

'Aren't you suspicious?'

'I'm getting a bit suspicious of you. Have you been drinking, Harry?'

'This isn't a joke.

'Okay, Harry. Enough guessing games. Yes, I was sick this morning. What of it, Harry? Maybe I didn't wash my hands well enough after looking after Leila?'

'Come on, Bonnie. You're a midwife.'

Bonnie blinked. 'What…?' Then it dawned on her what he was talking about. 'Don't be ridiculous. No! One time.' She shook her head. 'I have one word for you. Protection. That's why they call it that.'

She shook her head at his presumption. 'I thought you had tickets on yourself the first time I saw you.'

He glanced down at the floor and if she wasn't

mistaken she'd almost think he was disappointed. Good grief.

But when he looked up his eyes were sharp again. 'Then you've had a period since Bali?'

Now she was getting angry. And just a little worried as she calculated madly. 'Spare me. You may be a doctor but you're not my doctor.'

She stood up. 'Have a good flight tomorrow, Harry. If I don't see you, that will be good.'

Harry watched her walk away. Well, that hadn't gone well. Understatement. He'd been sitting in his office before his last patient when it had hit him. And nothing could *un*convince him that was why she was sick. He didn't know why he was so positively certain. He'd checked dates, they worked out. He'd checked the net, it was unlucky but possible, and all he'd need to do was find out if she knew.

She didn't but he still didn't rule the possibility out. And the really strange thing was, now that the absolute worst that could have happened might have happened, he actually felt euphoric.

It was ridiculous but curiously liberating. There was no use running away. If it had happened. And actually worked with his new plans, as long as she'd have him.

If he was lucky, he was going to have to watch a woman he loved go through a pregnancy and he would have to conquer his fear. As Bonnie was fond of saying, he had to trust Mother Nature.

Because he wanted to be there. Wanted to see every change, be a part of every new experience, see the things he'd missed out on last time, be there for the normal birth that he would have to learn to trust in. The birth of Bonnie's baby, and his.

Now all he had to do was convince her he was a sane and sensible man, which could be difficult given his behaviour over the last few weeks.

CHAPTER ELEVEN

BONNIE escaped to her room, steering down the empty hallway like a remote-controlled car, not sure who was driving while her mind raced.

She pushed open the door and pulled it shut behind her back. When she leant against it the wood was the only cool thing on her body. She stared at her pale face in the mirror on the wall and slowly closed her eyes.

Her fingers inched reluctantly down until she rested them over her pelvic bone. She was pregnant. No period, nausea, slight tenderness when she'd put her bra on that morning. Good grief.

How the heck had this happened and how could she not be absolutely devastated? Well, she knew how it happened but the lack of a sense of impending doom surprised her. Because it wasn't there. She was stunned and shocked but below those initial layers of disbelief lurked a tiny secret whisper of joy.

She was having Harry's baby.

And in the absolutely worst-case scenario she could tell her baby she'd loved its daddy.

Therapeutic, in fact, to admit it. Accept the truth of it. Stop denying the truth. She loved annoying, frustrating, gorgeous Harry with every cell in her body. And now she was sharing cells with him as they created their baby.

And if she'd gathered Harry's reaction correctly, he wasn't devastated either. Which opened up a whole new amazing realm of possibility.

When Harry knocked on her door three minutes later she opened her eyes. She knew it was him. Could feel the awareness through an inch of wood. They certainly had some talking to do.

She opened the door and he stood there tall and almost relaxed, which was a first since he'd arrived in the centre. She lifted her brows. When he smiled at her it held all the light and brightness and excitement she associated with the man she'd met in Bali.

Drat the man. He had too many good angles that made her forget how much he could drive her mad. These were all reasons he could sweep her off her feet but it was the question behind his eyes that really clinched it for her.

The wonder of his new self-knowledge, the warmth of a man who could feel complete with the woman he loved—and wanted her to feel the same.

'I've brought you a gift.' He held open his hand and the little silver baby he'd given her in Bali lay in his palm. 'I'd really love you to keep this.' He looked at her. 'Along with my heart.'

She knew she loved him, had done so since that magical night at his house in Bali, but he didn't deserve things to be easy. 'Do I have your heart, Harry?'

'If you let me in, I could try to convince you.'

They were married at sunset on top of a red sand dune overlooking the Rock. A wedding dune, with white

Balinese flags flying in a circle. Bernie was on the didgeridoo, playing haunting Aboriginal music, with a little dark-eyed girl in a white dress dropping white rose petals Harry had had flown in from Victoria.

Harry had flown down Bonnie's friends from Darwin and his colleagues from the RFDS had done a fly-past with white ribbons in the sky.

The bride and groom exchanged solemn vows, eyes only for each other as they held hands, and Steve as celebrant, pronounced them man and wife. Later there would be another wedding in Ubud and another circle of friends would be there.

When the stars came out the astronomer from the Sounds of Silence Dinner wove dreamtime stories of ancient love between planets, myths of romance and the Greek gods, astrology and the attraction of opposite star signs, and Harry and Bonnie smiled at each other as they watched their guests' rapt faces.

'We need to do this once a year for our anniversary,' Bonnie whispered. 'I love learning about the stars and listening to the stories.'

'And I love listening to you,' Harry teased. 'Even when I'm in trouble.'

Seven months later

Their car drew up outside the Uluru Birthing Centre. Bonnie breathed out the last of her contraction and put her hand on Harry's arm. 'Sacha can catch our baby.'

Harry looked across. 'I'll catch our baby.'

Bonnie raised her eyebrows. 'And how are you going to do that and hold my hand at the same time?'

'One-handed.'

Bonnie began to breathe as the next contraction built. 'Harry, I need your hand.'

Harry smiled at this woman he adored more than life itself. 'Sacha can catch our baby, my love. I knew your caseload midwifery would do me out of catching babies.'

'You don't really mind.'

He leant across and kissed her brow. 'I'll be the husband. I get the easy job. Have I told you lately that I love you?'

The pain eased and Bonnie sighed as she prepared herself mentally to stand up. 'Not in the last half an hour.'

'Sorry.' Harry leant across and kissed her lips gently. 'I love you.' He opened his door. 'Wait. I'll help you.'

She watched him climb out fast but still with that effortless grace he'd always had. 'I love you too,' she said to the empty car, and smiled.

LET'S TALK
Romance

For exclusive extracts, competitions
and special offers, find us online:

📘 facebook.com/millsandboon
📷 @millsandboonuk
🐦 @millsandboon

Or get in touch on 0844 844 1351*

For all the latest titles coming soon, visit
millsandboon.co.uk/nextmonth